ONE MORE ~~MORE~~ *Time*

RORY LECTOR

Blurb

Tyler Riley never thought he'd get the chance to leave home. In the small, coastal town of Perth, Australia, he can only dream of being the next big hockey star. But as luck would have it, opportunity knocks in the form of a prestigious hockey scholarship. Torn between his devotion to his family and his career, Tyler puts everything on the line to start over halfway across the world.

Brooding Bostonian Hunter Graves has one goal in mind: head down, focus on his career. A chance encounter with a transfer student from Australia, however, throws a wrench in his plans. Unbeknownst to him, Tyler is not only a fellow student—but his new teammate. Helmets clash on and off the ice, creating a level of tension that neither man can ignore.

Tyler dreams of a pro hockey career, but at what cost? Hunter finds himself falling for the new guy in town, but can he break down that wall he's hidden behind all these years?

With every electrifying clash on the ice—and in the bedroom—*One More Time* takes readers on a rollercoaster journey of love and self-discovery. Do these two men have what it takes to prove that love can truly conquer all?

Content warning

Content Warning: This book contains sensitive themes that may be triggering for some readers. Please be aware of the following content warnings: mention of past sexual assault (not depicted on the page and no idolization), explicit sexual content, profanity, homophobic slurs, physical assault, death of a family member, grief, mental health concerns including anxiety and panic attacks, sports-related injuries including concussions, and coming to terms with sexuality. If any of these topics are potential triggers for you, please take necessary precautions while reading. Despite these warnings, this book offers a high-stakes hockey romance filled with love and passion.

Happy to continue? Get your emotional support bottle ready, a cozy blanket and escape, Love Rory

Dedicated to my readers for being on this journey with me.

"Love is friendship that has caught fire. It is quiet understanding, mutual confidence, sharing and forgiving. It is loyalty through good and bad times. It settles for less than perfection and makes allowances for human weaknesses. "

Ann Landers

Contents

Chapter One

Tyler

This was potentially a life altering moment. The envelope in my hand trembled in my death grip. I couldn't help but chuckle at myself. I mean, labeling this as the most significant change in my life would be a bit of a stretch. That happened two years ago, and that was the day I realized that the world spinning on its axis was a lot like a ceiling fan full of dirty socks on April Fool's.

I used to find humor in pranks. So, I orchestrated a spectacle by hanging my smelly hockey socks on the ceiling fan for April Fool's. The resulting chaos mirrored the unpredictability of life. As I now stood on the brink of yet another crucial moment in life, I craved that thrill.

Weighing the thick envelope in my hand, I reminded myself not to over-analyze it. I glanced up to where Mum bounced on her toes in front of me, an eager smile playing on her lips. I'd always been told I had her eyes. I watched, heart pounding in my ears as her eager sea-foam eyes flicked from me to the letter as I slid it from the white envelope.

"Mum, stop. You're making me nervous," I grumbled, secretly relishing her enthusiasm. She'd been my number one fan since day one. Every time I stumbled; she was right there to catch me. Now, she stood there nearly buzzing with excitement, knowing that the contents of that letter could upend our entire lives.

"Come on, Ty! You know I hate surprises."

"Yeah, yeah."

With a sigh, I looked down at the page in my hand.

Dear Mr. Riley,

Congratulations...

I didn't need to read any further.

I froze on the spot, my heartbeat thumping in my ears. Mum snatched the letter from me, clearly having lost patience with waiting on me to speak. Her squeal should've snapped me out of my stupor.

This application was a long shot—the biggest fucking long shot of my life. My mind raced between each thud of my heart.

Should I? Shouldn't I? Can I do this?

"Tyler?" Mum squeezed my arm, and I turned to face her. She looked up at me with those eyes that could read me like the books she wrote for a living.

"Tyler, this was your idea. Even after my diagnosis I told you this was your dream, not mine—certainly not your dad's. You wanted the big deal. No matter what you do, you know I'll always be proud of you, right?"

Man, I hit the jackpot with my mum.

She wasn't wrong. The NHL was my dream, always had been. I'd watched games on TV growing up, hearing Mum yell and swear, eyes lighting up as she watched the playoffs. I wanted to be on that TV; I wanted her cheering for me like that.

That's where it all started. If I said my mom didn't have an ulterior motive for taking me to the ice rink, I'd be lying. I knew she secretly hoped it would give me a spark of inspiration.

Hockey itself wasn't in my blood, but we were an athletic family. My dad was an ex-fighter, Mum an ex-jockey. Not exactly pro hockey player magic, but I did partially thank genetics for my skill on the ice.

Though my dad wasn't really into the hockey scene, he never skipped a game. He was always there to give me a pat on the back—win or lose. I did pretty well, at least by Aussie standards. I had national medals, snagged a spot on the under-eighteens team, and made my way to the world championships. We played against some of the best players in the world and brought home a bronze—a major win for Team Australia. Now, with my golden ticket in hand, I was one step closer to being on the NHL's radar.

"Tyler?"

I hadn't realized I'd forgotten to answer her. The low hum and trickle from the fish tank were the only noises in the room.

"I know, Mum. I know you'll support me no matter what, but... this is huge. It doesn't just affect me anymore."

"You're not giving up your dreams because of little ol' me,"

My gut twisted.

Leaving her wasn't an easy choice to make.

"Oh, cut me some slack. I'm a grown woman; I can look after myself and Jamie." She laughed, but we both knew the grim reality of the situation.

Two years ago, life threw two big, dirty socks our way. The first hit was losing my Dad. He was a volunteer firefighter, who didn't make it home after fighting an out-of-control bushfire. He and Mum were high school sweethearts and a dynamic duo. She took his death hard—we all did. But the second sock hit when Mum got diagnosed with the big C.

"Mum, I can't do that—"

"You're young, Tyler. This has been your dream since you could pick up a stick. I don't want you living with the 'what ifs.' Yes, life dealt us the ultimate trump card, but we can make this work. I am not dead yet."

Tears began to sting my eyes. "That isn't funny, Mum."

As I reminisced over the last two years, my mind wandered to my little brother. Not only was mum grieving the loss of my dad, but she also had a schedule packed with doctor's appointments. I had to step up. I was a chef and a housekeeper among making sure Jamie made it to school and his MMA training. Mum was usually too wiped out from the treatment to do much of anything.

The idea of leaving them both felt like lugging around a ton of bricks. I tried to shield Jamie from as much as I could. From tucking Mum into bed when she was too drained to get up, to sitting with her during chemo. Keeping Jamie blissfully unaware of the harsh realities of life fell squarely on my shoulders.

"Tyler, talk to me." Mum's voice pulled me from my thoughts once more. I turned and pulled her into my arms.

"It's irresponsible. What if Jamie needs me? What if you need help?"

I yelped when she sharply pinched the skin on my side.

"You deserved that, call it a reality pinch. You've grown up way quicker than I'd have liked but you've become a young man I'm proud to call my son. On top of stepping up around the house, you still get good grades and have performed at an Olympic level. You can't put this opportunity on hold—they won't wait for you. I have family around; if I need help, I will ask."

I sighed, letting my head fall to her shoulder. Though I stood at least six inches taller than her, she never refused to hold me when I needed it

"If I didn't have cancer, would you have been on a plane before you reached the end of the letter?"

My heart tugged at the thought. Wrapping up high school while juggling things at home had been tough. What would the team setup be like? Guys from other countries would talk about constant rotations, but Perth didn't offer that luxury.

With just two ice rinks—one up north and one down south—your team was basically pre-determined by your skill level. The guys I played with had been the same ones I started pee-wee hockey with. They were practically my brothers. When life hit rock bottom, they were there. They always had my back, whether it was fetching Mum from her appointments or if Jamie needed a hand. Leaving meant ditching my family—my entire family.

I sighed. "Yeah, I'd be gone already. But that doesn't change the fact that you have cancer. And cancer or no cancer, Jamie needs his big brother."

She squeezed me tighter. "Yes, I get that. Motherhood has always been my priority, but I also had my twenties to... live. I got to figure out what I wanted, to party and be a bit silly—much to your dad's dismay. And as your mother, I will not have you waste your life away to support mine."

I closed my eyes as if the darkness could smother my racing thoughts.

Silently, I hugged her tighter, hoping it could keep her healthy and safe.

Hoping it would give me the strength I needed to do this.

CHAPTER TWO

Tyler

OCTOBER

I stood at Perth International Airport, gear bag and luggage in tow. My family surrounded me—both biological and ice.

My teammate, Holden, nudged me. His bright white smile was damn near blinding. "You gonna show those BU boys how the Aussies do it?"

"Hell yeah! We didn't earn that bronze for nothing." I tried to sound confident, but the nerves were setting in. Those guys in Boston lived and breathed hockey. It was one of—if not the most—prestigious college hockey teams in America. Getting in was a once-in-a-lifetime opportunity, and I had to prove my worth.

"I meant how we party, but sure; kick their arses on the ice too." Holden laughed when I shoved him.

"Dude, I can't legally drink there."

"Like that's ever stopped anyone. I can't wait to hear about all the college parties."

"Mate, not what I'm there for. The scholarship is grade dependent. If I screw this up, I'm right back here carrying you lot through another round of nationals." I bumped into his shoulder, trying to seem determined.

Holden sobered. "Fuck, we'll totally lose this season without you."

I laughed. Not only was it likely true, but I also needed to hear it. "You'll be right, mate."

This caught the team's attention and another one of my teammates, Beau, chimed in. "Mm, Holden's right. You're our captain, and you held us through those games. We're screwed." A chorus of grumbled agreements echoed him.

I shook my head, unable to fight the smile pulling at my lips. "Well, thanks for the ego boost, but I know you'll all be fine. Just don't show up hungover, and she'll be right."

I joined in with the laughter that followed. Telling a team of hockey boys, let alone Australian ones, to be sober in any capacity was like telling a baby cow not to drink milk: impossible.

My heart sank when my boarding number echoed over the PA system. I glanced at the faces around me; the faces of the people who'd supported me unconditionally through the toughest years of my life. I found a mix of sadness and comforting smiles. I made my rounds, giving each teammate a brief hug as they wished me luck. Then, my little brother stepped up. Who already nearly matched my height at the young age of fourteen.

"Love you," He hugged my waist tightly.

"Love you too, Bud." I hugged him back just as hard before he made way for Mum to take his place.

"Call me every step of the way, okay? Everything you need is in your pack." Mum's anxiety was palpable. "Sure thing, Mum. Love you." Despite the smile on her face, her eyes were glossy behind her black-rimmed glasses. I felt a tug at my heart at the realization of her weakened grip around my waist. I swallowed against the lump in my throat as she pulled away, her trembling fingers a silent plea for me to stay.

A hand clapped my shoulder, gripping me tightly. "I'll keep an eye on them, Ty." Holden's voice came from my side. My heart pounded in my ears; my eyes burned. I looked around and noticed I wasn't alone.

Mum averted her gaze to hide her tears, and my brother choked back a sob. Promise you'll call every day?" he asked, voice quivering.

"I promise."

As I walked toward the gates, I risked a glance back. Jamie's leg jittered as he fought back tears while Holden had an arm around his shoulders. I couldn't bear to witness my little brother's pain. So, I turned and walked away.

Boston was freezing—really fucking freezing. The bitter New England wind bit my cheeks as I walked to the admissions building, I sighed—it wasn't even winter yet. I wanted to love it; I always said how much I loved the cold, but this was a different kind of uncomfortable. My winter wardrobe from Perth was not designed for this. My hoodie was pulled tightly over my head, and my kit bag and knapsack felt heavier in the cold. Mental note: go shopping ASAP.

I was rudely snatched back to reality when I was shoved, crashing to the pavement with a resounding, *"Oomph."*

"Watch where you're going, man!" I blinked in the direction of the hostile, husky voice. *Didn't he walk into me?* I looked around, trying to ascertain where I was—I needed to learn to be more observant.

"Uh, sorry, mate," I grumbled, scrambling to my feet with the grace of a baby kangaroo.

The guy grunted in response. His amber eyes assessed me from beneath a knitted beanie as I took in his sweatpants and bomber jacket. "Whatever, just watch where you're going."

I blinked back at him, my first impression of Americans being they were definitely ruder than Aussies. I bit my tongue to keep from voicing my opinions. Instead, I simply nodded and strolled towards the admissions office, sensing Mr. Broody's eyes on me the whole way. Clearly, common courtesy wasn't a thing in Boston. But whatever, it's fine, I guess. I needed to get my attitude in check.

When I entered my dorm felt like hitting the jackpot. My living situation turned out better than expected—my own bedroom, a chill common space with a couch and TV, and a tiny kitchenette that seemed like it would do the job. I knocked on my dorm mate's door but found no answer. I pushed it open, finding an empty room— save for the explosion of clothes and books. I cringed, hoping the mess stayed contained behind closed doors.

After a much-needed shower, I flopped onto the bed. The springs protested against my weight, and I groaned at the stiffness of the mattress. Despite the jetlag, I decided to ring home. Mum and Jamie's faces lit up my screen, their voices a comforting melody for the pang of homesickness I felt. They shared mundane stories: what they had for dinner, the local shop's latest drama. Classic Mum, knowing everyone's life story. It felt reassuring, a throwback to dinners at home listening to Dad's tales of local chats. Jamie filled in details Mum forgot, and the smile on my face lingered.

When we reluctantly ended the call, I dozed off, dreaming of my coastal home where the wind played a nightly symphony on Colourbond fences.

I was awoken an undetermined amount of time later by the sound of Taylor Swift blaring through the walls. A lyrical male voice harmonized over the top, only to be interrupted by the loud whir of a blender. My arm flew over my eyes, and I huffed a laugh as the noises seemed to compete over which one could be the loudest.

I swung my legs off the bed—which gave its own creaky contribution to the cacophony of noises—and shuffled to the door. I opened it to reveal a blond guy dancing around the kitchenette. Despite the five-a.m. wake-up call, I struggled to be mad about it. The guy was practically skipping, wearing a T-shirt that was two sizes too small, but that hugged him perfectly and showed off his sculpted muscles.

I raised a brow. Not at the muscles, but at the pair of snug yoga pants that hugged his—

"Oh! Hi! Sorry, geez. I..." He fumbled for his words, and I stepped forward with a smile. I needed to put the guy out of his misery. I offered him a hand.

"I presume you're my roommate. Name's Tyler, but you can call me Ty." The guy looked at me like I'd grown a second head. His long lashes fluttered against his cheekbones, his mouth agape. My hand still floated in the air between us, and I was pretty sure it became the elephant in the room because he looked at it like – well, like I was holding my own dick or something. Seeing that he wasn't going to take it, I pulled my hand back.

"Ah well, sorry to scare you. You weren't in when I arrived yesterday." I pushed my hand through my hair, and his eyes tracked the movement.

"I was at my boyfriend's," he blurted. I didn't miss the way he cringed after. I shrugged. "Cool, I didn't catch your name."

He blinked his big brown eyes once more. "Cal." I smiled and his shoulders relaxed a little more.

"Well, nice to meet you, Cal. Uh, I'll let you—" I whirled my hand in the air to the mess that littered the kitchen counter, and the speaker that blared music through the small space.

"Clothes!"

I looked down and realized that I was still only in my undies.

"If you want me to have a genuine conversation with you, please wear more clothes. All of that—" He gestured to my body. "—is too distracting."

I instinctively covered myself, with a chuckle. "Sorry, mate. Didn't think much of it." Who wears a shirt in Australia? It's too hot.

"I wouldn't either if I looked like that. Geez." Cal, seeming to relax a little, went back to pouring his smoothie. I tried not to cringe at his less-than-expert smoothie pouring skills, the liquid dripping down the counter and the cabinet doors.

"More like growing up in hockey locker rooms on the coast of Australia."

Cal moved to lean against the bench, but I stopped him, saving him from sitting in a puddle of goo. Shifting him to the side, I grabbed a cloth and wiped up the mess.

"Australian hockey player with abs of steel saved me from getting smoothie on my ass. God help me now."

"I thought you had a boyfriend," I teased, guiding him around the kitchen to continue wiping up.

"Oh, I do. But I am gay and have eyes and ears," he suggested with a sing-song voice.

I couldn't help but laugh, grateful that this guy was way nicer than the one from yesterday.

"That doesn't bother you at all, does it?" It was more of a statement than a question, but I could hear the fear in his voice.

I turned my head from where I was clearing his dishes away. He was sucking on his metal straw, cheeks hollowing as he openly checked me out. "What, that you're gay, or you find me attractive?"

"Both?" Cal smiled genuinely, his eyes landing on my face instead of my crotch.

"I'm flattered that you find me attractive. And no, I don't care who you date."

A soft, grateful smile appeared on his lips. As I finished cleaning up, I heard him retreat from the kitchen "I have practice, then I'll be at my boyfriend's. So, I'll see you around."

"Catch ya!" I yelled at his back, feeling a bit down as he left. The dorm's air was now very quiet without his... well, him. I wondered if this would always be like this—me alone in an empty, quiet dorm.

CHAPTER THREE

Tyler

Mr. Boston Broody was on the team.

I stood in the doorway of the locker room, a dozen pairs of eyes on me like I was an animal in a zoo. And maybe I was. The moment I said, "G'day, mates," the room erupted in laughter.

Except for one person... he stood in the corner, those golden eyes sweeping over my body, once again sizing me up. The act had the ability to make me feel small, but instead, I straightened.

"Okay, boys!" Coach's voice thundered throughout the room, drawing everyone's attention. "This is Tyler Riley. He's come from Australia as part of the international exchange program. Tyler here led his team to a bronze at the under eighteens' world championship. So, I won't be treating him any differently from the rest of you."

Every head nodded in agreement, but their eyes remained fixed on me. I swallowed hard, fighting the urge to squirm.

I didn't like being the center of attention. I didn't do this sport for fame. Sure, I wanted my Mum to see *me* on the telly, but that was for her—not me. I tamped down that annoying little voice that made me question being here.

Coach showed me my locker where I dumped my bag and geared up for the ice. I needed to remember why I chose to do this. I'd been in Boston for a week and though it was my only time to sleep in before training started, I didn't complain when Cal woke me up at the crack of dawn. He was mostly absent, only popping in to change so I decided not to make a fuss.

Instead, I took the opportunity to have a sunrise jog through campus. I chatted with Mum and Jamie every morning and they seemed okay. Oddly enough, I was torn on how to feel about that.

A gentle hand on my shoulder pulled me from my spiraling thoughts. "Hey, man. I'm Colton—team captain. Everyone calls me Cap or Colt. If you need anything, here's my number. Don't hesitate to touch base. Being a fresher is hard enough, much less being so far away from home. That is unless you don't like home." He chuckled in an attempt to break the tension.

I took the piece of paper from his hand and flashed a smile. "Thanks. I love home, but we don't get a lot of chances like this. Hockey isn't really our national sport."

Colt grinned back at me. "That just means you'll take this seriously. On this team, there is an expectation of your performance. This is my last year, and my last chance at the finals if I ever want the chance of getting drafted, I need everyone to be on top of their game."

I nodded and began to strip down. I couldn't shake the feeling that I was being watched, and I turned to see those amber eyes peering at me from beneath long, dark lashes. His gaze darted down as he focused on the lone tattoo on my left pec. I turned away, avoiding the scrutiny of his gaze. I swiftly changed, then turned to face Colton.

"Look, I'm not here to fuck with spiders. I won't be late to practice. And you won't see me rocking up drunk or hungover. I didn't get where I am by slackin' off."

At first, I was met with silence. Wide eyes locked on me, until Colt burst out laughing. "Fuck with spiders?"

I rolled my eyes, realizing at that moment that it wasn't a normal expression. "It means I am not here to mess around." I forced an uncomfortable laugh as everyone began to mock my accent, which until now, I didn't realize I had. *Do I actually sound like that?*

"Man, this is going to be great. Do you really ride kangaroos to school?" a preppy guy asked.

Just to get back at him, I decided to roll with it. "Yeah, for sure. But you have to tame one first, mate. Crikey, they can be wild. Have you seen the videos of them boxing? Google it." I exaggerated my Aussie twang, sounding more like Steve Irwin than a country bloke from Perth. Which—unlike the rest of Australia—we don't have that strong accent that drives Americans wild —or so I thought. I watched, amused as my teammates scrambled for their phones. Rolling my eyes, I turned back to my gear. The ice was calling my name.

Slipping into my skates was like pulling on a pair of my favorite worn-in sneakers.

Though I tried not to compare mine to the others. I wasn't poor by any means. Before her diagnosis, Mum was a successful author, giving us a comfortable life with her royalties alone. Dad's life insurance money took care of most everything else, but we were still careful due to the unexpected fees of her treatments—though they were nothing compared to America.

Still, I couldn't help but notice the boys around me had gear more expensive than my first car. I noticed a couple of second glances but brushed them off. With my training kit on, I hit the ice, the only other teammate to join me being Mr. Boston.

His unwavering stare followed me as he did some warm-up stretches. The combination of his intense gaze and the rhythmic motion of his hips made my body flush hot. Given our first meeting, my body seemed oblivious to the fact that he was off-limits. I moved to the other side of the ice to begin my stretches until the coach began calling the drills.

I wasn't the tallest or the beefiest guy on the team by any means, but I put a lot of work into my body, keeping to a strict diet and workout regimen. Thanks to my rugby-playing grandad, I could handle hits like a pro. However, when we hit the speed drills, I knew it was my time to shine—even after being off the ice for two months. I was one of the forwards—and the only lefty—so I used that to my advantage. At least, that's how I saw it.

I had two players as my competition: Mr. Boston, a towering defenseman with a muscular build, and Colton, a forward with speed to rival mine. I contemplated letting Colton win in the speed drills but quickly dismissed the idea. After all, I was a Riley, and we don't shy away from a challenge. We tore our way up and down the ice, the delicious burn in my muscles keeping me going. I could see Captain's intrigued gaze as I passed him, but I refrained from teasing him.

"Shiiiiiit Aussie!" The preppy guy—Mouse—called out. "Cap's the fastest in the college league. You showing him up?"

I shrugged. It wasn't my intention, but I would be lying if I hadn't liked the competition. It was one of the many reasons we played sport, wasn't it? But I also had something to prove. My speed was my asset, and I was going to have to make use of it if I had any chance of getting noticed in this league.

"It's all good being fast, but can he use that speed with a puck on his stick?" Mr. Boston chortled.

Coach clapped his hands to draw our attention, "Okay, good work! let's finish up with a little skirmish to see where we're at."

He broke us up into teams, aiming for a balanced mix of age and skills. "Aussie, you could captain your team for this round, given your experience as captain last season." I nodded, but my stomach churned under the pressure. I wanted to work my way in and get to know the guys before being thrust into the spotlight. From what I'd learned, guys didn't appreciate a new face stealing the limelight.

As I faced my team, their jilted expressions didn't escape me. But having lived with a teenage brother, that was easy to ignore. I was relieved not to find Mr. Boston on my side of the blue line.

I'd kept a close eye on each player, sizing up their skills during practice. I didn't just skate; I dissected their every move. Game tapes from past seasons were my playbook, and aside from the other freshmen, I knew these guys' skills like the back of my glove.

With that wealth of knowledge, I rallied the team, bringing them together to lay out my game plan. To my surprise, they all nodded in agreement, some even throwing in their two cents about the other team's weaknesses. With a few taps on the back and a word of thanks, we were ready to hit the ice.

"Look, I hope there were no hard feelings about the captain gig. In my previous team, we worked together—no hierarchy, just respect and a shared goal to win. So, on three, we aren't here to fuck with spiders." I extended my hand, watching everyone's lips curve in amusement. Hands met mine, and on three, we yelled loudly, the sound getting my blood pumping. The coach covered his mouth, clearly hiding a smile though he tried to pass it off.

I met Colt on center ice and scanned his team placements, nodding in acknowledgment of his good choices on the first line. From what I'd seen of him in previous games, I hoped my plays matched up. I nodded to him, signaling that I was ready.

"Stay on two feet, Aussie." A familiar, husky chuckle came from my left wing. "Falling on your ass won't win you the game." Despite the annoyance that threatened to bubble up, I shot him a smile, not missing the raised brow from Colt.

The whistle blew, and the puck hit the ice. Colt was fast, but I was faster. My shorter stature gave me an advantage I swiped the puck, tipping it to Jarman—the player hovering behind me. The play was officially in motion. I slid to my mark, feeling the puck's solid weight against my stick. My blades carved through the ice, my focus sharp on the brooding, amber-eyed man shadowing my every move. His build was bulkier, but damned if he didn't almost match my speed stride for stride. A cheeky challenge played in my mind.

"Think you can catch me, Boston?"

I called his move before he made it. I ducked, passing the puck to Mouse. He gave me a goofy grin before effortlessly snapping it back. The crisp, satisfying sound of a perfect tape-to-tape pass reverberated through my stick, making my arm buzz and my pulse race.

Colt hustled to close the gap, but he was caught in my jet stream. I had my eyes locked on the goal. Only Mr. Boston kept up the chase. With a flick, the puck flew. The goalie leaped, their hand stretched out—but they were too slow.

The puck flew into the top right corner, missing their glove by a hair. A triumphant grin pulled at my lips, fuelled by the rush of the play.

The game unfurled like a rhythmic dance. I deciphered the play, orchestrated my team, and led us straight into the win. It was a fever dream of perfection. By the final buzzer, sweat dripped down my face, and my grin mirrored the satisfaction of a cat with a bowl of cream. The boys on my team collided with me by the boards, celebrating with bum taps and helmet knocks. Even if it was just a scrimmage match, I felt the coach's intention. He wanted me to prove myself, to show the guys I could be both skilled and supportive. A whisper of hope lingered, setting the tone for all the games to come.

Mouse clapped me on the shoulder. "Ausssieeee! Where the hell did you learn to do that?" I shrugged, unsure of what the answer truly was.

I headed toward the lockers, only pausing when the coach beckoned me over.

"Good work, kid. If you keep playing like that, you could find yourself on the starting line this season."

I flashed a smile and nodded. "I'm just getting started, Coach. Got something to prove."

"And that is?" His raised eyebrow demanded an answer.

"That an Aussie can make it in the big leagues." But it ran deeper; numerous reasons were driving me, and nothing would stand in my way.

"Well, if you keep it up, you won't have any troubles. If any of the boys give you a hard time, don't hesitate to let me know. Some have put in the hard yards since their freshman year to earn more time on the ice. Fresh competition, might not sit well with everyone."

I nodded confidently. "I can handle it, sir. Life throws more challenges than insecure men, trust me."

I strolled into the locker room, giving Coach a nod as I left him behind. Once inside, I kept my head down as I passed by my teammates in various stages of undress. I was a bit unsure about the locker room etiquette here. Back home, my team was my family—we'd have a conversation no matter what. But here, these guys were walking around in towels, some starkers others in their sweaty gear—those were probably the freshers. Banter, laughter, and stories about recent shindigs filled the air. I caught snippets here and there of them sharing details about girls they'd been with. It took all my self-restraint not to jump in and ask for a bit more respect.

At home, our talks about relationships had a different flavor—more about the long-term, grounded in respect. Occasionally, a nod about looks or a quick yarn about good or bad times, but we never got into the dirty details. Quite a few of us had sisters and as their captain, I made it bloody clear that any lack of respect wasn't on around me.

"What about you Aus? You coming to the party tonight?" I turned as I took off my sweat-soaked shirt, wet tendrils of hair whipping against my cheeks as I shook out my hair.

"Nah, parties aren't my scene."

A chorus of boos echoed through the room. "Don't Australians have a legal age of eighteen? I swear I hear you guys could drink us under the table." I couldn't help but laugh at Mouse. He had a point, "Nah-Yeah, Australians drink a lot. Half my captaincy was spent scolding my team for rocking up hungover. I just don't drink. Nor do I party—not my thing." I shrugged, wrapping a towel around my waist before making my way to the showers. There was never any time for parties. Not when there might be the need to rush my mum to the hospital or take my brother to early practice.

"What about girls?" Mouse called out.

I stopped, glancing over my shoulder. "What about them?"

"Well, Aussie girls are hot as fuck. Surely you at least partied for that reason."

"Yeah, there are some seriously good-looking girls, but I'm not a hit-it-and-quit-it guy. Girls are just a distraction. " My stomach churned at a painful memory that resurfaced, an old hurdle life tossed my way that had faded into the background when my dad passed.

"Dude, with that accent you could get any girly you wanted." I laughed at Mouse's attempts to get me to this party.

"More for you man. I'm already kicking your arse on the ice, least I could do is cut you some slack outside the rink?" I round of *oooo*'s round the room.

"I'll fill you in on what you miss!" Mouse shouted after me.

"Please don't!"

CHAPTER FOUR

Hunter

"Dude, you'll have no teeth left, what's your deal?" Colton skated alongside me as we cooled down.

I hadn't realized I was clenching my jaw so tight. Colton followed my gaze, laughing when he realized I was watching Mr. Australia gliding around the ice like a fucking figure skater.

"Threatened? Not like you."

He was right, but I'd never had a reason to be. I'd always been the most confident person in the room. Everyone knew me; I played with most of these guys through local teams and training camps. I was ready to dominate my senior year—be on the starting line, the hot topic in the locker room. I wanted to finish with a bang. Then this freshman from Australia swooped in and immediately captured everyone's attention. I hoped he'd be another average player, but even I had to admit that he was fantastic on the ice. He quickly stole the limelight from Colton—my high school teammate. We were supposed to be the stars, but we looked like rookies compared to Mr. Australia.

"He's just so..." I couldn't find the words to express how *frustrated* I felt. The guy was poised. He rolled with the punches. He showed up early, left late, and he even helped with the equipment—and he *never* complained. He didn't party, didn't drink, and he never showed up for the team meals. Yet, everyone loved him. He just had that charm about him. He took the time to get to know each member of the team—except for me. He looked at me and dismissed me like I was a waste of his time.

All I heard at gatherings was "Aussie this, and Aussie that." It was growing tiresome. On his first day, I saw a glimpse of vulnerability, and it made me want to crack his shell. Sure, maybe that look of vulnerability was because I was the one who knocked him to the ground. I'll admit, I was an asshole, but he caught me off guard with those crazy seafoam eyes. His reddish-brown hair warmed his complexion. He had beautiful, sun-kissed skin with a smattering of freckles over his nose. And that's why I ground my teeth. All it took was one look, and I was wrapped around his finger.

It was infuriating...

"Just so... What?" Colton chuckled, waiting for my answer. I couldn't say he was perfect, that would lead to another discussion I didn't care to have.

"Everyone just likes him, and he puts in no effort outside of practice."

Colton mulled over his next words. "True, but he puts in the effort when he is here, and if he gets us a win at The Frozen Four... I won't complain."

"Even if he outshines you?"

"I am good, but there's nothing to outshine. Tyler may be faster than me, but I still out-skate a lot of players in the NHL. I have some scouts watching me, and if I'm captain of a winning team, that looks a hell of a lot better than a losing one. So, get your attitude in check and try to get along with him. For the sake of the team."

I groaned, trying to think how I would survive an entire season with *Aussie*.

"How do I become friends with him if he won't come to a single party?"

Colton smiled. "Just give him time. We have our first game next week—we can try and drag him to an after-party then." Then just before he skated away, he added, "And stop grinding your teeth."

I rolled my eyes, not liking my chances. Though he managed to hide it from the rest of the team, I could see right through his lies about parties. I didn't miss the way he bit his lip or how his brow creased in the middle when he talked about them. Even during some of the locker room talk about women, his hands would clench into fists. Maybe he had someone back home, or perhaps he just didn't appreciate women being talked about like simple pieces of meat. I wasn't too fond of it either, but sometimes you had to play along—survival and all that. Like many of the guys here, this was my last year of hockey, and the key to success was undoubtedly getting along with the team.

Having my locker stall beside him was both a blessing and a curse. A blessing because I could knock into him as much as I wished—which was every chance I got. I couldn't decide what I liked more: the side-eye he gave me or the daily frown. However, the guy had a body any man—straight, gay, or otherwise—would die for. Seriously, he had to have zero body fat.

The week leading up to the first game—when my focus should have been on that and only that—my attention seemed to fixate on Mr. Australia. He quickly made himself at home, and I couldn't miss his attempts to find his team identity. He seemed to be a guys' guy—except when it came to me.

After another practice, I walked past him, deliberately bashing my shoulder into his. I heard a grumble, but he never bit back—which was disappointing. For some reason, I decided that needed to change—immediately.

"Something to say, Aus?" I taunted.

"You're not that big. Watch where you're going."

"*Not that big*." I had half a mind to show him exactly how big I was, but you know, locker room etiquette. I stood a whole five inches taller than he did and was a hell of a lot broader. The urge to crowd him against the wall grew with each passing moment.

"Sorry, *mate*," I smirked. "Didn't see you there."

His eyes fell to my mouth. "Just stop bumping into me. We're on the same team here. No need to be checked, yeah?"

"Just didn't see you." *Lie, lie, lie.*

"Just like you didn't see the puck in stick-handling drills," he said sarcastically before heading for the showers in an effort to keep avoiding me.

I went out of my way to stay close to him. "Noticed my stick-handling skills, did you?"

"I notice nothing about you, Boston, other than you have a tendency to run people over when it's not needed."

I hum and get ready for a shower, only to notice him turn and leave without showering.

"Something wrong with the shower?"

"I'm going to shower in my dorm." He said in a hurry.

"Aw, feeling shy, Aussie??"

"The only thing I'm feeling is annoyed."

He was gone before I could get in another word.

Colton walked in and sensing the tension, gave me a warning glare. I responded with my heart-stopping smile. There was something about making Tyler Riley feel *anything* towards me that got my blood pumping. His perfect game with his perfect eyes and his perfect hair may do nothing but piss me off, but I loved getting under his skin.

My need to irritate him lingered throughout the week. But when it came to our first game of the season, we were all determined to showcase that we were the team to beat. Tyler's easy-going nature took a different turn. He was still friendly, yet he clearly wore his game face.

And we came out on top.

I was in the zone, and though I wasn't too sure about the Aussie at first, he stepped up—big time. His on-ice chemistry was next-level. It was like he could read my mind. He knew every move before I made it. I'd had my eye on him since we first crossed paths. It was like that one simple touch put him on my permanent radar. Communication was almost unnecessary. I knew I could sling any pass his way, and he'd respond flawlessly. The energy was electric. You could feel it in both of us, especially when that final buzzer sounded and that victory grin spread across his face. I got swept up in the joy, like a moth to his damn radiant light.

"Man, that was awesome!" I exclaimed, giving him a pat on the back.

"I've never had that before! Nothing was ever that quick—that effortless," he admitted with a slight grimace.

"Oh god, please never tell my team I said that."

I chuckled. "Oh, I'm definitely holding that against you, Aussie."

Colton joined us, draping an arm over each of our shoulders. "My dudes! If we maintain that magic, we'll be on top at the end of the season. We have to celebrate!"

I refrained from touching Tyler, yet he flinched, nonetheless. Colton, however, didn't seem to notice He was already talking up the party at the hockey house.

"Kels is coming," I added to the conversation.

Colton smirked. "Still friends with benefits?"

My only response was a nod. Tyler, noticeably tense, made his way to his stall beside mine.

"Getting a third?" Colton threw in.

Tyler didn't miss the quip, if his side-eye was anything to go by.

"Who knows? She calls the shots. I'm just there for the excitement—and to get off, obviously."

"Get it out of your system now," Colton warned. "I don't think your dad will appreciate your polygamous ways when you're running the firm with him."

"Pfft, what he doesn't know won't hurt him. The more, the merrier." Tyler made a noise of disgust, and as I turned to him, I raised an eyebrow. "Didn't think your kind were prudes."

He ignored me, shaking his head.

My eyes were drawn south to his glistening abs as he stripped his jersey and protective pads. I'd never met a man who had me reminding myself to stop ogling. Seriously, his body was a tribute to the male body in his prime. Something that made me understand why artists sculpted it.

"Do whatever you fancy in the bedroom, mate. I just don't need to be hearing about it," Tyler quipped, his Aussie accent giving the words an extra edge.

"Aw, has it been a while?" I taunted, enjoying his discomfort, the subtle tick in his jaw. His icy glare told me I was getting somewhere, getting close to cracking that shell.

"Not everyone is a sex fiend, Boston. And not everyone takes pleasure in hearing about your conquests."

"Who were they, and what did they do to your libido?" I prodded, relishing the discovery of an imperfection in his pretty facade.

"No one," he grumbled, turning to leave.

Instinctively, my hand reached out, grabbing his elbow.

"So, you're a virgin? How long were you planning on holding that card? Wouldn't have wanted the guys to find that out."

His pretty eyes flared with anger. "Fuck you, Hunter," he spat. "I don't need to explain myself to anyone—especially a self-righteous Boston prick like you." He yanked his arm back, surprising me with his strength.

I didn't let his fighting words stop me; that little button was mine to press, and I was going to press it. My lips quirked at the knowledge of what I was doing to him. Wanting to rile him up more, I continued. "Come find me when you *are* ready to get the stick out of your ass then, Aus. Maybe I could direct you in the direction of a good lay."

"I'll do just fine on my own." He pulled away and headed for the showers.

A glutton for punishment, I followed him. "You obviously don't. You need to chill. I thought you Aussies were supposed to go with the flow."

I watched his shoulders rise and fall with each breath; his fists clenched at his sides. I opened my mouth to continue my tirade, but a hand on my shoulder stopped me. I turned to look at Colton and simultaneously caught the eyes of my teammates, all staring at me like they didn't know who I was.

"What the fuck, man?" Colton sneered. "Is that how you make friends?"

I exhaled, the sound laced with resentment, then resulted in grinding my teeth again.

I am going to have to send him my dentist bill at this rate.

Tyler Riley was *infuriating*. He paraded around like he had it all together, excelling effortlessly in everything he touched—and looking damn good while he did it. He was the type that got everything handed to him on a platter: friends, grades, skills.

I bit back any comments on his looks, fully aware of my own allure. I had that edgy, rugged vibe that pulled people in with the mystery. As for Tyler, he presented himself as untouched, save for that damn tattoo on his chest boasting an unread quote and a seemingly personal date. No scars, just the illusion of the boy next door. But he wasn't the typical golden prep boy you'd find around here. No, he was some golden Aussie. His voice had a seductive lilt to it, illuminating his demeanor and drawing people in like a siren song.

And here I am: resentful yet lusting after him. *Get your head in check, Hunt.*

"He just needs to loosen up. He can't waltz into our locker room and judge us for having a good time. Dude's wound up tighter than a preacher at a pride fest."

Laughter erupted from my teammates. "See? They get it!" I gestured to the laughing faces, but Colton simply shook his head.

"If it fuels his game on the ice, I couldn't care less. Respect his boundaries, would you? I want what we had today. And if it's 'cause he's choosing to stay abstinent, well, screw it, I don't give a damn."

The word 'abstinent' almost made me gag. But damn, there was this twisted desire to unravel what makes that guy tick. He was like a scratch-off ticket, the jackpot hidden beneath a cover. And damn if I didn't want to find it.

CHAPTER FIVE

Tyler

The fucking nerve of that guy! It was like he found the scab that needed scratching and kept picking until it started to bleed. I glanced at the time, noting it was nearing nine in the morning at home. Good, I needed some familiar voices. I shoved past Hunter and returned to my stall to get dressed.

"Ignore Hunter." I looked over to see Colton leaning against Hunter's locker. "He's all about the college experience. He just doesn't understand that it's different for us. Look, the party tonight is at the hockey house; it's not just sex and booze. We have video games, pool, and shit. It's just mates hanging out, and the guys get the deal; they won't try to force girls your way. We like you, Aus, and it would be good to celebrate our first win with you." I smiled, even though there was no way I was going, especially if Hunter was involved. Still, it was nice to have the invitation.

"Thanks. I'll think about it."

Colton clapped me on the shoulder, a broad smile on his face. "That's all we ask."

I packed up my gear and left, waving goodbye to the team as I dodged more attempts to get me to the party. I was already dialing home before the doors banged shut behind me.

"Hey, it's my college hockey star!" That was all it took for me to relax. I wasn't embarrassed to admit I was homesick.

"Hey, Ma, how's it goin'?"

Her chuckle sounded on the line. "I feel like I should be asking you that. You're the one exploring the world."

I rolled my eyes; grateful she couldn't see it. "Yeah, it's fine; we won our first game. I got to play in the starting lineup with the captain, got a couple of goals in. It was just a preseason game, so no biggie." I remembered the feeling on the ice and God, it made me... forget. Forget that I was thousands of miles away from home, forget all the new—forget Hunter.

"Tyler, it's hard to be happy for you when you don't sound it yourself."

"I'm just a little tired, getting used to the classes, the training schedule, ya' know."

"Mmhmm... I call bullshit," Mum hummed, knowing me all too well. I couldn't help but laugh, drawing a couple curious stares as I walked back to the dorm. The cold air stung my cheeks and nose, but at least I now had a jacket that could handle it

"I'm just missing home, you know? The team is great, save for one guy—the dude's got a mouth on him. On the ice, though, we're a killer combo. It's like we can read each other's minds. Though as soon as we step into the locker room... he just knows how to make my blood boil." I could feel my blood pumping at the mere thought of his glare, the way he studied me like he was trying to read me for weaknesses. It was as if he got off on making me squirm. That alone sent shivers down my spine, giving me that extra edge for the next match.

"I see..." I knew that tone; it was the one that meant, "I know something you don't." I swear that woman was a witch in a past life.

"See what?" The bite in my voice even made me flinch. I never spoke to her like that.

"Don't take that tone with me, Tyler Riley," Mumma Bear mode was activated, and my shoulders slumped.

"Sorry, Ma. He just gets me so riled up. What do you see that I can't?" There was a beat of silence on the other line, long enough for me to enter my dorm room. As usual, it was empty. Cal was the ghost that graced the halls, occasionally making his presence known by a lone sock in the living room or the stickiness of a poorly cleaned countertop. "Ma?" I began as I pushed through the door to my room, sitting on the bed that groaned like an Australian in the snow.

"Is he hot?"

Panicked, I looked around my empty bedroom like an idiot, as if someone else could possibly hear.

"Excuse me? Did my *mum* just ask if I found the dickhead teammate hot?"

She simply laughed. "Well?"

I blinked some more at the dingy-looking ceiling. Where was she going with this? "I am not telling you that! God…"

"So, I take that as a yes?"

I groaned, attempting to divert my thoughts from the guy who got my blood boiling. "Mum, he's a teammate." I could practically hear her eyes roll.

"I know something happened on that hockey trip years ago. Your dad might have mentioned the girl, but that doesn't mean you can't be attracted to guys. And, well…"

I stiffened, speaking through gritted teeth.

"But what, Mum."

"I do remember a boy who came to me *before* he slept with a girl, asking how does one know if he likes girls or guys."

"I was fourteen, Mum."

"Yes, but then you tried it with a girl — which we won't get into — then we lost your dad, and then I got sick, and you made it your role to protect both me and your brother. I worry you have decided not to explore yourself because there's so much responsibility on your shoulders."

I glanced around the room, desperate for something to capture my attention.

"Mum…" I was at a loss for words because, really, I wanted her to do all the work. I hated this topic for *so* many goddamn reasons.

"Tyler." She drawled out my name, knowing exactly what I was doing.

"Come on, son. This was your dad's game: making me fill in the blanks of his emotions so he doesn't have to. Not you. You come to me and work through your thoughts and emotions, which is why I'm assuming you're on the phone with your mum on a Friday night. Aren't your teammates out celebrating tonight win? You should be with them. So, talk to me, kiddo."

I sighed. Despite Dad being gone, she spoke about him freely. Two years passed like lightning, but the ache in my chest hadn't gone anywhere. "I don't know, Mum. I don't know what I am, *who* I am. All I know is I am a good hockey player. The guys here—all they talk about is sex, parties, hockey, and well, American college boy shit. I don't fit in. Sex…it wasn't something I enjoyed. How it all happened… I don't want that."

My mind went to sixteen-year-old me. I had the confidence of a kangaroo in a fistfight. Nothing scared me. I was cocky, loud, and nothing but smiles. Our Perth team beat the undefeated Canberra boys and we were on a high. Despite the loss, the Canberra boys threw a party that we all snuck out of the hotel to go to. Because we were the winners—that was it. But just as soon as I learned what that high felt like, I was also taught that life could slam you down quicker than you could blink.

I heard a soft sigh.

"Sex isn't meant to be like that. Yes, it can be casual, but it can also be earth-shattering. That's all I'll say on it. Just know that it doesn't matter who you like, Tyler."

I huffed a laugh. "I can't really explore that here, Mum. Sports aren't exactly the place for queer people. It's a liability, and the big leagues won't touch me if they find out. I have enough to worry about without trying to figure out if—" I paused, needing to take a breath "If I like girls at all."

There, I said it. And my heart was pounding in my chest, drowning out any other noise that threatened to compete.

I squeezed my eyes shut against the threat of tears. I could almost hear the gears turning as my mum processed what I'd just told her. "Honey, I don't know if that was any sort of coming out for you, but I'll say this: no matter how you identify, you're still you. You're still a young man with a big heart who doesn't shy away from who he is."

I sighed; I loved my mum, but she saw the world through rose-colored glasses. She was a romance writer that everyone fell under her spell, with her idyllic thinking of the world.

"Ma, you do realize I am in a predominantly Irish Catholic state, right? Half this country has banned books with even so much as a queer character. The sport that means the world to me banned rainbow *tape*."

"Fucking stupid," she muttered under her breath. "The lot of them, love is love."

I couldn't help but chuckle, "I know, Mum. I'm not putting a label on anything yet, but there's no point in denying it. You seem to still know me even from halfway across the world. Do I find guys attractive? Yes. Does that include one particular douchebag I know? Yes—annoyingly so."

Her laugh made me relax—slightly. "Do me a favor?"

"Hm?"

"Promise me that you won't stop yourself from experiencing... life. I don't want you to get your dream career and regret your path getting there. I don't think hiding part of yourself is good for your mindset. Having connections with people is important—whether that be a friendship or a fling. Sex isn't something you should be afraid of. What that girl did to you was unforgivable, but it's different when you're older. You have an opportunity now. You're a young college student. You can get to know another part of yourself. Go and find out who you are without being Tyler Riley the hockey star."

"I'll think about it," I muttered, but I couldn't deny the fact that her little pep talk had me itching. I began to wonder what it would be like—wondering how to do it without the team knowing.

"Atta boy. Go to that party, show face—don't be a hermit."

"Fine, I'll go."

I could hear the smile in my mum's voice. "Good! Now, wear something nice. You never know who you'll meet." Before I could protest, she signed off with a quick, "Love you! Buy your own condoms!"

My face was on fire, but for some reason she had me on my feet. She didn't need to know about the condoms I already had—I wasn't *that* clueless. I changed into dark, distressed jeans and a white top that was a little loose, so I tucked it in the back to show off my ass—ets. I threw on my new thick leather jacket and grabbed a beanie as I left, heading to the hockey house.

The party was hard to miss.

People poured out the front door of the brownstone, beers and red plastic cups in hand. I felt like I had walked onto the set of some reality show. I always thought the movies were exaggerated but as I moved through the house, I quickly figured out I was very wrong. I took in the guys who were obviously jocks, wrapped around girls who wore a lot less fabric than the weather called for. Then there were the edgy rocker types and the shy ones in the corners. The furniture had been pushed aside, leaving space for the drunken dancers in the living room. Girls stood on the coffee tables, men standing off to the sidelines watching. I wanted to laugh, but I was too busy absorbing the experience.

Back home, a party consisted of a small bonfire in a cut-in-half feed drum, people on deck chairs, drinking beers or whiskey and coke, girls sitting on laps, or singing along to the tunes that played on a tradies Bluetooth radio. You knew the night was ending when the last lot of dancing and singing hit, then people would crash in whatever they brought with them: cars, swags, or simply a sleeping bag.

This... this was next level. I walked through the house, not missing the heads that turned my way: fresh meat. There was a second TV and lounge set up where some guys played video games. The air hockey and pool tables drew a crowd that called out a barrage of insults to get their opponent off their game. A poker table was hidden past the kitchen on the dining table, and outside under some heat lamps was the beer pong table with a game going that drowned out the music.

"Aussie, Aussie, Aussie, Oi, Oi, Oi!" I spun to the noise, seeing half the team huddled in the kitchen, wide smiles greeting me. I couldn't help but return one of my own

"I feel at home already," I made the Australian lilt roll off my tongue thicker than usual. But it had the desired effect. They pulled me into the group, reaching out to pat any part of me they could reach—including my ass.

Colton wrapped an arm around my shoulders. "Good to see you changed your mind, Aus."

"Well, between you and the family calling me a hermit, I decided to brave the world of an American college party."

Jarman was the next to chime in. He was a typical hockey player, built like Colton but somehow even beefier. He was one defenseman I didn't want tackling me to the boards. His beard was something my dad would have envied. Thick and perfectly shaped to his jawline. His hair was buzzed short, and those muddy brown eyes always seemed to be smiling "What's so different?"

"Well, the turnout for one. We don't have huge house parties like this—they'd be shut down way too quickly. We have something called bush-doofs. We find someone with a bigger backyard or a large property. We have a fire, deck chairs, beers, and music. There's beer pong, but otherwise, it's just hard yakka and that, ya know?"

Pairs of wide eyes gaze back at me like I'm speaking a different language—maybe I am.

"Hard yakka?" Jarman echoes, testing out the unfamiliar word on his tongue.

"You know, banter, good chat, takin' the piss." I shrug, unable to find a better description than that, but the team seemed to accept it.

"You guys are a different breed. So, you just do bonfire parties and that's it?"

"Yeah, pretty much. But the legal age is eighteen, so most go out to clubs. Things like this—" I gesture around the house. "—are usually saved for special occasions." From what I can tell, the house is two stories and has people packing every inch.

The conversation seems to surround me for a bit, the guys eager to find out the differences between the two continents. It wasn't bad, it got my mind off the talk with my mum. Eventually, I messed around at beer pong until I started to feel buzzed, then I slinked off to a corner to people-watch.

My eyes caught a familiar face—Cal. He didn't notice me at first, which afforded me the opportunity to truly take him in. He was slimmer than me, but I could see the toned muscles pushing against his tight sweater. Though what made me approach him was the tenseness of his jaw, clenched so tight I was worried he'd break a tooth. I followed his gaze to find two guys making out under the staircase.

"You okay, mate?" I elbowed him, but softly, worried *I'd* lose a tooth if I spooked him. His face cut to mine, and I watched as he took me in, and realization hit his eyes.

"Well, you see that guy?" He pointed to the two guys going at it, and I wasn't sure which guy he was referring to. I cleared my throat—they weren't really my type. If I were ever honest with myself, I definitely had a type. One was edgy, with piercings and tattoos. The other was a clean-cut golfer-type guy, similar in height to me. The former was slim, reminding me of a skinny front band member, while the latter looked like he had an appreciation for the gym.

Cal watched me assess the two men, maybe trying to determine if I was uncomfortable. In truth, I'd never seen two guys kissing so... *passionately* in public. Their tongues danced together, wrestling for dominance. It looked messy, for lack of a better word.

"Which one? They're both guys."

Cal turned to me, and I realized he sort of reminded me of a baby-faced Chris Evans. He was attractive, a little on the smaller side but I appreciated his appearance nonetheless.

His expression changed, the agitation leaving his eyes even if it was just a little. He huffed out a laugh. "I suppose they are." He gestured again. "The one who looks like he plays golf on Sundays."

That had me laughing out loud, and a few heads turned my way. "Sorry, that's exactly how I described him in my head. What about him?"

Cal squirmed. "That's my boyfriend."

My mouth fell open in shock. I looked to him, then to the golfer guy who was sucking face of punker guy. My stomach churned in sympathy, because I thought they were really serious about each other. I had been at college for a few weeks, and I'd barely seen Cal.

"I hope that reaction isn't you wondering why he would go for someone like me," Cal grumbled.

I turned to look at him again, noting the way his teeth bit his lower lip. Then I looked back to his "boyfriend." He was attractive by societal standards, but Cal had much more going for him.

"One, I was thinking he's a dick for making out with that twink in front of you. Two, you're hot. Unless you're into the whole punk rock thing—which I'm not—he's downgraded. By a lot."

Cal's mouth curled into a wide smile. *Chris Evans eat your heart out.* I smile involuntarily. What can I say? Cal had a certain aura around him that was impossible not to like.

"You, uhm... you're into guys?" he asked sheepishly.

Nerves bubbled up in my stomach. "Uh..." I looked around to see if any of my teammates were nearby.

"Ah, not out then?" I didn't miss the disappointment painting his features.

"My life is complicated. I'm not from around here, and this is my opportunity to get on the NHL radar—"

Cal put his hand on my shoulder and squeezed. "I know. You've been the talk of the town: hot Aussie superstar hockey player—the girls are eager to get a taste of you."

I look away, disgust roiling my stomach at the idea. I'd had a couple girls come up to me, and thankfully my teammates stuck to their word, steering them in another direction. I don't know what they really thought of me. I didn't miss the whispers, and standing in the corner with an openly gay man was doing nothing to help the rumor mill... but I felt more comfortable beside Cal than I did when girls were squeezing my ass and asking me to speak Australian to them. "It's the same fucking language *darling*," was apparently the wrong answer, but the guys seemed to find it funny.

"Don't worry, I'll be the last person to out someone." Cal brought my attention back to him and I fought of a grimace.

"Your boyfriend is currently cheating in front of us, and you're consoling the guy who doesn't want the world to know that he might not be straight."

"I get it. There's this stereotype that you need to be this big manly man. And being a *man* means you have to be so fueled with testosterone that you only want to fuck pussy, right?"

I couldn't help but laugh out loud again, I turned to face Cal, ignoring some eyes drifting my way.

"Right, I'm kind of still deciding... what term fits. My life is complicated. I haven't had a chance to... experiment. "

Cal nodded, his boyfriend's drama forgotten as he looked into my eyes, his own a warm brown that radiated with sincerity.

"If you weren't the hockey star that you are, would you be dabbling in dudes?"

Instinct made me look around to see if anyone overheard what he'd said. With an eye roll, he took my hand and pulled me outside where the bonfire had been lit on the frosted ground. Outside of the cool frigid air, it was so much like home I couldn't help but smile while I looked at the flames. Cal added some wood to the pit before sitting down beside me on the wooden deck chairs.

"So? You don't have to tell me, but I am a good listener and secret keeper." Despite the cheeky grin on his face, I somehow believed him.

"You're just as pushy as my ma on the topic, you know that? But yeah, I suppose if my life was different, I would be. Maybe I would have explored something more. Or at least be open to it. I just don't want it to get in the way of my future... you know? There is only one Australian who had ever played national hockey league and he had to practically jump through hoops to get noticed. Add in the fact I may be gay..." I cringed at myself.

"I get it, being out can be hard, especially in sports. Then you have to actually find another guy who is openly gay to have a relationship. And at our age, the pool is a little small unless you want a Daddy. When you do find someone... well apparently, they cheat on you in front of everyone." Cal huffed.

I nudged him with my elbow.

"The guy is a dick stick. You don't seem like the type who golfs on a Sunday anyways. What did you have in common other than being gay?" It was brutally honest, but Cal didn't seem to mind.

He looked at me with that same smile. "I like you, you're honest. Really... nothing. The sex was good I suppose. He always knew the right thing to say, but seems he does that with anyone."

"Apparently good sex can be found anywhere, so you'll find someone who can be there both emotionally and sexually."

I took a sip of the beer I'd been nursing for a while. I really wasn't a huge fan.

"Apparently?" Cal looked at me with an eyebrow quirked, and I couldn't help but laugh again, the alcohol buzzing through my system.

"God..." I wasn't sure if it was because Cal was having a bad night, or if it was simply because I hadn't had alcohol since I was sixteen but I trusted him. "I've, uh, only had sex once. It wasn't great. I was out with the team celebrating, everyone was hooking up and drinking. I'd never really been one to let loose, but I was a confident guy. There was this one girl, real pretty, but she was very forward. I sort of let her kiss me and flirt with me. I tried rolling with it because I saw how everyone else looked jealous that she was giving *me* attention. She was apparently a big deal where she came from—had a reputation. But it made me nervous. I thought it was because I wasn't... experienced, but then she took me into some person's bedroom, and I started to feel really uncomfortable. She got more persistent with me and was touching all over me. I wasn't interested by this point, but she kept at it." I paused, turning my gaze to the ground. I saw that look on Cal's face—the pity. "I was young and stupid. I didn't want to upset her. I could have done something, could have said no... but I didn't. I let it play out."

Cal rested his hand on my knee, only briefly before he pulled it away. "You know that's not okay right? Did you express you weren't feeling it?"

I shrugged. "Not in so many words. I tried pulling away but she kept coaxing."

Cal took a sip of his own beer, mulling over my words.

"Still not okay," he decided. "If you want, I can always find her on social media and do a little karma. Don't underestimate my internet stalker game."

"Nah, it's fine mate, really."

"So, you haven't tried since—with anyone?"

The swell of the emotions that came with the last two years hit me like a ton of bricks. I blamed the alcohol once more because I hadn't touched it since that night. I also hadn't really let myself process any of it.

"My dad was killed a few months later fighting a bushfire. Then six months after that, Mum was diagnosed with stage four breast cancer. My brother was spiraling and needed me. Despite how strong Mum tried to be, she just wasn't present after Dad's death. She was a bit of a ghost. Sometimes it felt like I lost both my parents. She's better now, the cancer managed with her treatments. But with it all, the last thing on my mind was exploring that part of me."

Cal's eyes shone with unshed tears. "Jesus Ty, that's... horrible."

I shrugged, the knee-jerk reaction to just move on. I wasn't sure if it was Aussie attitude or pure dismissal. Because I couldn't afford break—not now.

"Well, you're here now. I think you should put yourself first. Explore that side of life, if anyone needs some good sexual therapy, it's you."

I barked a laugh. "Sexual therapy?"

It was Cal's turn to shrug now. "When you know, you know."

CHAPTER SIX

Hunter

"You're staring," Kinsley whispered in my ear as she sat on my lap. I trailed her smooth skin with my fingertips, letting them trail over her soft curves. I'd committed every inch of her body to memory, my fingers mapping out the points that would elicit a shiver under my touch. We'd had our little... arrangement since high school; a mutual agreement to help get what we needed without the complications that came with commitment. It was an easy, no-distraction way for us both to experience our sexuality.

"Am not." I totally was. It was impossible not to. He was wearing those fucking jeans that were tight in all the right places. His loose white shirt was tucked up in the back, showing off his ass and making me think of all the things I'd like to do with it—the most important being owning it. A picture painted itself in my mind of how he would look bent over for me as my cock disappeared between those cheeks. My dick perked up at the thought of taking power over Mr. Perfect.

"You *totally* are. Why don't you talk to him?" Kinsley cooed in my ear, though it came off more as a challenge than a suggestion. "No teammates. Also, the guy is celibate or something. He hates all talk of sex and practically recoils at the degrading of women."

She smiled against my neck, "I like him already."

"Don't get any ideas Kins," the tell-tale rumble of her laughter tickled my skin.

"Only idea I have is letting you have him tonight." I felt her shift on my lap, resting her head on my shoulder to allow her gaze to follow mine. They looked awfully cozy, though Tyler wasn't exactly showing any interest toward Cal—nothing sexual anyway. He was talking to him freely, with an easiness that was causing something inside me to shift. I knew I'd already made my bed with how prickly I had been to him, damn-it he had my attention. That stupid smile and the light in his eyes. The way his hair had that auburn shine in the light. He was so unaffected by himself, like he didn't care about how good he was. It was pathetic. He could at least be cocky or, I don't know, kick a puppy—give me some reason to hate him.

"He wouldn't want anything to do with me—especially in the bedroom."

She laughed at me and if I was honest with myself, I deserved it. There was a certain level of whine in my voice that made me cringe. I sounded like a kid who couldn't have what he wanted. I could bed anyone I wanted and to be fair, I usually did. Even though it was my last year in the game—not by choice—I'd never ruin my stats by getting involved with a teammate. Been there, done that, wouldn't recommend.

"Mm, the way he keeps looking over here suggests otherwise." I stiffened in my seat. I looked back in his direction to catch a small side glance my way. *Hmm, sneaky side-eye.* It was such a small gesture I wouldn't have noticed it if Kinsley hadn't pointed it out. "That's just him hating me," I said, trying to rationalize why he was looking at me. Surely it wasn't interest... right?

But then I saw him look again, disdain in his eyes as he took in me and Kinsley.

"He doesn't like you with me," she deduced, amused with her new game.

"He doesn't like anything that alludes to sex; you on my lap kind of tracks with that particular look."

She laughed again. "Ever thought he hates talk of sex with women because he doesn't *like* sex with women?"

I had to admit the thought crossed my mind, but it didn't even begin to answer all my questions.

"And he's friendly with Cal—the most out and proud person at this party," Kinsley added.

I rolled my eyes, "That means nothing, Callum would make friends with anyone. It's impossible not to like the guy."

With a huff, "True, but they do look cozier than he would if your Aussie was straight, and the way he looks at you with that heat in his eyes... I'm guessing he may be interested in a little taste of Boston."

I considered her words and began to assess his every look. I sipped on my whiskey my mind wandered to the possibilities. Maybe, just maybe, I could have a taste. Whether it was the booze clouding my thoughts, or the way the fire made the red hue in his hair shoot fire through my veins, there was one thing for sure: I wanted to taste that Australian.

Fuck my rules—one time wouldn't hurt.

CHAPTER SEVEN

Tyler

A swig of whiskey washed away the bitter taste in my mouth, the time ticked by as the flames in front of us flickered in the bitter New England weather. Though the alcohol and the fire weren't the only things heating up my insides. It took a lot of energy to keep my eyes on the fire, to avoid the gaze that poured gasoline over the one raging inside me.

"Dude, what did you do to make Hunter Graves look at you like that?" My gaze followed Cals, finally locking eyes with the person I was trying hard to ignore.

"Ugh, other than exist? The guy literally knocked me to the ground, took one look at me, and decided he hated me." Cal looked from me to Mr. Broody and back—then burst into laughter.

"The guy has the hots for you, that's why."

My head whipped around so fast it made me dizzy. Cal was no longer moping over the fact that his boyfriend publicly cheated on him, nor was a blabbering mess from our first encounter. After hours of sharing life stories in a drunken haze, his cheeks were flushed and smile bright.

"You're kidding me, right? The guy is as straight as an arrow. He talks about banging women every day in the locker room. Last time it rubbed me the wrong way so it didn't end well."

"Oh, this is too good—you find him hot." I didn't care for the mischief hiding behind his eyes.

"Well, yeah. He's... something. But he's my teammate. And I don't think I could handle it if I hit on him and he *is* straight."

"I get you, but I promise you're not barking up the wrong tree with that one."

My brow furrowed as my focus returned to the man who'd been nothing but a bindi in my side since I got here. After almost a month of being scrutinized under his glare, he's left me feeling uneasy in more ways than one.

"He has a girl sitting on his lap, nibbling on his ear while his hand is on her..." One of his hands had disappeared under her shirt to knead one of her breasts while the other slipped behind the waistband of her jeans.

My attention was recaptured by Cal's howling laughter next to me—and he didn't even attempt to stop as I whacked him on the arm., "Sorry, you know you *can* say pussy right? Hotty hockey boy over there is bi. His girl loves multiples, so they often have a third, who can be male or female—someone who can give them both pleasure."

I blinked, eyes raking over the couple. The girl was fully entranced by Hunter's touch, but Hunter... Those eyes never left mine. A shiver wracked my body. "And you know this... how?"

Cal shrugged. "I may have been their third once, but once Kinsley realized I only batted one way, it didn't happen again. Though she didn't mind playing voyeur for one night." Cal's smile turned sensual at the memory

"Was... was it..." Curiosity was getting the better of me, though my stomach flipped making me second guess myself.

"I got to ride him while she rode his face. He was... let's just say he knows what he's doing. If you want to dip your toe into the gay pool—secretly—he would be a good place to start. And from the fireworks crackling between the two of you right now... you'll find out that sex can be anything but boring."

I broke my stare-off with Hunter to look at Cal, my blood suddenly pumping a lot harder.

"The way I see it, big guy, is this is *your* chance to call the shots. You have one night to see if men really do it for you. We both know he's hot, and well... I suppose Kinsley's attractive too, so you can experiment there too."

I tightened my grip on my glass, surprising myself as I seriously contemplated it.

This is the whole reason I came to the party, right?

"Gimme your cell." I dropped my phone into Cal's outstretched palm and watched as he entered his number. "Call me tomorrow and we can catch up for coffee—which we'll both need after all this alcohol. I'm going to find my soon-to-be ex and tell him to shove it where the sun don't shine. Which he probably will: right up that little punk's ass. But hey, maybe next time you can be *my* wingman." Cal stood, tapped my shoulder, and strutted off. I wanted to call after him not to leave me here. To be honest, I walked here, and I was in no state to walk back to my dorm alone. I was kind of worried to get up at all.

I was unsure how long I simply sat there, staring into the bonfire. I was so lost in my own thoughts that I jolted when a presence made itself known.

Just like on the ice, I knew it was him.

His presence made my body temperature shoot up. He sat beside me, so close that our thighs brushed together. I swallowed hard. I only realized then that things had gone quiet. No one was outside—not even Kinsley.

Then he leaned in close. "I *can* keep a secret you know." His low, husky voice sent a shiver down my spine. My skin buzzed as the warmth of his breath tickled my cheek. A shudder wracked my body when his fingertips brushed the small of my back. Then those confident fingers snuck under my jacket, then under my shirt, once he pulled it free from my jeans. The slide of rough calloused fingertips had my skin pebbling up. My gut tightened as desire pooled low in my belly. The catch of my breath was visible in the cool night air.

"I don't know what you are talking about, Hunter." My voice came out hoarse and husky to my own ears. I closed my eyes for a beat, and my mind swam with images of what his hand would look like against my skin, intensifying my reaction.

"Is this why you hate it when I talk about women? You bat for the other team?" He was so close, I fought the urge to turn and look at him, because it would mean millimeters would separate our lips.

"I like women... I just don't feel the need to make them sound like meat."

He hummed, the sound shooting straight to my crotch. "I like women too, but there is something else. I saw you cozying up with Cal even though you could have your pick of any woman here. Though I get it, Cal has a movie star quality about him."

My loose, drunken lips spill without thought. "Baby Captain America." That had Hunter laughing, which lit up my libido. The sound alone had me hard as a rail. *Not gay at all, Tyler.*

"I can see that. Is that your type?"

I shook my head, staring blankly at the house in front of me, the only anchor keeping my arousal in check. "I don't know," I admitted all too honestly. Maybe I *should* have walked back to my dorm. Fingers met my chin, their touch hot against the cool of my skin. It only took a gentle tug for me to turn my head. His lips were right there, his golden eyes striking in the flames, dark hair mussed and falling in his face. My fingertips itched to reach out and brush it back.

"So, a baby bi then?"

I nodded, unable to lie under the deep scrutiny of his gaze.

"I can look after you baby," he purred. "I can make you feel good. You're safe with me. You can tell me what you like, what you don't, what's too much, what's not enough. Let me take care of you, Tyler." His words were a soft caress, my name rolling off his lips like a prayer. He was the snake in the grass tempting me to take a bite of the forbidden apple, and under my whiskey-soaked haze, I found myself nodding, my lips grazing his. Electricity flooded my system, and I was short-circuiting. I had never felt this—she hadn't felt like this. The anxiety that flooded my system all those years ago was clouded by lust and desire.

"I need your words, baby." His hand flattened on the bare skin of my back, and pictures came to my mind, of him taking control, pleasuring me from behind and a whimper left my lips.

It wasn't lost on me that the man touching me was the very same one who had the ability to make me angrier than a kicked hornet's nest. But through the fog, the only thing I could see was a man asking for my permission—something no one else ever had done. He had no idea what that was doing to me.

"Just for tonight, then—"

"We never mention it again." My heart pounded in my chest as he finished my thoughts for me.

I nodded, and then his hand moved, fingers lacing through mine a little too perfectly. I lazily followed behind him as he guided me through the sliding doors of the house. As we got inside, the realization of what I was about to do jolted my feet to a stop. I was about to protest, thoughts about the team rushing through my mind.

As if Hunter had a direct line to the shit show of thoughts in my head, he squeezed my hand. "Don't worry, everyone's turned in for the night. Kinsley is already in my room."

I stiffened. Cal said about Kinsley being a part of Hunter's... sexcapades, but hearing her name was like dunking a bucket of ice water over my head. The one simple word had fear flooding my body once more.

CHAPTER EIGHT

Hunter

Tyler stiffened and retracted his hand, which made me turn to face him. Those gorgeous eyes of his had suddenly lost the lustful gaze that had my balls tightening with need moments before. My heart broke when I saw what replaced it: fear. I flipped through our conversation, trying to figure out what it was that triggered him. Then, like a bell going off, it hit: Kinsley. He feared being in bed with Kinsley. I paused, assessing him. Two moments ago, I was on cloud nine. Tyler chose to spend the night with me despite me brooding over Cal getting his undivided attention. The realization that he was more like me than I thought had my blood rushing south. Then, he was shivering under my touch, eyes dilating at the thought of a secret rendezvous with me—and I had never been more turned on in my life. Something made me think this was his first time, which only made me hotter. But now? The idea of going up to a woman, which arguably should be the least scary part of that scenario, had him looking like he was about to encounter a wild animal.

"I, uh, I think I'm going to try and get home." Tyler began to back away, eyes darting from me to my bedroom door.

I frowned and shook my head, crowding into his space on the small staircase. I know the team called it a night. Those who hadn't made it to their bedrooms crashed on the couch, so in that moment it was just the two of us. His eyes darted to my lips, then back to my eyes, his dark lashes sweeping his cheekbones. My dick throbbed as if that gaze owned me. Which wasn't the idea: I needed to own him, yet this sudden vulnerability had me doing a total one eighty. I would take anything he'd give me in that moment.

"You don't have to touch Kinsley, she doesn't have to touch you. She can just watch… or I can send her away." I watched as his eyes shifted, and I felt a pang in my gut.

Was he scared of women?

I began to wonder what happened to make him that way, and my instincts kicked in. They were protective, primal—completely unfamiliar to me. I wanted to tell myself that it was because he was my teammate, we were supposed to have each other's backs—but I knew I was kidding myself. It was because it was *him…*

"Hunt…" His whisper hit my lips and I sighed, pressing my forehead to his and taking in a deep breath. The rich, earthy tones that were all Tyler mixed with the smoke from the fire and the sweetness of the whiskey he'd been drinking. I was drunk on that alone. I was dying to know what his skin felt like under my fingers.

"As I said, you make the rules. If it's too much, tell me. That includes Kins, okay?" His audible gulp betrayed his nerves, adding an adorable touch to the air. This guy, normally oozing with confidence turned into someone I hardly recognized—but that I adored just the same. His gaze pierced through those dark lashes, pupils dilated as if hungry to devour the sight of me. However it was still edged with vulnerability, so I knew I had to tread lightly.

I took another step closer, bringing our bodies together. Electricity crackled between us, his hard length finding mine. I was fascinated with how responsive he was. His lust-filled eyes fluttered shut at the slightest touch. His confidence mixed with vulnerability in the way he bit his bottom lip, creating an intoxicating blend that made him even more irresistible.

"Let me look after you, baby." I let my whisper fall over his lips. He nodded his head against mine, so I reclaimed his hand and began leading him to my room on the third floor. I shook off the thought of how perfectly his hand fit in mine Tyler held onto my hand like it was a lifeline and I loved it.

On the ice, we worked together in a synchronized dance, each knowing the other's move before it was made. I was dying to see if that chemistry translated to the bedroom.

Kinsley lay on my bed naked and warming herself up. Damn, she was hot—a fucking wet dream. She looked up with lustful eyes. I could see she was just as attracted to Tyler as I was. But she sure as hell was excited to see what had me so riled up. After seeing him with Cal, we both were eager to see if he would be our third for the night.

"His rules tonight Kins, he wants me." Kinsley didn't look upset. If anything, it turned her on even more. There was something we both wanted, something we hadn't checked off our list, but I wasn't sure if my baby was ready for that yet. Kinsley nodded, reading me like only she could before leaning back against the headboard and sliding her hand between her thighs.

Tyler looked her over, mouth slightly agape, but his eyes had lost that heat once again, as if the sight of her had him questioning his decision. I hooked a finger under his chin, redirecting his attention to me. He was shorter than me, looking up through thick, beautiful lashes. My thumb ran over his fuller bottom lip and he trembled. My dick was painfully hard against my zipper. I leaned in, brushing our noses together.

"Can I kiss you?"

Lust returned with a vengeance and without an answer, Tyler took control. With that same confidence he had on the ice, he speared his fingers through my hair, clenching hard enough to make it sting just the right way, His mouth crashed against mine and he sucked the breath right out of me. I'd kissed a lot of people before—men and women—but this, this was something else.

Tyler Riley was like an animal that was finally let out of his cage. His lips tasted like whiskey and pure man. His teeth tugged my bottom lip, commanding *more*. I groaned, reaching around to grip that tight-toned ass in my hands. I'd spent what felt like an eternity looking at it, trying to get a glimpse, but my Aussie was shy. Though a peek in the locker rooms could never hold up to how it felt in my hands. Hard, perky... and fucking *perfect*.

CHAPTER NINE

Tyler

I was on fire.

It was like the flames from the pit had absorbed into my skin and were burning for a way out, and the only reprieve was the broody Bostoner in front of me. I blamed the booze for giving me the confidence. The haze was strong, but it quieted the thoughts that wanted to take over.

Because kissing Hunter Graves was unlike anything I'd ever done. It was better than scoring a winning goal, better than the first feel of ice skates gliding on a freshly polished ice rink. No one had ever looked at me like the way Hunter was in that moment. Those dark, intense eyes locked onto me as if I were his sole focus. Like he hadn't eaten in days and I was his next meal. He had forgotten the woman in his bed, and so had I. I'd completely forgotten that I was supposed to be nervous about being in the bedroom with a woman. Because she was nothing, and he was everything. I didn't know this part of myself existed, and I wasn't going to lie—it felt good. Our gazes locked, our lips milometers apart as if he just felt the earth shake too. His body pressed to mine, the kiss leaving both of us panting. Was this what it felt like to be with a man? Or was it just him?

Him.

I knew I found men attractive, but up until then, I'd admired them from afar. But one look from those crazed eyes the first day on campus had me diving into the water head first.

"Ty..." I knew he was going to check in, I saw him assessing me, waiting for me to freak out. But nothing was going to stop me. I needed this. More importantly, I needed him out of my system.

I dove back in, sealing my mouth over his. His lips were soft but strong, warm and all-consuming. The fact that he was taller than me was an added turn-on. The way he angled my head to maneuver me to precisely where he wanted me to be, had me gripping my dick painfully hard to stop my oncoming orgasm.

"Clothes," I rumbled. I wanted them off. I wanted to touch what I knew to be a muscular chest, one that had tattoos over his pecs. The same tattoos that cascaded down his arms to the cuffs of where his jersey sleeves would sit.

Hunter smiled against my lips. "Anything you want, baby." The pet name had my body flushing from head to toe. *Fuck*, why did that do it for me?

He took a step back and shed his bomber jacket. His Henley was quick to follow, hitting the floor. Then his ripped chest was on show, the dim lamp light enhancing every bump and curve. My eyes traveled all the way to the V that disappeared behind his low-cut pants. I groaned. I wanted those pants off. I knew he had thick thighs, and an ass to die for.

But my hands shook, torn between taking my own clothes off or ripping his from his body. As if he knew, his hand took mine and brought it to his mouth where he pressed a kiss to the pulse point on my wrist.

"Let me take care of you." I nodded, completely under his spell.

He expertly worked his jeans open, my eyes studying the way his fingers turned his belt loose. Then the button popped and the zipper lowered. He shucked the denim, taking his CK briefs with it—and a purr left me, a fucking *purr*. I didn't doubt anymore how I felt about men—about this man. His erection jutted out proudly from between his thighs, long, thick, and cut. I licked my lips as desire tightened my gut. Hunter closed the gap, taking my wrist once more, and guided me to wrap my fingers around his engorged flesh. We both moaned at the slight brush of my fingers against his velvety skin. *God, fuck, fuck fuck. I am touching a dick. I am touching Hunter's dick.*

"How's it feel, baby?" His breath ghosted across my ear, and I wasn't sure when my beanie went missing but I was grateful for it. His hand curled around mine, helping me give his cock a tug. I felt its pulse, felt the perfect mix of hard and soft.

"So good," the words tumbled out of me as I began testing the weight of him in my hand.

Hunter bit my earlobe, "Can I get you naked now?"

I nodded. "Yes, please. *Fuck*, yes." The words tumbled out of my lips in a disjointed mess, a chaotic symphony of desire. I felt myself unraveling, succumbing to the allure of his husky, deep voice and the sight of him with his hand on his arousal.

"You have to let go, baby," he said with an amused lilt to his voice. I let go—reluctantly.

"That's it. Arms up; let me see the body I have been admiring for weeks."

My arms raised like I was a marionette and Hunter controlled the strings. Somewhere along the line, my jacket got taken off—I didn't care. I only felt myself get hotter as his calloused hands pulled my shirt over my head. Then those glorious hands mapped my body, dusting over my pecs. But I froze when he brushed my tattoo.

"Don't touch that," I growled.

Hunter nodded and true to his word, he moved on. I had to remind myself that I called the shots and set my limits. This was so unlike my first sexual experience that I found myself fighting back a sudden rush of unwanted emotions. I bottled them up and put them back on the shelf, returning my focus to the man in front of me. I focused on the darkness of his hair, the intoxicating color of his eyes, and the trimmed beard that felt like static under my fingers as I traced his cheekbones.

His hands landed on my belt. "Can I take your pants off? Can I touch you?" He pressed his lips to my neck as he fiddled with my belt, waiting for my consent.

"Yes, touch me. Fucking please touch me, Hunter." He groaned into my neck, nipping at the sensitive skin as my belt loosened. My jeans lowered, and his large hand cupped my dick through the fabric of my briefs.

"Fuckin' oath," I groaned, knocking his hand away to squeeze the base of my cock once more, staving off the orgasm threatening to race through my body.

"Mm, you're perfect, the way your body responds to mine. I could come to that sound alone," Hunter began to kiss down my abs, then his breath was at the waistband of my underwear as he lowered to his knees. I bit my lip hard, steeling myself to look down at him. My dick had already peeked out of the confines of my briefs, precome glistening on my stomach. I'd never been so hard in my life. Hunter's fingers lowered the fabric and my knees buckled when he licked the liquid from my stomach. Hunter's amused laughter fanned against my dick, his hand reaching around to cup my ass and keep me upright.

"Uncut..." he groaned. "Can I blow you?" I nodded sheepishly.

I took in a deep breath but as his lips sealed over my cockhead, I let out a string of profanities. I speared my fingers through his hair, loving the way it felt in my hands, how it looked between my fingers. The wet heat of his mouth was like nothing I had experienced before. "Hunter, god, fuck Hunter." He peered up at me through his lashes and began to move. I watched as he expertly took my dick to the back of his throat, sucking, slurping, and licking. I felt my balls tighten and yanked him back by his hair.

"I'll come if you keep that up." Hunter gave me that same cocky grin that irritated me only this morning. *Or was it yesterday morning?*

Now, though, it fired me up. I gave his hair another sharp tug to bring him to his feet, bringing our lips together once more. Our naked forms met, hard body against hard body as I rutted against him. Our hands mapped the curve of each muscle like we were starved for each other. I didn't know about him, but I was starved. I needed him.

I wanted to have him.

I dropped my hand, wrapping my palm around the both of us, shuddering at the feeling of his shaft against mine

"I want to fuck you," I whispered against his lips, pulling away just enough to see his reaction.

Fire licked the golden expanse of his eyes. "Yes, fuck yes. If it's okay, you fuck me and I fuck her."

I whipped my head around to the woman in the bed I'd completely forgotten about. I want to say no—I just wanted him. But I nodded anyway.

"Have you ever…" Kinsley's lust-filled voice trailed off, but I didn't detect a hint of judgment in her tone.

"Not anal," I answered. The nerves started to fire up in my belly once more.

Hunter wrapped his arms around my waist from behind, his lips kissing down my neck, his hand lazily stroking my dick. I felt myself relax into his embrace. "We'll talk you through the prep."

Although I nodded, I felt like I was navigating uncharted territory. I fought the urge to run. Despite the unsettling sensation, there was a steadying force that anchored me in that moment—Hunter's unwavering presence behind me.

"If I move, will you run?" Like he knew my thoughts, Hunter pressed himself harder against my back. Fear wanted to take hold, but something about him had me ready to dive into the scary unknown of sex.

Sex with a man.

Sex with a man who was going to fuck a woman at the same time.

I wish I could say I blamed the alcohol, but I'd been stone-cold sober since Hunter's lips touched mine. I was running on pure lust and adrenaline at this point.

"No, but I'm wearing a condom." I know it sounded stupid, weird even. I waited for his reaction, but he just kissed my cheek, then trailed his lips down the crest of my jawbone.

"Of course, baby." He pulled away slowly, like he was making sure I'd stay put. But just as I did before I hit the ice, I took a deep, steadying breath. I went to my jeans and took the condom from my wallet, rolling it on with tight strokes in the hopes that fear wouldn't make me deflate.

Hunter stood at the edge of the bed and grabbed Kinsley by her ankles. She squealed as he yanked her to the edge of the bed, rolling her over and slapping her ass. He put on his own condom and I watched as he slipped his fingers inside her, testing and teasing. "So wet for me Kins. Or is it for my man?" She moaned in response and my dick flinched. Me, he was claiming me.

You're only his for tonight.

It's just one night.

I moved in closer and Hunter looked over his shoulder. I watched as he lined his dick to her entrance. "I know who I'm hard for. Sorry darling, he has me close to exploding tonight."

Despite Hunter claiming he only had eyes for me, Kinsley moaned. He slammed into her in one smooth motion, causing her body to jolt—but she loved it. She clawed at the bedding, noises of pleasure filling the space around us.

"Baby, I need you to copy me."

Hunter's voice drew my attention back to him. I heard the click of the lube bottle. He lubed up his fingers, then pressed one into Kinsley's hole, drawing a louder moan from her. I watched, entranced by Hunter's body as he worked his finger.

"Your turn." He indicated the open lube bottle in invitation. I closed in, one hand on his hip the other picking up the lube. I copied his action, spreading the lube over my fingers. I flattened my other hand against his back, pushing slightly to bend him at the waist. I teased my fingers between his cheeks, slowly rimming him with one finger before I took the chance at pushing through.

He took it like he was greedy for it.

I worked him, keeping my gaze fixed on the way my finger moved in and out of him. His body clamped down on as if he wanted to keep me there. I added a second digit, curling it to feel for his prostate. "Fuck, Tyler! Please, please..."

I bit my lip, smiling at the sound of the Broody Bostoner coming apart over something as simple as my fingers. I wasn't a complete baby gay. I was no stranger to my prostate. I got myself acquainted with that magic button in private every chance I got. I angled my fingers as I worked him open. When I hit the target, Hunter's knees buckled.

"Fuck, you have to be perfect at everything—don't you baby." He was giving me the confidence boost I needed.

I leaned over him and nipped at his earlobe. "I only try to succeed, Hunter." Hunter's whimpers had me pulling my finger out, drizzling more lube over his hole to add in a third. I began flicking over his prostate, his words becoming more incoherent with every stroke of my finger. "Fuck me, Tyler. Please fuck me."

I pulled my fingers out quickly and slicked up my cock, my hand pressing on his lower back. I loved those two puckered dimples just above his perfectly toned ass. I took each perfect cheek in my hands, giving them a squeeze as I parted them and aligned my dick with his entrance. I heard both Hunter and Kinsley's bated breaths, waiting for the extra pounding from behind. I wiggled my hips, and met with resistance from Hunter's hole. I kissed down his back, my hand moving to wrap around his throat.

"Please, Baby. I can't take much more. Have me, take me."

I didn't need further invitation. This was what I wanted, everything I'd ever needed. Hunter Graves was the man I only ever dreamed of taking, I pushed through, pausing as I felt his muscles contract around me.

"Oh god. He's so thick, Kins—thicker than me. So fucking perfect."

Kinsley only groaned in response.

I began to move slowly, working him open inch by inch while he drove into Kinsley. She was a vocal girl, but I zoned into what I really wanted to hear, and that was Hunter's deep undertones. He was coming apart. With each thrust he chanted my name like a prayer, cursing as my cock grazed that sweet spot over and over. Every part of me was alive, more alive than I'd felt in a long time.

Life had taken a toll on me, and responsibility had become the collar and lead guiding me away from everything I should have. However, at that moment, a shift occurred. I was caught in that exhilarating high, where the heart plunges into free fall during the suspended moment at the pinnacle of a swing's arc. Unprepared for the impending descent, I clung to the experience, moving in and out of a man who had forever shattered the mold I once inhabited.

"God, Tyler, Tyler, Tyler." He chanted my name in time with each thrust, my body moving the way it craved; erratically, with no rhyme or reason. He came with my name on his lips and as he convulsed around me, I did the same. Release thundered through me so fiercely that my vision whited out. I rested my head between his shoulder blades, wrapping my arms around his waist. I held tight, not ready to let him go.

My vision returned in spots as I came down from the high. I could've blamed it on the whiskey, you know, chalked it up to a wild night. But I knew deep down, that it wasn't the liquid courage doing the talking. *He* was my whiskey. He was that smooth, warm sensation you get after a hard-fought game. Going down easy, leaving you with that lingering taste that makes you crave more.

It was like taking the ice. Like scoring a goal feeling the rush and wanting to stay in the game—even when you're running on fumes. He was my power play, but I couldn't let myself get caught up in the momentum. He left me hungry for more, a desire that echoed the adrenaline of an overtime goal.

But I had to play it smart, toe the line between the thrill of the game and the potential penalties. Just like in hockey, you can't afford to lose control on the ice. Your emotions have to be in check. So, as tempting as it was to go for the hat trick, I had to remember the consequences and keep my focus on the bigger picture.

This was a one-and-done. I quickly squashed the feeling that threatened to surface. The same feelings I'd kept under wraps over the years. I pulled away and moved into the ensuite bathroom. I discarded the condom and cleaned myself up at the sink. I looked in the mirror, and the man before me was flushed, different. Forever changed. Sex had a way of doing that to someone. I swallowed past the lump in my throat, hating the tears that burned behind my eyes. I was a fucking soft cock, overwhelmed by having so many emotions rise as the high I was feeling hit an all-time low.

A protective embrace took me by surprise as arms wrapped around my waist. I could sense a chin resting on my shoulder, and as our eyes met in the reflection before us, a shiver ran down my spine. Golden eyes, intense and searching, locked onto mine. Panic surged within me, a desperate desire to escape.

The yearning to run intensified, an instinctual need to evade his gaze and conceal the emotions etched across my face. I hesitated, caught between the comfort of the embrace and the fear of exposing my secrets. In that fleeting moment, I grappled with the conflicting emotions.

"Stay, Ty. Don't panic, don't go." His arms anchored me tight around my waist, his head buried in the crook of my neck. I didn't know what was happening, and I didn't want to look too deep into it. For him it was just sex, right? He liked multiples, a rotating mill of men and women.

And right then, I realized I couldn't do that. I couldn't be a notch in someone's bedpost. I got why women hated it. *I* fucking hated it. This guy made me feel something... something real. Something I had never felt before. Nothing lit me up like he did.

"I shouldn't. You said it was just one night, right?"

Hunter stood tall. I was waiting for him to rip the band-aid, for that cocky arrogant playboy to come out and play. But his arms moved from my waist, and I hated how cold I felt. I moved first, not wanting him to see the flash of pain in my eyes.

I was pathetic. Knowing the rules and limitations, I chose this—I *wanted* this. I wasn't sure if it was his soft touch, the tender kisses, or the sound of him calling me baby, but I was unraveling fast.

I was gay, like only wanted to fuck a man gay. Maybe even *be* fucked by a man, gay. I wiped my face and gathered my clothes, pulling them on hastily. This was a mess—I was a complete utter mess.

CHAPTER TEN

Hunter

I saw the panic in his eyes. He was spiraling.

I didn't even have time to recover from the best sex I'd ever had—and it had nothing to do with Kinsley. I felt guilty, but she took one look at me and knew that Tyler was the one I wanted sleeping in my bed tonight. I'd dabbled with my fair share of men and women, but none of them rattled my bones like Tyler Riley.

Kinsley left with a swift peck on my cheek, and her eyes told me the same thing I knew: Tyler was panicking. Which was confirmation enough that I was likely his first gay experience.

He also had zero interest in women. He hadn't touched Kinsley, nor did his dick so much as twitch at the sight of her. But me? Oh was he ever attracted to me. I knew people found me attractive, but having his desire? God, I was drunk on that knowledge alone.

My mind kept going to his lips on my back, how he fucked me with such confidence while his hands were so tender. He showed me with his touch just how much he appreciated every part of my body. It was different to everyone else.

For the first time, *I* wanted more than just one night. Outside of Kinsley, I'd never had someone more than once. It probably wasn't the smartest idea to go into this without her in it, but I could see Tyler wasn't completely into her being part of our sexual exchange. When I saw the look in his eyes in the bathroom, I could see the battle he was fighting. All I wanted to do was hold him together. I watched as he came to some conclusion in his mind.

I could see it then, the guy behind the blue-green eyes. He came here for the biggest opportunity in a lifetime: a way to prove himself. He wanted to show the world that a small-town Aussie boy *could* make it in the big leagues. If the last few weeks of being on the ice with him were any indication, I knew he could do it.

What we just did was like throwing a slapshot to an unguarded goalie. Tyler now had to hide a huge part of himself. Up until now, he was happy denying it, but now it came roaring to the surface. He'd only have to learn to bury it deep down again.

I tried holding onto him, but when he said, "Just one night," I let go, watching as he tried to find his clothes in the dim light. There was a war going on inside me. I didn't want him to go. I really didn't want this to be a "wham, bam, thank you man."

"Tyler, please. It's late and you've been drinking. Just stay, the guys will be sleeping well into the afternoon. I doubt they'd question you being here anyway."

He paused and mulled over my words. His head hung low as he fought with his indecision. I took a step closer. The wild animal that was unleashed moments ago was now outside of his cage, wondering where the fuck to go after a life stuck in captivity.

I stepped into his space. I had briefs on, but he was still naked. Every beautiful manly curve on display in the lamplight. I wrapped one arm around his waist, pressing him into my chest, the other hand spearing through his gorgeous auburn locks. He tensed in my arms, hands firm on my hips, ready to push away. But we both knew he didn't want to. I shushed him and held him tighter. His body trembled and I felt my own eyes burn in reaction to his overflowing emotions.

"It's okay, baby. it's okay." He shook his head against my shoulder. I alternated between rubbing his back and stroking his hair in an attempt to calm him.

"There is nothing wrong with you," I whispered against his temple.

"Why me? Why does shit always happen to me? Why can't I just be a hockey player like everyone else? All I ever dreamed about was going pro." His voice cracked as he fought against the threat of tears.

"You will, Ty. You *will* go pro. Everyone can see it. You can't help who you're attracted to."

He pulled back and looked into my eyes. God, that broken look had me all tied up. No one had ever torn me up like that man did. No one made me as angry, no one had made me want like that—no one had ever made me *feel* like he did.

"Yeah, but *you* can choose. You can still be with women. Fuck. I tried, but ever since..." The words died on his lips and shook his head.

Bile rose up in my throat. I didn't have a clue what happened to him, but I knew that a woman did it. And it only made me sick that I'd let his first encounter with a man—with me—trigger him.

"I can't choose who I have feelings for Tyler. Say I do fall for a man. I'd face the same war you're having right now. Look, I'll probably be the last guy on the planet to fall in love. I'm a dick, I know that. You know what I think, though? Fuck the world. It's messed up anyway. God knows we're living in a country with an outdated system but do they deserve to know the real you? Hell no. they aren't ready for that. But they *are* entitled to know you are going to be the best damn hockey player of our generation. And fuck you for that too—you took my title the moment you swept that fine ass in here."

Tyler chuckled and the sound fueled the fire in my belly. I lifted his chin higher, his lips close enough to kiss. "But that's all they are entitled to. *You're* entitled to your privacy. So don't let this—" I gestured between the two of us "Make you think you're doing something wrong. It's okay that you like men, especially my fine ass." Tyler smacked said fine ass, - "On behalf of all the queer men, we're fucking elated to have you on our team."

Tyler was breathing heavily in my arms, but at least the misery in his eyes was gone, replaced by desire. His tongue darted out to lick his lips and my eyes tracked the motion. I felt his dick harden against my own.

"For a complete ass, you really know how to bring a guy away from the edge."

My hands moved, cradling his strong jaw. "Seems you light up a sentimental part of me." I didn't know *what* he was doing to me. I never, never spoke like this, but just like on the ice, we were connected in a way I couldn't explain. The words left my mouth like his ears needed to hear them. All that frustration in the locker room made so much sense. Our bodies knew better than we did that we needed each other.

"We still have tonight, right?" Tyler murmured against my lips. *That* had my cock at full attention. I grabbed his ass and pulled him close, making sure he felt it.

"Mmhmm, the night is still young. Well... the morning is. What are you suggesting? Sixty-nine? Or a dual-hand job? I would say you could fuck me again, but I'm a little sore—you're bigger than what I'm used to."

That practically made him purr. "How about you do me?"

I froze, looking down at my baby gay.

"You sure?" I searched for any sign of doubt but found none. I only found those beautiful eyes blazing with heat.

"I want you to fuck me, Hunter. If this is the only night I can have, I want it to be with someone who makes me feel... safe, who turns me on like no one else. Please."

God, he didn't need to beg.

"You have no idea how many times I have thought of taking this ass while I'm ogling you in the locker room."

Tyler chuckled. "I had the same thought. Especially when you were winding me up. It only made me want to fuck the attitude right out of you."

I gave Tyler a nudge and he matched me step for step, backing up eagerly until his ass hit the edge of the bed. I took him in as he slowly lowered himself to the pillows, his hand stroking his dick.

Damn, he was so confident.

My first time with a guy was a fumble. It was an awkward jerk-off session in the bedroom, hoping the other guy was as into it as I was. Then it went to awkward blow jobs and eventually, I was able to find my first bottom. Later on, I dabbled in being vers.

Tyler was my first in a long time. And now? he was splayed out in all his Australian country boy glory. There wasn't an ounce of fear in his eyes. He went hard or went home and *fuck*, it was hot. I hoped to God he didn't ever go home; I didn't want to find out what that felt like. I crawled over him, bracing myself on the pillow on either side of his head.

I wanted to take this slow. I shouldn't have rushed it before seeing his reaction after was proof of that. I was chasing my own pleasure and somewhere along the line, I decided that I wanted it to be different with him. I wasn't sure what it was, but he was just different, and my usual way of doing things wasn't going to fly with this guy.

I feathered my lips over his, and he arched into my touch. His tongue prodded at my lips, begging for entry. My jaw fell open in invitation. I slipped my tongue into his mouth, taking my time and mapping out every available space. For the first time, fear of the morning after made my heart race.

Tyler must have read my thoughts because his hands cupped my cheeks and his tongue danced with mine, short-circuiting the worry cycle I was about to fall into. A noise left my lips, haunted by what hold he had over me. With one hand I fumbled for the lube, locating the bottle and clumsily flicking the lid open before I slicked up my fingers. I slowly stretched him to get him ready for me, loving the way he writhed against me, how his whispered cries called for me, and only me.

"Please, Hunter, I want you, need you, please." I kissed the pleas from his lips.

"Did you have another condom in your wallet?" I remember how hard he insisted on using his own, and I was gifted with a look of appreciation. Tyler nodded; eyes sparkling.

I moved quickly, hating the way the cold air stung my skin. I craved his presence again. I got out his wallet, finding the condom swiftly, and returned to the bed.

"Did you want to do the honors?"

Tyler bit his lip, and I quickly learned that it was his way of holding in his feelings. I really wanted to be someone he could voice those thoughts to.

But something told me, I wouldn't get that. I've only got this one night. After that, it's back to being his teammate.

Tyler snatched the condom, ripping open the foil and rolling it on me with care. He then grabbed the lube and slicked up my shaft. Silently, I lined myself up with his hole, the air sizzling with anticipation. I pressed in and heard his initial hiss as I breached the first ring of muscle.

I leaned down. "Relax baby. Let me make this good for you." I kissed him and reached for his dick. I stroked it slowly, getting him to relax and let me in. With each inch I gained his cock pulsed in my hand. We both spit out a curse as I bottomed out. I closed my eyes and focused on my breathing to keep from blowing my load too soon. Only Tyler Riley would have me coming like it was my first time.

"Move, Hunt. please." His words made me groan. And the lust in his eyes had me losing my breath. I'd been looked at many ways over the years, but nothing topped the way he looked at me in that moment. I gave him one experimental thrust, getting the feel for him. It was like I was feeling everything for the first time again. I felt his every pulse, every reaction to my movements. His body surged when I hit that spot, and I felt his toes curl.

I was going to make this man fall apart.

And fuck, did my baby fall apart.

He threw his head back on the pillow, mouth open as he tried to regulate his breathing. His body shuddered. I leaned down, needing to feel his lips. When our lips met, instead of the hungry, frenzied kisses I was used to, our mouths met in a soft, sweet dance.

He wrapped his legs around my waist, pulling me closer as he began to move with me. Our bodies moved in sync, each of us chasing our release. Our lips explored, only briefly separating to meet each other's eyes. His was... perfect. It was the only word that came to me. The slight part of those full lips had me wanting to kiss him and never stop. The flush to his cheeks made my heart stutter. My hand swept his hair back, kissing down his square jaw and his neck where I sucked a kiss to his Adam's apple. It bobbed under my touch, drawing a whimper from him.

I'd fucked men before, but this is completely different. This was not *fucking*. I was lost in him, entranced in his smell. So rich and earthy, with a hint of peppermint that I couldn't place. His body quaked as if my gaze alone made him feverish.

The way our bodies moved reminded me of how we were on the ice: our skates moving in time, knowing where the other one is without having to look, moving towards our goal together.

Just like that, I felt his cock swell and jerk, spilling over our chests. His body clenched around me, milking out my own release. My ears were ringing, but I knew we were cursing each other's names. Maybe it's because we knew this was different. Something more than just a one-night stand. It was to me at least. And fuck if it didn't leave me confused. I couldn't even begin to process it in my own head. And when I looked down at him, I could see the question in his eyes.

"*Is it always like this?*"

"No, baby. This is something different," I panted between shaky breaths. He nodded but didn't say a thing, didn't let me into his thoughts. I leaned my forehead against his, like a pathetic loser hoping those thoughts would breach the barrier.

"Will you stay?" I whispered against his lips. It was a sentence I never anticipated uttering to anyone else. It came out more like a plea, my brain realizing that the moment he was gone, I would be left questioning everything. In that moment, my own voice felt unfamiliar to me. He nodded, almost as if saying no was impossible. I planted a kiss on his nose and reluctantly pulled away, catching his hiss as I pulled out. "You alright?" I asked, my concern lingering in the air.

"Yeah, Hunt, I'm good." His smile revealed one lone dimple carved into his cheek.

I bit my lip to refrain from licking that little dip. I needed to hold back some of this vulnerability he was causing me to display.

I went to the bathroom to clean myself up, then returned with a warm cloth for him. His eyes tracked my movements lazily as I wiped his chest clean. I threw the cloth in the hamper across the room and slid between the sheets. Tyler surprised me by rolling over so we were eye-to-eye, and then his lips grazed mine. "Thank you."

Before I could think to reply, he found his way under my chin and rested his head on my chest. I worried he might hear how loud my heart was beating. I counted his breaths as they slowly evened out. My lips found his hair, my fingers stroking between the soft strands. I don't know when I dozed off, but I shouldn't have been surprised that like everything I did with Tyler Riley, it was a perfect sleep.

The cold sheets the next morning were like a torment I knew all too well.

Nothing perfect lasted.

"He isn't here," Colton's voice stopped me from scanning the open living area of the hockey house.

"No shit," I groused, joining him in the kitchen to help myself to some coffee.

"You know, when I said to become friends with him, I didn't mean fuck him."

"Who said anything about fucking? He just slept in my room because he was too drunk to walk home." I knew that anything I said would fall on deaf ears. Nothing got past Colton. He was the all-seeing eye.

"I'm going to guess he slept naked. Also, Kins left way before he did. Not normally your style. What would have happened if someone saw you? What would that mean for the team, Hunter?"

I looked away from Colton's hard stare. He was an old friend. I knew he didn't care what I did in my spare time. He never once outed me to anyone. Though, it wasn't lost on me that a good person in my books is one that will keep the fact that I am bisexual a secret. It should be common courtesy, but that wasn't the world we lived in

"Unless you decided to be a Peeping Tom, Colton, you know nothing. He slept on my couch because he was drunk. Kinsley left to make it less awkward. So you don't have to worry, Captain. Your precious forward and I are getting along fine."

I gave Colton a seething gaze, one of warning. He raked his hand over his face.

"I'm sorry, okay? I just don't want you messing with team members. I have no issue with your sexuality, you know that, right? Just… you have a way of sabotaging things, and I don't want the team to be one of them. Aussie doesn't give me the impression that he likes one-night stands, and that *is* what you do. So the last thing I need is you playing with his emotions okay? Don't you remember what it was like the last time you had a regular fuck buddy that wasn't Kins?"

I rolled my eyes. "This isn't the same." I cursed the moment the words left my lips. I'd just outed *myself*. I knew Colton wasn't stupid, but I wasn't going to out Tyler. Even if he did leave me without so much as a goodbye. "Because he slept on the couch," I jumped in.

Someone gag me.

"Mmhmm, right, so your banter back and forth is just that."

"Yup. We get under each other's skin, just drop it okay? Aussie and I are *fine.*"

"I'm sure you do get under each other's skin. But fine, I'll drop it. Just don't fuck with the team members, okay? This is *the* year, and I will *not* have your sex life get in between it."

I clenched my jaw so tight my teeth ground together and I nodded—if for no other reason than to end the conversation so I could go back to brooding.

Chapter Eleven

Tyler

I stepped into the coffee shop, the aroma like a jolt to my system. I suppressed a groan that threatened to escape at the imminent arrival of caffeine. It wasn't as good as the stuff back home, but it beat having nothing at all. I surveyed the shop, my eyes catching a hand waving at the far end. There sat Cal with a wide grin on his face. I felt one curl my own mouth, but it wasn't in response to him—it was the large breakfast and coffee he had waiting for me.

"You are a lifesaver; my head is pounding." Sliding into the booth, I cradled the coffee in my hands. It was still too hot to take a sip but it was the perfect temperature for warming my frozen fingers.

Cal looked at me with a cheeky grin. "So..." he drawled. "Spill. You're still in last night's clothes."

I groaned and let go of the warm mug to snatch my beanie from my head. I tried to shake off the hangover by tousling my hair. "Can't you wait until I have something in my stomach? What happened with you and your Sunday golf partner."

Cal rolled his eyes. "But don't think I'm going to bypass your first sexual encounter with a guy."

"How do you know there even was one?" But as soon as I said that my cheeks flamed. I brought my mug to my face in the hopes I could mask it.

"Because that kind of blush doesn't come from the cold. And your eyes have that post-orgasmic smile to them. Most importantly, my gay power is knowing when someone has been laid, and you have been thoroughly fucked."

I inhaled my first sip of coffee, making my nose burn.

Does that power also tell him I was the one who got fucked?

"Oh, hot damn, you totally bottomed!" *Busted.* "Is his dick as good as I remembered?"

That felt like a bucket of ice water had been dumped over me. The blood drained from my face, the realization hitting me like a ton of bricks—I was just another number. My own roommate had slept with the guy, for fuck's sake. If not for the pounding headache I might have bolted, hitting the pavement to blow off the tension building in my chest.

I woke up to Hunter holding me tight, his hand over my heart and his head tucked into my neck. Hunter was many things, but I never had him pegged for a cuddler. His body heat and strong grasp were something that caused a visceral reaction that had me scrambling from the bed and rushing out the door. I panicked. The last problem I needed was to fall for the team's playboy. As much as I wanted to believe that his behavior in the locker room was all an act, I'd been wrong before. And I wasn't making the same mistake twice.

"*No baby, this is something different.*"

The sentimental part of me wanted to believe him, but I knew I wouldn't survive another loss.

"Shit, Ty, I'm sorry. I have a big mouth. He never looked at me the way he looked at you. The night we shared was nothing but a quick fuck. I never slept over. No one ever has—not even Kins. But you did."

I shook my head, trying to clear the warring thoughts.

"What happened with you?" I was desperate to change the subject. I wanted to forget all about Hunter Graves. *Like that'll ever happen.* "Please say that preppy dipshit is now your *ex*-boyfriend."

"Yep, he is. I followed them back to his dorm and watched him fuck that twinky little punk with a dick piercing in *our* bed."

I made the mistake of taking a big gulp of my coffee just as he began to speak, and now I was coughing and spluttering, the hot liquid shooting out of my nose.

"Jesus, Cal. Fucking warn a guy when you are about to mention a pierced dick."

This was my life now, I went from blocking my ears of my teammates speaking about pussy, to apparently having a new friend that spoke about dicks and piercings.

Cal laughed. "Sorry. Forgot. you're a baby gay. To be honest, I kind of get my ex's fascination with the guy. If he hadn't already tainted him I'd be interested myself. Total waste if you ask me, being exclusively top and missing out on what that piercing—"

I raised my hand to stop him. "I get the picture."

Cal only laughed harder. "Okay, okay. Well, I walked in, made a big scene while he was balls deep in the punk's ass, then I watched as he pulled out and wailed that it was a moment of weakness, that he still loved me but I was so busy with my training that I made him feel alone. *Blah, blah, blah*. I told him to have fun, but at least let that pierced cock be used for good."

I wanted to laugh, but I refrained, biting my lip to choke it down

Cal smiled despite the pain in his eyes "Can we go back to talking about your night? Did you get the answers you were after?"

My gut tightened. "It was just one night. Life is the same, Hunter Graves will still be the pain in the ass he's always been."

Cal nodded at me, but his eyes sparkled. "I will ignore the pain in the ass comment, just this once."

I rolled my eyes and finished my breakfast wondering if I could ever forget the "Hockey Hottie."

That was Cal's idea. Not mine.

CHAPTER TWELVE

Tyler

NOVEMBER

The shrill ring of my phone through my Bluetooth headphones had my feet halting on the pavement, hunching over to catch my breath before touching my watch to accept the call.

"She won't stop vomiting, Ty. What do I do?" It was Jamie, his panicked voice making him sound much younger than he actually was.

I wiped the sweat from my eyes. The phone line echoed with the sound of my own breath panting back at me.

"There are wafers in the cupboard over the exhaust fan. Get her one of those and some Hydrolyte, two sachets in a bottle of water. Make sure she sips slowly. A cold flannel on the back of her neck also helps. Then call Auntie and get her to come over and help."

I heard a grunt and the telltale sound of a wooden chair being scraped across the tile floor. Then the old creak from the cupboard—the one I always had to spray with WD-40 to silence the old, rusted hinges.

Jamie didn't talk, nor did he hang up as he banged around in the kitchen. His footsteps echoed down the hall, accompanied by the unmistakable sound of retching. My heart sank. Years of protecting my brother from this exact scenario had me instinctively pulling my phone from my pocket to text Auntie Kay.

"Ty said to give you these."

"Baby, I am fine. Honestly, this will pass. You didn't need to call your brother."

I pinched my nose, the wave of emotions threatening to bubble up once more. *Hold it together.*

"Jamie?" Even with the distance, I could vividly picture his face. He was the one who struggled to express his emotions properly—that's why he was put into martial arts. He needed an outlet for his energy because when Jamie was upset, God help anyone in his path.

The bathroom door shut, and I counted his steps until I knew he'd reached his room. The door slammed, followed by a muffled groan as he screamed into the pillow.

"I can't do this, Ty. I can't. She couldn't even cook dinner last night. She fell asleep on the couch and when I tried to wake her, she was trembling so hard. I made toast because I didn't know how to do anything else! I am not you. I can't do this. I'm useless at caring for her."

Every feeling I had about leaving came rushing back. I sighed, knowing that following my dreams was too good to be true.

I steeled myself, realizing I was standing in the middle of the pathway. Students were giving me a weird look as I tugged at my hair. I heard shuffling, then another voice. "Jamie, give me the phone."

"Mum, he's just a kid. I have to come home."

"You will *not* come home, Tyler Riley. I'll have Aunt Kay come stay with us. We're fine. I promise."

The desperation in her tone did nothing to quell how not fine *I* felt. "Let me say goodbye to Jamie, mum."

I heard her sigh, and I knew this killed her. It's why I needed to be there, to protect her from thinking she was failing—to protect Jamie from the sight of our mum dying.

"Ty?" He was crying.

"Hey bud, awesome job. You did great. You *are* doing great. Auntie Kay will be there soon, okay? And if you ever need to talk just give me a call, okay? No matter the time"

"Okay," he said, though he sounded anything but.

"I love you, James."

"Yeah, you too." He hung up, and the silence was deafening. I clenched my jaw so hard my teeth ached. Quickly, I stuffed my phone into my pocket and sprinted back to the dorm.

The combination of music and the thud of each footfall on the treadmill battled with my thoughts. I was breaking my strict training routine, because even after this morning's run, my body was buzzing with a need for release.

Golden eyes appeared before me, breaking my focus enough to make me stumble. Luckily, I caught myself, bracing on the arms of the machine enough to regain control and pause my run. I jerked my headphones off, choice words sitting on the tip of my tongue.

"You know Aus, you can't run away from your problems. Through running does seem to be your specialty," Those infuriating golden eyes gleamed with mischief. With the help of the treadmill, we were eye-to-eye. I noticed a couple of scars that I was normally too short to see. They were more noticeable with his cheeks flushed from his own workout and his damp hair raked back out of his face one scar streaked across his forehead and disappeared into his hairline. The other sat on his right eyebrow. My hand itched to touch them, feel their depths. But I didn't. "Don't know what you're on about, Graves."

Hunter stiffened. "Don't call me that."

His tone made me stiffen. It was a lot like the one he used the day he knocked me over.

"What is your problem, Boston?"

His shoulders relaxed, but his face remained as stoic as it was before.

"Didn't think you would be the kind to abandon one date for another."

I scoffed. Was he *jealous?*

"Stalking me now? It was one night, remember? What I do is none of your business." I drew the line. My hand began to massage my chest as if it could rub away the ache there.

"Sure, if stalking is going to the only coffee house on campus and seeing you leave with one of my old conquests. I heard you loud and clear with the whole one-night shit when you were gone in the morning. Excuse me for treating you differently and letting you sleep over. If I'd known that's all you wanted I'd have sent you home with Kins."

I glanced around the gym, thankful we seemed to be the only two to get a workout in before practice. Hunter didn't miss my obvious concern. "Oh don't worry. Your secret's safe with me. But know this, Aussie: I know what you look like when you come, what you look like when you've completely come undone. I know you murmur in your sleep, and your leg twitches as you dream. I know you're scared of women and know every point on your body that makes you cry when it's touched."

My body shivered despite myself. "Good to see I still have that effect on you. It'll only be a matter of time before you come crawling back. The question is, Aus: will I let you in for thirds? Because that's not something I usually do."

His lips curled into a sneer. It was a threat rather than a promise, yet I couldn't ignore the unmistakable lust in his eyes. They raked over my body. His tongue grazed his bottom lip and I tracked the movement.

"You don't have to worry about that, Hunter. You caught me with whiskey glasses. Like any alcohol, it left a bad taste in my mouth in the morning."

He flinched and I instantly regretted my choice of words. But there was no turning back. He nodded, lips screwing to the side of his face.

"Right, Mr. Perfect got to dip his toe in the water. I am glad to have been your little experiment Aussie. Have fun with your baby Captain America. He's cute and all, but remember he's just a bottom. But you like the control right? Like holding the reins—both on and off the ice? Everything's perfect when you're in control, right?"

I felt the jab where he intended, sliding under my rib cage and racing toward my heart, just nicking it enough to let me know the knife was there. I bit my lip, head moving up and down as if sucking up his blow.

"Sure Boston, *pretend* you know me. You don't know a fucking thing about me. Enjoy your endless rounds of emotionless ass, pretending you don't give a flying fuck about anything on this earth other than being the cockiest man on and off the ice, right? But the game always ends. The high wears off and you realize you're all alone. You wouldn't know chivalry if it bit you in the ass."

The reality check was harsh; my conscience was slapping me hard. Hunter, in all his perceptive glory, peeled away the layers to reveal me for who I truly was. It all started with my desperate need for control, stemming from the very moment I found myself unable to say no. From there, it infiltrated every corner of my life: waiting anxiously for my dad's return that would never come, facing the unpredictable nature of watching someone fight cancer...

Life's unpredictability hit me hard. It forced me to play pretend, to convince myself I was in the driver's seat. But the truth was, I was gripping the wheel of a hydroplaning car, hurtling forward with no seatbelt and no brakes. Hunter's discerning gaze intensified my internal conflict, making me itch to reach out to him. Yet just as that impulse surfaced, another voice disrupted the moment, invading the gym and pulling me away from the emotional precipice.

"You two better not be fighting again. Are we going to have a problem?" Colton bellowed as he approached us, a towel slung over his broad shoulders.

"No problem," Hunter and I responded at the same time. But I could see it in his eyes. We very much had a problem—a big fucking problem. I hit my mark, and he worked his jaw like he was eating his final meal.

"Aussie here has made it clear where we stand, and I am glad to know. Don't you worry Colt, we agreed to be good hard-working teammates on the ice, isn't that right...*Tyler*." He stood confident, shoulders back as he commanded the boardroom. His smile was almost foolproof. It might have convinced others, but it didn't escape me. Hunter Graves was harboring pain and anger—a lot of it. And I knew I was the cause of at least some. I'd never spoken to someone that way. The echoes of my mother's disapproving voice resonated in my mind – "*I'm so disappointed in you*." She was right: that wasn't how she raised me.

She taught us early the value of addressing hurtful behavior Yet, in the presence of my broody Bostoner, all rational thought seemed to fly out the window. I nodded numbly, my remorse sinking in as I watched him turn his back and exit the gym.

"Sorry about him. He's an arrogant ass. If he is going to be a problem, let me know we can talk to Coach."

I nearly lost my footing on the treadmill, my eyes widening in disbelief. It was a shocking realization that our captain—someone I considered a friend—was willing to throw Hunter aside so quickly. In my eyes, Hunter was so much more than just a troublemaker; he was an asset to our team, a key player who knew how to navigate the complexities of the game. It pained me to see our captain so swift in betraying a friend. The camaraderie that bound us on the ice now teetered on the brink of destruction, and the ache in my chest mirrored the internal conflict I felt. I was torn between loyalty to a teammate and the disheartening reality of impending betrayal.

"Hunter is on the track to go pro too. I wouldn't discount him so quickly." I was defending him. Maybe it was guilt. Or the way he treated me when I was so vulnerable. Or simply because he was my teammate, but what Colton said wasn't sitting right with me.

No one speaks shit about Hunter. The thought was rich coming from me, but it played in my head as I clenched my fist.

Colton scoffed. "Sure he's a good player, but he fucks up everything he touches. Just you wait and see. Know that I have your back, okay? Don't get stuck in his orbit, all he does is bring down those around him."

I blinked at my Captain, feeling like I just got checked into a whole new game. It was like flipping between two periods: one where he's the chirping, supportive leader, and the next he's throwing me hit to the boards that's spinning my world faster than a slapshot.

"You have no reason to worry about that. But I will say, you need to cut him some slack. He's good on this ice and good on this team. Maybe it's you, Cap, who needs to let it lie and put some faith in your teammates. Because I know whatever shit is said off the ice is just that: shit."

I walked off, not bothering to look back at his expression. I didn't need to—his thoughts were radiating off him. I was starting to think I wasn't the one with the issue with Hunter. I just wondered if Hunter had anyone truly watching his back.

CHAPTER THIRTEEN

Hunter

"**B**ut the game always ends. The high wears off and you realize you're all alone. You wouldn't know chivalry if it bit you in the ass."

Tyler's words played themselves in a loop—a loop of hell… but one of truth. And it fucking hurt. It was the same kind of pain that hit me when I woke up without him next to me. I was all alone. Sure, I had Kins and if she called for help I would take off running. I didn't call anyone for help. No one needed to be caught in my storm. I'd rather protect those I care about and stay alone, wallowing in my own pool of self-pity when it all came crashing down around me.

I began stripping at my stall, ignoring the sound of the locker room door opening. I knew it was him without even looking—I could feel every time he entered a room—and I didn't dare look his way. I wished I'd never bumped into him. I wish he'd stayed in Australia. The only thing he accomplished was bringing up everything I'd worked so hard to ignore. Colton was right: I self-sabotaged, I did in high school, and I was on a one-track path to doing it again.

I felt his body buzzing beside mine, noticeably angrier than when I left him. It made me wonder what Colt said after I'd left.

Don't start caring. It doesn't matter.

"Hunter…" Considering he was hurling verbal bullets at me mere minutes ago, his voice was surprisingly gentle.

"Don't bother, Tyler. You were right. Let's just focus on being teammates." My voice lacked any hint of emotion.

"No, I need to apologize. I was an absolute cunt. I don't know you—not the real you. You were good to me and... I freaked out. I knew that we'd never be more than teammates and that scared me. I... I never speak to people the way I spoke to you, and I hate that I did."

I snickered, attempting to hold back my laughter. "Did you seriously just call yourself a cunt?" Maybe it was the tension in the air or him having the balls to apologize, but I couldn't contain it.

"I'm sorry... I forgot Australians have potty mouths compared to you—but it's the truth I snapped at you because you hit a nerve..."

I laughed, truly laughed for what felt like the first time. I was laughing at the guy in front of me, sweaty hair falling in his face as he called himself all the wrong names. And damn it if it didn't make him even more perfect. What would it take for this man to show me just one flaw? "Okay, okay—apology accepted. You can stop insulting yourself."

Tyler huffed. "Noted, while we're warning each other—" The door busted open before he could finish and the team piled in, shouting about girls and the normal drunken stories that came with a Monday practice.

I wanted to beg Tyler to keep talking, but Colton gave us his telltale whistle that meant sit down and shut up. I zoned out as he gave his normal spiel about the weekend being over and how we needed to focus. We had the Yale boys on our turf this week, which meant we had to stay on our toes. They'd had a few bad seasons and were looking to make a comeback. We were number four on the board and we needed to be number one. If we won this game, it would set a precedent for the Harvard game—they were tailing us on the leaderboard. Like us, both teams had fresh meat on their roster. Yale had some forwards that would contend with Colton and Tyler, and I knew Colton needed to outshine them to be noticed, but it wouldn't hurt for Tyler to get on their radar as well.

I didn't have my doubts about these next few games, as long as we kept up as we had been. However, what did make me nervous was the upcoming game against Merrimack. Particularly the presence of their defenseman, Zane Matthews. Zane and I had a past, one that could potentially influence the outcome of the game. My attention zoned in on Colton momentarily as he mentioned Zane by name. His expression spoke volumes, and the warning in his eyes was crystal clear: "Do *not* mess this up for us again." I nodded in understanding, sensing the weight of a particular Aussie player's curiosity.

Tyler's ability to read me was remarkable. He scowled in Colton's direction, oblivious to the fact that he had every reason to be upset with me. Despite Tyler's sharp tongue and the occasional bruised heart, his loyalty ran deep. In the end, he stuck to his word—I was his teammate. It was becoming increasingly apparent to me—and I suspect to many others on the team—that Tyler Riley would go to great lengths to protect his teammates.

As soon as my skates touched the ice, the tension faded from my body. The familiar earthy scent and my skates slicing through the frozen surface beneath me let all my worries melt away. My muscles relaxed and my mind cleared. I couldn't help but notice Tyler's occasional glances in my direction as we warmed up. I didn't get the sense that he was checking me out, more like he wanted to know if I was okay. I nodded in acknowledgment, and he visibly relaxed.

We were split into pairs for drills. Colton was partnered with Tyler, no doubt because of their speed. I had noticed a vast improvement in our speed—perhaps something to do with our new Australian teammate. Tyler trained with figure skaters, which wasn't unheard of. Many athletes trained with others in different sports to enhance flexibility and fluidity.

Tyler possessed a unique blend of grace and grit, moving at lightning speed before stopping on a dime, rotating, and propelling in the opposite direction like no one else I had seen. He navigated both sides of the blue line with tremendous confidence. He was never unafraid to deliver a hit, using his speed to catch opponents off guard before seamlessly returning to the play. Tyler frequently interacted with everyone else, offering tips on blade placement, leg angles, and demonstrating the techniques in the drills.

Coach didn't overlook Tyler's contributions or the team members willing to try something new. There were occasional stumbles as players adjusted to a slightly different gait, but Tyler was right by their side to pick them up if they fell.

"You better get that look off your face," Colton pushed my shoulder with his. I looked over and watched the tick in his jaw.

"What look? Can't I admire someone doing your job better than you?" I spoke nothing but the truth. Tyler would captain the team one day. Whether anyone liked it or not, they couldn't hold a candle to him.

"Fuck off. He can give all the pointers he wants but he's rattling the foundation we built this team on and you look at him like he's your next meal. We've finally recovered from your mistakes, Hunt. I don't want a repeat. That whole fallout made me miss the call to go into the leagues early, made me have to prove myself. I've put in a lot more work than your little Aussie. He didn't do the camps or the coaching skills classes. He didn't get a degree in sports psychology to read his players better. *I* did. I put in the work. I deserve this. I won't have our team crumbling because of you."

I saw it then, the same expression he gave me in the kitchen that made my skin crawl. We never really had big issues. We grew up close, we were always on the same teams. We were always a team on the ice and I thought we had each other's backs. He kept my secret from the team and turned a blind eye to me experimenting with my sexuality. Though as I noted that angry gleam in his eye, I saw something familiar. Something that had alarm bells sounding in my head.

Chapter Fourteen

Tyler

I t was game day, and I felt good.

The dust had settled between Hunter and me, and we entered a period of silent understanding as we faced the challenge ahead. I hadn't had the chance to give Hunter a heads-up about Colton, but as the days clicked by, whatever had possessed Colton in the locker room seemed to have faded. He went around to each team member—including Hunter—patting them on the back and giving them private pep talks. The tension radiating off him that day became nothing more than a blip on the radar.

I tried to convince myself that it was just that—a blip. The fact that he went back to his normal self made it easier. Perhaps Hunter and I staying out of each other's way played a role in all of it

"All right, boys! We've been working hard. I'm glad you've been trying some new skills but today I need your best. Don't try anything new if you're not sure it'll work. We need to show the Yale boys we don't waver, right?"

I got a *strong* feeling that he was talking about me. The hit felt so targeted I damn near flinched. I looked up and noticed he wasn't looking at me. Did I just imagine that?

Clearly not. I felt a couple of glances my way as if they were seeking out guidance. I ducked my head to avoid their eyes—I wasn't captain. I'd be lying if I said it didn't leave me irritated. In a show of silent support, Hunter's knee nudged mine, but I didn't dare look up. I didn't need the distraction. However, that didn't stop him from lingering in the darkest parts of my mind.

Colton didn't continue speaking until he received a chorus of confused murmurs in response. "Good—keep that shit in practice. Every single one of you has the qualities to do this. Do what you know and go out there and kick some ass! Let's hear it!"

A cacophony of noises broke out around me. I simply hit my stick against the floor, making noise despite my blood boiling over the obvious blow.

I shook off the insecurity and headed onto the ice. I paused as I crashed right into a large hand. I turned to face the towering mass that was Hunter Graves.

"Don't read too much into what he said. If those men know what's good for them they'll use the pointers you gave them as their best weapon. What's the point of leveling up and not using the skill upgrade, right?"

I smiled despite myself. "Thank you."

Much like the last thank-you I gave him, I watched something settle in those golden orbs. They softened as those beautiful green flecks came through. "Get out there and show them how an Aussie does it." He leaned in, whispering his next words in my ear. "I'll always have your back, baby."

His voice was a low purr that had my dick straining against my cup. I scowled and hit him with my stick. "No pet names."

Hunter simply laughed. "You will always be my baby."

"Cut it." I gave him a full shove that time. I skated out to start my warmups. I totally didn't watch him walk onto the ice and my stomach definitely didn't flip at the smile he flashed my way.

The anxiety that Colton attempted to plant in my mind dissipated. I hadn't realized the panic building in my chest. Despite a few shaky moments when calves and ankles protested the changes in angles, I truly believed my guidance was making a positive impact. It seemed like the team's overall speed had increased, and some of the guys were genuinely improving their forechecking techniques.

That flirty remark from Hunter had taken away every ounce of doubt. Suddenly, my mind stopped, and a stirring sensation down below signaled that my focus had shifted. A new fire ignited within me, a new surge of energy that needed an outlet.

Whatever works, right?

The game was lightning fast. Yale came at us with a burning desire to shatter our winning streak. They had fire in their skates, and they weren't holding back. Just to prove a point, I drew from the skills that somehow rubbed Colton the wrong way. I battled it out with our defense against Yale's lightning-quick forward: Justin Chisnech. I managed to dance with him, corral the puck, and hustle it back to the neutral zone, aiming straight for the goal.

On my wing, Hunter rode shotgun. He was hot on my left, ready to throw down or snatch that puck away—a true bodyguard on blades. The plays unfolded seamlessly and Yale's defense tried their best to steamroll me. Quick thinking led to a pass to Colton behind me on the right, the sound of the puck meeting the stick signaling his next move.

Scouting Yale's goalie, I spotted a chink in his armor. His left shoulder lagged, lacking the reflexes and reach of the right. The top left corner was screaming for attention and I needed to hit it fast. Signaling Colton, I saw his eyes on the goal, but two defenders were itching to pin him against the boards. The only way out was a pass, and Colton had to make his move.

There was a glance, a brief hesitation, and then Colton unleashed the puck in my direction. I could sense Chisnech closing in, and Colton's puck-hogging tendencies threatened to throw a wrench in my play. The goalie braced himself on the right, but the left was my ticket to glory. I faked right then flicked left, bracing for the hit that never came.

Cheers erupted.

I looked around. Hunter had leveled Chisnech, giving me a clear shot. Chisnech was fuming, confronting Hunter, who shot back with a cocky grin and a mock surrender. "Clean hit, man. Handle it. My forward just taught you a lesson."

A chuckle escaped me as we regrouped at center ice. As we skated back, I couldn't ignore Hunter's whispered words in my ear. "Told you I'd always have your back, baby."

Chapter Fifteen

Hunter

Tyler was right about the high of a game. Whoops and hollers reverberated off the walls as we walked down the corridor to the lockers, men patting each other on the back and smacking asses.

Aussie held the team together in that game. We won, but only just. That last shot on goal was magic, and it nearly didn't happen because of Colton.

He wanted that shot. Something he neglected to tell his team: there was a scout in the bleachers today. One who had his eye on Justin Chisneck. He wanted to show up Justin, but only succeeded in making himself look like a fool. I don't know why that made me feel good—maybe something to do with his digs at Tyler. But I was eager to celebrate, eager to keep that high going. Taunting Tyler had brought that spark back. He pretended to hate it, but I saw that glimmer in his eye. It's exactly what caused him to be such a menace on the ice. There was nothing hotter than watching him read the plays, and fuck, did he read that play.

I stood shoulder to shoulder with him at his locker, offering a congratulatory grin. "You showed them, baby," I teased with a playful lilt.

He whipped his head around, eyes wide. I couldn't help but chuckle.

"Didn't he!" Mouse whacked his shoulder, not even batting an eye at the use of the term. We were hockey boys, after all, and our locker room banter often included enthusiastic shouts of phrases a far cry from anything we'd say in the bedroom.

My baby gay, however, was cautious, not wanting to draw attention to us. I observed his shoulders tense briefly but then relaxed as he realized the nature of my comment.

Aussie shrugged. "The *team* showed them. You guys worked hard on the defense, and I saw a couple of you guys really strike off and close in on those Yale forwards. Your energy was truly something to be proud of."

I glanced at Colton, not missing the way his jaw ticked. "*Everyone* worked hard, though that last play could have gone really wrong. Graves, you were supposed to be on my wing. If you had my back, I would have had my shot. That's what we practiced."

"That's what we practiced if they played how we expected them to—which they didn't. Aussie had the perfect opening. Backing him up was the better option, and it worked. What nearly fucked it up was *your* hesitation."

Coach picked that precise moment to walk through the door. "Hunt's right, if the defense weren't solely focused on you, we would have missed that goal. Aussie was the one who saw that weakness in the net. I'm proud of how you all played today. I can see huge improvements with your footwork. If we keep this up, we'll kick some Harvard ass next week. Now, don't do anything silly tonight. I want you well rested for Monday's skate time. "

Colton didn't retaliate. Instead, he smiled and said "Yes, Coach," corralled everyone into the showers.

As we dressed to leave, I watched as every single teammate patted Aus on the back and said something to the tune of, "You'd better be celebrating tonight." To which they got a "maybe" or "I'll think about it," in response.

I made a point to match his pace as we left. My intention was clear: to catch some alone time with him and—hopefully—convince him to spend just one more night together.

Though the moment we walked out, Cal sidled up to Tyler's side. "Tyler, you're coming out with me tonight. My ex is going to be at the party and I need him to see I am *not* hung up on him cheating on me with Sir Punky Pierced Dick." Tyler groaned while I somehow managed to forget how to breathe and choked on my own spit.

"I'm sorry; Sir Punky Pierced Dick?" I could barely say it with a straight face.

Cal nodded, not bothered in the slightest about the pierced dick in the room. "Yeah, my ex decided to try a new stick. Though he took the test drive wrong—what a shame. That stick was meant for a power bottom but alas, Nathan's a greedy top."

I coughed again, barely covering the laugh that wanted to burst free.

"Can we *not* talk about the logistics of where sticks should be going?" Tyler grumbled.

Cal smiled, turning to face him. "What's the fun in that? I like making you squirm.

It's cute making a baby gay all flustered. One of these days I'll break you right out of that shell."

Tyler looked around the hall and seeing that it was only us said, "It'll be like waiting for rain in a drought man: not going to happen. And I am not cute."

Cal spun around to walk backward, holding his fingers up. "You are a little bit cute, right Hunter?"

I bit back my smile. I was about to reply when Tyler lunged forward, grabbing Cal's face and tilting it into the light. "What the fuck happened to your face?"

The sudden protectiveness of his voice surprised me. I saw the gash on the right side of Cal's head, held together by stitches and tape.

"Nah, see? You're cute," Cal cooed jokingly, but Tyler was having none of it.

"Cal, what the fuck happened?"

Cal sighed. "Sabrina was desperate to try a triple twist lift in our routine. Let's just say my face caught the third twist."

Tyler and I both flinched. "Are you okay?" Tyler took a step back and searched Cal's features. His voice was soft, sincere. I got that same pang in my chest that hit me when I saw them leaving the coffee shop.

You are not jealous; you are not jealous.

"I'm fine. I was more pissed at her yelling at me. Apparently, I didn't throw her high enough—she had some choice words. She said I need to take a few days to 'beef' up otherwise she was going to find a new partner."

"Sounds like a bitch if you ask me," I offered. "And it sounds like you need a good night out. I'll be your wingman--I know of a few guys who swing your way."

Tyler rolled his eyes. Cal, on the other hand, lit up like a Christmas tree. "Thanks, Hunt!" He then sauntered up to my side and not-so-subtly whispered, "but if you want the baby gay to be in your bed tonight, maybe don't mention all the guys you know that swing my way."

Damn it.

Chapter Sixteen

Tyler

"Aye! It's old Cap." I was surprised to see Holden's smile on the other end of the phone... sitting in my living room. I leaned in close to make sure I wasn't imagining things and noted my furrowed brow in the viewfinder as I wondered what the hell he was doing answering my brother's phone. I then voiced that very same thought. "Holden, what are you doing answering my brother's phone?" He kept the camera fixated on his annoying face, making me groan. That ridiculous smirk told me he was well aware of how much it bothered me.

"Good to see you too champ." His tone had me wishing I were there to knock him out cold.

"Fuck off. Where's Jamie?"

"Getting his shit ready. I'm taking him to his training. Kay drove your mum to her hospital appointment. Jamie didn't want to take the bus, so here I am."

Somehow, I found myself in a conflicting state. I was ecstatic that someone was watching over Jamie, but my gut twisted at the thought of Mum undergoing another round of chemo.

"Thanks, Holden. For real."

Holden's cocky grin faded. "You know I care for Jamie. I promised I would watch out for him. You two are practically family."

I relaxed into the couch, Cal's singing followed him from his bedroom to the kitchen.

"So," he drawled. "You been enjoying some college life, finally letting loose?" I could see the moment his gaze fell over my shoulder to where Cal was dancing into the kitchen shirtless.

"If you consider one wild night a college experience, Mr. Cute Australian boy, then yes—Ty here has lived his wildest self. Otherwise, he's just a robot—wake up, run, study, hockey, study, and repeat. Why don't you help a gal out and make him come out with me tonight?"

I shot a glare at him and clenched my jaw.

"Big wild night aye? I am all ears."

"And you still wouldn't listen because there's nothing to tell"

"I call bullshit. You haven't slept with anyone since you know who. And I know what that was like for you. So, she must have been a decent bird or... maybe a decent dude?"

I choked on my next breath. I heard a mumble from Cal behind me and his hand squeezed my shoulder. I met his gaze, understanding the unspoken apology in his eyes I hoped mine conveyed the anger simmering just beneath the surface. Apparently, my glare spoke volumes, as he retreated to his room. There would definitely be words exchanged between us later.

"So... now that the emu is out of the room, am I on the right track?"

My tongue felt too big for my mouth. I wasn't ashamed that I was gay. But it was new. I was still wrapping my head around it, much less trying to help other people along. There hadn't been a moment of the day where I hadn't had Hunter's face, or his muscles or his fucking ass flashing in my mind. Which when you share a locker room with the fucker... it was very inconvenient, to say the least.

"I take that as a yes, but your roommate? Is that smart? Like I see what you see in him, he is both pretty and masculine, but like... don't shit where you eat man."

A string of incoherent sounds that were meant to be words tumbled out of my mouth.

"W-no! What-uh-The fuck."

"Okay, but I'm clearly on the right track. It was a guy, wasn't it?"

I sighed and bit my lip.

Holden leaned in close and dropped his voice. "Your brother is still getting ready if you don't want him to know." His chocolate eyes were filled with warmth. I couldn't fathom why I ever doubted his unwavering support. Maybe it was just the toxic masculinity that came with playing any sport: you didn't want your teammates to think you were checking them out.

"Why do you have to be so perceptive?" I grumbled.

"Because we've been best friends since we were four. I have been through all the shit life has thrown at you. We slept in the same bed for years. I know you talk in your sleep. It's just what brothers and best friends do."

I huffed. "I suppose,"

"Guess I'm not your type though?" I knew he was joking by the smile on his face.

"Nah, mate. Your face looks like a bashed crab." I winked. He wasn't unattractive exactly, but he was... Holden. He was my brother.

"It's the mullet, isn't it? The moment I get rid of the mullet you will be all over me."

I laughed. "Sure, not the fact that being with you would be like being with my brother. Just not my jam."

"Fair, you're not my type either, your boobs are too hard, I need a pillow, you know?"

"You *will* need to shave off the mullet if you want your type,"

"Pfft. This mullet is iconic, isn't it Jamie."

I heard footsteps and the video bobbed as the couch sank with my brother's weight. "Keep telling yourself that as long as you want blue balls."

I watched Holden's hand go to the back of his, assessing said hairstyle and I couldn't help but laugh. Jamie's "no-bullshit" tone only added to the blow.

"You both suck. I'm a true-blue Aussie: it's a look!"

"It *is* a look, that's for sure," Jamie countered, just as dry as before.

My heart panged with homesickness over the memory of the simple days hanging in the living space with my two brothers. Holden fit in that category. God knows he was around enough.

"Go out tonight, Ty."

I didn't realize I was holding my breath, waiting for Holden to reveal something I had yet to disclose to my brother. It hit me in that moment: I'd appointed myself as his role model. Whether I liked it or not, I aspired to be just like our father. Disclosing that I wasn't anything like the man he idolized was something I couldn't bring myself to do. My own experiences were not something I wanted him to know about. The only wisdom I felt equipped to impart was that he didn't have to become a pushover like me—that he had the right to say no.

I glanced at Holden, hoping that maybe he could be the one to guide Jamie through the complexity of dating girls.

"You don't have to look after me or mum, Ty. Make the most of it," Jamie added, his tone loaded with undefined meaning. I looked at him, and though I knew I was half a world apart from him, it somehow felt even farther.

Holden being the amazing best friend that he was read the room and sat up., "Alright kiddo, get in the car so we aren't late."

"Not a fucking kid…" Jamie groused and left the shot, despite it being *his* phone that Holden was holding.

Holden sighed heavily. "I got it here mate. He's just a teenager. He'll be right. Go, enjoy a night with your mystery guy. We'll table this convo for now."

Before I could even answer he was yelling bye while disconnecting the call.

"Are all Australians hot? Or is it just the hockey players?" Cal's voice jolted me from my thoughts. I hadn't even noticed him sitting on the coffee table in front of me. He was dressed in a button up, corduroy pants, and a cardigan that suspiciously resembled something out of folklore. "You're barking up the wrong tree with that one. Straight as an arrow."

"Mmhmm sure. Are you coming or what?"

"Fine, but don't think we don't have a conversation to have."

After I changed, we headed to the hockey house. I found myself gnawing at my bottom lip, grappling with thoughts of what happened the last time I was there.

I will not sleep with Hunter Graves again. I will not sleep with Hunter Graves again.

We walked up the leaf-littered footpath to the door, Cal rambling away beside me. I was ashamed that I didn't hear a word he said.

"Dude, I could have just said I wash my balls with vinegar and you would be none the wiser."

"What?"

Cal reached over to ruffle my hair. "You had no clue what I had been saying as we drove over here."

"Sorry mate, just…" Just what? My mind was stuck playing an endless loop of Hunter's naked body, the feel of his skin against mine, the smell of his expensive cologne, the way he held me tight against his chest after sex. The way even when he attempted to rile me up, I ended up hiding a hard-on because his voice is something that should be recorded for an audiobook. *Fuck.*

"You thinking about mind-blowing sex?" Cal nudged me, his dimpled smirk beginning to grate at my nerves. My face must work better than my mouth because Cal let out a bark of laughter. "Fuck, man, he really did a number on you. I suppose it was your first, but God…. It's good you got a guy with experience; I wish my first time had me all daydreamy like that."

I shoved him—the only thing I could think to do. *Mum would be so proud.* Cal, only getting more revved up by my adolescent behaviors, threw his arm around my shoulders. "I think we could find another discreet male that would take your mind off Hunter. Someone for you to fuck, or—if you're like me—get well and truly fucked."

My stomach bottomed out at the idea. Could I do it? Sleep with another guy? Something about it was anything but appealing.

Cal led me through the front doors and my teammates called out as they saw me enter. I waved to my teammates, some approaching for those one-shoulder hugs, but Cal's idea ran through my mind like a derailed train. I wasn't picking up on a thing anyone said, absentmindedly nodding along to the conversation. Cal had already left the group, heading directly to him—Hunter Graves. He wore a dark black button-up shirt, sleeves folded to reveal his tattoos, paired with dark ripped jeans and boots. The entire look had my body heated like walking outside on a hot summer's day.

His eyes met mine, studying my body the exact same way I'd just studied his. Cal looked between the two of us, his grin giving us away as he publicized his excitement over our heated looks.

Little prick.

I looked away, surveying the room and noting the people scattered around the house. The house was warm, but a chill came through as doors opened and closed.

I spotted Kinsley sitting with a pretty brunette, watching as Lachlan and Preston played on the PlayStation. I didn't miss the way Lachlan Getz—aka Getzy—side-eyed Kinsley, whose full breasts bounced as she laughed. I scoffed, grabbed a Jack and Coke, and stole the seat beside Kinsley.

She looked shocked at first as I sat beside her; then, her eyes softened. "Hey, Aussie," she greeted. I smiled politely, trying not to flinch as she brushed her lips against my cheek. Getzy and Preston shot me a jealous look, adding to the nerves zipping.

"Hey Kins." I looked at the girl next to her and extended my hand. "I'm Tyler. Or Aussie, or Aus—whatever anyone wants to call me really." She greeted me with a warm-hearted smile and a soft grip on my hand. She was undeniably pretty – someone I could easily picture Hunter heading upstairs with tonight, perhaps even sharing her with Kins.

Kinsley, with her golden hair, blue eyes, and banging body created a beautiful contrast to the girl next to her. She had dark hair, hazel eyes, full lips, and an athletic body –the female version of Hunter himself.

"I know who you are. Great game today. I'm Kelsey Lienhart, women's hockey team." I suppressed a laugh and resisted the urge to point out the obvious. My gaze shifted between the two women, catching the glimmer in Kinsley's eyes as she seemed to soak in her friend's presence.

"Thanks. I haven't had a chance to watch the female team, but I'll have to now, see how you play," I remarked, unintentionally injecting a flirtatious tone into my words. Getzy and Pres smirked, obviously picking up on it. I truly just wanted to watch them play. Back home, I coached the younger female hockey team, and I firmly believed those women could easily compete with the men—even outplay us.

"She's very talented," Kels added. I couldn't help but smile. "The PWHL is looking to draft her, and she played for the under eighteens at worlds."

"Don't say that in front of Hunter," I teased, keeping my voice low enough for the three of us to hear. "He may get jealous of you moving on to a better-looking and more talented hockey player." They both blushed and I found myself liking the dynamic between them. However, it made me wonder where Hunter stood in this equation. I then mentally scolded myself for even thinking about him again.

I stayed engaged in the conversation, Kels eager to learn the differences between Australia and the States. I didn't blame her; Australia was a thirty-six out of fifty-six in the IIHF. When I said Australian players weren't on the NHL's radar, I wasn't joking. Regardless of all the time I spent training in other countries, the hours I spent on YouTube studying plays—it didn't matter. Mum even had coaches who watched remotely, guiding me as I trained to be the best I could be. I hated to think about the amount of money she invested in me over the years to get me where I was.

"It's crazy the amount you have done just to get that step ahead," Kelsey remarked, entirely unaware of the depth of my journey. I felt a hint of pride, a rare emotion for me. I'd never truly taken a moment to appreciate where I was—every step along the way. I had to look forward. I couldn't slow down. I always needed to be on top of my game. Because of that, I hadn't really taken a moment to pat myself on the back.

I looked away, feeling suddenly uncomfortable with the reality of it all. I was here in America, the top country on the IIHF leaderboard. I had a scholarship to a top hockey school. I was winning games.

Sure, I wasn't playing center like I was back home, I wasn't a captain. But I was in one of the first lines tonight. I was a forward and I was shooting goals, making assists with guys who had been on the draft's radar for years. They were only beginning to hear the name Tyler Riley. Scouts were at my games now. And for some reason, it had me feeling sick to my stomach.

As if she could sense my nerves, Kinsley passed me another drink. A quick smell of it told me she paid close attention—another Jack and Coke. She was an intuitive one and though I definitely didn't want to sleep with her, I could see her becoming a good friend.

When I glanced up to scan the room again, Cal was engrossed in conversation with a man the size of a linebacker. He was tall with full, broad shoulders. His deep skin glowed in the yellow ceiling lights, and I couldn't help but notice how the light accentuated the ridges of his muscles. He was undeniably attractive, his presence intimidating as he looked down at Cal. The combination of light and dark was stunning, and I had a strong feeling I would be hearing about him later—whether I wanted to or not.

Kelsey caught my line of sight and hummed appreciatively.

"Eric Davis. Often mistaken for his football twin, Ezra Davis. I may not be into guys, but if I were he'd be a top contender. The guy could be on the cover of the *Hot Guy Weekly*," she admitted.

I didn't react to her admission of her sexuality, too busy checking out Cal's current conquest. It suddenly struck me how obvious I was being, openly checking out a guy—and Kelsey didn't miss it either. I shifted my attention to where Getzy and Pres had been sitting, relieved to see they'd abandoned the video game, likely in search of new girls to chat up with since these two were clearly not interested.

Kelsey moved, taking a seat on the other side of me, reaching behind my back to keep some contact with Kins despite their physical distance. *Cute.*

"Don't worry; I think even straight males would agree he's hot," she assured me. "He would be anyone's hall pass."

I scoffed, observing the way Cal's eyes melted as Eric spoke animatedly about something. It was a rare sight to see Cal quiet, let alone starstruck. "Is Eric..."

Kel's was such a trooper. She didn't even bat an eye. "Yeah, he is. He's not closeted but he doesn't exactly go around screaming it. The only difference between the twins are their tattoos. He doesn't want someone to mistake him for his brother—he's a top draft pick."

I frowned. "So, the brother has to hide his sexuality for the sake of his twin's status?"

Kelsey nods. "Yup, sad really." She shrugs, but her hand reaches my knee and squeezes, the silent apology for the life I have to live—*we* have to live.

"Yeah, can we, ah, keep this… " Before I could finish, both women squeezed a thigh in turn.

 "Your secret's safe with us, Aussie."

I half-smiled, looking back to Cal and Eric. Cal had moved closer, leaving only a sliver of space between them. Eric gave Cal that same look of interest. I felt a pang of jealousy. There weren't many times I hated hockey, but as I sat there and watched those two shamelessly flirt, I questioned whether I'd made the right choice. I could have stayed home, pursued coaching or something, and found a guy who would look at me like that. It would just be simpler that way.

Sure, Australia wasn't without its homophobia. Perth, in particular, wasn't the most queer-friendly place to be. Still, I wouldn't have this heaviness on my chest, the guilt of not being there for my family.

I sculled my drink and poured another, Kins and Kels staying close to my side. They could have snuck away together by now, but maybe they sensed my unease. They stayed glued to me.

I watched as Cal's ex walked in, stopping in his tracks as his eyes landed on Cal. His jaw ticked, and he immediately went to approach them, Cal got to his toes and whispered something in Eric's ear. Eric's eyes lit up, and then they were making out.

Both girls leaned in, whispering, "hot!" They weren't wrong. I almost wanted to laugh at myself. For so long, I pushed this part of myself away blaming hormones and puberty. Nope, a lie. A blatant lie. Because I had two very attractive females beside me, and I wanted nothing to do with either of them. But watching Cal and Eric? I'd be lying if I said I wasn't a little jealous. Not of them specifically, but jealous of the fact that they could openly take what they wanted.

"I think you're making a certain someone jealous," Kins hummed into my ear. I looked around and sure enough, my broody Boston boy was staring a hole through me from the other side of Cal and Eric.

I took a sip of my drink, hiding behind the cup for more reasons than one. My face was flushed, and my eyes were clearly locked on three men in the room. The first two were hot enough on their own. That third one though, really got my blood pumping. There was something about the way he looked at me that made me forget every reservation I had over being with him. I felt a hand on either side of me—one from each Kinsley and Kelsey—as they pulled me away from the scene.

"Watch where you're going, big guy. You're not doing yourself any favors," Kelsey whispered in my ear. I listened as Kins led me up a familiar staircase

A lump formed in my throat as my body relived that night for the thousandth time. Upon reaching the top floor, I realized how drunk I must have been the last time I was there. It was almost like a separate apartment inside the house. I couldn't help but wonder how Hunter—who wasn't the captain—had managed to secure that space.

The bathroom was visible through the door that connected the living room to the bedroom, triggering memories of how Hunter had tried to comfort me mid-spiral. Oblivious to my surroundings, I pondered how we functioned on the ice with him seemingly becoming my new Roman Empire.

Kinsley and Kelsey closed the loft door, making their way to the couch and leaving me standing awkwardly in the middle of the room. The living room featured a small couch, where each of the girls chose a side and flipped it out to a bed, and decorated it with some blankets before browsing the TV for something to watch.

I walked to the furthest side of the room, where a messy desk sat piled with books and papers. Curious, I lightly nudged around to read the titles—Law. Hunter was studying pre-law. I felt like I should have known that, but then again, I didn't know half the majors my teammates were studying. Perhaps, when you don't see them off the ice, you never truly get to know them better.

I bit the inside of my gum, punishing myself for that. I wasn't like this back home. There weren't any secrets between myself and my teammates. While they didn't know I was questioning my sexuality, they were familiar with my home life and interests.

"You know," Kinsley called over her show. "You can make yourself comfortable, or you can go back downstairs. I just wanted to save you from getting caught out by your teammates."

I looked over to see the two girls cuddled under a blanket, Kelsey's head comfortably resting on Kinsley's chest.

"Thanks, I appreciate it." They smiled at me before going back to their show, their hands not so secretly exploring each other.

"There's whiskey over there on the bookshelf," she added. "Help yourself. There's also another TV in Hunter's room. The party tends to die down around midnight if you want to wait it out."

I went to the shelf, found a glass, poured myself some American Honey, and took my phone out as it buzzed in my pocket.

CAL: Hey, so I invited Eric back to our dorm…

I scoffed.

Don't stick your ass where we eat. Have fun.

CAL: Got it, sex stays in my room. I'll tell you all about it at brunch! Text me when you are on your way, I'll make sure all the dicks are away.

I laugh again, looking up to see the girls staring at me, "Cal's taking Eric to our dorm."

"Well, go get comfy in Hunter's room. He chills with the guys for a while before he makes his way up."

The door opened, and as if we'd said his name too many times, Mr. Boston himself entered the room. He took in his surroundings before his eyes finally landed on me. "Didn't know your voyeurism extended to lesbians, baby."

I rolled my eyes.

"Cal called dibs to the dorm for a bit," Kins offered. "I invited him up here." Did I mention I liked her? I could understand why Hunter was so loyal. Though I had a feeling he was going to have to say goodbye to their sexual rendezvous—Kelsey didn't give off the I share my girl vibes.

"Am I a good wingman or what?" Hunter smiled broadly. I looked away, my obvious defense mechanism against his disarming attractive looks.

"You did well. Now stop stroking your ego, we're trying to watch TV." Kins's tone was clipped, but I had the feeling she was up to something. I watched as Hunter took the hint, heading in the direction of his room before looking over his shoulder. "Feel like watching a hockey game?" Hockey was mutual ground between us, one I was kind of thankful for. The mischievous sparkle was gone from his eye, replaced by something soft and sincere. I nodded but paused to grab the bottle of whiskey and an extra glass for Hunter.

We watched as Boston fought against Florida, bonding over our mutual swearing at the opposing team.

"That was a fucking hold!" we yelled at the same time.

"Seriously, ref! Are you getting paid to miss their penalties?!"

"Remind me again why I like this sport?" I laughed, though with my recent worries, it was something of a non-rhetorical question. Hunter looked at me, brow quirked as if he was surprised by the question.

"Because your good at it. The moment you're in the rink you can't think of a reason why you *don't* love it? Bruises, sore muscles, and all."

And that had been pretty much it. It had been the one place I didn't seem to question myself. It was just me, my team, and the goal of getting that puck in the net. Perhaps it had been a caveman way of thinking, but in the craziness of life, sometimes it had been good to just hit something or check someone as hard as you could.

Hunter grumbled. "Wow, you didn't even preen at the fact I said you were good. Seriously, do you have any flaws? Please say you do, because you don't have a massive ego, you don't have a temper, and you always put others before yourself. Like seriously, there has to be something wrong with you.'"

I looked at him and his blazing amber eyes stripped me bare, as if my fatal flaw would be written somewhere on my body. I huffed a laugh. "You're just blind. I have many flaws. I'm a control freak, a perfectionist on so many accounts. Sometimes I wonder if there will be a day when I completely crack. I'm a chronic people-pleaser, even if I hate the person. You seem to be the exception to the rule and I'm not too sure how I feel about that."

The words rattled off my tongue, and I bit down on it in an attempt to stop any further ramblings. Hunter looked me over as if he could sense the tension in my jaw, and could taste the copper on my tongue as I sank my teeth in even more. The low glow of the TV made his eyes shine bright. My gaze traveled to how he bit his bottom lip, fuller than the top. I knew the taste of that bottom lip, knew how it felt sweeping over my own. My body reacted, heat prickling under my collar. I just hoped he blamed the alcohol. The heat in his eyes had me wanting it—wanting him—all over again. I was a man starved. Social construct dictated that I should push the bowl away when all I wanted to do was lick it clean.

Hunter leaned in. He was always so much braver, so much more daring. His lips ghosted mine, as if waiting for me to close the gap. His own honey—tinged breath mixed with mine, his head tilted so his nose just lightly grazed my own. "Those don't sound like flaws, baby. They sound like walls. Walls are there to protect, to keep you safe."

My eyes flicked up to his, those golden slivers shaded by thick lashes that were too beautiful to belong to this man. My heart couldn't take it. My heartbeat stuttered, only pounding when the heat of his lips grazed mine. I lunged. My lips collided with his, his groan sounded akin to relief.

Hunter pulled me to straddle his lap, the hard outlines of our erections meeting as he allowed me to take control. Control was one thing I didn't have when it came to Hunter Graves. My body was in charge, my mind was lost in a cloud of lust.

I took his face in my hands, pouring every ounce of my pent-up frustration into that kiss. His hands dug into my hips, guiding me to rock against his thick length.

"Fuck, baby."

His cries only fueled me. My hands moved, pressing heavily against his chest. The need to feel every crevice of his hard curves consumed me. I'd noticed them during workouts. I spent an extensive amount of time studying the hard lines I wanted to map out with my tongue. I found the hem of his shirt, working my hands underneath and guiding it up and over his head.

Hunter watched, eyes dark and heavy with lust. I only spared a moment to bite his bottom lip before I worked my way back down, doing exactly what I'd fantasized about. His smell, his taste had me high. His hands tightened on my hips as if he didn't want me to go too far. Though as I bridged his pants, he let me move. I nipped at the trail that led right to what I wanted, dipping lower... lower... lower....

"Ty... Tyler, fuck, fuck, fuck! What are you doing to me?"

I tugged his pants and boxers down with a little less finesse than I cared for, biting the inside of his thighs and then soothing the sting with my tongue. Hunter's whimper was music to my ears. That was *my* name on his lips, giving me the power to take him. I was inexperienced, but I hope I made up for it with my pure need for him. I licked a stripe up the underside of his cock and I couldn't tell you who's groan was louder. His salty taste hit my tongue, mixing with sweat and musk and... *Hunter*. It was too fucking good.

"Ty, God."

I chuckled, taking him in my mouth, alternating licking and sucking as I took him down inch by inch. I wanted more—I wanted to choke on him. But when he hit the back of my throat and triggered my gag reflex, he pulled me back by my hair "Take it easy, baby. You're doing great."

I only groaned in response because I was determined. This may be my last chance to do this and I wanted to make him come undone. The selfish, competitive, perfectionist inside me needed this to be the best he ever had. I had given in to being with him, and damn it I wasn't going to make myself live with the "what ifs.".

I needed this— needed him—out of my system.

I eased my mouth over him, loving the feel of his cut cock. The weight was heavy on my tongue, The deep, heady feeling taking over my senses. My tongue traced every vein, paying close attention to which ones made his hips jerk. I relaxed my throat and rolled his balls in my palm. As Hunter cried, I hollowed my cheeks, tongue flicking at the base of his cock.

"Oh fuck, oh fuck, oh fuck."

He swelled and throbbed in my mouth. I pulled back so his come could splash my tongue. I licked him right through his orgasm, aftershocks wracking his body. I licked until he pushed my head away, where I peered up between his thighs with a devilish grin as my tongue darted out for just one more taste.

Sensitive, he hissed and tugged me away with a rough grip on my hair.

So worth it.

Chapter Seventeen

Hunter

That orgasm was so strong it had me seeing stars. My head dipped back despite wanting desperately to watch that man claim my cock. And fuck, had he claimed it. No one had ever gotten my body buzzing like Tyler Riley. My brain was trying to catch up, my breath stuttering as I looked down at those sparkling eyes peering up through thick brown lashes. A dozen emotions swam through my mind, all battling for dominance but only one prevailed. Tyler kept his cards close to his chest. He was deep and mysterious, much like the enigmatic wizard in the tale of Oz. On the surface, he was confident, an all-powerful spectacle that left everyone in awe. Yet, amid the performance, there were moments like this when the curtain was lifted, allowing me a glimpse behind the façade.

In those rare instances, he revealed a vulnerability that made him undeniably human. His true, unfiltered emotions surfaced like waves crashing against the shore. I observed as bliss echoed through his beautiful seafoam eyes. Happiness, pride, *lust*, all directed at me. It was a sight so raw that my heart skipped a beat.

Unable to resist, I found myself drawn to him, yearning for a connection that went beyond the surface. His gaze alone had the power to make me forget the inevitable truth of how utterly gone I was for him. There was a lingering bit of hope that maybe, just maybe, he felt the same way. But such hope was perilous.

While I grappled with those emotions, he took the opportunity to capture his mouth with mine. His tongue explored my mouth as if trying to imprint the taste of our shared passion upon his senses. A guttural groan escaped me as I savored the mixture of my own taste combined with his whiskey-soaked flavor.

In that kiss, I felt the unspoken connection between us, a silent acknowledgment of a shared desire. Yet, the danger still lingered, threatening to unravel the delicate balance we had forged. As our lips danced, I couldn't help but wonder if he, too, understood the complexity of our entangled hearts. I needed some control back. I needed to be in charge again, because I was quickly becoming way too vulnerable when it came to him. I don't do vulnerable.

I quickly rolled so I was on top, all the while keeping our mouths locked together. I couldn't help the moan that left my lips as I tracked my hands over every defined muscle. I helplessly worked them south, and I didn't even bother to fight my smile at the way he squirmed beneath me.

I looked up to see that same look still in his eyes, his breathe coming out in short pants as he mumbled something along the lines of, "fucking dimples." Which only made me smile wider. He kicked his shoes off while I worked at his pants, pulling them free and tossing them aside. I teased up his thighs, licking and nipping at the skin while grazing over where he really wanted me to be. His body writhed beneath me, that beautiful Australian lilt letting loose a string of incoherent curses. I was hooked, desperate to hear him beg for me.

"Beg for me, baby."

"Just fuck me." He groaned, self control having flown out the window. I decided I liked that. I *really* liked that. I bit down on the goofy smile that was pulling at my mouth. He looked down and scoffed at me.

"I'm not going to say please, Hunter, if you continue to give me that adorable little smile I'll fuck your mouth until those dimples disappear."

My eyes went wide at that, and my dick swelled again at the though.

"Put a pin in that, Aus. I am *not* missing another chance to fuck that perfect ass again."

He groaned. "Either you fuck me or I fuck your mouth. Better make a choice before I do it for you."

I was torn between incredibly turned on, and kind of pissed off. This whole "one more time" ordeal had my palms sweaty.

That would be a fucking joke, and not a funny one. Having sex with Tyler had quickly become that addiction you couldn't let go. That one more chocolate bar you kept hidden for emergencies, that song you couldn't help but sing along to. Tyler and I couldn't help but fall into bed together, each of us needing that last hit—needing each other just one more time.

I reached into my nightstand for what we needed. I didn't fumble as I licked his leaking cock and my slicked up fingers teased down the smooth strip of skin between his balls. I wasn't gentle. There was no slow entry of my finger. I slipped one in to the knuckle, his sharp breath turning into a tortured groan as I worked him open. For someone who was new to anal, my baby was a pro. His body knew what it wanted. It was chasing that high like an addict. I was covering my cock with a condom when Ty demanded more.

"Fucking hell, Hunter. Just fuck me already."

I bit my lip, stifling back the urge to ask him, "What's the magic word?" Before I could, his strong thighs circled my waist and pulled, my dick bumping against his tight little hole. He drew me in, and I was quick to make sure my dick was angled just right, touching his taint. I went to inch in, but he had other ideas. One quick pull of those strong thighs buried me to the hilt.

"Fuck!" Our cries filled the air. His hole fluttered around me at my size, but my baby was a masochist. Tears peeked from the corner of his eyes, but before he was fully adjusted he threw his head back and rolled his hips in a silent plea for my body. "Move, Hunter. Fuck... *please*. Please, please, please just move. "

My jaw dropped and his eyes met mine for a split second. "Since you asked so nicely."

Then, I did as he asked.

This wasn't the slow sensual, sex we'd had before. My body slapped against his, while he arched his back, abs tensing as he angled himself so I hit the right spot with each thrust. His eyes were shut, head back against the pillow and God, it was a sight. I wanted that picture etched in my mind forever, anything to capture that masculine body begging for mine. His dick twitched with every hit of his prostate, the tendons of his neck straining against his pleasure. With each drop of pre come that fell onto his stomach, I felt my need to burst. But I needed this to last. I dug my fingers into his hips hard enough to bruise.

He loved it.

I smoothed my hands over his skin, over those rippling muscles in his groin. My thumb curved in on his pelvis, up to where his cock was glistening. With my thumb, I stroked a bit of the clear liquid away and brought it to my mouth. I groaned as his taste exploded on my tongue.

"Fuck, that's the hottest thing I have ever seen." The gravel in his voice had my eyes meeting his, pupils so blown that you could no longer see his irises. I slowly swept my thumb over the sensitive curve of his dick, as I pumped relentlessly into him. He threw his head back again and I was losing it. I thanked God when I felt him swelling in my hand, the combination of that and the abuse of his prostate making him soar to the edge. Every muscle bunched, his hands gripping the sheets so hard I wondered if they would rip. He cried out when he came, sweet liquid bursting between my fingers as it spurted over his chest. His whole body rippled with his orgasm. I had never seen someone come so hard. And I followed right behind.

There was no doubt someone would have heard the noise that left me. My vision whited out and my legs buckled. Tyler's strong arms grabbed me, pulling me onto his chest. I didn't care that it was wet and sticky. In fact, I kind of loved it. My head curved into the crook of his neck, my breaths shaky with the aftershocks wracking my body. I was well on my way to sleep, but the fear of being alone when I woke up stopped it from taking over.

It was my turn to beg. "Don't go. Please. Don't be gone in the morning."

Large hands traced lazy shapes over my skin. "I'll stay," he whispered. "Just this once."

With that knowledge alone, I fell into a peaceful sleep. One that had me wondering if I could somehow formulate a way to get this kind of comfort when he was gone. Something to keep the nightmares away.

CHAPTER EIGHTEEN

Tyler

I hesitated to open my eyes. I was lost in the rhythmic beat of Hunter's heart and the rise and fall of his warm chest. The feel of this solid, muscular guy holding onto me had every fiber of my being urging me to stay in that moment. I let myself relax in his embrace, blissfully unaware of the tension quietly building within me. Sure, I could blame it on alcohol, but I'd just be lying to myself.

It wasn't about being with a guy anymore; nothing had ever felt more right in my mind. I didn't have a single doubt about my actions last night. The real source of my unease was the stark reality of my life—Mum, my brother. I needed this dream of making it to the NHL to make all the sacrifices worthwhile. And that meant steering clear of complications.

Enter Hunter Graves: the colossal complication I never saw coming.

He is your teammate. You're fucking your teammate.

Yet, I couldn't muster the willpower to pull away from him. His scent, the warmth, and the steady thump of his heartbeat created a potent mix that induced something foreign in me: serenity. Something I hadn't experienced in... a long time.

"Your thoughts are loud, baby," Hunter's deep voice groaned, his arms tightening around me as if he could hug away the rush of thoughts. I sighed, reality seeping back in. Lifting my head, I rested my chin on his chest, meeting sleepy amber eyes. They held a softness I hadn't noticed before, though something still lingered around the edges.

Sighing again, I hoped he'd forget about the cacophony of thoughts that threatened to disrupt the tranquil atmosphere around us. His fingers found a stray strand of hair falling across my face, the brush of his skin against mine sending tingles over my body. Resisting the urge to lean into his touch, I marveled as his fingers adjusted the strand, subtly tracing the contours of my face.

My breath hitched in my throat as his fingers moved across my chin, ghosting over my adam's apple. "Beautiful," he mumbled.

That was it. In that moment, everything outside our little cocoon faded away.

I took a deep breath, leaning into the way my chest fluttered. A jumble of thoughts raced through my mind, the urge to reciprocate his compliment hanging heavy. He was more than just beautiful with that strong jawline, tousled hair and those eyes that shifted through an array of colors. When he let his guard down, they turned golden, a reminder of the summer sun kissing the ocean back home.

Ink swirled over his arm, painting pictures over the ivory skin that trailed over his shoulder and across his chest. He surpassed anything I could have conjured up in my head, more than anything I'd ever let myself fantasize about. Yet there he was, looking at *me* like that—like I was so much more than just a casual hookup.

I sensed a subtle reaction beneath me, a twitch of excitement, as his finger traced down my neck, gliding over my chest to follow the words inked there. The question lingered in his eyes, but he didn't say a word.

"One more time?" His breath fanned over my lips. I was so swept up in him, so stuck in a trance that I didn't see him lean in until he was right there, lips brushing mine.

My body acted of its own accord, my leaning in until our lips brushed. Like he always did, he knew exactly what I wanted. He rolled on top of me, kissing me slowly and savoring every inch of my skin. He prepared me—almost lovingly. I simply watched as he did it, mouth slack, vision hazy as I gave myself just one more selfish moment. He filled me, moving in that way that hit me just right, his lips grazing mine with each thrust. Pleasure zapped through my body, intensified by the lingering sensitivity from the night before. My hands tangled in the longer strands of his hair, desperate to hold onto the moment for a little bit longer.

"Fuck, baby, I can't hold it. I want to... it feels too good."

But I was right there with him. I let myself go, fighting back a rush of emotion that had tears burning my eyes. As if they knew this would be the end. He rested his forehead against mine as I came, groaning as he followed me over the edge.

Our breaths were heavy as they tickled over each other's lips, too scared to part—too scared to put words to how we were feeling. At least, what I thought he was feeling. If it was even half of what I was feeling, this was way more than one more time.

My phone buzzed beside the bed, pulling us from the moment. Hunter sighed, pulling out of me, and kissing my cheek tenderly. He handed me my phone as he left for the bathroom to dispose of the condom and clean up.

I didn't look at the screen. Instead, I looked to the ceiling as if it would give me some answers. Soft, silent tears rolled down the side of my face. I hit the bed with my fists before rolling to the edge, feet cold on the wooden floor. I rested my arms on my naked knees and looked at the text.

> **CAL**: Hey bestie—coffee, my treat, obviously. I won't take no for an answer.

I huffed a laugh. I could practically hear his voice in my head.

"Something funny?"

I looked to my side to see Hunter dressed in his jeans, handing me a wet washcloth. I took it and wiped my chest clean.

"Just Cal demanding my attendance for coffee. No doubt to tell me way too much information on his hookup from last night."

Hunter nodded, something indiscernible flickering in his eyes. I chose to ignore it and instead got myself dressed. I fired off a response to Cal, pausing to listen to the girls. I knocked and waited for them to declare themselves decent before pulling it open. Both girls were dressed, cuddled together and both wearing the same blissed out smile.

"Where are you off to Ty?" Kinsley asked.

"To see Cal. He owes me coffee after consecrating our dorm."

"We'll come with you," Kinsley gave me a broad smile.

"Well, if the girls are coming, can I tag along? I'm starving." I looked over my shoulder to see Hunter leaning in the doorframe, bracketing me with his strong arms. My eyes betrayed me, drinking him in hungrily. *Fuck me.* My attraction to him was going to be the death of me. Hunter, like always, read my thoughts and pulled his bottom lip between his teeth. *Torture, looking at him every day was going to be torture.*

I nodded, too scared to speak as my body reacted to him. There was no doubt my voice would give me away. I looked away from him, catching knowing grins from both the girls. I rolled my eyes.

"Come on," I told them. "No doubt Cal is itching to spill the beans about last night."

"Hopefully that's the only thing itching," Hunter cracked. I smacked his chest, trying to deny the fact that his laughter was the most beautiful sound I'd ever heard.

Kelsey kept a firm grip on my hand as she pulled me through the house. In the midst of the bustling crowd, I couldn't help but notice Kinsley's playful antics with Hunter. Jealousy prickled under my skin, but I quickly redirected my attention forward, feigning interest in a girl who met my gaze.

Kelsey being the skilled actress she was, smoothly maneuvered my arm around her, placing my hand strategically close to her chest. The room erupted into catcalls, adding to the electric atmosphere. To play along, Kelsey drew me even closer to create an illusion of intimacy. She sealed the act with a kiss on my cheek, accompanied by a look of sheer adoration that masked the inner turmoil I felt.

I whispered my gratitude in her ear, but I couldn't shake the burning in my chest. The words clashed with the uncomfortable truth settling in the spot inside me where Hunter had taken up residence. The façade was taking its toll, and with every step, the lie burrowed itself deeper into the tangled web of emotions.

Cal sat in the cozy corner booth in the back of the café, his eyes lighting up when he spotted me. He sprang to his feet with infectious enthusiasm, excitedly waving me over. Despite the somber undertones that clouded my mood, I couldn't help but smile.

Cal's energy was contagious, breaking through the anxiety that had a death grip on me. The warmth in his greeting worked its way into my disposition, momentarily lifting the weight that had settled on my shoulders.

"Someone's in a good mood." I accepted the hug that he threw in my way, his arms wrapping around my neck as he bounced in my grip.

"You made my night. If it wasn't for you, I wouldn't have met and slept with the man of my dreams."

His grin lit up the room. He pulled back and gestured to the table, where my omelet and coffee sat waiting for me.

"I even got them to make it with egg whites. It took a lot of bribing, but anything for my future best man."

I chuckled, trying to bite back my concern—and a comment about him hopping into this like a kangaroo on a freeway. I looked behind me and saw Hunter's gaze, his darkened eyes slanted as he looked at Cal.

"Too soon to be jumping into wedding planning, don't you think, Cal?" Hunter nudged him, but Cal didn't let skepticism sway him.

"You two grumpy butts can keep your negativity to your side of the booth, I will bathe in the light of optimism that I've met my soulmate."

We all settled into the booth: Hunter to my side, Kinsley to his left and Kelsey beside Cal, we ate our food while Cal spilled every sordid detail of his evening. It was more than once—he made that abundantly clear. A permanent flush seemed to cling to my cheeks throughout the entire ordeal. Hunter's presence beside me felt like a constant source of distraction, his wandering gaze creating an uncomfortable awareness. I tried to dismiss the sensation of his knee pressed against mine, even though the warmth of his thigh seemed to burn through both layers of denim.

As the awkward atmosphere persisted, Hunter's whispered words cut through the ambient noise, sending shivers down my neck. "He thinks this is hot, but it doesn't top us last night." The provocative statement hung in the air, an arousing reminder of the intimate encounter we shared. My elbow met his stomach, but he simply chuckled.

A pout involuntarily formed on my lips as I realized that Hunter's ability to grate on my emotions had become a recurring theme. The delicate dance of tension and humor between us only added another layer to the complex emotions swirling within.

Cal gave us a sideways glance—one that told me exactly what we'd be talking about behind closed doors.

"There I was talking about chemistry, and you were burning my fire with the electricity between you and Hunter. You fucked again."

"And yet again, Cal, I don't talk about my sex life." The sharpness in my tone was uncalled for, and Cal's expression told me as much.

"Geez, you're the only guy I know who gets fucked—by Hunter Graves no less—and remains in a pissy mood. I've had some amazing sex in my life, but Hunter definitely still tops the list."

I couldn't help it—I growled. My frustration bubbled over as I stormed past him and to the kitchen. Intent on my meal prep, I ignored him, but I couldn't ignore the knowing smirk playing on his lips. I rolled my eyes and—barely—refrained from commenting, silently hoping he'd just drop it. My mind was already occupied by thoughts of a certain dark-haired individual. I certainly didn't need any assistance from my friend.

Cal sidled up behind me, his arms enveloping my torso. He wasn't one to shy away from touch, but I bristled under the embrace, a mix of annoyance and discomfort coursing through me. Despite my body's reaction, Cal remained unfazed, squeezing me tighter with his chin casually resting on my shoulder.

"One day, my friend, you will be comfortable with who you are. And until that happens I'll stick right by you."

A weak, pathetic laugh left me, my non- chopping hand resting on his as I let my weight fall back into him.

"I guess you'll be sticking around for a while then; being gay in the NHL isn't exactly trending."

Cal let out a weighted sigh, one that said that he knew I was right.

We were in an age where pride was both celebrated and shamed, where hockey pride jerseys were no longer worn in warm ups because it was "distracting." I let out a sigh of my own and continued preparing the food for the week. Cal hugged me for a bit longer, knowing I needed the comfort, before he pulled away and began to work silently alongside me.

Nothing else needed to be said.

CHAPTER NINETEEN

Hunter

That morning's bliss dissipated the moment Cal whisked Tyler away. I tried not to let my teeth grind as I watched the easy way they interacted; the public affection Cal was able to give Tyler. It was something my body ached to do myself.

He shut me down the moment we left my room. Tyler Riley knew how to give a cold shoulder that would make Frosty the Snowman jealous. It didn't matter how much I tried to melt the ice by pressing my thigh into his. That was my little sign that we *could* be more. We could have each other and our careers too. God, I'd take any little morsel he gave me after last night.

My reflection was one I barely recognized. Wistfulness lingered in my eyes, masked by the façade I wore for lunch with my father. I knotted my tie like a soldier would his uniform: methodical, robotic, and tight enough to mimic the hold that man had over me.

"Why are you even going?" Kins asked from the bed, fidgeting with her hands. "Couldn't you come up with some excuse?"

"You mean like I've done twice already? The last thing I need is him showing up unannounced. What if he saw me with Tyler? We both know I'm holding onto that team by a thread. The only thing keeping me on is that winning makes him look good. The second hockey makes me look anything other than perfect, he'll pull me from the team faster than you can blink."

"I don't like it. I don't like who you are around him. Don't think I haven't noticed how you've pulled away from me before. Last time it was weeks before we slept together again."

I let out a heavy breath. "Kins, we agreed not to sleep together anymore, so why does that matter?"

Kins rose from the bed, lip trembling ever so slightly. "It's not about the sex, Hunter. It never was, and you know that. It's the fact that you hid whatever that man did to you."

I pulled her into a hug, less for her comfort and more for my selfish attempt at her not seeing the lies written all over my face.

"He's never done anything other than let me know what a disappointment I am to him, but he's still my father. He's the reason I'm here—he's the only family I have left."

Kinsley pulled away, eyes blazing. "He isn't family, Hunt. Family doesn't treat you like that. He'll have you follow in his footsteps, and marry a trophy by graduation. I can see pieces of your beautiful soul crumbling away every time you see him and he doesn't even care. I can't lose you like that, Hunt."

I drew her close again, burying my face in her soft golden curls. "You will never lose me, Kins. It'll always be you and me. But I only have this year left to enjoy myself, and I'm going to make the best of it. That means keeping Dad happy. Otherwise, it's bye-bye hockey." The words hung in the air, a heavy acknowledgment of the sacrifices I felt compelled to make for the sake of keeping the peace.

Kinsley nodded in my shoulder. "And Tyler?"

The simple sound of my name made me freeze. "What about him?"

"Where does he fit? Because I've never seen you as happy as you are with him. I didn't even know you could light up like that. It feels like I've been looking at you through a filter my whole life. Then Tyler walks in and someone hits the enhance button. I want that for you, Hunt—all the time. not just in private."

I want that for me too.

I shook off the thought, pressing a kiss to Kinsley's head and grabbing my suit jacket.

"I am not the guy who gets his dream man, not when Tyler's dream is the NHL. We both know it, and we're both better off being each other's dirty little secret." Those words cut deep—I hated referring to Tyler as anything but what he was: perfection. In a different world, I'd be the first one to hold his hand on pride float while my lips claimed what was rightfully mine.

Kinsley's glossy eyes told me she thought the same.

What was the point in loving someone when you couldn't love them out loud?

The black town car halted outside my father's Beacon Hill condo. The thick black lacquer door extended a cold welcome. I glanced back at the driver, Silas, lightly tapped his shoulder with a polite thank-you, and ascended the stairs.

Ignoring the erratic rhythm of my heart, I forced each step, feeling like the protagonist in a movie. Although, I wasn't sure if the music score in that moment would be a cinematic suspense piece or something from an intense action movie.

Before I could even knock, the door whooshed open. Then I was staring up at an older, matured version of myself. He scrutinized me from head to toe, and decided if I was worthy enough to stand in his presence. This was our family home, not a country club filled with his colleagues, yet the same standards were upheld. "Hunter."

"Dad."

His outstretched hand became the closest semblance of a loving touch I would receive from the man who raised me. I took it, careful not to apply too much pressure—just enough to convey strength without posing a threat. It felt like a carefully choreographed dance. One I had to perform flawlessly to meet his expectations. Did other families engage in these calculated exchanges? I couldn't be sure; my exposure to "normal" people was limited.

I grew up in a world where straight meant more than just posture. In terms of sexual orientation, it noted your beliefs and your place in the hierarchy as men and women. The misogynistic, patriarchal ideals I was raised with left little room for individual expression. A woman's role was to be a trophy: defined by her ability to bear children and keep a home. That was the straight and narrow path I was expected to follow—the quintessential American man.

I followed my father through the house, feeling more like I was entering an old-fashioned parlor. Leather, wood, and a flickering fire provided the only warmth in the room. I took a seat on the unworn leather couch, ignoring its protests while my father settled into an armchair, his back turned to the cold streets of Boston. Despite the early hour, he held a snifter of whiskey. I eyed that golden liquid as if it were my only salvation to make it through that afternoon.

"Your team is playing well it seems." His voice was cold, void of any emotion.

"We'll take The Frozen Four this year, I can feel it. Scouts are watching us."

I regretted the words as soon as they left my mouth. My father's stern mouth hardened. Scouts weren't a part of his plan. As the head of Graves Law, it was decided that I would transition into the family law firm.

"Well, that may be true, but understand this: old money did not come from boys being pansies on a slab of ice. Our legacy, was built on decades of hard work and preserving the family name. I followed my father just as he followed his. We built this company—the Graves legacy. We have every CEO and every senator; we have *America* in our hands. They want us to represent them. It will not end with me. *Hockey* is not an appropriate career for a Graves man."

My nails bit into the palm of my hand.

"If you even consider talking to those scouts, I will make sure everyone suffers. Not just you—your entire team. Do you hear me? How would you feel if a certain Australian boy lost his scholarship? I see how you two are on the ice. I can tell you two have a... connection."

My skin itched like fire ants tore into every cell. Tyler's face haunted my thoughts. Of course, my father noticed. And of course, he hated it. My protective instincts took over.

"He's my teammate, sir. But I know my place. You have been kind enough to let me play these last few years. I promise I won't talk to the scouts."

The words alone cut through me like a knife. That small, broken part of my soul would always be left crying in his presence. He didn't have a conscience—he sat poised and perfect, back straight and shoulders square as those around him crumpled.

"Good. Now, your grades."

That was the moment I realized I wouldn't leave that pristine black door unscathed.

I tried not to flinch with each tug of my jersey, hiding the offensive skin underneath my long-sleeve skins. Both Tyler and I remained silent, though he still casted glances my way. Both of us had a single focus: the game. We were often the first at the rink and the last to leave, training harder than anyone else. Though I waited until I was alone before I changed.

We still found each other in the gym before the sun, but I no longer took my shirt off to flirt with him. His eyes still sought mine out, as if he wanted to capture even a fleeting moment of that connection we once shared. But we knew better. We pushed it deep into the shadows. We had to play the straight card now. My father would have been proud, but my soul ached.

I felt a kinship with the men of the past, those who secretly lusted for another man but were constrained by the illegality of it. Unlike them, I'd never felt guilty about my sexuality. Everyone who needed to know did. I was proud of who I was. I was good in bed, and I enjoyed it, But now, being hung up on someone I couldn't have left me hating the turmoil of feeling this way about a *man*. What made it even more gut-wrenching was seeing the same emotion in Tyler's eyes.

Coach clapped to capture our attention, breaking me away from my thoughts. "Alright boys! We have a home game tomorrow with UMass Lowell. We have quite a few away games lined up so please make sure they're in your diary. Your roommates have been emailed to you and I won't be taking any feedback. This is a good chance for team bonding."

I couldn't grab my phone fast enough. My heart raced as I saw the email notification. My thumb hurriedly tapped the screen, clumsily opening the email. Beside my name, Tyler's somehow seemed larger and in bold. I bit back a smile and glanced beside me, only to see Tyler far from impressed. My heart shattered. That team list was my chance at just one more time.

Before I could say anything witty to play off my disappointment, Tyler's phone rang. Anxiety worked its way across his features. His head twitched as if he were about to look at me, but he thought better of it. He swiped the screen and brought the phone to his ear but before he could say anything, another voice sounded through the speaker. I couldn't discern who it was, but the smile on his face made my stomach drop.

Tyler got his bag and swung it over his shoulder without so much a second glance. I wasn't the only teammate looking at him like he sprung two heads. His voice changed as he spoke to whoever it was, more vibrant than I'd ever heard it. An unusually thick Aussie twang echoed down the hall. *"How are you? I missed you. What have you been up to?"* .

Mouse and Jarman appeared to either side of me, leaning against the lockers.

"Aussie has some serious game! First Kins and Kels, now an Aussie girl?" Mouse bellowed, broad smile beaming at the possibility of our Aussie being a secret player. He was a player alright, playing my heart like a piano.

"It's always the quiet ones," I muttered, trying and failing to hide the disappointment in my voice.

Jarman's eyes briefly locked onto mine. He was the type that didn't miss much. But thankfully he always kept his findings to himself.

"That's for sure! But with the fire he has on the ice, it's no surprise." Mouse turned his beady little eyes on me. "*You've* seen it firsthand though! One of these days I'll get you drunk enough to know what happens in that room of yours."

I chuckled. Mouse was all bark and no bite. He let the girls fawn over him, but he only had eyes for one. Too bad she wasn't the type to be into hunky hockey players.

"I think it would burn your innocent little eyes, Mouse, to see what your mentor is like when he shakes off that straight and narrow act." I bit my tongue. *Straight and narrow—fucking hell, you idiot.* "I mean, Kinsley has no complaints, that's for sure." *Shut up, shut up, shut up.*

Jarman's eyebrow quirked. Like I said: doesn't miss much. *You did not just out Tyler; you did not just out Tyler.*

"Sounds like you're losing your regular hookup to an Aussie, Hunt" Mouse teased, jostling my shoulder.

"Oh, I'll never lose Kins. But I'll never refuse her a double dicking."

Tyler is going to fucking hate you.

I ducked to hide the shame creeping under my collar. Out of the corner of my eye, Jarman's lip quirked as if he'd figured it out. Instead of calling me out, he jostled my shoulder. "Mouse is just jealous, you and Tyler both manage to juggle two of the hottest girls on campus and he can't get the one he wants. He hadn't realized all he needs is a manga and a band tee and she'd be wrapped around his finger."

I laughed, feeling my heart rate begin to slow. I shot him an appreciative gaze, maybe I was laying too many cards on the table, but he was my teammate, and I was going to hold onto that a little while longer. Because who knew if I would still have my team when I was forced to drop hockey and work for my father.

CHAPTER TWENTY

Tyler

"Hey, sweetheart." Mum's voice was like salve to a wound. It felt like we hadn't had a proper conversation in weeks and with the lyrical questions that came through the line, I felt like a kid again. I answered each one with enthusiasm, letting her hear how excited I was about my success so far. Her praise made all the pain worth it. I was winning games, drawing attention for my skill and I hadn't truly taken a moment to absorb it all. Because the second I stepped off that ice, I was planning the next one, berating myself for every little mistake. I knew I was doing it, but I wouldn't get where I needed to be by taking it easy. I couldn't let her down.

"So, that's hockey covered—I'm not surprised you're excelling in that department. But what about friends, or maybe... girlfriend? Or a boyfriend?"

I opened the door to the dorm quickly, hoping no one overheard. Cal stood in the kitchen, humming to his music while staring into the open fridge like it would materialize what he wanted.

"Ooh, is that Mama Riley?"

Most times, I strategically made it to my room for calls home. I wasn't embarrassed by Cal, but after the last encounter with Holden, I didn't trust him to keep his mouth shut.

"Oh, is that your roommate? Let me see!" Mum's bright eyes widened, and I bit back a curse. They'd both been excited to meet each other—even it if were only a video call.

As if that were invitation enough, my phone was ripped from my hand. Boundaries were something we needed to discuss—quickly.

"Hey Mama Riley! Oh, your son didn't mention how gorgeous you are!"

I groaned, letting him have the spotlight as I grabbed a water from the fridge.

"Oh, you are too sweet. I hear you torture my son with Taylor Swift music. I thank you for your service. He might pretend it's annoying but it makes him feel right at home."

"We both know he sings her songs in the shower."

My cheeks were on fire. "I do not!"

"It's nothing to be ashamed of, Ty."

"It's okay Mrs. Riley, he seems to like the closet. Closet Swiftie, closet gay—maybe one day we'll get him out of there."

I gaped.

Mum laughed.

My stomach fell through the floor.

Cal never once looked at me, continuing on as if he hadn't just outed me to my mum.

"Aha! So you know who he's seeing? What's he like? Do we like him?"

"All broody but heart eyes only for your boy. It's cute."

"Cal, give me the phone." He looked at me, not a shred of guilt on his face. Though I hoped my anger was written all over mine.

"Ty don't be mad..."

"Cal, give me the phone." I bit my words through clenched teeth, blood pulsing in my ears

"Fine, I was just giving you the little push you needed. You won't talk to me about him I thought you would with your family."

"That was for *me* to decide, Callum." I snatched my phone, not even caring about the hurt that crossed his eyes.

"Tyler!" Mum gasped.

"What, Mum?"

I turned the phone back to me, not bothering to hide my anger.

Her face fell and she started to speak as my brother stepped into view. I shook my head, hoping I could stop her before it was too late but it was in vain. "Tyler, Cal's right—you can talk to me. I thought after our last conversation you'd know that I love you regardless of if you're gay or not."

I watched Jamie's face contort. "You're gay?"

Before I could respond, he rounded the couch to get closer to the phone. "How long have you known? Were you ever going to tell me? Or was that something else you were going to protect me from?"

"I- I didn't want you to feel like you lost a role model in me."

"You thought I would care? You think that I would look at you less because you fuck men? Is that how little you think of me?"

"Jamie, it's not like that." That temper of his flared. His jaw twitched, his eyes blazed.

"Yeah, right. You know what, Tyler? I didn't just lose Dad the day he died. I lost you. You stopped being you. You stopped being my best friend. Now you keep secrets and talk down to me like I'm a kid. I might be younger than you but you aren't the only one who had to grow up the day he died."

My chest ached, desperate for the air that caught in my throat. I watched my brother storm out, the echo of the front door slamming ringing in my ears.

Mum tried to break the tension. "Tyler—"

"Forget it, Mum. Just... forget it." I ended the call and threw the phone across the couch. The lack of a satisfying crash only made my blood boil more.

I saw Cal approaching from the corner of my eye.

"Don't, don't come near me, mate. When will you ever learn to keep your fucking mouth shut?"

"I thought they knew—"

"You know what they say about assuming."

I got up and stormed to my room, changing back into my gym gear and stuffing my feet into my sneakers. I headed for the door. "Where are you going? Didn't you just finish training, shouldn't you be resting?"

"I'll rest when I'm dead."

"With the way you're going, that'll be sooner than you think." Cal snapped back. In return, I slammed the door in his face.

I barely slept. Despite being exhausted from way too much exercise, my mind just wouldn't relent. I'd tried calling Jamie—more than once. I just needed to know that we were okay. His words played over in my mind like a hit of crystal, keeping me wired as they seeped into every corner of my mind. I was one step away from bailing on the game and flying home.

As if the universe knew, my phone lit up with Mum's name. I contemplated ignoring her call—even though it wasn't entirely her fault. I wasn't even mad at Cal anymore. It was *my* secret that caused Jamie to be upset

"Hey, Ma," I sighed.

"Have you heard from your brother? He hasn't come home." The panicked tone in her voice had me bolting out of bed.

With nowhere to go, I paced in a circle around the room. "What? No? I have been trying to call him to clear the air."

I could hear her heavy breathing. "Okay, don't worry, he might just be... I'll find him, get some rest. Good luck on your game tomorrow."

"You think I'm going to rest without knowing he's okay? I'll call around, see if anyone can help find him."

There was a pause while she mulled over my offer. With a sigh, she relented.

"Thank you. I'm sorry. If I could drive, I would be out looking for him."

I frowned. "*If* you could drive?"

She let out a breath, one she'd been holding for way too long.

"I told Jamie not to tell you. I got in a bingle the other day. No one was hurt, minimal damage. I blacked out just for a moment. They took my license off me because the chemo is making me unfit to drive. I can try and get it back, but the doctors want me to finish this treatment and see how I recover."

My knees buckled, I dropped back onto the bed. My hand fisted my hair. *Why am I even here?* I needed to be home.

It was my turn to sigh. "I'll call the guys and get them to help. But no more secrets. There's no point in breaking up this family even more."

"Thanks, Ty. I *am* sorry, so sorry. I'm failing you both." I didn't need to see her to know she was crying.

"You're not. We're lucky to have you. I'll find him. Love you."

I disconnected the call and dialed Holden immediately.

"Mate, isn't it like two a.m.?"

"Have you seen Jamie?"

The line went silent.

"Not since yesterday. I took him to his training and dropped him home. Why?"

I explained everything and Holden spit out a curse. "Fuck, okay bro. I'm getting in my car now. He didn't mean all that, you know. He loves you. All he talks about is how much he misses you. He just wants you to let him in on your life, not you just worry about his."

"It's hard, okay? He hasn't been himself since we lost Dad, and now we are losing Mum, and I just felt like I need to protect him. I can't lose him too, Holden, I see that look in his eyes, and I worry that one day he might..."

"He wouldn't," came Holden's gruff voice. "I would never let him do that."

Despite everything, my lips tugged into a grin. It meant the world knowing someone like Holden was looking out for him.

"I'll find him, Ty, don't you worry. We are *not* losing him."

The last bit sounded more for him than me. The call ended and I simply sat on my bed looking at my screen. I wasn't a praying man, but I couldn't help sending a silent call to anyone who would listen that my little brother was okay.

The mirror reflected my exhaustion. Dark circles seemed insignificant compared to the fog that surrounded me. It had been three hours and there had been no sign of my brother. I needed to be at the rink in an hour and a half. I couldn't move. I was frozen in place, waiting for the call, while also hoping it didn't come. My mind swirled with all the possible outcomes—most of them not good.

I left the bathroom and shuffled to the kitchen. If I was going to be dumb enough to play this game, I needed some fuel in my system.

"Any news?" Cal tentatively asked as I entered the kitchen.

I shook my head and mindlessly prepared the breakfast I may not be able to eat.

I stood at the bench, pushing my egg white omelette around the plate.

"Ty, you need to get going, I can be on call for your family if you would like?"

"I am not going until I get a call."

"You'll get kicked off the team if you don't show. Then all of this would have been for nothing."

For the first time ever, I dumped my full plate in the sink and grabbed my bag, wondering why exactly I was doing this.

Then my phone rang. It was Holden. I wondered if something happened to Jamie, who it would be to call me. I closed my eyes, and hesitated. If it was bad news, I wasn't sure I wanted to know.

"Ty?" I tried not to read into the tired tone of Holden's voice.

"Found him."

"And?"

"He's fine. He's going to stay with me for a while just to have a break. He isn't..." There was a deep sigh that followed that told me too much.

"I'm coming home."

"No, you're not. I am perfectly capable of this. You need to finish what you started. If any of us is going to go pro, it's you. He wants that for you, you know? He tells me all the time. He just misses what you had before... you know."

"How bad is he? Be honest."

"He isn't great. He thinks you're too focused on protecting him to be his big brother anymore. He just wants that back. Give him time, then call him and just be real with him. Tell him about your man, about your life, and he'll be happy to open up to you. He'll feel less alone."

"I don't know how to be okay when he isn't, Hold. I can't lose him."

"You won't, I have him. I promise you that. I will *always* have him. But right now he just needs some time for himself. Your mum's chemo is really bad so your auntie is moving in to help."

I checked the time and groaned. "Okay, I have to get to the rink; I'm running late. But please keep me updated, on all of them. I fucking hate this, man."

"I know you do, but trust me. They're my family too. You've done so much for me—the least I can do is let you have this. Just win that game."

I'd never been so late to the ice in my life. My head was a mess, and I was just trying to focus on the last words Holden said. *I need this win.* I didn't miss the look on my teammates' eyes as I approached. I was never late, and I could tell I looked less than stellar. When Hunter's eyes met mine and widened I knew I looked like a train wreck.

He rushed over and grabbed my elbow, dragging me behind the private wall of the showers. "Dude, I've been calling you. Where have you been?"

I shoved him away and went to my locker. Ignoring his questioning look, I dropped my bag with a ceremonious thud as I started to strip.

Hunter returned to my side, backed by Mouse and Jarman.

I angrily put on my gear as they waited for an explanation for my tardiness. "Yes?"

"Dude, you're never late," Mouse admonished. "Was it the bird you were on the phone with when you left yesterday?"

I should kick his ass for referring to my mum as a bird... I shook away the thought—humor aside that wouldn't get us anywhere. "I slept in. I was uh, distracted last night and forgot to set my alarm."

"Bullshit," Hunter spat. "You don't sleep in—no matter how distracted you were the night before." I spun and shot him with a look that I hoped sent daggers into Hunter's skin. Jarman's eyebrows lifted in response and if I wasn't late, I would be taking Hunter somewhere to bash his head in.

Mouse *ooh*-ed and the very small thread I was holding onto snapped. "I was up late dealing with family shit. Can you please let me get ready? I want to be on the ice for warm-up."

Jarman and Mouse jostled me affectionately and headed to their stalls to finish taping their sticks. With them gone, my mask began to slip. Those same cries from earlier echoed in my mind. Hunter, as if he could read my thoughts, sidled in as close as he could without drawing the attention of the others.

He was so close that his breath tickled my cheek when he spoke. "I get it baby, you're homesick. But remember why you're here, what you're trying to achieve. You've been on top of your game all week, making plays, calling them out. You came here for the big leagues and you're going to take them by storm. You've already got people talking, and today they'll see you blindsiding UMass with those Aussie moves."

His words soothed my skin. Washed over me like his lips did when we were in bed together. Each word, each brush of his lips soothed the itch that crawled underneath—the one that made me want to get on the next flight home. It brought me back to the present, where Hunter was close enough to really take my mind off everything.

He cupped the back of my neck, briefly but firmly enough to do what I wished his lips could. "You got this, baby. Head in the game. Think about the ring of that buzzer when you get a goal, the buzz of the crowd, the sound of your pads slamming against your opponent. Everything else will be right where you left it: outside of this locker room."

Then his hand was gone along with the kiss of his breath. He sat next to me, taping up his stick like the others.

I did exactly as he told me: got my head in the game, forgetting all about the way he brought me back down to Earth with his touch alone.

Hunter's words were on repeat in my head as I hit the ice and between the cold air and solid ground, I'd never felt more centered.

Warm-up was a blur. Hunter kept me on my toes by testing all of my blind spots. Thankfully, Cap didn't dare make anymore digs towards my plays or what I'd been teaching the guys.

The first-period buzzer rang with a play that I'd practiced with Amon. Colton was under the thumb of a pesky Umass defenseman, leaving me with Amon on the right wing and Hunter backing me, reading the play perfectly to keep me clear. The puck flew between Amon's legs, pulling it forward for the shot.

I knew this goalie—I'd watched his every game, saw the way he favored his right side. He was ready for that puck. What he wasn't ready for, was Amon's new footwork. There was a slap of puck meeting stick, but not from Amon. His almost pirouette sent the puck to me with his skate while his stick looked like a follow-through. and I watched as the sound registered in the goalie's ears and he lunged right—but his reaction time was too slow as I hurled the puck into the top left corner.

Hunter wrapped me up from behind yelling, "That's it, baby!" in my ear before Amon skated over to knock his helmet into mine.

"We did it, Aussie!"

Chapter Twenty-One

Hunter

Nothing rattled me more than seeing Tyler walk through those doors with that look on his face—one of a man about to give up. He looked ready to jump on the next flight home—and my heart was ready to go right along with him. A twinge of jealousy hit me at the simple thought of him spending the night with someone else. A small, stupid part of me still worried that he might take the easy way: appearing straight. Though when he mentioned the phone call home, the puzzle pieces began to fall into place.

I knew I had to do everything in my power to remind him why he was here. I hoped that everyone took my hand on his neck as a brotherly embrace, though Tyler and I knew it was anything but. His pulse spiked beneath my fingertips and his breath hitched as my lips hovered close to his. His eyes tracked every movement of my mouth, silently begging for a kiss.

That firm touch and my words seemed to break whatever had him in a chokehold. I watched as he came to life on the ice, that smile he reserved for a select few spread wide for the cameras. The world was catching a glimpse of the Aussie glow, and the crowd loved it. I knew then that I would spend my night replaying that video, waiting to hear what the commentators had to say and to see the public's reaction. I had no doubt they were falling for that golden Aussie boy as much as I was.

By the third period, we had it in the bag. We were up by two with eight minutes left on the clock. UMass was furious, fighting hard to breach the blue line and challenge our goalie, Preston McLean. Preston stood poised, but I couldn't ignore the slight jitter in his glove as the UMass forward closed in. I accelerated to intercept the puck, sensing the looming threat of another player aiming to knock me off course to create a clear path for their forward to the net.

The sound of a collision echoed through the rink. I gained control of the puck, swiftly directing it back to my team. Jarman guided the puck toward the blue line when the referee's whistle pierced the air. Confused, I scanned the ice, certain that Jarman wasn't offside. Then, my attention focused on the scene behind me.

Tyler laid crumpled on the ice. The UMass defenseman towered over him, shouting in his face. The towering UMass defenseman had him pinned, shouting fiercely into his face.

"Fucker! You think you can hit me!" He grabbed Tyler's visor, lifting his head then smashing it to the ice with a sickening *thud*.

I saw red. Before I could blink I had his jersey in my fists, pulling him off and poised to lay a blow to his face when hands on my biceps held me back.

"Chill, man. Chill." It was Jarman, his voice smooth and calming. "He's getting a penalty."

"He fucked with my man! He fucked wi—"

"I know And he'll pay on and off the ice," he assured me. "You won't be any good to anyone sitting next to him." He only loosened his grip once I relaxed and he gave me a pat on the back as he stepped away. I looked over to see Mouse helping Tyler to his feet. Without hesitation, I rushed over, not stopping until I could see those beautiful eyes of his.

"Guy can't take a hit. All I did was check him away from you, and he lost his shit," Tyler explained. He shook himself off as if being laid out on the ice was no big deal. He laid a hand on my shoulder and I swear I could feel the heat even through the pads. "I'm fine."

I studied him, wondering if he could see my desire to take him somewhere private to see how "fine" he really was.

Jarman led Mouse to position to give us a few moments alone. Finally, Tyler smirked at me and lowered his voice. "Keep those bedroom eyes to yourself, Boston; someone might see."

During the power play, Tyler added an assist to his game stats. If he was hurt at all by the hit, he didn't show it. If anything, it fueled his fire. The cameras captured that cocky grin of his, and the crowd went wild for it.

For the record, so did I.

I had an addiction, one that became increasingly evident—especially in the locker room. My eyes couldn't help but study my teammate in a way they shouldn't. Pink slowly darkened on Tyler's skin, showing the first hints of bruises from the hit. In another universe, I'd be soothing every inch of sore skin with my lips. But reality was a nasty bitch, and I was forced to tear my eyes away. I tried to ignore Tyler's jerky movements as he tried to rush out of the change room.

"In a hurry again, Riley?" I attempted to keep my tone light, but the quirk of his brow meant that I failed... epically.

"Got things to do and people to see, Boston," he quipped back. Without so much as a second glance in my direction, he effortlessly threw his bag over his shoulder and left before I could blink. The lingering tension hung in the air as I resisted the urge to follow, realizing that some desires had to remain confined within the walls of the locker room.

CHAPTER TWENTY-TWO

Tyler

I counted the dots of the popcorn ceiling as I waited for the phone to connect. *Pick up, pick up, pick up.*

"Hey." Though it was dry and disinterested, the sound of Jamie's voice made me sigh with relief

"Hey, James." I hoped that the name only I was allowed to call him would soften him a bit.

"How was your game?".

I was finally able to relax, tearing my gaze away from the monotonous ceiling. "We won. I got laid into but it was worth it."

"Win the power play then?" The lightness creeping into his tone made me relax even more.

"Yeah, got an assist."

"Sweet."

The conversation lulled and the silence stretched on, feeling much longer than it actually was. I knew it was then my turn to break it.

"I'm sorry, James; really. I only figured out I was, uh…"

"Gay?"

"Yeah," I sighed. "I only figured it out once I got here. To be honest, I wasn't going to come out at all—not exactly encouraged in professional sports."

"That's fucked."

I laughed.

"It is."

"So, you have a boyfriend?"

I choked on air, feeling like the simple word got lodged in my throat. "No. We... we can't be together. We fooled around a couple of times, but it's over now."

Jamie went silent again, long enough for me to pull my phone away from my ear to check that he hadn't hung up. Instead, I saw a request for a video chat. I accepted instantly, revealing a younger version of my dad staring back at me.

"You like him?"

I could have laughed at the scrutinizing glare my brother gave me. He was much like Mum in the sense that he could read you like a book.

"Yeah, I like him. It'll never work though."

He seemed to think over that. "Have you ever liked *anyone*?"

At first, the question surprised me. Then again, our age gap meant that I wasn't having the same conversations with him that I was with Holden and the crew—though I was the one who had to answer all his questions.

"No, I have only been with one person before—a girl. So, I can't say I have a lot to go off. But I do like him."

"And with the girl, did you like her?"

I winced, and my face must have answered his question. "What happened? If you didn't like her, why did you sleep with her?"

My eyes closed, almost of their own volition. As if I could somehow shield myself from seeing his face as the truth revealed itself. According to Holden, this was what we needed—honestly. So, summoning every ounce of courage I could muster, I confessed everything; that I'd been too scared to say no. I told him about how I regretted every second of it. And then, the truth: I wasn't comfortable that night because I wasn't interested.

"If she lived in Perth, I would fucking punch the bitch." I couldn't help but laugh, "Seriously Ty, that's fucked up. I might be younger than you but even I know that's not okay."

My heart warmed knowing I'd at least taught him that.

"It is what it is, I know now to speak up when something doesn't feel right. I hope that you are the same. And you always feel you can talk to me."

"You know you can still be my role model if you're gay, right?"

That caught me off guard. "I can't really teach you…"

"I don't need you to teach me how to…" He shook off the thought. "That's not why I look up to you. I look up to you because you're out there living your dream. Because one day, I know you will be cheering *me* on when I am winning fights around the world. You're my role model because you're my big brother. I'm sorry for what I said…"

"Don't be, you were right. I've been trying to fill a space that I never can."

"You may not be Dad, Ty. But I didn't realize how much you truly protected me until you were gone. There are days I feel bad because I want you to give it all up and come home."

My heart shattered so fiercely that I was surprised I couldn't hear it. "And if you say the word I'll be on the next flight home."

"That's not what I want. I want you to fulfill your dreams. It's what Mum wants—it's what Dad would have wanted."

I nodded back to him. "I wish I could be in two places at once, James. I really do."

A sad smile graced his lips, and I watched as Holden's bedroom light flicked on to reveal his glossy eyes.

"Yeah, me too. But we'll see you at Christmas."

A hum escaped me, a subtle acknowledgment fueled by a gut feeling that I wouldn't be seeing them as planned. We planned for them to fly out to me, but I had a feeling they were keeping the severity of Mum's condition under wraps.

"Yeah, can't wait," I responded with forced enthusiasm, masking the unease that lurked beneath the surface. I redirected the conversation, losing myself in his stories about training and his upcoming fight. Holden's assistance with his grades became a focal point—a welcome relief, given his perennial struggle to concentrate in class. Though when the conversation shifted to his friends, a palpable frustration emerged. They were forging new connections, moving on, and leaving him behind. The timing stung. He was in a place where he needed his friends the most.

When there was another beat of silence, Jamie surprised me. "You know, you should really see where it goes with your guy. We both know life is too short."

"He's my teammate,"

His eyes went wide. "Did you know he was your teammate before it started?"

I looked away to hide the flush creeping over my cheeks and he burst into laughter. "What is so funny?"

"My perfect brother fucked up by fucking his own teammate!"

"Aye, I'm not perfect!"

"You try to be. This is too good. Like bad if you guys get caught, but kind of funny to see you do something you shouldn't, literally."

"Ha-Ha, laugh it out, its over."

"Sure—let me guess who it is!"

Despite everything, I couldn't help but share a laugh with him, playing along as he speculated with a finger to his mouth about who it could be.

"It's one hundred percent Hunter Graves. The tall, dark, and dangerous type. Also, I've watched the tapes you've sent me; you two are too in sync not to be sleeping with each other."

I only responded with a playful eyeroll. "On that note, I'm going to bed."

"I was so right, wasn't I?"

"Goodnight, smartass. I love you."

"Love you too."

That conversation finally lifted the weight off my chest. Almost on cue, my stomach rumbled—loudly. I tried to remember the last time I ate—and I couldn't. I'd somehow played a hockey game on an empty stomach. I needed to refuel, and fast. As I went into the kitchen, I mentally calculated the calories burned and tried to figure out what I needed to replenish.

Cal's voice broke through my thoughts as I cooked. "Hey, how's things at home?"

I flipped the chicken breast on the skillet and faced Cal, noting the hesitance in his pose. "I can't speak for Mum, but Jamie's home. We're better, I think."

"Ty, I'm so sorry, really. I'll do better. I don't know why I can't keep my mouth shut sometimes."

As I looked at him, truly studied him, I wondered if anyone could stay mad at that face. He resembled a golden retriever, with big brown, mopey eyes that made anger difficult to sustain. "I want to say it's fine, and we're cool. I'm over being mad at you, but when I share things with you, I need you to keep them private. I get to tell my own story."

"I know, trust me. It was a douche canoe move, and it won't happen again. It was just a friendly rib at each other. I thought I could do that with your family, but I was sorely mistaken. I regretted it instantly. A big mouth is good for one thing and one thing only. So, I'm sorry."

Even in one of the most serious moments we'd ever shared, he made me laugh. "We're good. But I don't need to hear about your big mouth; you keep that all for Eric."

"Oh, and he loves it. I have so much I want to talk to you about! It's been eating me up."

"It's barely been two days," I laughed. "What else could have happened since then?"

Turns out: a lot.

And just like that, we were okay. I listened to the saga of Cal and Eric, finding relief in the fact that hearing about his very normal problems distracted me from my own... even if it was only a little bit.

CHAPTER TWENTY-THREE

Hunter

It's the day before an away game, and I was eager to get away from campus.

Let's be real: I was eager to spend the night in a hotel with Tyler.

It had been weeks since we'd been together, and I was starting to go mad. But every time I even thought about bringing someone else home, my stomach leapt into my throat.

With winter break coming up, the parties were constant and we only had a few games left. Puck bunnies were coming after me left and right, so I was spoiled for choice. But all I could think about were those blue-green eyes that peered up at me through dark, dense lashes as I drove into him. I couldn't stop picturing the way his mouth parted when I did something he loved, or how he somehow topped from the bottom.

He might be a baby gay, but he damn sure knew how to play the game.

I groaned, pressing a palm to my erection that raged at the mere thought of him. Seemed Little Hunter was only wired to stand at attention for one person now. *How rude.*

"You seriously need to corner Riley and just have sex already, I have never seen you this wound up." Kinsley slipped into the booth in front of me and I readied a smart remark to throw back, only to stop dead in my tracks. Her eyes were red and puffy, her nose irritated. Without a second thought, I bolted out of my side of the booth and slid in next to her to get a closer look. She pulled away, feigning interest in the menu I knew she had memorized.

"Did something happen? Is it Kelsey?"

She shook her head, lip quivering as the emotional wall she'd erected crumbled. She knew better than to attempt that around me: we'd grown up together and I knew her inside and out—no pun intended. I wrapped my arms around her, guiding her head to the crook of my neck. Instantly, her shoulders shook and her tears stained my skin. I held her until she settled, but my own stomach churned with worry.

"Kins, please—you're scaring me."

"It's not Kelsey; we're fine."

"Then what is it? I doubt school would do this to you and I just brought you a period pack two weeks ago so I know you're not pregnant."

"No, you're not going to be an uncle anytime soon." I huffed a weak laugh, though she still hadn't revealed the real reason she was upset. I could count on my hands the number of times she had broken down in our entire friendship. Each instance was one I'd rather not relive, and right then, she was giving me serious déjà vu. "Kins..."

"He's getting out. Good behavior."

My body went rigid, my arms instinctively tightening around her.

"No, he isn't."

"Yes, he is. His lawyer called to warn me that he's going back to the house."

"I won't let him go free."

Kinsley pulled away, looking at me as if I'd grown a second head. Maybe I had lost it, but that man couldn't be anywhere near her, and I'd do anything to ensure that.

"Hunt, he's on parole. He'll be monitored, and if anything happens to him, they'll know."

I couldn't help but laugh despite myself. She just assumed I'd resort to murder. She didn't even care about ethics—she only cared about me getting caught.

"Kins, I promise murder will be my last resort. I'm calling my father."

Kinsley jerked out of my grip.

"The hell you are. I would never ask that of you—he's just as bad as mine."

"At least mine still wants me alive. Keeping yours in prison is the only way to ensure that you are as well. You're my best friend, Kins. I'm not going to sit and just hope he plays the good Samaritan this time around, especially when I'm traveling so much."

Kinsley looked at me, tears streaming down her face and I could see the war going on behind those eyes.

"Promise me you won't put yourself on the line for this—that you won't let him control your life as a result. I could never live with myself."

I kissed her forehead in an attempt to appear sincere, but I couldn't make that promise.

She had done so much more for me than I had ever done for her, and if giving up my dreams was what it took to keep her safe, then that's what I would do.

I remembered that day in our senior year when she'd first called me for help.

"Hey Kins, what's up?"

"Hunt! He won't stop, he won't stop!" My best friend's ragged sobs echoed through the line. My heart raced. In the background, distant but audible, I could hear the screams of both her parents.

"Hey, shh, shh. What's happening?"

More sobs followed, though more muffled than before.

"Dad... he won't stop hitting her. I'm scared, Hunt, I'm so scared."

Adrenaline flooded my veins. I swallowed against the rising panic in my throat.

"Hold on, Kins. I'll get help." My feet were already moving. I went to the corded phone in the kitchen and quickly dialed 911.

"He'll kill me if he knows I called it in, Hunt.. Oh god... Mom's hurt."

"I won't let anything happen to you; I promise."

"Hunter."

Dad sounded surprised, and rightfully so. I never called; he was lucky if I answered when he did. Taking in a deep breath, I tried to gather the strength to say the words I never thought I would utter to my father.

"Dad, I need a favor."

The line was silent, and I could practically hear the gears in his mind turning.

"Is that so?"

"Yes. Kinsley's father is getting out of prison early for good behavior."

I knew I didn't need to say more. Kinsley's father was a lawyer as well. He worked in the same circles as my father. Though he went to prison for assault and battery, he had dirt on a lot of people—which undoubtedly got him the lowest sentence possible.

"And let me guess: you don't want him to be released early?"

I ground my teeth. "Yes."

My father chuckled. "I was hoping that you and the Morrison girl would be bored of each other by now, but I suppose it's better than the alternative. Fine, I think I can work some strings to get him to finish his sentence. But you'll owe me."

"It needs to be more than a few years. He can't be released—period." I felt the nail go into my metaphorical coffin as the words left my mouth. I was selling my soul to the devil.

"Fine, but you know what this means, son."

"I know."

I'd never regret keeping Kinsley safe, but I still looked to the sky, feeling the tiny pieces of my true self being ripped away

CHAPTER TWENTY-FOUR

Hunter

I looked across the hotel room to my roomie. His auburn hair was longer than when we first met, his stubble a little thicker on his face. My mind often wondered to what that new facial feature would feel against my stomach as he looked at me with those eyes, working his way lower... and *lower*.

As if he could sense my thoughts, Tyler turned his gaze on me, warming me inch by inch as he studied me from head to toe. I stood half-dressed, wanting nothing more than to get lost in his body. It had been too long since I felt his touch, and there was nothing I wanted more than to ask for one more time.

"You've been M.I.A lately, everything okay?" Tyler asked, concern melting together with the heat in his eyes. He was the only one that could read me like a book. Kinsley hadn't even noticed the cloud hanging over my had the last couple weeks. My fake smiles and extroverted bravado had kept her concerns at bay. But my Aussie? He'd been shooting me questioning glances for the last couple weeks.

"Just family shit, you know?"

Ty's lip quirked, an all-knowing look coming to his face. "Want to talk about it?"

I let my gaze flow over his torso, wishing he wasn't wearing a shirt, wishing I could drown in his dips and diverts of his muscles.

"I rather forget."

He huffed out a breath and cast his gaze down as he shook his head. Each back-and-forth shake was like his mind swinging between yes or no. I stood to one side of that swing, hoping he flew my way so I could catch him.

Just as I thought he was going to swing the other way, he picked up his phone and started to swipe across the screen. "I'm Into It" by Chase Atlantic began to play. He looked up, eyebrow quirked, and his lips splitting into a sexy smile that had me rushing across the room, tugging his shirt off, unbuttoning his jeans and sinking to my knees—for him.

CHAPTER TWENTY-FIVE

Tyler

Hunter Graves on his knees was a beautiful sight. Fuck, the man was sexy as sin. My heart skipped a beat seeing his eyes sparkle again, but I didn't want to read too much into it. He hadn't fooled me with that fake ass bravado, he was *too* happy. He wasn't my grumpy Mr. Boston, the man who shot me glares that could kill and pushed me to my limits more than anyone ever had. *My Boston.*

I wasn't going to read into that either.

It was our last away game before the winter holidays, and I was itching for a break—to see my family. Just like Hunter, I needed to forget. I needed just a little bit of space from all the worries that had built up in my head. Hunter Graves was doing an amazing job at helping me forget. His initial hunger to have me bare-chested and at his mercy slowed as he worshiped every inch of skin on my lower abdomen, his lips and tongue alternating as they traced the planes of my body. He worked lower, nipping along the V that guided him to the part of me that ached to be touched.

"Fuck, Hunt.... Hurry up and suck me already."

I felt him smile against my skin. He worked his hands over me slowly, the torturous drag of his skin against mine leaving embers in its wake—making me impossibly hard.

"You're going to make me come before we even get to the fucking."

He hummed in response. "I know you have a great recovery time, Aus. There's nothing hotter than watching you get hard while I'm inside you."

My breath hitched in my throat. It was enough of an answer for him to continue.

He moved his hands around to my knees, pushing up toward my groin and eliciting an obscene noise from my lips. "Hunter."

My Jens were pulled to my ankles and he mouthed along the outside of my cock, dampening my underwear with his saliva. He gripped the waistband in his teeth, pulling the fabric down in one swift move. His warm breath fanned against my rigid length. I watched, entranced, as his gaze was locked on me and only me. My underwear hit the floor and his hand cupped my balls, rolling and massaging them to the beat of "Forever" by Labrinth.

"Hunter..." I groaned the last half of his name as his tongue finally landed where I wanted it. I speared my fingers through his hair, latching onto a thick fistful. My hips jerked into his mouth, a silent plea for him to keep going.

I lost myself in his golden eyes as he looked at me through thick lashes. His mouth *worshiped* my cock, his tongue tracing the line of the thick vein that ran on the underside. He worked his way to and from the head, dipping his tongue into the slit and playing with the foreskin. It was sloppy, it was dirty—and I was drowning in it. He pressed two fingers to my lips and I eagerly sucked them in, mimicking his pace on my dick. He moaned around me, vibrating my skin. My balls drew higher.

"Not yet, baby." The hand that wasn't in my mouth tightened around the base of my cock, staving off my orgasm. "Not when I have so much more to give you."

I bit his fingers in protest, his low chuckle did nothing to my impending explosion. Hunter pulled his fingers out and dropped my erection, moving both hands to my ass.

"Fuck, this ass torments me to no end." Hunter stood, both hands gripping my ass in a claiming hold. He ducked his head down, claiming my mouth in a hot, heavy kiss. Teeth clashed and tongues collided before he parted with a slow slide of his tongue. I whimpered, *fucking whimpered* at his mercy. Before I could take back what I wanted, he spun me around, using my jeans around my ankles to his advantage. I was bent over the bed, completely exposed to him. Somehow, having my pants at my ankles only added to my arousal. Being at his disposal sent a thrill up my spine. He flattened a palm between my shoulders, pressing me into the mattress. His teeth grazed my neck, his tongue priming his favorite spot before he bit down. Then his fingers, slick from my own saliva, began to tease along my taint.

"Oh, god."

"Mm, I have been wanting to take this ass." His hips lurched forward; his arousal evident against my ass. The mixture of his hard length between my cheeks and his soft breath on my neck had me wanting to beg, plead, *cry* for more. I needed this just as much as he did.

"Please," I begged. "Just one more time."

"I will make sure it's something you remember baby," he purred.

And oh, did he ever.

Hunter worked his way down my back, kissing each knot in my spine until he sank to his knees behind me. He mouthed down my crack, warmth filling me as his tongue met my eager hole, working me over in unison with his fingers. He hummed as I spit out an incoherent string of profanities. He was loving this as much as I was. Damn… he was loving *me*.

"Hunt I'm about to—*fuck!*-" I couldn't take it anymore. Hunter stood; I heard packets ripping. The pause in time as he covered his cock in a condom and lube was torturous, enough for me to thank him when he slammed home. That one hard thrust sending me crashing over the edge without a parachute. He gripped my hips hard, bruising them; *claiming* them as I strangled his cock.

"Gods, Ty, baby…"

He slowed his pace, gently milking every bit of my orgasm out of me. But as he promised, the constant hit of his thick dick against my prostate had me thickening again almost immediately. I whined when he pulled out, "No, come back! I'm still hard."

Hunter chuckled, kissing my shoulder and guiding me to turn over. His heated gaze left me speechless. He discarded my pants and my underwear and tossed them aside. Then his large body blanketed mine as we positioned ourselves in the middle of the bed.

"I want to watch you fall apart this time, baby."

My breath caught in my lungs. The song playing softly from my phone only heightened the tension— "I See You" by MISSIO. He positioned my legs around his waist, then slowly slid into me. His thrust were calculated this time, slow and measured as he seemed determined to last as long as he could. The lyrics pooled over us. My hands combed through his hair, my hips met his beat for beat. Our lips danced together until we both hit climax once more, our orgasms fading with the music. We breathed heavily over each other's lips, each of us brushing sweaty strands of hair away from the other's face.

We didn't say anything, afraid that words would take away what we just shared. Instead, we made our way to the shower, silently but intimately washing away the evidence.

We walked out of the bathroom as close as we possibly could. We both paused and looked at the two double beds in the room, then to each other. We didn't have to speak to know that the same question lingered in both our minds.

Hunter made the decision, grabbing my hand and pulling me to the bed we just... fucked in? No, it was so much more than that.

We curled up in the bed and Hunter pulled me to his chest. I couldn't help but feel safe—safer than I had in a long time. I closed my eyes and settled into his arms, into the feeling of being safe.

Only for them to fly open at the sound of Jamie's unmistakable ringtone. The digital clock flashed midnight. My blood ran cold. Hunter pulled back at the feeling of my body going rigid.

"Need to get that?"

In place of an answer, I jolted out of bed, grabbing my phone and answering the call as I ran into the bathroom.

"Jamie?"

"It's Mum," he sobbed, his words barely recognizable.

"Jamie, take a breath. What's going on?"

"She-she had a stroke, Ty. I saw it – an-and—" Jamie was choking on his sobs, and tears began streaming down my cheeks.

"Who are you with right now?"

"Holden's on his way. Auntie went in the ambulance with her. I couldn't- I couldn't go. I don't want to see her die, Tyler,"

I swiped my hand over my face, ignoring the wetness that came with it.

"I'm coming home, okay?"

"I'm sorry. Ty, I—I need you. I'm sorry."

"Don't be sorry. I have to talk to coach and book flights and everything but I'll be there as soon as I can. I'll call soon, please text me with updates, okay?"

"Okay, Ty?"

"Yeah, James?"

"I'm scared."

I braced my head against the door frame. "Me too."

"Love you."

"Love you too, James. See you soon."

I disconnected the call, bracing myself against the bathroom door. Every part of me wanted to fall apart, but I knew I needed to collect myself to be strong enough to get home. I needed to derail the train running rampant in my mind if I was going to handle the situation.

I flinched when a pair of strong hands squeezed my shoulders. "Baby, what's happened?"

"I need to go home."

His hands then moved to my waist, as if he was trying to prevent me from leaving. "What? No, you can't."

"I have to. Mum's just had a stroke and my brother's all alone."

I choked on my words as Hunter spun me around, cupping my cheeks in his hands. I could barely make him out through the haze of tears. "Fuck, okay. We'll go to Coach. What about your dad?"

It felt like my heart split in two. "Died two years ago in a fire."

Hunter's face broke, and he pulled me into him. As he held me tightly, he didn't realize he was giving me that little bit of strength that I needed. He let go of me and wandered into our room, surprising me by packing for me before taking my hand again.

"Will you be back?"

I closed my eyes against the sudden, overwhelming rush of emotions. I couldn't answer this question. Thankfully, I didn't have to—my silence said it all. His lips met mine. "If you need anything, baby, just call."

I nodded, feeling his forehead against mine. He kissed my temple, my cheek, my chin.

"Do you want me to come with you to see Coach?"

I shook my head—I wouldn't be able to let him go.

"Okay, baby. I'll organize the Uber and your flights, you go talk to Coach. I... hope you come back."

I nodded and pulled him in for one more passionate kiss, one that was heated, demanding. Because I wasn't sure if I'd ever kiss him again.

I stood in front of Coach's hotel door, my legs shaking in an attempt to quell the emotions that threatened to burst out of me.

"Come on, come on, come on…" I let out a deep breath.

A bleary-eyed Coach pulled the door open, then those eyes widened as they took in my tear-filled eyes and my over-packed duffel.

"Tyler… what the-"

"I'm sorry, Coach," I interrupted. "I don't have much time; my Uber is on the way—"

"Uber? What the fuck, Riley?"

"Sir, my mum has cancer. My dad died two years ago and I just got a call from my brother that she's had a stroke and been rushed to hospital. I'm all he's got and—"

"Go. I'll take care of everything here. Keep me updated. But for now, be there for your brother. And I hope your mom is okay."

I nodded, biting my lip as the tears continued to pour down my cheeks. Coach did the one thing I didn't expect; he took me in his arms and squeezed me tight. "You have talent, kid. I hope you can come back."

I pulled back, speechless, and answered him with a simple nod before making my way to the awaiting car. My phone buzzed just as I opened the door.

Boston: Flight confirmation is in your email. I hope your mom is okay. And I hope this isn't goodbye.

Amidst the swirling thoughts about what awaited me back home, I couldn't help but feel that I was losing something else entirely.

CHAPTER TWENTY-SIX

Hunter

*T*yler Riley is gone.

The sentence flashed in my mind like an emergency broadcast, over and over. I wasn't sure what broke my heart more: the look in his eyes, or watching him walk away. The moment his phone rang, I knew something was wrong. We never talked about family. I didn't even know his dad died, much less how on top of it, his mom was fighting cancer and possibly dying. One thing was clear: I never wanted to see his face broken like that again. Ever.

Confused murmurs circulated through the team as we headed to the rink.

"Where's Aussie?" Mouse whispered to me.

I shook my head. It wasn't my place to say. I only dodged more questions once we got to the locker room. My stall didn't feel the same without him beside me. I had been playing for years, many of them with the same teammates, but I had never felt so disjointed in my time in hockey without my Aussie beside me. He gave hockey a whole new life— a whole new meaning.

Coach cleared his throat, dragging me from my somber thoughts. "Okay, boys. I'm sure you've noticed we're down a team member. Tyler had to fly back home to Australia. His mum had a stroke, and due to his family circumstances, he needed to be with them."

Rumbles went through the room. I looked around at the faces that mirrored my own. Aussie had no idea who he had become to all of us. He was more than a teammate: he was the glue that held this team together.

"Is he coming back?" Mouse asked a slight quiver in his voice.

"I would love to say yes, but the truth is: I don't know. His family circumstances are unfortunate. He may need to look after his brother."

"What about their dad?" Mouse asked, not reading between the lines.

Jarman put his hand on Mouse's shoulder. "His dad died two years ago."

I tried not to let the fact that Jarman knew this over me affect me. I was too busy trying to shake the fact that I may never see my Aussie again.

But it was all-consuming. Tyler's absence was evident both on and off the ice. It affected the whole team. We weren't connecting our plays, weren't communicating right, and it led us to our first loss of the season. We silently retreated to the locker room and prepared for the journey home without a word. No one needed to talk because we were all wondering the same thing: how we were supposed to pull the season off without him.

I tried calling him on our way home, but his number was disconnected. It suddenly dawned on me that he may have a different number in Australia. The rest of the trip home involved me trying to cyber-stalk him, and I wondered why I had never done this before. He was a hockey legend. I didn't find a Facebook, but I did find an Instagram. There were multiple videos of him and his team in Australia with the same few guys showing their face in his photos. The most recent picture was posted over two years ago. Hesitantly, I opened up a direct message thread.

> Hey baby. How's everything?

Read

> Is there anything I can do?

Read

> Hope everything is okay

Read

If he was reading the messages, it meant he was okay, right?

He had to be.

Chapter Twenty-Seven

Tyler

Realizing the concept of time is life-altering. I remember being a kid and being picked up from Holden's house a little too early for my liking. I would put my little hand in the air and yell, "Please, Mum! Just five more minutes!" My hand seemed so big back then, just like the amount of time I thought I had with her.

Then, there's a shift; a moment in your life when you realize the significance of just five more minutes. I think mine was during my first real hockey competition. We only had a few minutes left on the clock and we were down by two. All I wanted was to win. The time that once felt like the longest in the world suddenly didn't seem like enough. Yet once I slammed that second puck into the net I realized: that anticipation and adrenaline warped the concept of time. The plays felt like they were in slow motion but if I watched the tapes back, sometimes all it took was a fraction of a second to change the game.

I sat beside my brother, holding his shaking body in my arms. I had to wonder if I hadn't stopped to kiss Hunter one more time if I would have made it in time. Maybe I wouldn't have hit every red light. Or what if I'd run a little faster from the car?

What if I didn't leave at all?

Would I have been there to say goodbye? Would it have mattered? Would she have been able to hear me? I was aware of time passing, but somehow I was still stuck in that moment where I found my little brother crying over Mum's body, flat lines on the monitor. I watched as Holden tried to pull him off, tried to console him—but failed. If there was any mercy, it happened when I finally arrived. If I could do nothing else, I could hold Jamie together.

A nurse crouched in front of me, but I couldn't hear what she said—I had to read it off her lips. She was telling us to go home. It seemed as if my brain refused to process sound to protect my heart from the sound of Jamie's sobs.

I gathered my brother in my arms. He wasn't small by any means, but in that moment it didn't matter. I didn't care how big he was, I would have found the strength to carry him out. We found our way into Holden's back seat, and I watched the world pass by as he drove us to what was once our home. At some point, Jamie had cried himself to sleep. I worked on autopilot, guiding him through the front door and into my bed. By the time I tucked him in, hoping he would sleep, I felt arms around me.

I turned and let them pull me into Holden's chest. There was once a time when my best friend's arms would have been comforting, but now it just felt wrong. We were the same height; I couldn't tuck my face into the crook of his neck. Nor was he as thick as Hunter. I missed those bulging biceps, the way I could rest my head on his chest. I missed his smell, and I missed the way he called me baby.

I missed him.

"I'm so sorry, Ty."

I pulled away and gave him my best attempt at a smile, but it came out more as a grimace.

"What can I do?"

I shook my head because there was nothing he could do. Nothing would bring her back.

The door opened and my aunt stepped through, looking so much like Mum before the chemo drained her. She sat on the armchair, eyeing me like I was under a microscope.

"Right, I have a plan. It's what your mum wanted so I just need you to listen."

Her words being in past tense felt like sharp needles stabbing me in the chest. But I did as I was told and waited for my auntie to let me know what the future held.

"Jamie is on summer break, and I think you should take him with you back to America. I know you have your studies and hockey to focus on, but a change of scenery would be good for him. He can still train, maybe even learn some new skills. Most importantly, he can be with you. Your mum said under no circumstances were you to quit—and I'm inclined to agree. You boys have lost enough, but you have each other, and your dreams."

Hockey wasn't the dream that had me liking the idea. It was the fact that I could be in Hunter's arms. Even just a few minutes would make me feel at least a little better.

Auntie continued. "She left everything to you boys—royalties, the house, and her life insurance. You two won't have to worry about *anything* in terms of money. Once school starts back, I'll care for Jamie, either here or at my place; I'll let him decide. This house has a lot of memories, but it also holds a lot of ghosts."

Didn't I know it.

"If he needs to stay with me, he's more than welcome," Holden offered.

"I'm going with Tyler," a groggy voice sounded from the door. Jamie's eyes were puffy and devoid of light.

I held out my hand, and he came toward me like a magnet. I was thankful he wasn't closing me off. He sat next to me, curling into my side.

"I think that's best," Auntie agreed. "We'll do this as a family. We'll find you a program to keep up your training. Tyler will have some time over winter break to help settle you in."

I held Jamie tight as Auntie went over the logistics. Mum was to have her funeral, then both Jamie and I would fly back to Boston where he would stay with me in my dorm. It dawned on me that I would no longer be homesick. I looked around the room filled with memories, good memories of a childhood most people would die for. Despite it all, I couldn't cry. I felt my phone buzz in my pocket, and my heart skipped when I saw his name pop up on the screen: *Hunter56 messaged you.*

I read his worried messages and felt that ache in my chest. That meant it was all real. I wasn't ready for it to feel real.

Jamie had slept in my bed every night, cuddled to me like I was his lifeline.

Today was the day. I wiggled myself out of his grip and walked outside into the summer air, heading to the back granny flat that was Mum's sanctuary. The scent reminded me so much of her: roses and agapanthus. The porch swing came to life with the early morning summer breeze. I could almost see her there, sitting with her laptop or a book, sipping a cup of coffee as she watched us play in the garden. I swallowed past the lump in my throat and stepped up to the door. With a creak, I was welcomed to the smell of books and gingerbread candles: her favorite scent. Her desk remained cluttered and messy, quintessential Mum. Yet, her shelves were neatly organized. Her books were her prized possession. There were pictures of us on the walls by the soft plush velvet couches. I lay down on one, looking up at the ceiling fan. Finally, I dialed his number and prayed he would pick up

"Hello?"

The sound of his voice had me covering my mouth to stifle a choked sound. I don't know when Hunter had become the place my heart had decided it could be vulnerable with, but he was.

"Baby? Is that you?"

"Yep," I sobbed.

"Talk to me, what's happened?"

"She is gone, Hunt. She is gone."

I heard his inhale of breath, then the heavy exhale. It was as if he was trying to suck in the pain through the line and let it go, taking it away from me.

"Baby..."

"Her funeral is today, and I don't know if I can do it, Hunt. I've been holding it together for my brother but I don't think I can anymore. I'm hanging on by a thread, counting down the hours until I can come back."

"I will be right here waiting when you get here, baby. I'll make sure to catch you when that thread breaks. But right now, you should focus on being with your family. Be strong for your little brother and say goodbye to your mom without any regrets. I'll be right here when you get back."

I nodded, even though he couldn't see me. "I need you."

"You have me. I'm here, no matter what time it is."

"I am sorry about the game."

He scoffed. "Fuck the game, baby. All I care about is you."

I fought against tears, knowing the second I gave in it was over. "I'm not okay."

"That's perfectly okay. I know you can get through today. It's just like pee-wee hockey, one foot in front of the other. Don't be hard on yourself if you stumble. Before you know it, I'll be waiting for you at the airport."

Hunter didn't realize how much I needed to hear that. I found myself hugging the couch cushion, wishing it was him.

"Can you just talk to me for a bit?" I asked. "Tell me about school, or Kins, or your family. Anything."

I heard him consider the thought before he spoke again. "Well, I study law-"

For the next half hour, I listened to his voice like it was my favorite podcast. He distracted me with his talk about pre-law and how his dad was some big-shot lawyer. He didn't delve too deep into his family, only mentioning that he had to follow in the family's footsteps.

It was ridiculous. He was a phenomenal defenseman. I could easily picture him in a pro league. I told him as much, and made it clear that I wasn't just saying that because we were involved. His laughter soothed my open wounds. "Nothing on you baby. If I could go pro, I'd want to do it with you."

"So do it. We may not get the same team straight away, but someone's bound to see our chemistry."

"Our chemistry, huh?"

Despite everything, the smile that tugged on my lips was real. "On the ice, Boston. I meant on the ice."

His amused hum told me he didn't believe that one bit. Our chemistry was so much more than two guys on the ice. I was flooded with guilt over the fact that I actually felt relaxed. It was the day of my mum's funeral for fuck's sake.

"It's okay to have a moment of peace in the storm baby. She would have wanted that."

"How do you always know where my head is, even so far away?"

"The same way I can connect a puck to your stick without seeing you. I feel you baby."

A whole load of new emotions began to come over me. So, I did what I needed to do.

"I better go. I'll send you my flight details. It's a long story but Jamie's coming with me. He'll stay in my dorm."

"Well, you'll be home soon. And your brother is lucky to have you."

"Bye, Boston."

"Bye, Aussie."

I disconnected the call, took a breath, and went back inside to get Jamie fed before we said goodbye.

I hated funerals, but Mum had made it easy on us. She had every little detail planned. I choked down the resentment that she seemed to know this was coming. I said my eulogy and because of the impact my parents had on the local community, it was a big turnout. I talked about how lucky I was to have such dedicated and devoted parents, how she was my best friend, and how I wouldn't be where I was without her. It was all true but despite everything, I still couldn't cry. I couldn't forgive her for leaving. I knew at heart it wasn't her fault. But I couldn't believe she was not there. She'd never see me go pro. She wouldn't watch Jamie grow up. I knew none of this was her fault. But the longer I sat there listening to how great a life she lived, I could only be mad that it wasn't long enough.

The wake was short and sweet and the next thing I knew, we were shopping for Jamie's winter clothes. We packed our bags, and got on a plane. We hadn't talked much during the funeral, but as we sat on the plane, Jamie turned to me. It hit me then how tired he was, and I knew I probably didn't look much better. I hadn't really looked in the mirror—probably for the best.

"Since we talked last, did you end things with your teammate?"

"He's meeting us at the airport," I groused, knowing the teasing was coming.

Jamie smiled. It didn't quite reach his eyes, but it was genuine. "So, you're still together but not together?"

I sighed. "I don't know, James. We keep swearing each time is the last. We hardly know each other."

"Do you *want* to get to know him?" Jamie studied me, his eyes sincere as he waited for my answer.

"There's just... *something* about him, James. I don't know. He makes me feel safe, and despite how little we know of each other's lives, we know each other beyond that, if that makes any sense."

He shrugged, "I get it. You're different when you talk about him. I get a glimpse of that light in your eyes that I haven't seen in years. I look forward to meeting him."

"He makes me feel... a whole lot. But he's my calm in the storm."

Jamie smiled, and we sat in silence for the rest of the journey.
Nothing else needed to be said.

Chapter Twenty-Eight

Hunter

I listened to the overhead announcements, waiting for Tyler's connecting flight. I needed him in my arms. *Seeing* his broken expression was one thing, but hearing that break in his voice and not being able to hold him was ten times worse.

I breathed a sigh of relief when their flight finally landed. It felt like an eternity until I saw him emerge from baggage claim with his arm around a blond boy whose head reached his shoulder. His eyes were covered by the cap on his head, but I didn't miss the beard he had grown over the last few days. It was as auburn as his hair, and I itched to get my hands on him.

I didn't know what the protocol was. I wasn't sure if I was allowed to go to him. Did Jamie know who I was? But like he knew I was watching him, his eyes met mine, and I wasn't oblivious to the dark circles framing his.

I began to move, and he said something to his brother who then pushed him in my direction. Tyler sped up, I got a glimpse of his lip quivering before I swept him up in my arms. I felt the shift of his breath as he tried to hold his composure, which only broke my heart even more.

"I've got you, baby. I've got you."

I took the hat off his head, needing to thread my fingers through his hair. His head was firmly buried in the crook of my neck, and I took a deep breath in, relishing the scent of *him.*

He turned his head to the side, seeking out my lips. The kiss was quick and chaste, but

I understood. I held him for a little while longer before I pulled him back and brushed his tears away with my thumbs.

I wanted nothing more than to hold his hand, but I pulled away. I hated how we had to act like that extremely intimate moment never happened. He replaced the cap on his head and turned to his brother to make introductions.

I held out my hand to the little Aussie. He took it in a firm grip with a smile, but his eyes told another story: don't fuck with his brother.

We reached his dorm, and I felt torn. Every part of me urged me to stay with him. Sensing my hesitation, Tyler grabbed my wrist and pulled me in behind him.

I had never been inside before. The small living and kitchen area were tidy but lacked any personality. I expected to see at least some trace of Cal. As if he thought the same, Tyler froze and frowned.

"Cal?"

Upon hearing his name, Cal ran bolted from his room and threw himself around Tyler, mumbles of condolences muffled in his shoulder. tried not to let my teeth grind with the green-eyed monster that wanted to take over seeing Tyler embrace him back. I felt an elbow to my side and found Jamie rolling his eyes at me.

Tyler pulled away from the embrace. "Thanks, but what happened to the couch?"

"Well, you said your brother was staying with us. So, I got us a new couch; it's a pull-out so your brother can have a bed to sleep on."

I wish I had thought of that. I watched Tyler's face soften, his hand clasping his roommates. "Thanks, Cal."

There was a moment of introductions between Cal and Jamie. "So, Jamie, how about you and I go do some sightseeing? I happen to know of a few mixed martial arts gyms in the area. Maybe we can get you signed up somewhere."

Jamie smiled softly. "Sounds good. Is that okay, Ty?"

Tyler nodded, but I didn't miss the warning in the look he shared with Cal. "*Protect him at all costs."*

"I'll bring some food back for us. Hunter, are you staying?"

I looked to Tyler for guidance, and he took my hand.

"I'll take that as a yes," Cal answered. "See you two hunks soon." He winked and Jamie scoffed.

"Please don't corrupt my brother!" Tyler called as they disappeared through the wooden door.

The soft click was like a wall going down. The man who was holding everything together turned to look at me, and I saw every ounce of pain behind those eyes. I took his hand and led him into the room I presumed to be his. I don't know how I knew my guy would be the stupidly organized type, but I did. His bed was made so tightly you could bounce a coin off it. It was much like him as a person—the outward display of perfection, but only a cover for old worn sheets of someone who has gone through too much.

The moment his door closed, I grunted at the impact of his body hitting mine. He snuggled into the crook of my neck, his breathing heavy enough to make me sweat.

"I've got you, baby. I got you."

His cries were spontaneous and unforgiving. I held onto him tightly, even as he began to buckle under the weight of his grief. "They're gone," he wailed. "They're both gone."

I held him silently. I couldn't say anything—there was nothing *to* say. Nothing made any of this okay. Voicing that wouldn't make anything better. It sucked, that was the reality of it. The shittiest things happen to the best people. He never deserved to lose one of his parents, let alone both.

"I don't think I ever really processed it, you know?" he sniffled. "That fact he was gone. Because right after Mum was diagnosed with cancer, then it became about looking after her while protecting Jamie and pretending that I was okay. Fuck, Hunt—all I've done is pretend to be okay."

The tears that fell from my eyes were as much for him as they were for me. I knew what that was like, putting on a mask for everyone. Though I could handle it—my burden was nothing like that of Tyler's. I led him to the bed, laying down and pulling him close.

"I just keep thinking about how I won't be able to call back home and tell her about my day. She'll never be at my games; she will never get to see if I go pro."

"You *will* go pro. And whether you believe in an afterlife or not, baby, I believe she'll be watching. She'll see you shoot that first NHL goal, win that first game—and she'll see you win the Stanley Cup. That I know for sure. You're impossible not to keep tabs on, even in the afterlife."

I wasn't sure if I was saying the right things. But when those teary blue eyes looked at me, they told me something I said helped at least a little.

He dipped forward to kiss me, and all the emotions he couldn't put into words were instead tattooed upon my lips. I felt every hint of grief, but I also felt his affection towards me. I didn't stop him because selfishly, I wanted any bit of Tyler Riley he would give me. He lifted onto his elbow and the kiss grew in passion. When he rolled on top of me, I placed my hand on his chest to make him pause. His heart beat fast and heavy under my palm.

"Baby, are you sure? We can just lie here together." Again, I questioned the right and wrong of supporting the person you loved through grief. If there was a textbook it likely would say "Don't let them fuck the emotions away."

"Yes. I need you. I need to feel you, feel something that will bring me back from this all. I need to be grounded. You do that for me."

My heart stilled in my chest. I wanted him to feel that, because he was more than wanted. He was becoming my center—my home and that was scary. Despite the voice that told me I shouldn't, I nodded. I let him take off my clothes, then I did the same for him. I kissed every freckle, every groove of muscle, hoping he had the ability to know how I felt for him with my touch alone.

He matched me touch for touch and when it was time, he leaned over to his side drawer and pulled out what we needed.

He rolled the condom onto me before I took my time prepping him. I stretched him, getting him good and ready for me as his head fell back. The cords of his neck were taut with the pleasure I gave him. His breathing was heavy, his groans bouncing off the bare walls of his bedroom.

He tugged my hand from his ass in silent demand and I watched, entranced as he took control, angling my cock to his entrance. My breath came out in short, stuttered pants as he sank down, enveloping my shaft in the warmth of his body. My balls drew tight.

Tyler paused, but only for a moment. I didn't know whether it was for him to adjust or to keep me from blowing my load right then and there.

Then, he began to move. He rocked his hips at a tantalizing pace. I fought against letting my eyes close, desperate to keep my eyes on the image of Tyler riding me like he was designed for it. I brushed away the hair that fell over his face so I could fully appreciate the soft light from the window filtering through the curtain to highlight every perfect angle.

I sat up, needing to be closer. With my arms wrapped around his waist, I let him take everything he needed from me, occasionally bucking up to hit just the right spot. His lips molded with mine, and we let ourselves get lost in one another. It wasn't lost on us that this was no longer just fucking, and with it, our orgasms didn't hit hard and fast like before. The build was slow, but twice as euphoric. The tingle of pleasure built until we crashed over the edge together, melting into each other with our mutual climaxes.

We stayed there wrapped up in each other's embrace, sweat cooling on our skin and the scent of sex heavy around us. As our noses brushed and our foreheads rested together, I thought about the amazing man laying on me. His strength was beyond admirable. He showed impeccable strength in the darkest of times. But despite all that, I wanted to be there for him, through the good, the bad, and the ugly.

I leaned in to give him one more kiss before we eventually fell asleep.

The creak of the front door jolted me awake. A gentle knock followed that signaled Jamie's arrival.

"Dinner's here," his youthful voice called out through the door.

Tyler mumbled back a drowsy response, prompting me to steal a glance at him. His hair was tousled, eyes tired, yet a newfound relaxation graced his features.

We quickly got dressed and as I attempted to tame Tyler's unruly hair, I couldn't help but wonder how much he cared about his brother's perception. Tyler caught my hand, rolling his eyes, "She'll be right, I need a shower anyways."

In the living room, a subtle, suspicious exchange of glances passed between Jamie and Cal. Tyler held my hand as we settled on the couch, where he wrinkled his nose at the pizza on the table.

"Told you!" Jamie laughed, pointing his slice at Cal. Perplexed, I scanned the room, trying to determine what was going on.

Cal interrupted my thoughts, "Fine, you were right. I also bought chicken and salad, it's in the fridge. Jamie told me you wouldn't eat the pizza but I thought you would want some comfort food."

"If you think I am dropping the ball on my meal plans now, you're horribly mistaken," Tyler declared, rising to retrieve his preferred meal.

Jamie seemed to read my confusion and chimed in. "He never *ever* breaks his meal plan during hockey season."

"That's not true! I drank alcohol!" Tyler defended himself.

"Baby, you drank alcohol twice," I said. "And I would bet that you went on extra runs to burn the calories, am I right?" Even with that knowledge, Tyler's commitment to the sport went beyond what I initially grasped. He was the lone figure on the team who was strict about his meals during team dinners, and aside from those two parties, I couldn't recall a moment when he deviated from his pursuit of perfection.

Cal chuckled. "Oh, your baby definitely did."

Tyler lightly smacked Cal over the back of the head, which I knew was more for the baby comment than anything else. The room filled with laughter, a mixture of camaraderie and revelations about the meticulous planning behind Tyler's seemingly flawless game plan.

I didn't think much of calling him the pet name, but it hit me that he may not like me calling him that in front of others.

"It is scientifically proven that the right intake of food, will keep an athlete on the top of their game," he explained. "I don't need anything weighing me down. If the pro's do it, so will I."

"Baby, the pros still eat pizza."

He gave me that adorable eye roll that told me though I may be right, he wouldn't be listening to me.

Right then and there I made it my mission to eventually get my Aussie to have some American pizza.

I never really felt like I had a proper family. Kinsley was the closest thing, but sitting there on Tyler's living room floor with him sandwiched between my legs, our fingers twisted together from the arm I had over his shoulders- was the closest thing to a *family* I ever had. Cal was spinning his wild stories, and Jamie, now comfortably in his bed, was cracking up at Cal's crazy tales of failed romances and wild skate partners.

I sometimes got a bit jealous thinking about Cal being a big part of Tyler's life but in moments like these, I was glad Tyler had a friend who could distract him from all the pain. My eyes kept drifting to the brothers, especially the way Tyler watched Jamie. Every time

Jamie laughed, Tyler squeezed my hand, like he couldn't get enough of that sound.

Simply holding Tyler like that, in such a casual way, meant a lot to me. Silently, I began to plot in my head. I wasn't sure how I'd keep it going, but I wanted it to.

I woke to the blaring of my phone, my Aussie clinging to me like a koala. I let my arm fall to find the offending piece of technology and with it in my hand, I looked down. Reality smacked me in the face with the image of my dad's name was lit up on the screen.

As if he could sense the change in my demeanor, Tyler lifted his head, and despite the cuteness of the small crease between his brows, it did nothing to settle me. I leaned to kiss his hair.

"My dad—I have to take it. I don't know how long I will be so, I'll see you later?" The two lines between his brow didn't leave as he watched me change and head for his door. "If you need anything, please call, okay?"

"Um, sure." Tyler said, his confusion evident, and it broke me that I couldn't stop to explain.

I stepped into the quiet hallway, grateful for the early hour that kept the place barren.

"Yeah?" I answered the phone, the nerves already settling in.

"Is that how you answer the phone to your father?" Even his tone made me flinch.

"Sorry, sir."

"Mmhmm, remember that I helped your little friend. Don't think I can't take that away with one simple phone call."

A chill ran down my spine. The memories of that night flooded back. Kinsley's mom was confined to a nursing home as a result, trapped in her own body. Every visit echoed with the haunting thought that it could have been my best friend lying in that bed. The fear of that man seeking revenge on his daughter for putting him in prison lingered heavily in my mind.

"I'm sorry, sir," I muttered, grappling with the weight of those memories.

I heard a noncommittal grunt before he steered the conversation to the reason for his call. "I need you home for a couple of evenings. Bring your best suit *and* your best behavior. No repeats of last year."

The mention of last year triggered a pang of unease. After a particularly hard set of exams, Kinsley and I drowned our sorrows in alcohol which led to some pretty reckless behavior. I could still hear my father shouting about how we disrespected him in his own home.

"Yes, sir." He signed off, sending me the details of the event in a detailed email.

Though it nearly killed me, I chose not to return to Tyler's bedroom. I wanted to avoid those prying eyes that could read my expression. He'd only pry for more information, and I wasn't sure I could keep it from him. Conflicted about my connection with Tyler, I knew I had to distance myself with the upcoming events. Tyler occupied every corner of my mind, yet I needed to withdraw.

I needed to protect him.

Choosing between avoiding Tyler and playing puppet for my dad was like a game of Pick Your Poison. The whole soiree was happening in some posh gentleman's club, a space filled with people who probably voted against everything I was. They were all smiles and laughter, pretending everything was hunky-dory under my dad's scrutinizing gaze. But he was keeping his word—Kinsley's dad stayed put, thanks to some prison brawl. Kinsley's ecstatic call was the silver lining in this unrelenting thunderstorm.

In the middle of it all, was Mr. Nolan White, with his slimy, veneered smile shining under the lights. It's the kind of smile that lures you in, only to chew you up and spit you out. The rumors trailing behind him are as nasty as the smell in a high school boys' locker room.

"So, your dad says you're off to Harvard to finish your undergrad?" he asked, his eyes gleaming with some twisted power trip. I was half-tempted to dial child protective services or find someone who would. But before I could fire back, my dad slapped his hefty hand on my shoulder. I've always wondered if letting me play hockey was his way of justifying the bruises.

"Why didn't you start there in the first place?"

My immediate response was an eye roll, but before I could say anything smart back, my dad butted in. His grip on my shoulder made it clear that there was no escape. Our unspoken family dynamics lingered beneath the surface, hidden behind forced smiles and polite small talk.

"I wanted him to get this little hobby out of his system while he studied. His university was the best hockey team in Boston, but they also do a lot for our firm."

Nolan gave a knowing smile. "Of course, let him get all the rough and tumble out. I do follow your team; quite a season minus that one game."

I nodded, not wanting to cue him in as to why we had a blip in our winning streak.

"That young Aussie was quite some player."

The mention of him had me tightening my fists involuntarily. Before I could tell that fool to keep my Aussie's name out of his mouth, Dad dug his fingers into my shoulder so hard I winced.

"He is," I replied, hoping that he'd drop the topic and my father would ease his grip.

"What's he like to play with? Is it true what they say about Australians?"

"Just like any other player, sir. Good at what he does, has something to prove," I deflected. Nolan, having decided he wasn't going to get the gossip he was after, politely excused himself from our presence.

I'd hoped my father's grip on my shoulder would relent with Nolan's departure, but each finger left its mark. I was already calculating how to hide these bruises from the team—especially Tyler.

"Next time, I expect you to keep the topic off hockey, you hear?"

My instinct was to spit back, but what was the point? This was a gentleman's club, where they talked business, sport, and women. It just so happened that I played a sport popular in the state of Boston. But I decided it was better to hold my tongue.

"Yes, Sir," I relented, another piece of my soul chipping away as I let my father walk over me again.

The feeling of my phone buzzing made me jump. The heavy sigh behind me revealed my father's displeasure with the interruption.

"Take that and then turn it off," he instructed. I nodded and scurried away into the dark hallway, pulling out my phone to see Kinsley's name.

"Hey, I'm kind of busy. Is everything okay?"

"Well, I was calling to ask you that. You've been MIA for weeks. The last time I heard from you was when I called about Dad—way before midterms. One would think you're avoiding me."

I sighed, instinctively reaching to comb my hand through my hair. But just as quickly as they grasped the roots, I pulled them away, mindful of where I was. My father's potential reaction to my disheveled appearance echoed in my head. *"Gotta keep up appearances, Hunter."*

"I've been busy with training and midterms, that's all. Everything is fine. Can I call you later? I'm out at the moment," I attempted to keep my voice light and nonchalant, but Kinsley knew better.

"Hunter, where are you?"

I hesitated, not wanting to add any stress to her plate. I loved Kinsley, but sometimes she could be a bit overreactive. I didn't need that right now.

"At an event with my father. It's completely voluntary, and there are people from the firm here I need to know for when the time comes," I fabricated, cursing myself for the silly lie. She gasped, and it was all I could do not to pull at my own hair.

"Hunter, you're *not* going to work with that man. You've never wanted to. Your dream is the NHL—to fund your own life and play hockey."

I sighed, contemplating my response just as I spotted my father at the end of the hall. His expression said it all, and a condescending touch of his watch was his signal that my time was up.

"Look, Kins, you've caught me at a bad time. I'll call you later."

She began to protest, but I quickly hung up and turned my phone off. A small part of me was already working up excuses in the back of my mind, fully aware that Kinsley would demand real answers—answers I wasn't ready to provide.

Returning to my father, I couldn't shake the disapproving look in his eyes.

"Go mingle, make us look good. Then you're to come back with me to the house."

I sighed and nodded, swallowing the dread that the latter half of that sentence brought up.

CHAPTER TWENTY-NINE

Hunter

"I gave you what you wanted, didn't I?" I braced myself and took the blow that was sent my way.

"Yes, sir."

"Why wasn't it good enough? I've given you everything you could ever want and you still fall out of line."

I had no clue what I'd done wrong this time. Sometimes, I never did. Nothing I did would ever please him. I did wonder what would happen if I crept a little closer to that metaphorical line he was talking about. Would he stop hitting me?

But stepping onto the ice made me feel like myself. Tyler made me feel more like myself. I'd tried being with women and outside of Kinsley, no one stuck. I couldn't see a future with any of them. Ha, some future I pictured for myself.

Yes, I found women attractive, but the only time I'd been in anything resembling a relationship was with a man. Yet another thing my father didn't approve of. Could I give up being with men?

I suppose I could, but Tyler's words echoed in my head. It didn't matter that I was attracted to both men and women; what mattered was who I fell in love with, and that happened to be a man. I knew then I couldn't give up Tyler Riley.

Fear embedded itself deep into my body, deeper than the bruises he pounded into my skin. I was afraid of what he would do if he found out I was sleeping with a man. I didn't want Tyler involved in my mess—he had enough on his plate. Could I add my father to that mix? But could I bring myself to walk away? My heart tugged me in one direction while my head pulled in another. I would stand next to Tyler no matter what, I'd help him weather any storm. But what if *I* was the storm? I could be the one to destroy everything.

My father swung again, this time knocking me to the ground. "Hunter Domonic Graves, are you listening to me?"

What was there to say? Sorry for not being the son he wanted, sorry for the rules I couldn't seem to follow despite how many times he tried to beat me into submission. But that's what I said in the end—sorry. I groveled like a pathetic loser.

My "reward" was him walking away. I was free to go.

Hey, I'm exhausted. I'm just going to crash in my room. I'll see you at tomorrow's game. Hope you're okay.

Aussie: 'M fine but something tells me you're not.

Why wouldn't I be? Just studied too hard. See you tomorrow.

Aussie: Fine, g'nite.

CHAPTER THIRTY

Tyler

I threw my phone across the room, sending it clattering onto my desk as a stack of textbooks fell to the ground.

Hunter and I weren't officially an item. I wasn't ready to come out so we hadn't had the "boyfriend" talk.

Damn it! In light of my situation, I wasn't in the right mindset to be thinking about calling Hunter Graves my boyfriend.

However, if we weren't on the same page, I at least thought we were reading the same book. I thought he wanted to be around me as much as possible. He claimed he was there for me. He listened to my thoughts, he held me while I cried.

He had sex with me.

I was hesitant to call it making love because we weren't there yet, right? In the midst of my mental spiral, the door opened and Jamie leaned against the frame doing what he did best: reading right through my bullshit.

"What did he do?" Jamie asked, knowing me well enough to pinpoint a certain guy as the cause of my outburst.

"He didn't do anything."

"And I suppose that's the problem? One moment he's picking you up from the airport, comforting you, holding your hand and, calling you baby—now he's AWOL?"

Ding Ding Ding.

I only nodded in response.

"He did go running out of here like a kangaroo with his tail on fire," Jamie said. "Something happen?"

I think back how he was wrapped around me one second, and stiff as a board the next—all because of a phone call.

"He got a call from his dad."

Jamie frowned. "He not a good guy?"

"Hunter's pretty private about his home life. All I know is that his dad practically has his whole life planned out for him."

Jamie hummed, and in that moment I realized that I wasn't the only one who had to grow up quick.

"And that annoys you," Jamie deduced, breaking me from my thoughts. "You've been vulnerable with him, and now he won't do to the same for you."

"Okay Dr. Freud—yes it annoys me. We haven't established what we are or where we want to go with... whatever this is. But he hightails it out of here, goes radio silent all day, then sends me a vague message. It just rubs me the wrong way."

Jamie barked out a laugh. "And they say girls are difficult."

"*Emotions* are difficult," I grumble.

Jamie nodded and pushed off the door. "Let's eat. I'll even watch hockey tapes with you. I am bored out of my brain."

I didn't miss the way Hunter avoided me as I entered the team gym, or how he ducked into the toilets to change instead of doing so at his stall. The other guys hadn't arrived yet, but I was eager to hit the ice after having some time off. Being away was the longest week of my life. As I began to change, the Coach's gruff voice echoed through the locker room's open door as he poked his head in. "Riley, got a minute?"

I nodded and followed him to his office, shoving my hands into my hoodie as if it could provide some sense of comfort. I had a feeling this was going to be a difficult conversation.

I sat in the seat he indicated while he took his desk chair. There was a beat of silence as he looked me over, almost as if I'd crumble right before his eyes. *Been there, done that, sir..*

Logistically, I knew that wasn't how grief worked, and the guilt of moving on weighed heavily on my chest. But this was what Mum wanted. I needed to do this.

"How are you, Tyler?" There it was: the magic question..

I wondered if I looked as bad as I felt, if my exhaustion was showing on my face.

"As good as can be, sir. I'm more than okay to still play if that's what you're asking."

The smile he responded with was full of sympathy—maybe even pity—and I didn't like it. I didn't want to be seen as the boy who just lost a parent. I just wanted to be Tyler Riley: the hockey player.

"It's okay if you're not. We have a game in two days, and I think it might be best to have you as a healthy scratch. It'll, give you some time—"

"No. Please, I need to be on that ice. This is what my mum would have wanted—she wanted me to play."

I hated how my voice thickened, how my body vibrated as I fought to hold myself together.

Coach looked at me, really looked at me. I felt as if every detail of me was under intense examination.

"Fine, but if I think you need to be benched at any point during the game, that's what I'll do. I think you should also visit the university's counseling services given that—"

"I'll consider it, sir," I interrupted—but it was a lie. There was no way I was going to sit in some therapist's office while my carefully constructed walls were broken down. There would be time for that once the season was over.

"Good. I am sorry for your loss Tyler, truly. Please know we're all here for you—the staff, and the team. I hope it's okay that I kept them informed. Your absence was noted and the team really cares about you."

I nodded because I had expected as much. There weren't very many secrets kept when you stayed in such close quarters with people.

Unfortunately, the locker room was filled with my teammates upon my return—except the face I truly needed to see.

A horde of sympathetic eyes met mine, and I endured all the awkward hugs and condolences. Though the only thing I wanted in that moment was to return to a time when I was just the new kid from another country.

"Thanks, everyone. I'm getting through it, but please don't treat me any differently. I'm not some fragile doll that's going to break at the drop of a hat. I'm here to play hockey and *win* hockey, and we can't do that if you're pussyfooting around me, okay?"

They nodded and all took turns patting my back before they thankfully went about getting into their gear. Once we were on the ice, it was all systems go. Coach was on a mission to iron out some cracks, and I couldn't be more thankful.

What I couldn't ignore, however, was Hunter. I was laser-focused on Hunter on the best of days but that day, he was a red flag on skates. With every move he made, every swing of his stick, his face twisted. I had never seen him play so... shit. Coach seemed to agree.

"Graves, what's up your ass!? Do I need medical to check you out? You're as slow as a sloth and as stiff as a board."

"Sorry, sir. I'm fine." After that, I watched him push himself harder, and to give credit where it was due, he did look better. But it was as if I felt his every flinch in my core. Something wasn't right.

If anything was going to break me, it would be if something happened to him.

I stayed on the ice until Hunter and I were the last ones standing. I knew the rest of the team had already showered and changed to get lunch before we sat down to watch tapes. "Alright, boys, that's enough!" Coach called. He'd been more than generous with our ice time. "Cool down, get ready and eat. See you in the media room in an hour!"

Hunter moved as quick as his body would allow. I kept a close eye on him as I trailed him into the locker room. The steady hum from the Zamboni filtered into the empty space, bouncing off the walls and making our silence seem even louder.

Seeing that I wasn't going to back down, Hunter took his shirt off, a hiss escaping between his teeth. Now it made sense why he didn't want to sleep over: so I wouldn't see his black and blue torso.

"It's nothing, Tyler," he said, his tone void of emotion. I didn't like it.

He started toward the showers, ignoring the fact that I'd already taken in how bruised his body was. It didn't take much for me to put it together. I was no stranger to knowing someone with abusive parents—it was a horribly common occurrence.

But it had never hit so close to home. Never had it pulled such a visceral reaction from me. I was behind him in an instant, spinning him and softly pressing him into the cool tiles with my hands on his waist. He didn't look me in the eyes, but he didn't fight me either. I didn't like this version of him at all. I wanted my hot-headed Boston boy back. I wanted him to challenge me, show me that whoever did this to him hadn't broken him.

"Boston, look at me," I nudged his chin up with my own, crowding his space and not caring if anyone saw. Our eyes finally met, and my heart sank.

"Who did this to you?"

I felt when goosebumps pebbled over his skin at my bare chest touching his. I was mindful not to touch the bruising.

His eyes fluttered, long black lashes fanning against his angular cheekbones.

"It doesn't matter who did this to me." The words assault my lips.

"It matters to *me*, Boston. Do you think I could survive something happening to you?" *You are my home now.*

The realization hit me like a freight train, and I was close enough to confessing how I felt about him right there and then. His eyes closed, but he didn't give me an answer.

Instead, our noses brushed before he tilted his head to bring our lips together. He ate up my mewls of pleasure, fingers possessively clenching my hips.

A clatter from the locker room had me jolting back and desperately trying to adjust myself in my underwear. "Fucking stupid" I mumbled. "Promise me you will come to me for help, with whatever this shit is going on in your life? Because seeing you like this makes me go all ragey and when I go ragey I'm clearly not thinking straight."

He laughed at my choice of words so I gave him a playful shove, regretting it instantly when he winced. "Shit! I'm so sorry."

I lightly brushed my hand over his bruises., "I don't like this." The words meant more than just his bruises, and the softness in his eyes made me think that maybe he understood that too.

But he didn't say a word. He didn't promise that he would let me in. I pulled away, unable to leave without kissing his cheek. I left wondering if I would survive a heartbreak like losing Hunter Graves.

CHAPTER THIRTY-ONE

Tyler

We stood in our suits outside Merrimack's ice rink, a light snow falling around us. It was the last away game before Christmas break, and five days since I'd proven to Coach that I could do this. It was a close-to-home game, so there was no hotel room to share with Hunter. He'd returned to being nothing but my teammate after our encounter in the showers.

It was fine, totally fine. Standard practice these days, it seemed. Hunter had managed to hide his bruises—mostly. I could only hope that he would eventually tell me what happened.

Kinsley called me a few days before the game, asking if I had much contact with Hunter. She didn't say anything other than he seemed to be avoiding her. All I could say was, "Same."

I even went to Jarman, who'd known Hunter since high school. He confirmed that Hunter was always one to keep to himself—loyal on the ice, always down for a good party, but insanely private. Even at parties, he seemed to only be there to hook up. He never stayed around to chat with the team. Armed with that knowledge, I told myself not to worry. It was a blatant lie, of course. I already missed the attention.

Hunter nudged my arm but didn't look me in the eye. "How are you liking the snow?"

I scoffed. "P-pretty," I forced out, not wanting to seem like a wimp, but my traitorous body made me a liar. My limbs shook and my teeth chattered.

Hunter laughed, wrapping his arm around me and giving me a squeeze. "Too bad this isn't a hotel stay; I'd be able to keep you warm, Aussie."

I felt my body react, and I nudged him off me. He winced, but my expression was enough to make him back off, as if he could sense the beast lying within that fought to be released.

He thumbed over his shoulder, "I'll see you in there, Aus. Better hurry, or your teeth may fall out with all that chattering." He turned and walked off so fast I would've had to jog to catch up.

Jarman appeared beside me, laughing. "Not this cold in Aus, huh?"

I snorted. "Not in Perth, no. Coldest day on average was about fourteen—and that's Celsius, not Fahrenheit."

Mouse sidled up to my other side, looking overly puzzled. "So, what's that in normal numbers?"

"You guys do realize you're the only country in the world who don't use Celsius, right? It's about fifty."

Mouse's eyes widened. "*That's* the coldest? That's a breezy summer night here."

I nodded., "I quickly learned Perth hoodies wouldn't cut it."

They laughed and Jarman jostled my shoulder, "Some hockey player you are, scared of the cold."

I frowned, "I'm not scared! Even on the ice it's hard to stay cold. I'm just not used to it." I nearly sighed with relief when the central heat washed over my face as we entered the rink and headed to the locker rooms. This was game one of two—we'd face off against them again at home before breaking for the holidays.

"Let's hope bad blood doesn't get Hunter into trouble," Mouse muttered across to Jarman, who only grunted in response as his face twisted up.

"Uhm... what's that supposed to mean?" I question.

Jarman stayed quiet while Mouse was happy to fill me in on the gossip. "Well, their star defenseman, Zane Matthews, used to play on our team. The two were inseparable. Then we were in the locker room before the grand finals—looked like they were having a pretty heated talk. Next thing we knew, Hunter broke the guy's nose and made him miss the game. Matthews had an agent *and* a scout there; he was hoping to go the AHL route. Colton and Matthews cornered Hunter after the game and lost their shit. Hunter was benched and Matthews was scratched—we lost that game."

I cringed, a part of me trying to match the guy they were describing to the one who monopolized so much of my mind.

"It was way out of character for Hunter," Jarman added, seeming to know where my mind went. "I think it may have had something to do with Kinsley." Then without another word, he squeezed my shoulder and went to his designated stall.

Colton commanded everyone's attention, and the team gathered around to listen. "All right, boys! We need to go out there strong, make them scared for the game tomorrow. But also, keep it clean; we need you all in top shape for our home-ground game."

A cacophony of noises broke out around the room before we headed toward the ice. I followed close behind Hunt, noting the way he carried himself differently, minding the injuries to his ribs and shoulder. I gritted my teeth tighter.

"Riley!" The sudden sound made me flinch. I spun to see Coach calling me. He stood beside a man in a suit with a blinding smile.

"Yes, Coach?"

Coach angled himself to face both of us. "Tyler Riley, this is Connor Bellamy."

My eyes went wide as it dawned on me who I was meeting. "Holy fucking shit" I blurted, smacking a gloved hand over my mouth as soon as I realized what I'd said.

The man only laughed, but I was spiraling. Connor Bellamy, the former star defenseman from Boston, was standing right in front of me. He had two Stanley cups under his belt and there he was, standing right in front of me—and smiling. Connor Bellamy was smiling at me. "I am so sorry, I am working on the language..."

Connor waved me off. "It's all good. You've made quite an impression this season. And since you know my name, you clearly know your hockey." His hand came out, and I fumbled with my glove to shake it.

"I promise I'm not usually a fumbling idiot. This is just... you're the first NHL star I've met and..." I stopped when I realized I was still holding his hand.

Coach cringed out of the corner of my eye. I was totally messing this up.

"Trust me, I've been where you are: looking my idols in the eye and making a fool of myself. I like you, kid. And your coach has spoken very highly of you. I'm here for a couple of reasons. I do represent young hockey players trying to get into the league, but only ones I think can make the cut. You're showing great potential, so I wanted to introduce myself. If you keep it up, you may be hearing from me."

I felt like I was shaking. Wait... I was. I nodded more than was necessary before I saw Coach's eyes widen—a silent warning to say something. "Crap sorry, I'm in shock here. Yes, I'll keep it up. Actually, I'll do better. I really want a chance to prove myself. The NHL is my dream."

Connor laughed and Coach scrubbed a hand over his face. "Awesome to hear, kid. Now get out there and show me what you got."

I bounced on my skates, saying a round of thank-you's, and Coach mimed for me to go away because I was making a bloody fool of myself. I skated onto the ice with new energy, the smile on my face big enough to attract a few questions from teammates. But I shook them off—I didn't want to jinx anything.

As we got into position, Hunter slid by me. "Told you the NHL will be calling at your door! Bellamy is one of the biggest agents in the league now. You got this, baby. Your mom's going to see you go pro in no time."

Before I could say anything, Hunter was gone. The puck hit the ice and Colton fumbled against their centre who shot the puck to the blue line. Sixty seconds was a long time in the hockey world, and that first minute revealed that this game was going to get messy.

Mouse had already been put into the penalty box for slashing. Jarman, our biggest player, took a nasty hit from a defenseman that had less business on the ice and more being at the top of a beanstalk. The dude missed his calling as a goalie or a grid-iron fullback or something. Jarman was getting checked out by the team doctors, and I was starting to get a bee under my bonnet.

That first period felt like the longest of my life. I hadn't even thought about the agent until I was heading to the locker room. I didn't get a chance on goal; their defense was tight, and our boys were getting penalty calls so often, we spent the whole period trying to get past them. We were currently down by two, and I could see Preston stewing. We all knew better than to try to give him a pep talk: no one ever messed with the goalie when he was trying to stay in the zone.

Colton stood once more before all of us. "Boys, what the hell?! We're a mess out there. What's with all the penalties? We need to skate smart and clean."

I scoffed, perhaps a little louder than I intended to. Everyone's eyes shot to me—everyone except Hunter. His eyes stayed fixed on the ground as he rolled his shoulder.

"We *have* been playing clean," I defended. "Mouse got that penalty because he was getting roughhoused. The play wasn't going to work: the team was too spread out. Mouse needed backup. They know our usual plays. Cap, I hate to say it, but fast breakaways aren't going to help us here. That team is all muscle; they want to play rough, and they're getting away with it. If we let them do nothing but beat us up, we'll have nothing left for tomorrow."

Colton looked at me, eyes blazing with fury. Coach waited in the background, ready to step in if needed. "What do you suggest then Aus?" Colt's tone was anything but welcoming, and the rest of the team nervously wrung their hands around their sticks.

I didn't let Colton scare me. "One, we need to be a fucking team. You're skating ahead and expecting us to be there, blind to the fact that their defense is all over us. They have big guys who are blocking the goal, but if we use that to our advantage and switch it up with a lot of passes, they won't see it coming. But it means we need to hold our own—speed won't work. We need to use shoulder checks to keep the passing lines free."

I knew this strategy *heavily* depended on working as a team. We couldn't go in there with the intention of showing off. The first period only proved that Colton was only interested in getting his goal percentage up.

Coach spoke up. "Aus is right. They've altered their game to match us. The clean lines aren't working anymore—they can see it coming We're spending all of our time in the defensive zone and that's what they want. We need to get some hits in, throw them off their game."

Colton ground his teeth. "Yes, Coach."

The rest of the team agreed and we reset before hitting the ice once more.

My plan worked. Finally, we were moving the puck between the lines. Though my plan wasn't without its downfalls because I was getting checked left, right, and center. Those guys did *not* want me to have the puck. The moment it hit my stick, I needed to keep it moving or I'd lose it. I hit it towards Mouse who had a free pass to Amon, but before I could press forward, I was checked against the boards.

"What the fuck!" I spat, whipping around to see a familiar number sixty-six: Zane Matthews.

"You his new boy toy then?" he chirped, making me flinch.

The sound of puck hitting a stick made me get my head back in the game.

The puck soared back to the neutral zone when Merrimack defenseman intercepted it. I bit out a curse, jumping into motion.

But the second I got it back, I was hit again.

"He'll only wreck your chances of getting signed too."

I shoved him off. I wasn't going to let him get me. I followed the puck and the whistle blew right before I my face met the boards again.

"Dude, the play's stopped!" I shouted at the mass towering over me.

The refs made their way over and pulled him away from me—and the bastard had the audacity to smile.

"I'll get my answers soon pretty boy," he sneered.

I blinked in disbelief, and the next thing I knew, Hunter and Mouse were by my side closely watching Matthews.

"What the hell is that guy's problem?" I asked.

"You okay? Did he hurt you?" Hunter was in my face, and I looked to him, desperate for answers. It was starting to dawn on me that I truly knew nothing about him, and it was just another thing that caused a fire in my belly.

"No, I'm fine. But whatever your beef is with that guy, keep me out of it." I skated off and ignored his calls that followed.

The game continued with a lot of back and forth—then my plan finally worked. The tic-tac-toe of passes let us soar the puck into the net.

"Fucking finally!" I pumped my fist and skated to the bench to tap the outstretched fists of my teammates. It was a much-needed confidence boost for us all, and it seemed to kick us into gear. We followed up with another messy—yet efficient—goal.

Period three began on a tie, and the rage simmering in Merrimack's eyes told us they were not going down without a fight.

Jarman sent the puck flying to me. He'd been cleared to play, and he was back with a vengeance. I passed to Hunter as I felt him approach my right wing. I went forward, waiting for the pass back. Matthews was hot on his heels, crashing his shoulder against the boards. Hunter stiffened, and I knew he was struggling. I went in and stole the puck.

It was enough to distract Matthews, but I didn't like how labored Hunter was. I kicked the puck to Mouse as I felt Matthew's incoming approach. He checked me, and I lost my balance, ass hitting the ice.

"Fucking dick."

Hunter yanked me to my feet, pushing me back into play. "Keep going, baby," he called, returning to the defense to clear space for Mouse.

But Matthews crashed into Hunter, driving his stick into his back. The whistle blew.

I saw red.

I leapt onto Matthews. Fists clenched to his jersey, I yanked him to his feet. Hunter clutched to his injured shoulder, which only fueled my rage.

I clenched one fist around Matthews's mask, driving the other into his ribs. He held his own, but it only spurred me on. His size didn't bother me.

Helmets came off, and fists kept flying.

"That's enough, boys!" The ref called. "Otherwise I'll call for another penalty."

I pulled back spitting out a mouthful of blood. I felt hands grab me and go to pull me away.

"You fucking faggot!" Matthews shouted. "He'll fuck you over too, just watch."

I schooled my features. That fucker wasn't going to out me., "I back my teammates wanker! Watch who you're calling faggot."

The moment those words left my lips, my anger shifted to a different focus.

 Matthews knew Hunter liked men, and something told me their feud was more than friendly fire.

I shoved the hands off me and skated to the bench, wiping the blood from my face. The pain hadn't hit yet, but I knew I was going to feel a world of regret for getting involved in any mess to do with Hunter Graves.

CHAPTER THIRTY-TWO

Hunter

H e wouldn't look at me. No matter how many times I tried to catch his eye, he deliberately avoided me. I needed to explain—right then and there. He needed at least a little bit of the truth. Maybe not the whole truth, but enough to convey my intentions.

As the power play unfolded on the ice, Tyler insisted on being part of the action—against Coach's advice. Meanwhile, I found myself benched due to my shoulder. Coach had seen the strain, and now I had to figure out a way to clear it without disclosing too much. My attention shifted to the game, focusing on our first line with Colton, Amon, and Tyler as forwards, while Jarman and Lachlan held down the defense.

Tyler's expression was something new, a fierce determination I hadn't witnessed before. Usually, he straddled the line of a serious go-getter or a golden retriever. Now, he was poised like a relentless bulldog. The defense from Merrimack was solid, and time ticked away on the clock as the power play neared its end. This play could either make or break us.

The puck danced back and forth, Tyler weaving through checks, searching for an opening. Then came the denial, followed by Tyler's quick recovery. He circled back to the blue line, assessing the situation. In a seemingly solo effort, he dodged opponents and passed the puck to Amon, orchestrating a distraction that let the puck to glide between Amon and Jarman. With a flick from Jarman, the puck met Tyler's stick midair and in one fluid motion; it soared over the goalie's right shoulder. The team erupted in celebration, sticks banging and shouts echoing through the arena.

Amid the jubilation, a Merrimack defenseman slammed Tyler into the goal post. The sickening crack of helmet meeting metal resonated through the now silent arena. Tyler sprawled awkwardly, the culprit conveniently extracting himself from the scene. Jarman quickly intervened, blocking my view as he shoved the guy away from Tyler.

My heart froze.

Mouse appeared beside me. "Dude, is he okay? He's still down."

"Boys, stay here—too much traffic." Coach demanded. He, along with the teams' trainers, bolted onto the ice.

It was all my fault.

I leaned sideways on the bench, trying to peer through the traffic. Eventually, I saw Jarman help Tyler to his feet, though he was a bit unsteady. Amon adjusted Tyler's helmet before he got nudged away by the trainers. Ignoring the concerned faces around him, Tyler raised his hand in a signal that he was fine. I let out a sigh of relief, keeping my eyes fixed on him and silently urging him to look my way.

"Come on, baby, look at me," I muttered.

As if he'd heard me, Tyler turned in my direction. However, the expressionless look in his eyes left me feeling defeated. I sat down on the bench, a sense of disappointment settling in. Tyler was promptly taken to the locker room for a checkup as the remaining teammates managed to hold the lead for the last minute, securing the win. Despite the victory, our team was visibly shaken. Between Jarman, Tyler and me, we'd taken some hard hits—and we still had another game to go.

The team quietly descended the chute, exchanging occasional taps and careful pats on the shoulders with affirming expressions. In the locker room, Tyler was stripped down to his boxer briefs, flinching away from the light the team doctor shone into his eyes.

"I'm fine," Tyler growled, hating the attention. Coach quickly joined them to hear the verdict.

"He's battered and bruised, but no signs of a concussion. If you experience headaches, dizziness, or nausea at any point, you need to inform one of us immediately. A scratch tomorrow is better than risking a prolonged absence due to a repeat head injury."

Tyler rolled his eyes, displaying no signs of impending issues. "I'm fucking fine."

The team doctor raised his hands in surrender, accustomed to moody twenty-some-things eager to get back on the ice. Coach didn't press further, exchanging a meaningful look with Tyler that told him to speak up if anything happened. Tyler nodded his head in understanding and grabbed his towel, storming off to the showers.

The rest of the team parted ways, perplexed by the sudden change in Tyler's demeanor. He wasn't known for having a temper. As I hurried to strip down and join him in the showers, I couldn't help but shake off the thought that, despite the circumstances, there was something... sexy about it. Yet, as I entered, he still avoided eye contact and purposefully ensured that not a single inch of his skin touched mine. "Ty..."

The locker room buzzed with the team's lively chatter, providing cover for my next audacious move. I threw caution to the wind and gently touched his shoulder.

Though I flinched as he whipped his head towards me. The fire burning in his eyes wasn't of a sexual nature, but I couldn't say it would have bothered me if it was. A twisted desire grew within me, yearning for him to channel that frustration towards me, to hold me, to deliver some kind of retribution.

"Don't fucking 'Ty' me. Next time I'm gearing up for a game and one of us has a target on our backs, you better tell me, got it? I don't like being blindsided and I don't appreciate someone seeing right through me. *And* also, I don't like discovering things about your exes while on the damn ice. I feel like an idiot for defending you when I clearly don't know a fucking thing about you."

His chest rose and fell with each breath, his voice a restrained whisper that lashed at my bare skin.

"Ty, I'm sorry, really. I didn't think he'd target you."

Tyler rolled his eyes, and I couldn't help but bite back a smile over how that simple gesture stirred something within me.

"Well, surprise, surprise, Hunter: You have this stupid magic fucking dick that makes everyone remember you."

With that, he grabbed his towel and stormed out, leaving my mouth hanging open in stunned silence.

Despite my best efforts, I couldn't snag a seat beside Tyler on the bus back to the university. Instead, I found myself sitting in an empty seat, staring at him like some smitten teenage girl. Jarman settled in beside me, his knee unintentionally knocking into mine. "You two good?" His voice was low, almost conspiratorial.

"I messed up," I admitted, the weight of my mistake heavy in my chest.

Jarman responded with a low, rumbling laugh. "No shit. Not telling your guy about your ex, and then having your ex rile him up with an agent in the crowed is pretty fucked." I looked at him, wide-eyed, my words stuck in my throat. Jarman seemed unfazed, an amused expression on his face. "Dude, I've known you since preschool. We've played on the same team our whole lives."

He wasn't wrong, but his observation left me feeling guilty. I realized I knew practically nothing about him, except for the fact that he had a lot of sisters.

"But..."

"But nothing," Jarman interrupted. "I saw how you looked at Zane. Your little secret smirks weren't so secret to me. Maybe growing up with sisters means you learn to see things that others don't."

"You saying you're a girl?" I snarked, earning myself a well-deserved smack across the back of the head.

"No, it means I'm not just another meat-headed guy who only has his head in the clouds."

I nodded, silently urging him to continue talking. I didn't want to admit to anything. Plausible deniability was my refuge.

"During that last term, you'd been with Kinsley more than anything. So, I assumed you and Zane had a falling out. I still don't understand why you punched him, and I was a bit disappointed in your behavior. Despite you never noticing me, you were a nice guy, in a way. I mean, you were never rude."

"So, that's the low bar for a nice guy?" I quipped. "Just not being mean? But you're not necessarily nice to people either, just indifferent."

Jarman shrugged. "Sometimes, being nice is doing nothing at all. You had shit going on. I got the impression you didn't have the best family life. I never saw your parents at games and once I saw your dad drag you by the back of your neck and shove you into a car. So, I think you not being a royal asshole because your life sucked means you're a nice guy."

I didn't say anything, hating how ignorant I'd been all those years. He knew I was queer the whole time and never once said anything.

"Since you won't say anything—and please note that I hate talking—I don't care about your sexuality. But I see you with Tyler, and he's different than the rest. I know you care about him."

I deflated at that "Yeah, he's..." I sighed, not sure how to put it into words. Because I only wanted to say perfect.

"Do you have a plan?"

I looked back to Tyler, who stared blankly out the window, letting Mouse animatedly talk to him about the amazingness—his word, not mine—of the star-nosed mole. Mouse was none the wiser that Tyler was tuning him out and that his unamused grunts were only for show. Jarman scoffed, and I looked back to him, dark eyes glimmering at his best friend.

"No plan. I need to be able to explain, to apologize. But I shouldn't be getting close to him—for more reasons than one."

Jarman took his attention away from Mouse, still smiling. "The reasons are?"

I shot him a look and he rolled his eyes in a way that meant, "Spill."

"His entire life just fell apart. He's lost both his parents in a span of two years and his little brother is hiding in his dorm room until he needs to go back to school. Between the loss and the responsibility, he doesn't need to take on my bullshit."

"Stupid reason because he needs you now more than ever. Next."

I furrowed my brow yet again.

"Come on, Hunt, I don't have all day. Accept the fact that I know you better than you know yourself."

I did just that and continued. "The NHL isn't exactly rolling out the rainbow carpet for gays."

He nodded, seeming to mull over that information. "It won't be easy, but what they don't know won't hurt them. You get to the league, show them how amazing you are, and then come out. Use your big lawyer knowledge to sue for discrimination if they try anything silly."

I had to love his optimism. "Jarman..."

He sighed. "Yeah, yeah, I know there's the timeline between you graduating and him doing what he does, but time is just that: time. You two have something that could withstand the test."

I rolled my neck out, considering it. Even just a month with Tyler Riley would be a dream.

"So, next concern."

"My dad. He… isn't a nice guy, Jarman. I don't want him anywhere near Tyler. I'd never forgive myself if he got hurt."

His hand clasped my shoulder. "You are out of his home, Hunt. He surely can't have that much reach."

I gulped, meeting his warm brown eyes. "I'm only here because of him. I don't have a scholarship—he owns me, Jarman."

Jarman's face contorted. "Well, is there any way you can get an agent? Or even enter the AHL without him knowing? You're good enough, man. That way you can start your life on your own terms."

I shrugged. I hadn't been approached like Colton and Tyler had. But I wasn't exactly reaching out for agents either. The thought seeded itself in my mind, and Jarman smiled proudly.

"I'll look into it," I relented.

"For what it's worth, I think you two are good for each other. If your chemistry on the ice says anything, then you can get past the hurdles, however many they are. I like you two together."

"You're making me feel like a dick," I grumbled half-heartedly, and he chuckled.

"I've always considered you a friend, Hunt, even if you didn't realize it."

I patted his knee. "Thanks, man. I am sorry. Really, you're a good guy—and a good friend."

We left it at that. During the drive back to our rink, I concocted a plan to try and win Tyler back.

CHAPTER THIRTY-THREE

Tyler

The hardwood floors protested my weight as I dragged myself through the door. My temples throbbed with the painful reminder of my collision with the goalpost. Note to self: helmets can only protect you from so much.

Two worried faces greeted me as I entered the dorm room. Jamie's concern only worsened when he saw how I rubbed my temples. I tried to reassure him by gathering him into my arms. "S'fine, Jamie, just a little bang. You get hit worse in your fights."

He groused but held onto me tight. "You weren't moving," he mumbled into my chest, panic clear in his voice. "That brute from Merrimack had me pinned. I'm fine, really. Even got cleared by the doctors." He nodded without another word, but his embrace said it all.

"I'm not going anywhere, James. You're stuck with me for a lifetime."

"Better be." We stood there for a moment and my eyes met Cal's over Jamie's shoulder, who offered nothing but sympathy in that one gaze.

Eventually, Jamie must have felt secure enough to let go. Given the unpredictable nature of our lives, I couldn't really blame him for thinking I'd vanish into thin air. He asked the question that sat heavy in the room, "So, what did that fucker say to make you crack on with him? You never fight."

"Called me a..." I glanced around the room and considered my audience. "Not so savory term for gay people." Cal and Jamie's eyes widened, and I made my way to the kitchen to prepare dinner.

Jamie's voice followed me. "Why would he call you a—"

"Why would he call you that?" Cal interrupted, sparing me the horror of having to hear that word any more than necessary.

"Pot met kettle, that's why. He's Hunter's ex." The simple feeling of his name in my mouth made my stomach flip. The tension in the room was palpable now.

"Awkward," Jamie mumbled before he began helping me cut vegetables.

"He is just jealous you have him now, that's all," Cal offered.

I barked out a laugh. "Quite the opposite; seems Hunter screwed him over. He was set on letting me know I'd be next."

And I swore then that I was done with Hunter Graves—something I should have done months ago. Our first encounter should have been the universe telling me to stay away—even if he did have that deep, soothing voice, and those ripped muscles and those captivating eyes... *Fuck*! Even when I was angry at him, he had me in a chokehold.

"It's fine," I said in response to their silence. "I'm done with it all. I don't need this drama."

I chose to ignore the knowing look Cal and Jamie shared. I was moving forward; there was another game tomorrow and we needed to win. I needed to show both Hunter and his crazy ex that they couldn't get under my skin. Even if I had to fake it to make it.

Thankfully, we eased into a comfortable conversation. I listened to Jamie's excitement about his new club where the owner had taken a liking to him. Cal had been helping and between the two of us, we made it work. They also let Jamie hang around during the day, helping with odd jobs so he wasn't cooped up in the dorm. Jamie spoke about the fights he watched, about the dynamics of the guys. But through it all, I could only focus on his smile. Even Cal melted at the sight of my younger brother coming to life. There were times when grief hit him hard, but this escape from reality was doing him some good.

Eventually, Jamie talked himself to sleep, resting with his head on my chest. Cal took himself to bed while I continued to sit there with my brother. It didn't matter that I was wiped, I knew I wouldn't be able to sleep. The least I could do was sit there and comfort Jamie.

Though I grumbled when a soft knock at the door forced me to disentangle myself. Thankfully, Jamie slept like the dead. I gently laid him down on the couch before moving to open the door.

"Hunter, what are you doing here?" Apparently, that was an invitation enough for Hunter to close the gap between us, his non-injured arm reaching up to grip the door frame. I couldn't tell what was more attractive: his lips just tantalizingly out of reach, the way his hoodie slid up to expose the sexy V of his muscles, or the way his rolled-up sleeves gave me just a peek of his tattoos. I steeled myself before I forgot what I'd decided

"I'm sorry, Tyler," he said. "I'm really fucking sorry."

His presence alone was enough to break me, but I kept my cool.

"For what, Boston?"

His lip quirked into a sad grin. "For everything I suppose—the hot and cold, acting like a dick, not telling you about Zane. Though despite what he thinks, it's his own fault he didn't get into the AHL."

I sighed, "Hunter Graves: damaging everything wherever he goes. Thanks for the apology. See you tomorrow, Boston."

I made to shut the door, but his large palm stopped it. "Ty... please, baby."

I closed my eyes because my heart was beating out of my chest. I couldn't think straight when he called me baby.

"I really am sorry, okay? My life is complicated, but I talked to Jarman, and—"

"Jarman fucking knows?" The fury in my voice was purely driven by the anxiety of being outed to another teammate.

"He already knew. I didn't have to tell him."

I'd had enough. "Leave, Hunter." Then I shut the door in his face.

"Baby..." His voice was broken on the other side of the wooden door. I scolded my heart for wanting to comfort him.

"I am *not* your baby."

Once I made sure Jamie was tucked in, I retreated to my bedroom. I couldn't shake the feeling that something just within my grasp was going to be yanked away once more.

The second game against Merrimack was almost the same: the hits came hard, but my "don't fuck with me" attitude seemed to work in our favor. Despite our tension off the ice, Hunter and I were magnets in the game. Our passes were flawless and he set me up for two goals that had our home crowd cheering. Hunter tried the post-goal celebration each time, but I was quick to return to the bench and celebrate with everyone else. I just couldn't look at him. Looking at him would mean I would cave, and I couldn't cave. Not anymore.

We finished the game with a one-point win once again. This time, spirits were high as everyone cheered in the locker room, sticks banged against the floor in celebration for a good closing game before winter break. Coach caught my eye and inclined his head to the door, indicating for me to follow. There, just outside the locker room doors, was Connor Bellamy, wearing that million dollar smile. "Hey, kid, great couple of games."

I hoped he didn't notice the way my own smile didn't meet my eyes. Those games were some of the sloppiest I'd ever played. Scrappy wasn't normally my style, but that team deserved it. "I liked seeing the two sides of you. You're a versatile player, which is what the league would be interested in."

Before I could say anything, the doors opened and Hunter approached, his showstopping grin on full display. "Hunter Graves, it's good to meet you." Connor outstretched hand to greet him. Hunter made me a fool by acting calm, cool and collected in front of NHL royalty.

"I should be saying that to you, sir. You're the legend here." Hunter oozed charm, and I found myself naturally fumbling with my gear to appear busy.

"I'm glad you're here. I wanted to say how much I enjoy you two on the ice I have been watching closely, and your connection is great. I hope to see more of it."

"Oh, you will, sir. Aus and I have great chemistry on the ice, but as much as I'd love to take credit, it's all him. He has a striking ability in being able to read his team."

I shot daggers at him with my eyes. What the hell was he doing? Connor gave us a smile and handed a business card to each of us. "It doesn't go unnoticed. Here's my info. I'd like to set up some meetings, and talk about your future."

I took it eagerly, as did Hunter. "Again, good game. Coach, thanks for the tip." Connor waved goodbye to us. I looked down at the card as if it could hold my future. *Do you see this, Mum?* My stomach churned and I bit my lip to fend off my emotions.

"I knew you'd make it to the big leagues, baby." Hunter bumped into my shoulder, but I pulled away.

"Come on, Riley. You can't stay mad at me forever. You at least have to let me explain."

"Hunter, I'm not in the mood, okay? I saw what I needed to see: a scorned ex who gave me a black eye."

"I was only trying to protect him." Hunter's tone was shaky. I turned to look into his eyes, seeing a disheartened look that got my own heart lurching with the need to comfort him.

"How does breaking someone's nose protect them? Is this some American thing I don't understand? Because where I come from, you call someone a cunt and call it a day."

Hunter choked on a laugh. "Dude, seriously, your language."

I rolled my eyes. "Sorry: a dumb dog, a wanker, twat—any insult. Fists are for a drunken bogan who's sloshed off two cartons by five p.m."

Hunter looked at me like I'd sprouted a second head. "Okay... I was protecting him; he needed to realize I was bad news. He wasn't taking a hint."

"So you'll do the same to me if I get too close? All you have to do is tell me to fuck off."

"No," he whined, looking around as our freshly showered and dressed teammates filed out of the locker room.

"Ausssieeeeee! You celebrating tonight?"

This time, the guys were meeting at a local bar before the after party at the hockey house. I had to think about it, knowing I'd be leaving Jamie alone. "I don't know, man. I don't want James to be all by himself."

"Bring him!" Mouse suggested like he'd just discovered gravity.

Thankfully, Jarman came to my rescue. "He's not bringing his fourteen-year-old brother to a college party."

I gave him what I hoped was a grateful gesture. I hadn't really looked Jarman in the eyes since finding out he knew about me and Hunter. But looking at him now, I could tell that he was someone I could trust. I pulled my eyes away, not wanting to think too hard about the gold-eyed Boston boy standing next to me. Even though I knew that would be near impossible.

Jamie all but shoved me out of the dorm that night. "Dude, I can be alone. I am not five. I have my PlayStation and you meal prep enough to feed a shelter. Go have a night out."

I pulled out my dark jeans, my black Henley, and a thin black jacket, throwing my parka over my shoulders. Cal waited by the door, his eyes scanning me up and down. "Dude, are you robbing a bank or something, or did you just listen to Paramore too much in 2009?"

"Don't diss Paramore," I argued, nudging his shoulders. "They're a vibe."

"I am just saying: normally you're a *Folklore* era kind of guy—Not *Reputation*. You're even wearing combat boots, my man."

I rolled my eyes. "Nothing wrong with *Reputation* either; it's a vibe too."

Cal just scoffed. "Boy, did Hunter do a number on you. If you get with another guy, I am totally getting the boombox out and blasting 'Look What You Made Me Do.' outside your bedroom door"

We headed to his car, the whispers in my mind clinging onto that part about the other guy.

Maybe it was time to move on.

CHAPTER THIRTY-FOUR

Hunter

I was sitting in my room when I heard the chorus of yells downstairs.

"Aussie!"

My body straightened at the sound of his name. I looked down, suddenly regretting the choice to be a couch potato—gray sweats. Because knowing he was downstairs only gave me enough time to grab a hoodie and rush out the door.

I watched him smile as the men from the team jostled him about in greeting. His auburn hair stood out against his all black clothes, his cheeks flushed from a combination of the cold and the attention from the team. I stood frozen on the stairs, silently begging him to look my way, just once.

Almost on cue, I watched his shoulders stiffen., I saw him blink a few times and knew that if I were standing closer I'd be able to see those dark lashes fan against the sun-kissed freckles scattered across his cheekbones. He was fighting it, telling himself not to look up, not letting himself get drawn in by my presence. But like me, this thing between us was too big to ignore. His head slowly rose, like a puppet on an invisible string and his eyes connected with mine. His Adam's apple bobbed at the sight of me, and I knew he was taking in my disheveled state. He was seeing me for the first time—the real me. The one behind the cocky smile, behind the mask I put on for the rest of the world.

His eyes held mine for what felt like an eternity. I watched Jarman come beside him, his eyes flicking between the two of us. We were completely oblivious to the party going on around us. We were apart, yet he was my home base, his heartbeat with mine, his mind and mine connected. I was dying to cross the inevitable barrier that held us apart.

Jarman said something to Aussie, and I stood in anticipation because it looked like he was saying to give me a chance. If I was reading his lips right, that was—he was telling him to talk to me. Aussie gave me one final glance over and slowly shook his head. With every shake, I felt my heart cracking. I tapped my fingers on the railing, then retreated back to my room.

CHAPTER THIRTY-FIVE

Tyler

Do not think about how broken he looks. Don't you dare.

My head pounded, and I told myself it was the stress—the constant racing thoughts battling each other like prize-winning boxers. Their blows pounded against my temples, further intensifying my headache. It was all his fault—I'd had the headache since the game the day before. No matter how many shots of whiskey I downed, it didn't drown out the voices and pictures in my mind.

How sexy he looked under me, how sexy he looked *over* me. *"I'll look after you, baby.,"* That vulnerable look as I took in the bruises on his body.

"Baby…" The rejected look just before I closed the door on him.

His tousled hair as he stood on the staircase meant he'd been pulling at it the way he does when he's stressed. I could see the tracks from fingers sliding through the roots and where he attempted to flatten it, but there were always a few strands that protested.

Then a different face flashed to the forefront of my mind; Zane Matthews. My gut churned at the hate in his eyes, that fucking slur being sprayed across the ice.

Australians often used many insults as terms of endearment, but that one had a universal meaning. I rolled my eyes and sighed, coming back to the present. The smooth burn of the cheap whiskey warmed my body as I tipped my head back. Most guys had already found their hookup for the night and had begun to retreat to their bedrooms. Mouse stood opposite me on the bench, animatedly talking about… something. I hadn't paid much attention to what but I knew that at least it wasn't a mole. I blinked back the dizziness, trying to focus on what he was saying.

"Dude, she looked at me! She actually looked at me!" Mouse practically bounced on his toes.

Jarman hummed and sculled back another shot, pouring one for me. I followed his lead, but as I lowered my head again the room began to spin. *Fuck.*

"That's good mate. Just ask her on a date," I slurred. I hadn't had *that* much to drink, had I?

I shook my head in an attempt to clear it, but that only made it worse.

"How? She's so perfect, and I'm ... well, me." Mouse's jovial tone went uncharacteristically flat.

"Just ask her what her perfect date is. Then ask her when she's free and take her out to do exactly that. You're a good-looking guy, she'll say yes."

He beamed., "Oh, em gee, Aussie. Yes! I'll try that!"

He clapped me on the shoulder and ran off. I looked beside me to see Jarman's gaze locked on him with a pained expression.

Well, fuck. I knew that look all too well.

"Jar..." I started.,

"It's nothing, Aus. He's my best friend, that's all. I worry." He took another shot, not giving me any confidence in what he just said. He then clapped me on the shoulder as well before saying he was going to head out.

I stood there on my own, looking around at everyone's happy faces. There was something about being alone in a crowded room full of happy couples that made the world seem so small. There was only me, myself, and I. I had the depressing thought, and my heart protested the idea—the one that told me this was my future: surrounded by a team but no one to go home to at night.

That lonely thought had me picking up the rest of the whiskey bottle and heading out into the cold.

Chapter Thirty-Six

Hunter

Like something out of an angsty teenage movie, I watched the snow fall outside while I pretended to study the constitutional law book in front of me—that had been open to the same page for an hour. A lone figure stumbled out the front door and onto the snow-patched lawn, lifting a bottle to his lips. He looked to the sky, the small fire pit light catching the reddish hues of his hair. His breath misted out in front of him as he... laughed?

I noted the way the air mingled with his short exhales, the way his chest rose and fell as he shook his head like he was shaking off his thoughts. My body reacted before my mind, and I charged from my room and into the yard.

I opened the sliding door, and despite the increase in noise, he still didn't notice me. I stood on the porch, watching him move around the fire, sipping whiskey like it was the answer to all his problems.

I'd seen Tyler cry before, held him as he broke down in my arms. But I'd never seen him like this. This was a different type of broken, and I didn't like it one bit. His feet didn't know left from right, and his face was void of all emotion.

I took a step closer.

"You know, I never used to be this pathetic," he said, letting me know he was aware of my presence. I moved to take another step, but he pointed at me with the hand holding the whiskey.

"I've always been able to control this stupid feeling. Because I told myself, I could be alone. I was fine, being the guy everyone depended on. I always performed no matter what life threw at me. I prevailed. I proved that I didn't need more than who I already had beside me. Right?"

My eyes began to burn as his pain-infused words hit the frosted air.

"Right?" he repeated, a little louder this time—loud enough to make me flinch.

"Ty...."

"That should be enough: my team, my brother, and hockey. That should be all I need, right?" His voice got louder as tears fell down his cheeks. Though he continued to rub at his temple with his free hand, as if every word hurt.

"But no, one fucking night with you turned into another and another, then poof! "His hands flew out to his sides, whiskey sloshing out of the bottle and splattering onto the fire, sending the flames high. I stepped forward, needing to get that bottle from his hands, but he brought it back to his mouth and turned his back to me.

"Poof, I've lost my mind. Do you know why, Hunter?" He looked over his shoulder.

"Why, baby?" My voice was barely a whisper.

He spun on a growl, charging up to me and stabbing his finger into my chest—right over my heart.

"Because of *that*, because you made me yours. *You* called *me* baby like I was *yours!*" He screamed loud, too drunk to care if anyone heard. I glanced to the door to see if anyone noticed the scene he was making.

His cheeks were red, face soaked with tears. He had a black eye and a small knot on his head from colliding with the goal post, along with a nasty bruise forming on his chin. Frankly, he was a mess—my beautiful fucking mess.

"See what you just did there? Looking around to see if anyone sees the gay hockey star losing his mind. That's my fucking future: always looking over my shoulder, pining after what I can't have. Looking at you with hearts in my eyes, even though I'm destined for the same fate as Zane: throwing punches at your future lovers who fall for your smart mouth or that soft touch that makes me feel like I'm the only one," he choked out, one jab of his finger before withdrawing from me once more.

"Before *you*, Boston, I was happy being in the closet. My friends and family were enough. I told myself that one day, when my dreams were said and done, I'd run back home and move to a small country town and meet a country boy and settle down. "

The thought alone was enough to make me snap. I lunged, pinning his arms to his side and holding him tight to my chest so he could feel the low rumble in my chest—my sign of disapproval at the very idea. The whiskey bottle fell to the ground, glass shattering at our feet.

He let out a sob, crumbling in my embrace. "But then *you* fucking happened, Boston. *You* saw me, *you* made me feel. You showed me what I was missing. You gave me another dream that I shouldn't even be fucking thinking about. Because this dream, you and me, could destroy everything."

I held him tighter. "It *is* you and me, Aussie. I see you, and you see me. That's all we need in this world. I don't care what the future holds, whether it's being miles apart or behind closed doors, I will always be yours—and you'll forever be *mine.* You *will* fulfill your dreams, and I'll be right by your side to cheer you on—no matter what. Then when your dreams are said and done, fuck that hypothetical country boy. You'll have the man from Boston who will follow you wherever you go."

His fingers dug into my sides and he shook his head against my shoulder like my words weren't true.

"How do I know you won't break my heart? I don't know if I could survive heartbreak like that."

I sighed, holding him even tighter, like I could keep him there forever. "I can't promise perfection, but I can promise that you'll get the best version of me possible. And if I do, I'll grovel at your feet until you forgive me. I never want to break you, baby. Come to bed and when you're good and sober, I'll explain everything. Then you can decide if you still want me."

He laugh-slash-sobbed into my neck. "I wish I could hate you."

I'd taken many hits in my life, but his words hurt more than any fist I'd ever taken.

"Tomorrow, baby. I'll tell you *everything* tomorrow. And if you still feel that way, if you still want to hate me, I'll help you forget. If it makes you happy to hate me, I'll make that happen."

He scoffed, soaking my shirt with snot and tears. "You make that sound romantic."

Even through all the hurt, he still made me smile. "Just give me one more time to look after you tonight."

He hummed his approvals. "One more night."

I could tell that the alcohol was taking its toll the more he sank into my touch. "Yeah, baby, one more night." I shifted to put his arm around me, trying not to let my bad shoulder buckle under his weight. Somehow, I managed to trudge his muscular ass across the snow and into the house.

"Oh-ho-ho Aussie is hammered!" Mouse screamed.

In response, Tyler mumbled an almost incoherent "snot-shammered."

I couldn't help but laugh, though with the way his head hung on his shoulders, I felt like I was holding up a ticking time bomb.

Cal rushed over, Eric at his heels. "Fuck, is he okay?" Cal moved in and lifted Tyler's gaze to his.

Aussie barely had it in him to give a lazy smile. "Hi Capt'n 'merica."

"Oh my god, this is all my fault. I should have been watching him."

Cal flustered, to which Tyler replied, "S'fine, I's a big boy."

That only made me laugh again. "Okay big boy, let's get you to bed." Then I turned to Cal. "Let Jamie know he's crashing here?"

Cal agreed, but his concern didn't waver. I took pleasure in knowing that if Tyler did want to hate me at least he wouldn't be alone.

Tyler's dead weight flopped onto my bed. I rolled my injured shoulder as he groaned and rubbed his head again.

"Head hurts." I wondered how much of that was from the bump on his head and how much of it was booze.

"Alcohol does that, baby." I filled a glass with water from the bathroom and plopped in two aspirin tablets.

"Snot alcohol. Punches and goal posts hurt."

"You have a concussion!" I gritted my teeth. "Why did you play today? That's fucking dangerous, Tyler."

He shrugged lazily. "Hads points to proves."

His slur did nothing to ease my concerns. Again: concussion or booze?

"And what if you got hit *again*? What if you had permanent damage? You feel like leaving your brother with no one?" I growled.

Even in his drunken state, he stiffened. "Worst brother ever," is what I thought he said.

I bit back a curse—that wasn't what I intended by scolding him.

"You're not the worst. Stupid maybe, but not the worst." I stripped him down to his boxers and tucked him under the blanket, holding his head up so he could have the water. "Drink, baby."

He did and gagged on the first mouthful. "Bleh, that's fucking rank."

"You will thank me tomorrow. Sleep now."

He frowned the most adorable little frown, "One more time."

My dick threatened to rise but I told it off, because the way he said those three words had me thinking he wanted to fuck me goodbye.

One, he was way too drunk. Two, if we did fuck again, I'd want him to remember every touch. I didn't think he was ready to hear those three magic words, nor was I ready to be rejected by the only person I'd ever said them to. So, I'd make damn sure to *show* him how much I loved him.

"Sure, baby. Let me get changed," I lied, knowing if I waited long enough, he would pass out. After a shower—a cold one—and pulling on clean underwear, I found Tyler curled up with my pillow as if he were chasing my scent. The sight both melted and broke my heart. Because the next morning all of that could be gone.

His auburn hair flopped over his eyes, his long lashes fluttering against his skin. Little grunts and murmurs escaped him before he tightened his grip on the pillow. Some might call me a creep for watching him sleep like that, and maybe I was, but Tyler rarely let his guard down. To most, he was an overachiever, a golden retriever with a bulldog edge. But in truth, there were so many more layers to him.

I noticed things about him that no one else did: the way he pressed his forefinger into the skin of his thumbnail, which was always red and raw. He gnawed at his cheek and lip when he was deep in thought—which was often. If he was made to stand still, his leg would bounce to some internal rhythm—like he was counting the steps he could be taking. When he was focused on the ice, he mumbled to himself inaudibly— a ritual he kept hidden from most.

I lived for the moments when he sat beneath me, eyes ablaze with lust, his mouth slack and free from the day's worries. He moaned without a second thought, clinging to my body like a lifeline. If he spent all his time in a world filled with stress and heartache, I was his relief, his breath of fresh air. No one had ever made me feel so strong, so... worth it.

CHAPTER THIRTY-SEVEN

Tyler

I had dreams of someone waking me up through the night. The husky voice reminded me to drink water and asked me over and over how my head felt. Then, once I took a drink of the disgusting bubbly water, the voice would soothe me back to sleep. The warm, cedar smell washed over me, sending me deeper into unconsciousness. I woke up thirsty as hell, but remarkably, my headache was dull compared to the night before.

I shifted my head on the pillow, only to notice the pillow was hard, and had skin—soft skin that was bathed in that smell I'd been clinging to in my dirty clothes for weeks. An involuntary murmur of pleasure left my lips. A hand threaded through my hair, massaging my scalp and making me almost purr.

"That's nice," I whispered.

"How are you feeling?" Hunter's quiet murmur tickled my hair.

"Surprisingly okay." My hand began tracing lines over the planes on his stomach. I was fighting the urge to cringe as the events from the night before played on a blooper reel in my mind. But I remembered every little word he said—and I wanted to know if he meant them.

"Good, how much do you remember?"

I could have lied. That was my chance at an out, but I didn't want it. "Everything until I laid down, then it's a bit blurry."

He huffed against my hair, letting me know his lips were close enough to kiss if he wanted to.

"I am sorry—for everything, Ty." The words infused themselves into my hair, lulling me into a sense of comfort.

"Why'd you hit Zane?"

I felt the rise and fall of his chest as he readied himself to tell me, my chest tightened in anticipation.

"So he'd hate me."

I shifted to rest my chin on his chest so I could look him in the eyes. They had a haunted appearance that made me want to reach out for him, but I waited. "Why?"

Hunter looked away from my eyes to the roof. "He saw my father hit me."

"Hunter..." I shifted so we were eye-to-eye.

"Zane had snuck into my bedroom one night, and my father happened to walk in when we were... fooling around. To say he was angry would be the understatement of the century. I kicked Zane out, but I didn't realize he was watching through the window when my father hit me. When I got to practice the next day, Zane cornered me and said he'd report it. His dad was a judge, and he was determined to see my father punished. I panicked. I already knew I wasn't going to play my best that day: my ribs were broken, and I hurt all over. I had nothing to lose. So, I punched him. If he challenged my father... he would have had so much more than missing a game to worry about."

"You protected him the only way you knew how..." I murmured.

Finally, his gaze met mine again and he nodded. "I've tried so hard to stay away from you the last few months, Ty—and I failed. Sharing a room with you on the road... it was impossible to not have you. We kept saying each time was the last, but every time only meant that much more to me. Every time you walk away I fall into a pit of self-hatred. I can't have him hurt you. Being with me is more than just being gay or being my teammate: you'll have a target on your back. My father is ruthless. I was trying to protect you by staying away. But I am *so* fucking sorry."

I rested my forehead against his, closing my eyes to take in his words. My brain processed his words, and I found myself torn. Self-preservation would have had me leaving him, but my traitorous heart wouldn't let that happen.

"I spoke to Jarman—after he called me out on a few things. He got me thinking about finding a way out. So, I called Connor Bellamy today. I'm not a draft pick, but I explained my situation and he thinks I have potential. My stats are good, and if I can't get into the NHL I said I'd settle for an AHL contract."

I opened my mouth to protest because he deserved better but he silenced me with a finger to my lips. "I know what you're going to say, but any contract I get promises my own income that doesn't rely on him. Then, I'll work my ass off to be noticed by the NHL."

I let the big question leave my lips. "And us?"

Hunter brushed his knuckles against my cheekbone. "Well, it depends on where I end up and when you get called up—because you will. Then we decide if we can do long distance.

I wanted that, anything I could get. I'd take stolen moments over nothing at all. I nodded the action quicker than forming the words to say it.

"You have to decide if I'm worth the risk, Aus. My plan was to finish this year, complete my pre-law, and secretly sign a contract. I want to slowly and quietly extract myself from him, but it doesn't stop the fact that being with me comes with its own set of risks..."

"Look..." I began.

Chapter Thirty-Eight

Hunter

In my experience, nothing good ever came from a conversation that started that way. I braced myself, waiting for the rejection.

"We both have baggage," he began.

"I know..."

"I'm not ready to run up to the rooftops and announce that I'm gay—"

"Aussie," I interrupted. My heart stuttered.

"Will you let me know if your father is being a wanker? If he lays a finger on you, will you let me take care of you?"

I huffed a laugh. "The one time you can use 'cunt,' and you choose the word 'wanker.'"

He rolled his eyes. "Hunt..." He warned.

"I promise I will stop at nothing to protect you," I replied.

He frowned at that., "Did you not hear me? If this is going to work, I need you safe. I've lost a lot of people I care about, and I refuse to lose you. I *cannot* lose you, Boston."

I bit my lip, unsure if I could promise not to sacrifice myself if it meant saving him.

"I will tell you—that's as much as I can promise. Because if it comes down to it, I will always protect you." Tyler didn't seem to like the answer and I half expected him to pull away.

"So, are we doing this then? No more one last time? We'll be exclusive but... secret?" My heart pounded my ribcage. I was suddenly aware of his weight on me, his scent washing over me.

"I've only been with you since that first night."

I watched his smile light up his face, loving how it washed away the heavy creases between his brows. "So, yes? Exclusively secret couple?"

"Yes, baby." I lunged to crush his lips in a bruising kiss. "You're mine, and I'm yours."

Tyler rose onto his knees, throwing one leg over me until he straddled my lap. I felt his hard length against mine as he leaned over. Our lips collided, desperate and needy. The feeling of his muscled back flexing under my touch sent a shiver down my spine. With a deep breath in, I grazed my nose against the crook of his neck..

"Mm you always smell so good."

"I think I'm sweating out cheap whiskey."

"No wonder I'm getting drunk off you."

Tyler barked out a laugh. "You did not just say that." Still, his eyes sparkled.

"I did—deal with it and fuck me already."

His eyes lit up. I loved making my Aussie fall apart beneath me, but in that moment, he needed control. He pressed a quick kiss to my lips before reaching into the bedside drawer and dropping our supplies by my hip. The look he gave me took my breath away. Those turquoise eyes shone through thick lashes, combined with a devilish smile that promised exactly what I wanted. He kissed a slow path down my stomach, paying special attention to my still-healing bruises. When he reached the waistband of my boxer briefs, he hooked his fingers behind it and pulled them down so his lips could seamlessly continue their path down my body. The combined sensation of the fabric against my heated flesh and his lips leaving behind a trail of goosebumps in their wake had my cock throbbing.

Tyler's last kiss landed on the inside of my ankle, and I couldn't tell you why, but it sent a thrill through me. It must have been the intimacy of it all, to be touched with such tenderness, knowing that he intended to destroy me. It had me melting into a pool of submission for the man who would own me—forever.

His lips made their way back to the inside of my thigh before he flattened his tongue against the curve of my ass, licking a path over my taint and my balls until he reached the head of my dick. I arched towards his touch, chasing the wet heat of his mouth. I writhed beneath him, crying and pleading as he fondled my balls with one hand, while he used two lubed fingers to stretch me open. When he closed his mouth over my cock, my vision whited out.

"Aussie." My voice broke and I hoped he could hear the desperation, hoped he could tell how close I was to ending things before they even began.

He hummed around my shaft and it took every tactic I had not to shoot right down his throat.

"Ty, baby..." I panted. "I'm ready. Please, please just fuck me."

My body arched as he skillfully tapped my prostate, which had me gripping the base of my cock tightly to stave off my release.

Tyler groaned and kissed the inside of my thigh. Then he hooked my left leg over his shoulder and rose to his knees, aligning his cockhead with my entrance. He pressed a soft kiss to my neck and pushed through, his groan rolling through me. I hissed when his teeth sank into my neck, marking me, claiming me as his. I didn't care—not in that moment.

My hips bucked, seeking out friction. Tyler read me perfectly, rolling his hips in a way that made my body light up. I arched into his chest, my dick rubbing against the silky skin of his abs. My eyes shuttered involuntarily. It was all too much—Tyler stretching me, filling me. The way he rocked his hips to graze my prostate with every move.

I couldn't hold back.

"God, Ty, I won't last."

His lips met mine in a sloppy kiss. "Good, neither am I. You feel fucking amazing. So tight, so *mine*."

I took his lips once more as my body combusted, come smearing my chest and Tyler's stomach. I had never felt so... *owned* by anyone in my life. Tyler Riley owned every part of me: mind, body and soul. He shuddered above me, his lips pulling away to release a shaky breath that said more than words ever could.

Aftershocks made our bodies tremble as we took in each other's breaths, wrapping ourselves in each other's smell.

I wrapped my arms around him and pulled him close. He didn't seem to mind the mess between us as he curled against my chest.

I felt as every rigid muscle softened, curving into me like it was where he belonged. And in my mind, he did.

Wrapped up in each other, we slowly drifted off to sleep.

Chapter Thirty-Nine

Tyler

I moved around the kitchen, the rhythmic clatter of utensils and the sizzling of ingredients filling the air as I did my weekly meal prep. Cal lounged on a bar stool, his eyes fixed on my back like it held the answer to a puzzle he was hellbent on solving.

"Cal..." I warned, sensing the mischievous grin spreading across his face.

"What!" he exclaimed, feigning an innocence that had me biting back a smile. "What kind of best friend doesn't spill the details of a drunken escapade? I think it's in the handbook that you have to. What if you needed an alibi for something?"

"Okay, Baby Cap, this isn't a crime drama. I didn't wake up next to a dead body, and I don't need you to prove my innocence."

Cal huffed dramatically. "You never know! It's crucial information, Ty."

I shot him a look over my shoulder. He sat with his hands outstretched as if he were dead serious. Which, with Cal, was always a possibility.

"I had way too much to drink and word vomited all over him," I explained. "He apologized, put me to bed, and agreed to talk when I was sober—end of story" I stayed focused on the stove, knowing that the heat creeping under my collar would give me away if I looked at him.

"That story being your pages glued together?" I risked a glance to see Cal waggle his eyebrows.

I grimaced at his odd analogy. "One doesn't kiss and tell, Cal."

"Ha! You don't need to tell—the carpet burn on your neck does it for you."

My heart raced and my hand shot up to cover my neck.

Cal erupted in laughter. "Got you! That was too easy."

I returned to the chicken and vegetables on the stove with a scowl. "Fine, we're... something. I don't know what the something is but we're exclusively, secretly something. So, if you could refrain from mentioning how you two..." I shuddered, unable to even say the words.

Cal jumped down from the stool and wrapped, his arms around me from behind. "I'm genuinely happy for you, Ty. Even if I think the whole closeted gay thing sucks."

When the hockey guys crammed into our dorm room, I suddenly became aware of the limited space. With their broad frames and towering builds, our apartment was transformed into something reminiscent of *Alice in Wonderland.* It felt like everyone had taken a potion that made everything shrink—including Jamie, who was wedged between Jarman and Mouse. I stood in the kitchen, putting a little too much focus into pouring a glass of water to calm my nerves. I struggled to keep my emotions in check when it came to a particular teammate of mine who hadn't shown up yet.

Though it was right on cue, a knock at the door made me flinch. Jamie rushed to answer it and Cal's boyfriend, Eric, shyly greeted everyone as he settled into Cal's side. Cal beamed as he kissed Eric's cheek, but then Eric pulled away, leaving Cal stand there awkwardly.

I shot Cal a questioning look, but he shook his head. I guess best friends didn't tell each other everything after all.

The door thudded again, distracting me from the internal struggle as Hunter walked in. I couldn't help but stare with hearts in my eyes as he chatted with Jamie and exchanged greetings with everyone else. I couldn't ignore the way he inquired about training, hanging onto Jamie's every word. I took the opportunity to take in his appearance.

Distressed jeans hung onto every curve, hugging his hips and thighs. A leather jacket hung open over a white tee, making me squirm. I guess a man in leather just did something to me.

Hunter glanced over and saw me staring, giving me a heart-stopping grin. The look in his eyes said everything his mouth couldn't in that moment, but he still leaned in to whisper, "Glad you like what you see baby."

Between Jamie's bed being folded into the sofa and the beanbags Jarman brought with him, everyone found a seat. Jamie chose to sit beside Cal and Eric while Hunter pulled me down between his legs and casually suggested, "No point sitting on the floor, Aus— we can share." I didn't get a chance to argue—it was less of a suggestion and more of an order.

Mouse did the same with Jarman, hopping onto the same beanbag without a second thought. Though no one missed the way Jarman tensed.

"Oh, come on!" Mouse whined, "we shared a bed all through middle school. You can handle sitting with me for a couple hours."

Jarman nodded, but it was tense with gritted teeth.

Hunter squeezed my shoulders—I wasn't the only one noting the tension between those two. As everyone sipped on fizzy drinks or beer, we settled in to watch the Hanukkah holiday hockey game. The dim light of the room afforded Hunter and I the privacy to exchange heated glances and soft touches. Eventually, I settled into a sense of comfort.

Maybe this wouldn't be so bad after all.

Chapter Forty

Hunter

The comfort of having Tyler between my legs while we watched the game went unnoticed by the others. I massaged his shoulders, relishing the way he melted under my touch. As the game concluded, Mouse commandeered the conversation and steered it toward his holiday plans.

"Jarman and his family usually come on after Christmas, and help eat all the leftovers. It's great! I get my family, and then my best friend and his family come the next day–like a second Christmas. Oh, and I'm trying to invite Jenny. I have a date with her tomorrow. Do you think it's too early to invite her to the cabin?" We all groaned simultaneously.

Eric, who'd been relatively quiet all night, scoffed, "Way too early. If someone asked me to meet their family within the first few months of a relationship — scratch that, the first *year* — I'd call them a stage-one clinger."

The room fell silent, and all eyes turned to Cal, who exchanged an awkward glare with his boyfriend.

Tyler appeared a bit irritated. "I don't know about that. It depends on the connection you have. Some people are married after a year."

I whipped my head down to my secret boyfriend. Marriage? Was this about us or his protective instincts toward Cal?

Eric shrugged. "Those people are crazy if you ask me."

"Or you could just have a commitment issue?" Jarman chimed in. "Because I think if you know, you just know. Time is just a social construct," Jarman's tone made the whole room tense.

Mouse, blissfully unaware of said tension, added, "Well, I think I'm going to ask her. I can always introduce her as a friend. I think she'd like skiing. If not, how romantic would it be if I taught her? It could be like one of those adorable rom-com movie moments, don't you think?"

Cal gave Mouse a soft smile. "Yeah, Mouse, I think that's super romantic. I'm tired and have an early morning skate, so I'm going to call it a night." He kissed Eric's cheek and headed down the hall to his room.

Tyler shot daggers at Eric. The air hung heavy with unspoken tension, until Tyler spoke "Thanks, Jarman, for organizing this. Really it's been great."

Jarman read the room. "Yeah, of course." Jarman tapped Mouse's shoulder and whispered something in his ear which had my hackles rising.

"Oh man!" Mouse groaned. "But I was just getting started," Mouse moaned. Jarman then followed his rebuttal with a simple look, and Mouse grumbled his way to his feet and out the door. Jarman's eyes followed him before he looked to Eric, who lingered with his eyes on Cal's door.

"Let's get out of their hair," Jarman said with a pointed glare at Eric, who finally got the message. I watched as they headed to the door, then, Mouse turned to me. "Hunter?"

"I'll help clean up. I'll see you back at the house. " Mouse shrugged and left, and I didn't miss the way Jarman's lip turned up in a knowing grin.

Once the others had left, Tyler grabbed my hand and led me to his room, he yelled goodnight to Jamie who was re-making the futon into a bed. As I entered, I couldn't help but notice the meticulous organization. His desk, adorned with anatomy books and a notebook filled with detailed sketches and descriptions, caught my eye. Not a single thing was out of place, even his stationary meticulously arranged in a line.

"Baby, your highlighters aren't even out of place," I observed, impressed by the orderliness.

Tyler shrugged nonchalantly and sat on his neatly made bed. "I try to keep control where I can."

He looked at me, seemingly expecting me to find his organization unusual. It dawned on me that perhaps he had faced judgment for being meticulous. "Has someone judged you for being a little over the top with it?"

Tyler lifted his hand, tilting it side to side. "My teammates always called me a little neurotic. Mum used to say I was always an organized kid, but then dad died, and Mum got sick…"

I joined him on the bed and wrapped my arms around him, finding comfort in the fact that he didn't resist. We lied down—fully dressed for once—and curled together on top of the sheets. "I think you are perfect just the way you are," I reassured him.

Tyler remained silent, pondering my words. "What about you, Hunter? What's your quirky trait?"

I thought about it before confessing, "I'm a little impulsive—I don't always think things through. The only time I do is around my father. Maybe that's my way of taking back a little control. So if there ever comes a day we live together, you get to point out all the annoying habits I have. Now, knowing you're a bit of a control freak, everything I do is going to annoy you. Sorry in advance."

Tyler chuckled, but then pulled away, a serious expression in his eyes. "Hunter, your dad: you said he was bad and controlling… but how far does that go? Other than him hitting you— which stops now, by the way."

I released a deep sigh. "He hits, he has money and people in high places." I wanted to leave it at that, hoping the expression on my face conveyed how much I didn't want to talk about him. It felt like discussing him in the same space as Tyler would somehow tarnish the air around us.

"I don't want you around him, Hunter. I know I have no place making that decision for you, but I refuse to see you like that." His blue-green gaze hit me right where it hurt. I pulled him to my chest in the hopes that having his lips close to my heart would heal the ache there. "I am doing everything I can to cut ties with him, Ty. I promise you that."

And I meant it. In the hours between him being in my bed and me being at his place, I met with Connor Bellamy. I half expected Tyler to comment on my attire, as it was fancier than most would wear to watch a hockey game on the couch.

I met Connor in a small diner away from campus, in an area my father wouldn't typically pass through. It might have been a bit excessive, but it was necessary. If my father caught wind of me making deals that didn't align with his expectations, it wouldn't end well.

I didn't want to tell Tyler yet that I had been talking to Connor about potential offers, I'd asked him to put out feelers to see if anyone would be interested in signing me. I had good stats, and that year was my best yet. The risk would be that I could throw away the chance of better offers after the season ended, but I'd have to cross that bridge when I got to it.

"Listen, kid, you've got talent. I've seen it, and my contacts have seen it. The consensus is clear: — they're eager to assess your potential post-season—, after the draft—to see if you're a fit for their team. They're looking for consistent performance, just like what you're delivering now."

I nodded, anticipating that very scenario.

"I know this isn't your normal case, sir, and I know you usually have clients who probably want bigger things. It's just... I need a contract. I need it bad after this year. I need to cut ties with my father, and he isn't the nicest of men. Breaking free of him is the dream first, sir. As I mentioned on the phone, I'm happy to settle for AHL and work my ass off to move up."

Connor's face tightened and he gave me a grim nod. "You may not fit the usual profile of my clients, but I recognize significant potential in you. Ordinarily, I'd advise waiting until the season concludes. However, what I can share is that my contact coaching the Vancouver AHL team is actively seeking skilled defensemen. If we navigate this strategically, considering the imminent retirement of their NHL defenseman and no plans to trade for another player, there's a chance they might bring you forward. It's a calculated risk, but are you up for it?"

My heart raced. "Yes, sir. That would be an amazing opportunity—and the farther away from my father, the better."

Connor smiled sympathetically. "I thought as much. I've already had a chat with my associate, and he's genuinely eager to secure you for the upcoming season, having reviewed the videos I forwarded to him. Now, I've got this contract for you to go through. If it aligns with your aspirations, you'll be an official AHL player by Christmas. The plan is for you to kick off the next season, allowing you to conclude your current season with your existing team."

A stark white wad of paper hit the table, and suddenly, all the noises around me became pronounced. The chime of the bell had me looking at the door, as if my father might walk in at any moment. But it was only a group of college kids, their laughter almost mocking my paranoia.

"Do you mind if I read it now? Or are you in a rush?" I asked.

Connor signaled to the passing waitress in place of a response "Hey, can I get the burger with fries, please?"

She blushed, nodding frantically, "Of course, sir."

I laughed, spinning the papers right side up, and began to read. "You must get that a lot."

"You will too one day, but just wait until you're in the leagues. But the last thing we need is a kid with scandals following him around." I tried to swallow the lump in my throat, knowing that Tyler and I could become the biggest scandal in the history of hockey.

"I know, sir. Hockey first, I promise." I lied.

Half an hour later, I'd read through every line of the very detailed contract. The money was decent—not NHL money, but enough to survive. I tried not to think of the man I had in my bed that morning and the promise that we would be a team both on and off the ice. My freedom meant his safety, and I had no intention of swaying his future.

The pen felt heavy in my hand, the scratch of my signature like an arrow shot into the air toward my future.

Connor nodded and took the papers from me. "Take it as reassurance, kid; this isn't selling out. Maintain the level of play you've been delivering, demonstrate to the league what they've been overlooking, and mark my words— I'll be dialing you up to announce you're getting the call-up."

"Thank you, sir." I put out my hand, and he just laughed.,

"I'm your agent now, just stick with Connor."

I rephrased my thank you and watched him leave, the bell of the door signaling the finality of my choice.

My teeth anxiously gnawed on the inside of my gums, and the feeling in my stomach felt far from elation. I closed my eyes tightly, telling myself I just needed to get through to the end of the season. Finishing this college year would be my new beginning—**our** new beginning.

Chapter Forty-One

Tyler

Finally.

Finals were over. I was exhausted, but relieved. It felt like I could finally breathe, and I'd have time to shift my focus entirely on Jamie.

As I stumbled into the dorm, he looked up from his book, offering a nod of acknowledgment. Red-rimmed eyes met me, and the weight of the day laid heavy in the room—it was Mum's birthday. We had an unspoken agreement not to mention it, and I respected that as I gave him a silent kiss on the forehead before going straight to the kitchen. As I scoured the fridge, a thought crossed my mind to break my diet. Though what I really wanted was a drink.

Dad was always the one who orchestrated week-long celebrations for Mum's birthday. After he was gone, I kept up the tradition, though it always felt like rubbing salt in the wound. Jamie, never one to fake smiles, made it clear that my efforts were in vain. Now with Mum gone, I wondered how dad would keep her memory alive.

A knock on my door interrupted my thoughts. I shot a look at Jamie, who was engrossed in his book. When he looked at me and shrugged, I moved to open it. Then my heart skipped a beat.

Hunter stood there in dark jeans and a hoodie, wearing that brown leather jacket that made his eyes shine.

"Boston," I sighed. I intended on sounding puzzled, but the smile he gave me swept that right out the window.

"Hey baby," mischief sparkled in his eyes as he held up a pair of skates. "So, I know a certain special someone in your life had something they never got to check off their bucket list..."

I clenched my teeth as rising tears blurred the image of Hunter in front of me. He remembered. It was one of those mindless conversations we had while cuddled in my bed, but he remembered. I peered over my shoulder to Jamie, who looked at Hunter with glossy eyes.

"Let me get changed." He shot off his bed and rummaged through his bag before darting into the bathroom.

"Hunter..."

"Don't thank me, Baby. Just because she isn't physically here doesn't mean we can't celebrate with her. Let's embrace the life she wanted."

I launched myself into his arms, the skates clattering to the floor so he could accommodate me. I wondered if this would ever get old, being in his arms—a loud voice in my mind shut that thought down almost as fast as it disappeared.

"Tyler, stop molesting your boyfriend and get changed!" Jamie demanded. "I want to skate!"

I let go of Hunter to see my brother rugged up to the nines with his own pair of skates in his hand. Jamie did like to skate, but MMA was something that he and dad could have together. It didn't hurt that he was good at it either. I saluted him and quickly went to get changed.

I came out of my room to see Hunter flicking through the book Jamie had been reading. "Have you read all her books?"

"Nah, I uh... Only just started," Jamie flustered. "I know they're for adults, but it kind of makes me feel closer to her. I hear her voice and ..." Jamie trailed off, cheeks fire engine red.

I scuffed his hair. "I get it, kid. I never thought of that before but maybe now I'll start."

I watched his face relax. Mum did tend to write... let's be honest, it was smut. Maybe it wasn't appropriate for someone Jamie's age to be reading it, but I wasn't going to be the asshole to stop him if it was the one thing that brought him some comfort.

We stepped out of Hunter's car, greeted by the sight of an open ice rink. Families laughed and skated around, a distant melody of Christmas music filling the air. Inhaling the crisp, cold air, I took a mental snapshot of the scene before me as if I could capture it on a postcard and send it to wherever Mum might be now. Snowflakes clung to my lashes and my now too-long hair— a feature I hadn't had the heart to trim since it was Mum's favorite. Though the frigid weather made me miss my beard.

"It's cold as balls," Jamie exclaimed, rubbing his gloved hands together.

Hunter laughed. "Bloody Aussies," playfully mimicking an Australian accent that sounded more British. I went to playfully shove him, but he caught my hand and brought it to his lips for a kiss.

"Ugh, you two are nauseatingly cute. Let's go skate," Jamie suggested, heading to the concession stand to get our tickets.

I paid over his shoulder, and soon we were lacing up our skates. The first glide on the ice brought a familiar sense of peace. "Mum would have loved this," Jamie said with a mix of sadness and wonder, his gaze taking in the twinkling fairy lights above us. My hand found his shoulder and squeezed, knowing that my traitorous voice would betray the emotions I felt. Hunter's hand squeezed mine, offering me the strength to move forward.

Nestled between my guy and my brother, we slowly circled the rink, silent witnesses to the world around us under the night sky. A couple of kids zipped past us, the sound of their skates cutting through the ice serving as music to my ears. I smiled unconsciously.

Inspired by the kids, Hunter leaned forward and locked eyes with James. "So, James: are you as quick as your Ty here?"

Jamie grinned, never one to back down from a challenge. "Not even close. But I'm faster than you."

Hunter's lips played with a rare smile. "Oh, yeah? Want to bet?"

Jamie raised an eyebrow, meeting Hunter's gaze beneath his snug beanie. "If I win, I get the bedroom, and you two get the couch."

Laughter erupted from all of us in acknowledgment of the amusing proposition.

"Sure, kid. Shake on it?" Hunter said, and they sealed the bet.

I positioned them side by side, my scarf in the air. "On the count of three."

The race began, and I leaned against the boards, watching as they dodged people in their pursuit. Hunter's longer legs effortlessly covered distance, but my little brother showcased surprising speed with his nimble legs. I caught the moment Hunter feigned exhaustion, and Jamie took the win. With a victorious grin, Jamie declared, "I won! Sofa for you two! Just keep it down because we all know Cal is the type to peek."

Bent over with laughter, Hunter and I enjoyed the banter. "Ah yes. But what you don't realize, is dorm beds are all springs. So the couch is softer—and un-christened."

Jamie's face twisted in disgust. "Ew! Okay, can I just have a hot Milo instead?"

Hunter looked confused.

"A hot chocolate," I explained. "But while we're teaching you Aussie terms, we call it hot choccy."

Hunter smiled, gliding to my side and wrapping his arm around my back. "Okay, baby, let's get you Aussies some hot choccys." His 'Aussie accent' may have been terrible, but I found myself enjoying it from his lips. Unaware that I was staring at them, Hunter leaned down and kissed me, soothing me when I tensed in his arms.

"No one knows who we are here, so right now, you're mine."

I bit my lip in an attempt to restrain three little words from spilling out. We skated out of the rink, Hunter holding my hand under the twinkling lights. Even before the hot chocolate hit my system, I could feel the warmth of Mum watching over us. If she were here, she would be on the sidelines, a soft smile gracing her lips.

Chapter Forty-Two

Hunter

I found myself drifting around Tyler's body in the kitchen, following his directions carefully as he walked me through what to do. I had zero skills in the kitchen, so I soaked up every word, trying to commit them to memory.

"You don't eat carbs?" I questioned, noting the lack of any in the meal. I was fully aware of his strict diet, but it only unveiled another layer of his need for control.

"I try to avoid them. I don't want extra shit to work off if I can avoid it. I don't really drink either but there's something about certain hockey parties that always gets me sloshed."

I chuckled. "Sloshed?"

Tyler shot me a smirk over his shoulder. "Uhm, you know, drunk, hammered, smashed?"

"You have the weirdest sayings."

He playfully pointed the spatula at me, wearing his favorite fake frown that I found adorable. "Don't get me started on American slang."

I raised my hands in surrender. "Alright, baby."

He hummed, his gaze flickering to my lips before he peered over my shoulder to make sure his brother was still engrossed in the book he was reading.

I inched closer, trailing my fingers over Tyler's firm ass in his sweats. A muffled moan escaped him as he shuffled on the spot, doing little to appease my growing desire.

"What are you doing to me?" he whispered. I bit my lip to suppress a happy chuckle.

I glanced at Jamie—who was either oblivious or intentionally ignoring us—then edged even closer, blowing a breath across the back of his neck. He leaned back into me, his head finding a resting place on my shoulder.

"Miss me, baby?" I murmured, evoking a whimper from him. It had been over a week since we last had sex, and it seemed the craving was mutual. I wrapped my arms around him, grazing my lips over his neck. He carried a scent of earth and oceans, a combination that never failed to clear my lungs. We stayed like that while he continued to cook, his body enveloped by mine. I only looked up with the distant notes of music playing in the background.

Jamie stood by a record player, seemingly unfazed by our canoodling. "Mum loved records," he simply stated, returning to his book without another word.

I sensed Tyler's uneven breaths and held him tighter. I felt him move against me, and as we began to sway over the simmering dinner, I rested my chin on his shoulder, choosing not to acknowledge the wet tears that landed on my arms. "Mum and Dad always did this," he explained. "Dad was the cook, so Mum would put a record on and hug him from behind. They would sway to the music as he cooked."

He didn't have to tell me that it was something he always wanted for himself. I kissed his neck, letting him know without words that as long as I was around, he'd have it—even if I did have two left feet. I would die to give him anything he wanted.

We stayed that way for a couple of songs until he turned off the stove and began to dish up the plates.

We ate in a circle on the floor. Tyler explained that it was his dad's favorite meal, and I watched as Jamie closed his eyes with the memories that came with the flavors on his tongue. Eventually, we sat in silence, watching hockey on mute as my mind swirled with memories of the day. Jamie eventually dozed off, snoring softly from the bed while Tyler rested his head on my shoulder. I closed my eyes, savoring the feeling of him nuzzling into my neck. I couldn't even find the energy to mock him for taking in a deep breath to inhale my scent—because I did the same thing to him any chance I could get.

We stayed like that for so long that my ass began to hurt. I pulled away, only for him to lay me down on the hardwood floor. His weight had the same effect I'd imagined from those overpriced weighted blankets. Tyler's breath was like the soft, summer breeze off the coast of the Hamptons, sweeping away a lifetime's worth of anxiety.

We didn't talk. It was almost like there was too much to unpack. Instead, we chose to sit in comfortable silence.

My lip twitched every time Tyler grunted or let out an annoying huff at the game, but I couldn't bring myself to focus on it. I found peace in my fingers going through his still hair, the strands turning more auburn as it grew. The golden hues sparkled in the lamplight as it fell from my fingertips.

There were many moments the word love popped into my mind when it came to Tyler Riley, many moments where I tried to deny the fact that I was falling for him.

But it was all in vain. And it was such a bittersweet feeling.

Because come summer, I would be gone.

CHAPTER FORTY-THREE

Hunter

I sat in my driver's car, engrossed in the videos Cal sent me while fighting off the surge of longing that passed through my veins. I wanted nothing more than to be there with Tyler, Cal, and Jamie, sharing in the warmth of their holiday festivities. My gaze shifted to the brownstone home I'd grown up in, and my stomach churned.

I weighed my options. How bad could it possibly be if I left now? How long could I resist the urge to witness Jamie and Tyler unwrap their presents in person? I decided to bide my time and catch a glimpse of the joyous moment.

I'd recruited Cal weeks ago to capture the gift opening. "We should wait for him to get back," Tyler suggested. Despite being in their dorm room, Cal had transformed the space into a place Santa Claus himself would be proud of, determined to infuse the holiday spirit into their lives. Both Tyler and Jamie were adjusting to an American Christmas already and though they were more inclined toward a quiet celebration, Cal wasn't having that.

"Nope, he wants you to open them now," Cal insisted, unwavering in his commitment to creating a spirited Christmas for his friends. The air buzzed with anticipation, and I couldn't help but share in the excitement, even from the confines of the car. Cal eagerly shoved the presents in their faces, and I watched the video anxiously as Tyler and Jamie began tearing at the wrapping paper.

Jamie went first and though it was a challenge to find something for a fourteen-year-old boy, I did my research. I discovered special editions of their mom's books, signed and unique. Alongside them, I included purchased photos from the ice rink. Before the books, a framed picture caught Jamie's attention: a moment frozen in time with Tyler's hand on his shoulder, both looking up at the lights in awe. Jamie studied the image, biting his quivering lip, then moved on to the books. As he opened them, his fingers traced the edges, discovering his mom's cherished signature. I glanced at Tyler, hoping the stunned expression on his face was a good one.

With tear-filled eyes, Jamie urged Tyler to open his gifts. Tyler unwrapped a hockey stick signed by his favorite player and a smaller package containing a leather bracelet with a gemstone orb. Tyler brought it to his eye, revealing a picture of us kissing at the ice rink. It was a silent declaration, a way to show him that even if we couldn't make our relationship public, we were bound together forever. The video cut off as Tyler looked at the gift thoughtfully, leaving me yearning to be there, to ask him if he liked it, to share in the joy of the moment. I could imagine what he would say.

"That was too much, Boston. But thank you."

Aussie Baby: Fuck you for making me open this without you here. Not fair when I can't show you how much it means to me. Hurry up and come home.

Home.

I flinched as the tell-tale sound of knuckles on glass pulled me from my daydream. I looked up into the disapproving face of my father, then opened the door to the black four-door coupe. My eyes briefly met Silas's uncertain glance from the driver's seat.

"You have a Merry Christmas; tell Delta I said hi," I told him, attempting to keep the interaction as cordial as possible under my father's intense glare. "I sent some gifts over for you and the kids."

Silas managed a smile, though it didn't quite reach his eyes. "Thank you, Mr. Hunter. What time would you like me to come pick you up?"

"Don't worry about it; I'll organize my own ride. You go enjoy Christmas with your family," I replied, my decision firm.

Silas hesitated, gaze flickering to my father's. "Be safe, Mr. Hunter," he finally said.

I pondered if time was on my side. Should I have said more? Attempted to offer reassurance that I would be okay? Instead, I opened the door and bypassed my father on the way to the front door.

Inside, I was greeted with a directive from my father. "I need you to be on your best behavior. I have a guest with us tonight, and she was important to me, so no backtalk, do you hear me?" The once-masculine house now resembled a scene from a Bloomingdale's catalog, Christmas having overtaken my father's space. I rubbed my chest, trying to massage away the ache of a boy who once yearned for that time of year. Memories long forgotten resurfaced but the music, once a source of joy, had become closer to torment.

I took in the festive scene as I watched my father effortlessly navigate the room until he stood in front of an attractive blonde. She showed no sign of aging, looking timeless in a black dress with her hair swept away from her face. I couldn't help but wonder if she was closer to my age than my old man's. His expression softened as he gazed at her, his tall frame leaning in for a kiss where her golden hair met flawless skin. I caught my dad's eye, and he exchanged a glance with the woman before taking her hand and leading her my way.

"Hunter, this is Brittney. Brittney, my son, Hunter."

She flashed a confident smile, the kind a lioness would wear as the head of her pride. "So lovely to meet you, Hunter; your father speaks so highly of you." She initiated a polite kiss on the cheek, and I reluctantly followed suit.

My brain fired off snarky comebacks, but I swallowed them all and played the part. "Likewise, you look lovely this evening."

Before I could attempt a conversation, my grandfather appeared behind me. "Hunter," he greeted with a firm hand on my shoulder holding me in place.

I was well aware of my father's posture straightening in the lingering presence of *his* dad. Shifting sideways, I escaped the tight hold on my shoulder, but the relief was short-lived as I now found myself under the judgmental gaze of two Graves men. As always, the conversation shifted to business—even on Christmas. My father fielded relentless questions about cases and profits, defending our status as the top law firm in the country as if he were in a courtroom.

"Don't worry, son. Young Hunter will be with you soon and then you'll have everything straightened out. Isn't that right, Hunter?" my grandfather remarked.

I could do nothing more than respond with a forced, "Yes, sir," concealing the fact that it was a lie. My father shot me a gaze that sent shivers down my spine.

"But I believe Dad's done an amazing job since your retirement," I deflected, hoping to please my parental figure by defending him in the presence of his own. "He's added some big names to the portfolio—and don't forget the Turner case.".

My grandfather let out a disapproving chuckle. "Got your son trying to make you look good? That says something, doesn't it, Dominic?"

Well, there went my hope for a good Christmas. The festive cheer was steadily slipping away, replaced by the weight of crushing expectation.

I quickly turned to the fire to work my jaw, which ached from all the fake smiles and schmoozing. The clock on the mantlepiece told me that I had been at it for two hours. Surely it had been longer than that. A waiter gave me a much-needed reprieve by announcing that lunch was ready to be served. *More like dinner at this rate.* I found myself wondering if other people's Christmases came with placement cards and foreign faces. The younger male sitting beside me looked all too eager to be here, and I fought the urge to roll my eyes. Maybe one day he'd figure out that the grown-ups' table wasn't all it was cracked up to be.

The young, bright-eyed man turned to me with, a broad smile on his face. "Hey, I'm Miles You're Mr. Graves' son, right?"

I nodded, not really wanting to engage in any more conversation. *Where the hell was this food?* I gulped down the glass of red wine in front of me as an excuse not to talk, but the smooth burn of the alcohol was needed.

"You play hockey, right?" I froze, feeling more than one set of eyes hit me from either end of the table.

I nodded again but kept my eyes forward, hoping that the guy would realize I wasn't interested in the conversation. I caught the glare from my father and my stomach twisted.

Unfortunately for me, Miles kept talking. "I've watched your games. Man, you are good. Especially this year. You're on fire—especially with that Australian dude. I'm a bit of a hockey lover myself. Can't play for the life of me, so I make it up by the number of games watched."

A plate was set in front of me, and I was grateful for the distraction. The food should have been amazing—Dad would expect nothing but the best—but it might as well have been chalk in my mouth. I couldn't taste anything, and the texture only made me sick as I felt eyes on me throughout the whole meal.

I checked the time, knowing I only had about an hour left for dinner before they retreated into the lounge for refreshments. That's when I would politely excuse myself and get the hell out of dodge so I could be with the people that truly mattered. My phone buzzed in my pocket for what felt like the hundredth time, but I ignored it like I had for the last few hours. If my father caught me looking at my phone, I knew my chances of getting out of there would be slim to none.

"So," Miles knocked my shoulder playfully. "Were you planning on going into the league, or will I be seeing you in the office?"

"Last year of hockey," I mumbled, hoping he would get the message.

"Oh, that sucks. It's not like the office is going anywhere; surely your father would love to see his son in the big leagues. You really have the potential."

Would this guy ever shut up? I looked over to my father, who eyed me with his hands folded on the table.

"No, I want to work for the company. Hockey is just a hobby," I said again, keeping my tone flat as I downed another drink. I looked to my father again, who'd looked away to say something to Brittany. I let out a sigh of relief, hoping I passed his test.

Thankfully, young preppy Miles changed the subject and began rambling about gold stats. I kind of felt sorry for the guy—nowhere to be for Christmas except this dull party, with my snooty family and 'future work colleagues.' If things were different, I may have even liked the guy. But instead, I sat with a glass in my hand feeling like I was in the hot seat.

With lunch finished, I was finally able to snag a private moment to check my phone.

As soon as the screen turned on, multiple messages popped up.

Aussie Baby How's your day going?

(11:00)

Aussie Baby : Are you nearly done? I want to thank you for your gifts.

(14:00)

> **Aussie Baby:** I'm probably being paranoid, but is everything okay?

(16:00)

> **Aussie Baby :** Can you just text me telling me everything is okay? Tell me you're stuck in a boring family event and that's why you haven't messaged me.

(18:00)

> **Aussie Baby:** Okay, I know this way past one message too many, but can you please let me know you're okay?

(19:00)

> **Aussie Baby:** I know I'm acting like some crazed boyfriend, but past experience of you being with your father is making me worried. And you said you would be here after lunch—hours ago.

(20:00)

I hadn't estimated the lunch running late, and now I was stuck in the refreshments room trying to escape. Every time I inched towards the door, another person pulled me aside to talk nonsense about things ranging from current affairs to my professors at school. I'd begun to grow tired of keeping my mask up, and it was getting hotter with every drink I had. The fire blazed with no reprieve; even taking off my jacket was inappropriate—God forbid I looked anything other than professional. Also, my father hated my tattoos; if they were on show, he would not be pleased.

Time passed, and it was like my father knew every time I tried to duck out—I was intercepted every time. I felt my phone vibrate in my pocket, letting me know someone was calling. Having had enough of talking to Mr. Hayes, who was discussing the current stock market, I gestured to the device in my hand. "So sorry. I have to take this."

I left the stuffy room full of even stuffier people and ducked into my dad's office. I perched on the large, wingback chair and answered the call.

"Boston?" That familiar voice soothed me more than the copious amounts of alcohol I'd consumed.

"Hey, baby." I sighed in relief.

"What the hell, have you not heard of replying to a text? A simple 'I'm okay' would have sufficed."

I leaned my head against the cool leather. "I know, baby. I'm sorry. My father has been watching me like a hawk, and I haven't had a chance to get away at all. Every time I try, I'm cornered by some stuffy businessman."

"Okay...Promise you're okay?" I didn't like the weariness in his tone.

"Yeah, baby. Not a single mark on me. I just need to find a safe escape out of here, so my father doesn't get mad."

Tyler hummed. "Okay. Well, come home soon, yeah?"

"I'll work on it, baby, promise." Those three magic words lingered on my tongue, but it wasn't the time or place.

"Good, see you soon, Boston."

"See you soon."

I hung up the call and stood, shaking off the nerves. I shimmed the handle and went to pull, only for it not to budge. I frowned and tried again—nothing.

My brain registered that it was locked, but I continued to try as the panic set in. I rested my head against the hardwood and listened to the distant clinking of glasses, knowing that no one would hear me if I called out. My father's soundproof office was designed that way and could only be locked on either side by a key—that my father kept on him at all times. I gritted my teeth, looking around even with the knowledge that the room had no windows. All I could do was wait it out. I considered messaging Tyler, but I didn't want him caught up in that mess. If there was nothing else, I learned from an early age, it was to never get anyone else involved.

I tried that once—and instantly regretted it.

My head began to pound, and not from the alcohol.

I slid down the wood until my ass hit the ground, dropping my head into my hands as I fought off the memories.

"Please, I'm sorry. I'm sorry!"

"Sorry for what? Huh?"

I stood in the kitchen, legs shaking nervously. I fiddled with the sleeves of my black suit, fighting the urge to loosen the tie that was getting tighter around my neck by the second.

"I didn't mean to! I didn't! But he was saying horrible things about mama, and I couldn't take it."

The replay of my grandfather calling my mother a pathetic, useless drunk made me snap. I remember the looks on everyone's faces as I called my grandfather a fucking asshole—but it was my mother's funeral.

"You never **ever,** talk to your elders like that. Show some respect!" His hand slapped the bench in warning.

"He called Mom a drunk!" I yelled, forgetting my place.

"Your mother **was** a drunk, she killed herself because she drank too much and decided to drive! We have drivers for fuck's sake, son. Your mother was a stupid woman! So, you have no right to call out your grandfather for telling the truth!"

His hand came across my face hard enough for me to fall to the ground, clasping my face, tears falling in a mixture of hurt and hatred. I didn't want to believe a thing coming out of his mouth.

"You're wrong! She was side-swiped coming to pick me up from hockey!" I yelled, the fire in my body too hot, the fury having my mouth running despite knowing the consequences. I'd never believe them…She loved us, she loved **me**. She'd never have driven drunk. My father's leather shoe dug into my exposed ribs, stopping me from saying another word. I coughed and spluttered, vomit creeping up the back of my throat.

"You will not speak to me like that! You never yell at your father!"

He kicked me again. I saw the black shape come in. Kaiser—-my driver, and more of a father than anyone had ever been—swung his fist, connecting with my father's jaw. Despite the pain, adrenaline had me sitting up, watching with wide eyes as I watched my father figure defend me against my actual father.

"Hunter, leave. Now!" Kaiser called as he swung again.

I backed up, but I didn't leave, unable to tear my eyes away from the scene unfolding in front of me. Kaiser wasn't a big man, much smaller than my father, but he defended me like a heavyweight champion going for the gold.

Until he took a single hit.

One hit of my father's fist to his temple had his eyes rolling back in his head, then he hit the corner of the counter. Somehow, I knew he didn't feel its impact.

I was frozen in my spot, looking at Kaiser's chest, and praying to anyone listening that it would rise. I prayed and I prayed, and I prayed and. When I realized that my prayers were going to be unanswered, a broken sob tore through me.

"See that as a warning, son. You will toe the line, you will never make a scene in front of colleagues and family, ever. Because it's not only you I can put in place."

My father stood tall and after shaking out his bloody fist, he left the kitchen. I sat sobbing in the corner, watching as security guards took Kaiser's body away.

"Fuck." I swore, looking into the empty fireplace. I took out my phone and fired off a message to Tyler.

> Hey baby, sorry I won't be able to make it there tonight. Don't worry, I'm fine, but I need to show face. I'll just stay here tonight. Merry Christmas, Baby.

> **Aussie Baby:** What? You're serious?! I don't like this. I'm coming to get you out of there. I don't like you being around him, Hunt."

All I could do was turn my phone off and watch the clock.

I'd moved to the wingback chair and didn't realize I'd had fallen asleep until I felt a foot roughly knock mine. I briefly opened my eyes, taking in the mahogany wood that closed in around me, the large body of my father in the center of its walls. He undid his suit jacket with calm indifference, rolling his sleeves up and transforming into a much less professional version of himself. I swallowed hard, knowing it was in my best interest to stay quiet.

He walked to the drink stand, pouring himself a whiskey before leisurely going to the front of his desk, leaning against it, and lifting his glass to the light, admiring the golden liquid swirling against the crystal.

"So, I heard the funniest thing." He took a sip of his drink before hanging the glass at his side, his dark eyes now seeking out mine. I stayed still, trying not to act like I had something to hide.

"No? Not going to bite? Okay…" He nodded his head before continuing, "I overheard a rumor of a certain agent visiting the ice. I *also* heard he took a particular interest in my son."

I involuntarily gulped, heat beginning to flush my body as my heart began to race.

"I thought to myself, surely my son would shoot him down. We had a deal, an arrangement. Not to mention my son is now in my debt." My father closed the gap between us.

"Sir, I—-"

A smack rang out in the quiet room. My cheek burned, a line stinging across the flesh telling me that his signet ring had broken.

"I did *not* say you could speak." His voice reverberated off the walls.

I could do no more than nod obediently.

"So, imagine my surprise when my informant sees you at a cafe with said agent, signing papers you have *no fucking right* to be signing!"

That made me shoot to my feet. "You had me followed!"

My father laughed and I flinched, anticipating another hit. Instead, he walked around his desk.

"Yes, because you have *never* stayed in line, son. You openly have threesomes with both men and women on a regular basis, you get your body tattooed, skip class and frankly, find every way you can think to rebel. So, I need to keep an eye on you. One, to stop the PR nightmare you could be for me, and two, so I know when to rein you in. You should be lucky I've cut you so much slack."

I wanted to roll my eyes, but I tightened my lips and kept my eyes on him. He shot me a smarmy smile that made my blood run cold.

"I gave you some free rein to be young and stupid because you sure as shit won't be doing that when you work for me."

I ground my teeth, the words on the tip of my tongue: I don't want to work for you.

Seeing my answer in my eyes drew another evil laugh from the man. "Oh, you *will* work for me, son. Whether you like it or not. I'll make sure of it."

The silence that fell over the room was deafening.

"It seems threats don't work on you, son." He smacked some photos onto the desk, and I stood, blood rushing in my ears as I saw pictures of me at the ice rink with Tyler and Jamie.

I snapped, "Don't you dare go near them!" My body vibrated, my hands balling into fists at my side with the need to hit something.

But my father wasn't threatened by me. He only laughed. "Well, that depends, son. Will you continue to play this happy little family thing?"

I blinked. "It's my life, Dad. I'm done with this. You can't keep threatening to hurt people just because you don't like them."

"That's where you are wrong. Who will touch this boy when they find out he is gay? A gay Australian who's only been on the radar for half a season? No one; he's a PR nightmare."

Tyler's fears rushed through my mind. His entire life was in my hands.

"I see we have reached an agreement. You'll cut ties with the boy, and then I'll stay away from him."

I nodded, because there was nothing else I could do. Though my heart threatened to burst right out of my chest.

"Now for our other issue: hockey."

I took a step back, noting the change in his tone.

"You took a contract, and you thought I wouldn't find out?"

 I retreated another step.

"It's what I want to do, Dad. It's what I love; it's what makes me happy. Doesn't that matter to you?"

"No! You belong to me; you are destined to work *for me*!"

I heard the crash before I felt the splash of liquid. Alcohol burned the back of my neck as small pieces of crystal stung my flesh.

I tried to shake off the resounding echo of smashing glass.

Hands gripped the lapels of my jacket. I was no small guy, but unfortunately for me, neither was my father. He was half an inch taller than me, and he weighed more. I gripped his hands, trying to pull him off me.

"I'll make sure you never play hockey again."

He shoved me hard against the wall. I fought him, driving my knee into his groin. He swore and bowed over, freeing me from his hold. I bolted for the door in the hopes it would be unlocked.

It wasn't.

I spun on my heel, about to look for a key while he was down. My head slammed into the door as he grabbed the back of my head.

Black spots blurred my vision. He knocked the breath out of me with a blow to my ribs. I tried to wrench out of his grip, but he pounded my ribs until my knees buckled.

Then he let go and watched me fall.

I brought one arm up to protect my head as his foot hit my stomach.

I tasted blood on my tongue.

He reared back to kick me again, but I caught him by surprise, wrenching his leg and sending his large body hurling to the ground. A crash rang out as a leather chair toppled over. I scrambled to my feet, thoughts of escape running through my mind.

My father went to get up, but I caught the glimpse of the key shining around his neck. I knew then what I had to do.

It was time for my father's reign of terror to end.

 I lunged for him, getting a blow to his face just as he did the same to me.

My ears rang from the punch that hit the side of my face but I fought.

It was my only choice to fight.

I wrapped my hand around his throat, tightening my grip with the little strength I had left.

My father grappled under me, latching his hands around my neck.

My lungs began to burn from the lack of oxygen.

I tightened my grip on my right hand, my left reaching for the chain.

With one swift tug, the metal snapped under my grasp.

I had the key.

I closed it tight in my first and let it dangle in front of his face. The shock was enough to make him loosen his grip—just enough so I could get free. I bolted to my feet, driving one into his stomach for good measure before rushing to the door and fiddling with the lock.

My heartbeat thudded in my ears, ticking down each second I had to get the door unlocked. I felt like a character in a horror movie with the killer on my heels. My hands shook as the key finally found its slot and I turned the handle.

The shuffle of feet had me panicking to open the door, my heart stuck in freefall as a hand clasped my shoulder.

"Get your fucking hands off him." I staggered as the door flew open and a fist hurled past my face and landed in my father's jaw.

Aussie?

My shoulder was freed as my father stumbled.

"You will pay for that! don't think I won't press charges!" My father seethed, attempting to launch himself at Tyler.

I moved to block his path.

"Easy." *Jarman?*

"I would *love* to see you try," Tyler said with a confidence no man should have when taking on my father.

"You think people will believe I laid a hand on my son? He has a history of being a hothead on the ice. They'll only believe that my brute of a kid hit me first. He has a history of assault, you know? That broken nose was a hard charge to drop when that kid's dad was a barrister. But money and favors always talk. *This* was just self-defense."

Tyler laughed and took a step.

Then a younger voice shouted a warning. I looked to the door to see Jamie's wide eyes.

"Ha! Is that what you think? That you'll have your own son arrested? You wouldn't dare tarnish your family name like that. *You* would ruin the legacy you've worked so hard to build. What will the media think? That your own son hates you enough to touch you? Or that you bashed him shitless because of your fragile masculinity?"

I cried out when my father lunged for Tyler. Fears of the past flooded the present as I waited for the blow that would make history repeat itself.

Tyler took the hit to the chin but kept his composure, spitting blood in my father's face. "Admit it *Mr. Graves*, all you have is fists and no heart. All you want is to beat your son into submission but it hasn't worked up to now, has it?"

"He is my son, and I'll discipline him any way I like!"

"And that's with your fists, *you* hit him. So, what? He can't play hockey anymore? So he can finally be yours?"

"That stupid game started off as a great cover for the bruises he *earned* every time he failed me. But now he wants to use it as a way to get away from me. That will never happen."

I flinched as he lunged again, but this time it was Jarman who moved and held him back. I watched in awe as Tyler didn't move.

Tyler stood in front of my father's struggling form and, despite being shorter, he'd never looked bigger in my eyes.

"Here is what is going to happen, Mr. Graves. You will let your son go, or *he* will be pressing charges. There are multiple witnesses to what happened today. I have some amazing connections; you see, my mother was a world-renowned author, and I happen to know of a huge audience that would love to hear the story of someone with your power abusing your own child."

"And it's all on record." A man skirted around Jamie to enter the room with his phone in hand—Jarman's dad: The chief of police.

My father's face paled. I saw fear in someone who'd never felt it in his life.

"Hunter, if you would like to press charges, you have the chief of police backing you. We could have your father put away for a very long time."

"Son, don't do it." For the first time in my short years, my father begged.

I stood with a newfound strength, sneering down at the man that was supposed to protect me. "As Tyler said, *Father*, you will let me go. You will let me play hockey and live my life the way I want. You will never speak to me, touch me, or anyone I love again. If I find out you so much as looked at anyone, I will press charges, for so much more than my own abuse. I still haven't forgotten what you did to Kaiser."

The room went silent, and I heard my father grinding his teeth. His head jerked. It was barely a movement, but it was a nod.

"Fine."

Tyler backed away from him, instantly rushing to my side. He cupped my cheeks in his hands, scanning my body from head to toe. The pain that was written in those beautiful eyes of his outweighed the feeling of unconsciousness threatening to tug me under. His hand found mine, our fingers knitting together perfectly.

Somehow, despite the pain, I had never felt stronger.

I would have never been able to walk out of that house, knowing I won, without the man by my side.

CHAPTER FORTY-FOUR

Tyler

I knew something was wrong the moment I got that text.

In an instant, I was off the floor and getting dressed. I had my phone in my hand, calling the one person who knew Hunter better than I did: Jarman.

The next thing I knew, I had Cal driving just in case we needed a getaway car. I instructed Jamie to record no matter what. We followed Maps to Million Dollar Row.

The eerie silence of the house did nothing to quell my anxiety but the one thing I knew was that I was *not* letting the world take another person from me. Not now, not ever.

Jarman and his father were out of the car with us, and we entered the home, thankful the front door was unlocked. I followed the sound of a doorknob rattling until one swung open, revealing my man—covered in blood. My mood reflected the red that splattered Hunter's crisp white top.

Like exposing a weakness on the ice, I had to expose his father in order to secure my goal: to have Hunter free of his wrath once and for all.

With his final jerky nod, I knew we won. I rushed to Hunter, who was pale and bleeding. I had seen so many things in my life—my dad in a casket, my mum wasting away, but seeing his broken gaze and blood covering every inch of him broke me. I took him in my arms and Jarman was quick to help me with his weight.

"I've got you, babe," I whispered in his ear. "I have you."

"I want to go home."

His father needed to see my man walk out; he needed to see he couldn't break him.

"Use me as support and walk out of here, babe, one last time. Then it's done. You won, babe. It's you and me from here on out."

Glazed golden eyes looked back at me, and even though I knew he was in pain, he stood proud as we made our way out of the house that had been his prison.

As we got to the pavement, Jarman's father called out to us, "Get Cal to follow me; we'll get him checked out properly."

I nodded and slid into the back of the car. Hunter's head fell into my lap, and he looked up at me with tears streaking the blood that coated his face.

"You came."

"Always."

My hand brushed his blood-soaked hair off his face, noting the cut above his eyebrow—the one that used to be just a scar. I shifted, pulling off my cardigan, and blotted his head with it. Hunter didn't even wince, just looked at me like I was the only person in the world.

"I'm free."

"You're free, babe, now to get you healed so you can finish out one last season with me."

He sighed. "Why does it have to be the last?"

Hunter

I didn't really want to be sitting in that ER—and neither did Tyler. But that didn't stop him from sticking by my side the entire time. I could only imagine what this was like for him. He held my hand every second he could and if he was struggling, it didn't show. Other than worrying his bottom lip as they checked me out, he was my rock. I was cleared with nothing more than a minor concussion and a few cracked ribs. I got stitches just above my brow yet again, which had been sewn up too many times in my lifetime. After I gave a few reports, I was finally released.

Tyler visibly relaxed, letting out a sigh of relief as we stepped through the sliding glass doors. Snow fell around us and we'd barely cleared the threshold before I stood from the stupid, mandatory wheelchair and closed in on Tyler. I pulled his chin up so he would look at me, his turquoise eyes glistening with tears.

"Baby..."

"You fucking scared the shit out of me, Boston." The waver in his voice was like a knife to my heart. Despite how every move sent ripples of pain through my body, I held him close. He fisted my blood-soaked shirt tight, careful not to put his full weight on me. It would have been so easy to say how I felt right then and there. But I didn't—we'd been through too much that day and my brain hadn't had a chance to catch up.

"Lets go home," I said as I saw Jarman waiting patiently. We both got in the backseat and I clicked myself in the middle, resting my head on Tyler's shoulder. Somewhere between the methodical movement of his fingers in my hair and the slow hum of the engine, I fell asleep.

My Aussie woke me up with a gentle kiss on my forehead when we got to the dorm. I leaned over the middle console and patted Jarman on the shoulder. I hadn't gotten a glimpse of myself, but Jarman's sympathetic eyes had me believing I looked like utter shit—which wasn't far off from how I felt. The cold air hit my body in all the wrong places, my aching muscles tensing in protest to the frigid air. I bit back a groan as the pain flushed through my body in a wave that was enough to warm me up from the cold. Tyler didn't miss a beat, throwing my arm over his shoulder and helping me into the small two-bedroom apartment that had become more of a home than my million-dollar mansion.

Once we were in Tyler's dorm, I stood back as he checked on Jamie and tucked him in a little tighter before guiding me to the bathroom. Both of us too exhausted to speak, Tyler stripped me to my underwear and began running a cloth under warm water.

He gently brought the warm cloth to my bare skin, attempting to wipe away the evidence of the night. I watched as he took care of me, sparkling eyes taking in every mark and wiping the excess blood and iodine. I noticed the bruise blooming on his cheek and my blood began to boil. I kissed the mark, like my love could heal what my father did to him.

He turned his head just for a moment, resting his temple against mine, and breathing me in. I had no doubt I didn't smell great but if it bothered him, he didn't say. I watched as he found strength in himself to pull away, and then he left. I stood there wondering if that was it, if I was supposed to find him, or stay put and wait for him to return.

His quiet footfalls heading back in my direction somehow made me smile because my baby had grace even without the ice around him. He came in holding a chair, which he placed in front of the sink. "Sit," he commanded.

So, I did.

He softly guided me without his words, angling me so my head tilted over the basin. It was awkward at first, his body towering over me as he turned on the tap to warm water. The moment it hit my scalp, I let out a weighted sigh.

With the warm water running through the strands of my hair, I felt the night wash away.

With Tyler's fingers stroking through the strands, I felt him wash the past away.

With his fingers massaging the shampoo, I felt him building me back up, giving me strength with his fingertips.

As he began to wash out the soap, he swung his leg over my lap, sitting on my splayed-out legs. Soft kisses found my jaw, my Adam's apple and finally, my lips.

As he completed my hair, peppering kisses in between conditioning and its final rinse, I felt him love me. Tears fell without permission as my body absorbed everything that he was. Though I had cared for people and even loved before, I had never had a love like that. Never felt someone give over themselves like Tyler Riley gave himself to me.

As I sat on the chair with nothing but my briefs, Tyler's body seemed to tower over me in his Perth Hockey hoodie. Tears began to fall. It felt like Tyler was the one being vulnerable, showing me exactly how he felt, with every little touch. He might as well have been standing there stark-naked spilling his every emotion to me—telling me that he loved me.

That was the love that people wrote about, the love that lasted forever, through every fucked-up life hurdle. Tyler Riley would forever be the man I loved. Him and only him.

And he made me believe that I was that for him too.

CHAPTER FORTY-SIX

Tyler

I woke up more times than I could count, just to watch the rise and fall of his chest. Jamie even crept in a couple times to do the same, giving me a knowing look before retreating back to his bed. If Hunter seemed the slightest bit uncomfortable I adjusted him, hoping to make it even a little better.

Hunter's face when he opened that office door was etched into my memory. I'd seen Hunter smash men twice his size like a bug. But that look of pure fear as he tried to escape the grasp of his father… Fuck. I wish I'd one more than punch the fuckhead in the face. It took every last bit of restraint to not strangle him for what he'd done.

I found myself playing with the soft strands of Hunter's hair like it could keep him safe with me. "Mm, never stop doing that." His breath tickled my collarbone. *Never.* Despite everything, my lip quirked. I stayed quiet, but did as he requested.

Hunter lifted his head, letting my hand fall to his back. Hunter winced as he attempted to roll so he could see me. I pushed him to lie down and lifted myself on one elbow to look down into his honey-toned eyes.

Hunter's finger traced the outlines of my tattoo. "I've been curious about this…" 'What fire does not destroy; it hardens' 2.2. 2021' Oscar Wilde, right?" I nodded, watching him trace every curve of the script.

"Dad was a volunteer firefighter; he lived by those words, though they can be interpreted very literally. He always thought about how a fire affected the community. In times of trouble, people band together and become stronger in the face of destruction. I suppose when he died, the fire didn't destroy our family—not completely. It hardened us. We only got stronger and did what we needed to survive together."

Hunter looked up to me, bringing his hand up to cup my face. "*You* were stronger for your family, baby. You were hardened by what happened and made sure those you love were safe and cared for."

Part of me wanted to say, "Fat lot of good that did."

Logically, I knew I couldn't have saved Mum, but that ridiculous part of my brain spun with all the what-ifs.

What if I'd seen the signs sooner or pushed to see more specialists. "*What if, what if, what if.*"

Then there was Hunter. I *knew* his dad was bad news—I'd seen the evidence. And yet, I didn't do everything I could to stop him from spending Christmas there. The bruises that spanned the majority of his body were proof of that.

Most frustratingly, he read every thought that ran through my mind like they were tattooed on my forehead for him to see. "Baby, unless you magically could become a cancer-curing doctor before the age of seventeen, there was nothing you could have done for your mom. And there's no way to make my father a better man—except maybe a lobotomy. I'm the idiot for giving him so much control."

I growled. Yes, fucking *growled*, like some deranged Tasmanian devil, "He's your father, and your only family, you're not an idiot for giving him the time of day."

Hunter laughed, then winced. "Even if he hit me every time I was with him? You don't have to baby me, Ty. I'm an adult. I'm weak. Until I met you, I never considered following my own dreams. It was you who made me strong—strong enough to sign that contract and actually get away from him."

I blinked. Hunter's eyes widened.

"Contract?"

I pulled back in an attempt to read his features better. He scrambled in a mass of awkward limbs as he fought to get up, only to give in to the pain. Though it did nothing to quash the anger boiling my blood.

"I was going to tell you..."

I felt myself blinking at him, a kangaroo in the headlights, wondering if I stand my ground or get the hell out of the way or if I jump to the other side.

"It was after you slept in my dorm, before I came here for the game night. I saw Bellamy, and he got me signed to the farm team. I wanted to be free, to be a hockey player even if it isn't the NHL…"

I knew I looked like a blubbering fool, doing nothing but stare as I counted every time we'd seen each other leading up to Christmas. He never told me.

"Wh-where? When?" Hunter made to grab my hand, but I dodge just out of reach. I felt like I was back in that living room, dodging another flying sock on April Fool's.

I am not entirely sure if he paused before he responded, or if time simply slowed. But when he spoke, I heard him loud and clear: I had half a season with him, then he would be in *Canada*. I nodded, torn between being sad for myself and happy for the person I lo—liked. The person I *liked* very much.

I did the math: we would have until April.

Four months.

Fifteen weeks and five days.

One hundred and ten days.

But who was counting?

More than a summer fling, yet it was less than half a year.

Again—who was counting?

Would I stay and fall more in love with him?

Or would I be nothing more than a teammate and let him go so he could follow his dreams?

"Baby, we said through whatever happened…" Hunter reminded me of the conversation we had the morning he signed that very contract. But, all I could see after those one hundred and ten days was him in Canada and me in Boston. He'd be playing professionally, and I would be here, still trying to prove myself. I barely had time to take a shit, let alone manage a long-distance relationship. Hunter had wedged himself into my life *now*. In a perfect mold of sex before sleep, and sex before training. I knew it was so much more than just sex, but we'd gotten to know each other in between the heat and the passion. Again, I was stuck in between the what-if's of the future and the man before me.

I needed a break. I dressed in my running gear and grabbed my water bottle. Hunter followed me to the kitchen, wearing nothing more than his briefs—which was awfully distracting. Cal entered the room, eyes wide as he took in the muscular, bruised god trying to get my attention that I was somehow ignoring. I could be childish just this once, right?

"Can we please talk about this?"

I grunted, trying and failing to sound unaffected. "What is there to talk about, Hunter? I am happy for you, This is everything I wanted for you."

"What about us?" Hunter's voice was practically begging, and I almost halted. Almost.

"What about it? We have the rest of the season, then you'll be in Canada. From there, only time will tell." I shrugged, and I tried not to take note of his hurt expression because the moment I caught a glance of it, my chest constricted.

"You going for a run?" Cal interjected, and I hoped he saw the relief on my face at the interruption.

"Yeah, want to come?"

Cal rushed back into his room to change and I prayed to whatever higher power was listening that he wouldn't take too long.

"Baby..."

"Hunter, there's nothing to talk about."

Hunter assessed me, nodding but not looking any more dejected. He walked back to our room, ass looking annoyingly perfect in those undies.

"You are *not* going to lose him too, Tyler." I looked to Jamie, who'd silently watched the scene unfold from his bed. I wanted to protest because I felt like I was on a tightrope about to fall the moment Hunter was gone. My body reacted, the threat of tears imminent. I used to be able to push back emotions, but the more time I spent around Hunter, the more those walls crumbled.

Cal thankfully chose that moment to reappear fully dressed. I saluted like an idiot to my brother, not even bothering to call out to Hunter.

Don't judge me— I never claimed to be emotionally smart.

I was grateful that Cal waited for me to run out my tension before he gave me the third degree.

"Jamie isn't wrong, you know. Hunter isn't going to leave you."

Each heavy breath I took misted in front of my face. "I've never done any kind of relationship before, much less long distance. I just don't know—"

Cal slowed to a stop and reached out for my arm. "Ty, I've been in a lot of shitty relationships. I've spent every single one of them wishing I had something like what you two have. You two are Hawk and Skippy—in a more appropriate era the Jack and Ennis. *You* are the great love story that——"

"You just listed characters who either died from a hate crime or never got to be together because one was married to a woman."

My brain took that thought and ran with it. What if Hunter fell in love with a woman in Canada.

"That's not what I meant. You two have what most people can only dream about. But you don't have to work with an archaic timeline."

"It's not particularly inclusive either."

"Oh, shush. You two can be best friends for the cameras. There have been questionable friendships in professional sports since the dawn of time."

"That doesn't change the fact that he's leaving and I'm not."

"No, but I saw that bruised, broken man with the adorable puppy eyes and those tiny little briefs—that left nothing to the imagination by the way—who wanted you and only you. For now, and forever. God, that could be a Taylor Swift line. Maybe I should call her agent. Oh, maybe I'll tag her in a TikTok and hope she comments back!"

I burst into laughter and Cal smiled, his ridiculous rant having its desired effect.

"Ugh, I'm just waiting for the inevitable heartbreak, Cal. I'm holding on by a thread here and losing him... I don't think I could—"

Cal squeezed my arm with sympathetic eyes. I gave him a warning glare when he held on a little too long. He only gave me a wide smile in response. "Hunter will hold onto that thread for you, that's all I'll say, Ty."

And by God, did I want to believe him.

CHAPTER FORTY-SEVEN

Hunter

I didn't realize I'd fallen asleep until the scent of the ocean woke me. I didn't know how he still smelled like that after being in Boston for so long, but I wasn't going to complain. Tyler was tucked into my neck, his soft breath tickling my skin as he dozed with one arm lightly draped over my torso. I didn't know if that meant we were okay, but the arm over my torso claiming me was enough for me to have a sliver of hope.

As if he knew I was awake, I felt the flutter of his long lashes under my chin.

"Boston?"

My heart quickened at the sound.

"Yeah, baby?"

"I'm sorry I freaked."

My hand found his forearm, squeezing like I'd never get the chance to hold him again.

"It's okay. I get it."

Tyler lifted his head, sleepy turquoise eyes meeting mine.

"No, it's not. You had a shitty christmas and then told me this big thing, and I ran. It's just... I've lost too many people in my life, and you mean a lot to me, okay? And it hurts me that I will be losing you in one hundred and nine days."

I smiled. He was counting every second we had left together. I knew that somehow he was including the Frozen Four because there was no way in hell we wouldn't get there. I wouldn't even entertain the thought.

"Don't laugh at me!" he whined, and that Aussie twang popping out in his voice only made my smile widen.

"Baby, you counted."

"Oh, like you haven't."

I *hadn't*— because I was in denial. I also wasn't someone to think five steps ahead. I was too busy thinking about the present—and maybe getting back on the ice. But the one thing I knew for certain was that Tyler was my here and now. Whatever the future held, that wouldn't change. No one could put him higher on a pedestal than me, and that would always be that.

End of story.

"It's sweet of you to think so, but I don't think like you do. I think in the moment. And right now, I know that I want you—I will *always* want you."

Twin spots deepened his cheeks, and I fought the urge to kiss him senseless. One, because I knew it would give me a serious case of blue balls and two, we were supposed to be having a serious conversation. So, in the true form of having a healthy relationship, I resisted.

"Just—what if—"

I took his cheeks into my hands. "What if the world ends? What if our bus crashed on our way to our next game?—"

"Don't even joke about that, mate."

I laughed, and gave in enough to kiss his nose. "You know what I mean. Life has been shit to you—real fucking shit, and you didn't deserve it. But you can't live in fear of the what-ifs. You can't control *everything*, baby."

He groans. "If you weren't broken, I would shove you off the bed right now."

Another kiss to his cheek. "You're only saying that because you know I'm right."

"Yeah, yeah." He sighs, going back to nuzzle into the crest of my neck.

"So, we just... —see where this goes?"

"Yes, baby." I smiled, knowing that Tyler was anything but the "go with the flow" type of guy.

He hummed and we relaxed into each other until he suddenly jolted out of bed.

"I never gave you your Christmas present!"

"Baby, you *are* my Christmas present." I waggled my eyebrows, earning an eye roll in response.

"Ha, ha," he deadpanned. "You're not getting sex; you look like a bruised peach. Pain isn't my kink, babe."

A low growl starts deep in my chest. Not only because he took sex off the table, but because he called me "babe."

"So even BJ's are off the table?"

A flicker of heat passed over those pretty eyes, "Depends on how good you are." He winked before sliding away and strutting that toned brief-covered ass away from me and out the door.

Seriously! Does no one wear clothes around here?" Jamie calls down the hall.

"Nope!" Tyler responds, re-entering the room with a small package. His cheeks were flushed and though I didn't need a gift from him, I was eager to know what it was.

"It's really silly, and then you got me something so personal and thoughtful, it's nothing compared to that—"

"Hand it over, Aussie."

Tyler sat on the edge of the bed and passed me the perfectly wrapped box. I looked at it for a moment, holding onto the present tightly.

"I don't remember the last time I got a christmas present..." I fought the urge to rip into it, instead slowly slid my finger under the tape in an effort to preserve Tyler's wrapping artistry. The adorable, Australian-themed wrapping paper revealed a plain cardboard box. I looked up at Tyler to see him gnawing on his lip.

I fought the urge to pull his lip from his teeth, tossing the lid aside to reveal a Boston jersey. I picked it up just to see a matching one underneath.

"Turn them over," he instructed with a slight waver in his voice.

I laid one jersey out on the bed, then the other next to it. There, I saw us.

Riley 28

Graves 56

I looked up to him to see the look on his face. Every concern was written across his features. Would I like it? Had he gone too far? I carefully returned the jerseys to the box—then cupped his cheeks in my hands and claimed his lips. He whimpered as I pressed against his bruised cheekbone, so I moved that hand to cup the back of his neck—I was *not* breaking that kiss. His tongue teased at my lips, begging me for entry. I let him in, letting him seek the comfort that he needed from me.

"Do you—"

"Love them, baby. Thank you." *And I love you.*

Through all the emotions battling in my chest, it didn't escape my realization that

Tyler's number was half of mine. I wasn't a religious man. I wouldn't even call myself spiritual. But I couldn't help but think that it was a sign.

CHAPTER FORTY-EIGHT

Hunter

S itting out on practice was torture.

Considering my condition, I'd missed weeks. I sat beside the coach with my eyes glued to Tyler. He flew across the ice, practicing with his line—that didn't include me. I tapped my stick against the boards as I watched the scrimmage, his face a mask of indifference as he was put at center instead of on the left wing.

The puck dropped, and he was lightning quick. Colton swore as the puck was stolen from him. Tyler shot across the ice with a clean pass to Amon who sent it right back. He checked one of our defensemen—his opponent for the sake of practice. He scrambled him by dragging the puck between his legs, knocking it to Mouse who passed it back to avoid Jarman—on the rival team. In a tic-tac-toe fashion, he faked left then let the puck soar over Preston's right shoulder.

It was a beauty.

Preston simply shook his head, his smile visible even from behind his mask. My Aussie skated to rest, preparing himself for center ice without a single celebration over his goal. Coach made notes in his little black book—and I wasn't the only one who took notice. Colton's jaw ticked as he saw the lineup.

The energy was palpable in the locker room, the anticipation of the upcoming games radiating through the air. It was a challenge not to be captivated by the man before me. Amidst the animated banter and shoulder knocks exchanged among teammates, he remained indifferent. We shared a bond that felt stronger than ever, gearing up for another road rotation leading to the end of the regular season, all with the hopes of securing a coveted spot in the Frozen Four.

Tyler's gaze met mine, eyebrow quirking at the intense look I was giving him. The atmosphere crackled with electricity as we geared up for the challenges ahead, the promise of the Frozen Four hanging in the air like a shared dream.

"Easy, Boston," he whispered in my ear as he passed me on the way to the showers. I caught the backward glance, a slight smirk playing on his lips—the only thing to break that stoic mask. I muffled my groan, trying to calm my body's reaction to that little quirk that was a promise of what was to come. He'd been holding out on me, hell-bent on me recovering—save for a few blowjobs. But I was hoping that I showed him I was completely fine and ready to make that body of his *mine*.

I sat at the dining table with Jamie, bouncing between studying and catching up with the kid engrossed in his book next to me. I kept a close watch on Tyler, who buzzed around the kitchen. Rice was cooking, bulk chicken and vegetables were in preparation, all part of his meal prep for both of us.

"Baby, are you sure you don't want any help?" I called out, seeing the frown deepening on his face as he monitored the food while reading a textbook, mumbling to himself.

"Yeah, nah, s'fine." He waved his hand in the air while reciting more information about muscle connections.

"Yeah, as in yes, you want help, or nah, you don't want help?"

His gaze shot to me, and I got the perfect view of his angry face—it was adorable. He was no doubt pissed at me for breaking his concentration. I'd learned the hard way that getting in the way of that man's hyperfocus was equivalent to trying to clip a small dog's nails—a guaranteed way for your fingers to get bitten.

"No, I am fine. If it was nah, yeah, then it would mean I need help," he elaborated like Aussie slang was common knowledge, returning to tending to the meal prep.

I could only watch his next move helplessly from my seat. Time seemed to slow, but I couldn't move quick enough. His eyes turned back to the textbook while his hand reached for the saucepan—missing the handle completely and grabbing the hot metal. I jumped up and rushed over as Tyler let out several choice swear words.

I cradled his hand, taking in the red lines on his finger and palm. I dragged the cursing man to the sink and shoved his hand under the cold water.

"You are juggling too many things, baby."

"Too many things that need to get done, Boston. Let me go; I need to tend to the food so we can eat."

"Yeah, nah," I said, taking in the amused sparkle in his eyes. "You stay where you are; I'll take the food off the stove." I didn't miss that maddening little quirk of his lip. I left him by the sink, elated that he listened to me while I finished the meal prep.

Another thing I learned about living with Tyler: he's the most disciplined man in the world. All his meals are thought out to give him the exact calories and nutrition he needs. He also tracks his calories burned so he knows how to adjust his diet accordingly. The guy was nuts. I'd never craved sugar more in my life.

Once the food was sorted, I returned my attention to Tyler. He was leaning against the counter looking at his injured hand I made my way over to him, looking at the angry red marks that would leave blisters on his dominant hand.

"Stay here." I went to grab my first aid kit from my hockey bag and returned to find him muttering to himself yet again.

"Fucking idiot," he mumbled with his head hanging low.

I stepped into a space, using a single finger to lift his gaze to mine. Not many people saw this side of Tyler Riley—the side that didn't have all his ducks in a row. But God, my man was his own worst critic. He never accepted failure; never accepted being anything but the best. Making mistakes... that led to this, him cursing himself for being an idiot. I didn't like it, not one bit.

"Hey, baby, guess what?"

"What," Tyler pouted, and I couldn't help the smile. Even angry he was fucking adorable.

"Even professional chefs burn their hands sometimes. You juggled cooking while trying to recite the entire chapter on muscle composition." Tyler huffed, and I caught it with my lips, kissing him hard enough to wipe that adorable frown away.

"Go sit down and relax for five, baby."

"I have to take Jamie to his class then I have to write an essay for my sports psych class, and I need to practice my stick handling because I lost that pass from Mouse earlier when I shouldn't have. And I want to re-watch the tape for Harvard's game before we play them again."

I leaned my head against his in exasperation. Did I mention the other reason we weren't having sex was that my guy didn't know when to stop? If he wasn't studying, he would help his brother, carting him to and from practice. Then he was watching tapes or playing with a stick and puck. His need for perfection on every field made me realize that he had little time for anything else.

Though every time I got him alone and tried to talk to him about it, he would drop to his knees and suck the words right out of me. Before I could reciprocate, he would crash only for his alarm to wake us up at fuck-me-o'-clock to do it all over again.

"You need a break, Ty. You never stop—ever."

"I can't. The moment I drop the ball, everything will turn to shit, Hunter."

I'd be lying if I said we hadn't had this conversation before.

"You sit down and do your essay," I commanded. He looked at me, posed for a fight. I could sense the words on the tip of his tongue. "This is not negotiable. James; you got your stuff together? I'll take you to practice."

"Yep! It's only an hour's class, though. Tyler was going to stay and watch."

Crap on a broomstick. "I'll watch and record it for him. He needs to do his essay." Jamie shrugged and hitched his bag over his shoulder.

I saw Tyler's mind ticking, but I had him cornered. I kissed him quiet. "Essay. Now."

"But—-"

I dropped my voice so Jamie didn't hear. "The only but you get is from me, tonight. Let me help you, Aussie."

"Ugh, fine."

With a final kiss goodbye, I left his dorm room and took Jamie to practice.

I don't know why it had taken me so long to ever watch his brother fight. The kid was good—real good. I could see the trainers thinking the same thing.

I gave him a broad smile when he stepped up to me after. "Dude, that was awesome."

Jamie shrugged, which made me laugh because it was so much like Tyler. There was something about those boys that had them undermining how good they actually were.

"So, this is your dream—to be an MMA fighter?"

Another shrug. "Yeah, I guess."

In the short time I'd known Jamie, I realized he wasn't a man of many words. In his early teens—he was exactly that: a man trapped in a teenager's body.

"You guess?" I shook my head. "You are so much like your brother. You just whooped that guy's ass and he has to be at least five years older than you."

Jamie chuckled. "He just had bad form. You see it in guys who have come from boxing to MMA. They can throw a punch like a boss but don't have the technique from learning multiple disciplines. Give him a few years at the gym and Johnny will show him."

It didn't escape me that he was purposely avoiding answering the question.

"Jamie…"

That earned me a signature Riley eye roll. "I don't know. I thought I would fight competitively for a while. Then I'd become a volunteer firefighter like Dad and help him run his gym. But we had to sell it. Mum couldn't run it, Tyler didn't know how and I was too young. So, one of the coaches bought it off us. I haven't told Tyler any of this but it fell apart after it sold. I worked there, but Holden found another gym smaller, more professional kind-of how we once were, you know? I know if I told Ty this, he would stop everything to reclaim the gym and then give me my dream. It's what he offered in the first place: to quit hockey and run the gym until I was ready."

My eyes blew wide. Tyler giving up hockey? I couldn't imagine him without it, though I knew he would have done it for someone he loved.

"Mum stomped on the idea before he could even get it out of his mouth. I also vetoed it because Tyler *is* hockey; that's all he has done for himself. When he isn't doing hockey, he was helping me, or Mum, or Dad, or his friends. It's just who he is."

"Does he know you want to be a firefighter?"

Jamie laughed at that, "God no—and never tell him. Could you imagine? I'm surprised he still lets me fight. I am lucky I am good, because if I got beat up every session, I think he would be trying to get me into a safer hobby like… crocheting."

None of it surprised me. I kind of hoped that—for Tyler's sake—Jamie didn't go into firefighting. Really, on behalf of the man I loved, I hoped that Jamie would be wrapped in bubble wrap so he didn't have to lose anyone else.

As we drove back to the dorm, I directed the topic to safer grounds. Jamie told me about his plan to return to Australia in February for school, staying with his Auntie for the term. It hadn't been discussed with Tyler, but they planned to sell the family home and put everything in storage. Since Tyler was set to be in Boston for another two years—hopefully longer if he got a contract—she didn't see the point of keeping the house. With all the memories attached, Jamie didn't want to return either.

It dawned on me how much caring for Tyler made me learn to worry about others' feelings. Because right then, I suddenly was holding onto knowledge that could hurt him.

"You should tell him, James."

"I will—after the Frozen Four. He needs to have a clear head for that."

I nodded, worrying my lip.

I walked into Tyler's room, pleased to see the worry lines between his brow gone as he read over his essay.

"Hey, babe," he called without even looking my way. "How was Jamie's training?"

"Your brother is the new Daniel LaRusso.,"

Tyler laughed. "He does mixed martial arts, not karate."

I shrugged, plonking myself on his—our—bed. "Semantics. He whooped the ass of an eighteen-year-old. I don't think the coach wants him to go back to Australia."

Tyler stiffened a little at the mention of his brother leaving, and I instantly regretted the words. "Yeah, I don't want him to leave either, but he really can't stay in my dorm forever. He needs to go to school. There's little chance of a school shootings in Australia."

"I hate to admit it, but you got me there."

Tyler chuckled and lifted his finger, signaling he would only be a minute—but I was done waiting. I circled my arms around his shoulders, nuzzling into his neck. One hand met my forearm and squeezed. "Hi, babe," he said again. I hummed against his skin, knowing I'd never tire of hearing that. "Just submitting it, and then I am all yours."

"Shit, you got that done quick."

He shrugged. "You gave me the time I needed without distractions. Thank you." It never ceased to surprise me how easy it was to please Tyler Riley.

I stayed curled over his shoulders until he pressed submit, glad he didn't seem to mind my sudden onset of neediness. "Done."

It happened so quickly I couldn't react. Tyler moved and pushed me to the bed. His strong muscled thighs straddled me, and his hands found their way into my hair, wrenching my head back to make me look at him. His pupils were so blown that only a thin sliver of blue remained around the edges. I swallowed a grunt as his lips crashed into mine, biting, nipping, taking everything.

He could have it.

I fucking missed him. Every moment with Tyler Riley was one I would savor, but those stolen, heated moments were everything I lived for. He rocked his hips, grinding our erections together. If it weren't for his kisses swallowing the sound of my moans, I'd be worried about his brother hearing me.

"I need you so fucking bad, Boston."

He didn't have to tell me twice. In a rapid tornado of hands and limbs, clothes flew off, teeth biting and lips kissing each other's flesh as it became exposed. I scurried back to the headboard, grabbing for the lube in his bedside table. I lied down and invited him between my legs—only for him to shake his head. Silently he straddled me again. "I want you to take me like this," he whispered, before claiming my mouth with his.

I lubed up my fingers, sliding my way through his cheeks and pressing against his entrance. Tyler's breath hitched as I teased and taunted the puckered skin. His little whimpers were music to my ears. So much so, I felt the telltale dampness of precome against my stomach. I tried focusing, holding off my body's desire to explode before I could get inside him. I pushed through, curling my finger to the spot I knew well which turned Tyler into a crying, writhing mess. I added another finger, spreading and scissoring them inside him so he was ready. It had been a while, and I wanted this to be enjoyable for him— *needed* it to be. "Fuck, babe, I can't wait any longer, fuck me, please."

I was at his command. I leaned over to the drawer to get a condom, only for his hand to stop me.

"No."

I felt my eyes go wide "Baby, we ..."

"I know we're clean, I trust you."

It was something I suggested a little while ago, especially since we were exclusive—but he wasn't ready. Now that he was, I wasn't going to deny him. My body responded by milking another drop of clear liquid onto my stomach. I slicked myself, then lined up my cockhead with his entrance. With my first around my shaft I squeezed, hard enough to stave off my orgasm at the simple thought of taking him bare.

I couldn't stifle a shout as he sank down in one smooth move, taking me to the hilt.

Fuuuck

Before words could leave at the feeling of Tyler's body strangling my naked cock his lips were on mine, hips rolling as he claimed his own pleasure. Between that, his mouth owning me and his hands roaming my body, my brain short-circuited.

"Fuck, baby, fuck," I swore, and he groaned as he found the perfect angle to hit that magic spot.

He drove home in a perfect dance of pleasure, where he pulsed around my dick with each hit of his prostate. I clenched his ass in my hands—though he needed no guidance. I knew I wasn't going to last much longer, and from the sounds he was making told me he wasn't either. I moved one hand to pump his dick in time to the rolling of his hips.

He broke first. I felt his body convulse on top of me, and with it, I crashed over the edge without a parachute. I thanked the sex gods when he came hard at the same time, his legs twitching with pleasure, the rhythm he once had now slow soft jerks as he rode our explosive high.

Tyler collapsed slowly to my chest, which was sticky from sweat and come. He slid to the side, still too scared to put too much weight on me. His lips kissed at the fading yellow bruises. He did that every night, kissing the marks as if he could make them go away.

He lay in silence.

"Baby?" I whispered, only to smile when I looked down and found him fast asleep.

CHAPTER FORTY-NINE

Tyler

APRIL

"Baby, did you read this?" Hunter called from the stool as I made breakfast.

"Read what?"

"This article about you." I looked up to see his beaming smile. I walked around the table to rest my chin on his shoulder. Front and center was a picture of me from our latest win, shooting a goal from the blue line.

"I don't read articles about me," I answered, about to circle away when two large hands grabbed at my hips and brought me between his legs.

"Well, you should, Mr. Bigshot. Listen to this."

He held me tight, not letting me budge as he began to read aloud.

Australian Sensation Tyler Riley Dominates American College Hockey Scene

"In a remarkable turn of events, nineteen-year-old Tyler Riley, has become a rising star in the American hockey circuit. Having honed his skills on the beach coast of Western Australia since the tender age of four, Riley's journey has been nothing short of extraordinary.

As the former captain of the under-eighteen international team, Riley has not only amassed multiple state competition victories but also led the Australian team to their highest-ever win in the nation's history. Now donning the colors of Boston University (BU), Riley has seamlessly integrated himself into the college hockey scene, making a significant impact from the left wing and eventually maneuvering to center.

His ascent to the forefront has not gone unnoticed, especially as he pushed out seasoned player Colton Sanchez, who had been under the watchful eyes of NHL scouts. Riley's record-breaking performance this year includes scoring a goal in every game he has played, showcasing his unparalleled grit, strategic prowess, and uncanny ability to seize goal-scoring opportunities.

Coach Rod Martins of BU speaks highly of his prodigious talent, stating, "It's been a great pleasure to have this kid on the team. He has brought a different mindset to his teammates, one where the communication between the lines has vastly improved. He has a lot of potential and his growth has only just started. His stats speak for themselves. I have no doubt his dreams of being in the NHL will come true."

As the spotlight intensifies on Riley, all eyes are set on the upcoming Frozen Four competition. Having propelled his team to a winning season, the young Australian phenom faces the ultimate test to showcase his skills when the pressure is on. With expectations soaring, Tyler Riley's journey through the American college hockey ranks continues to captivate fans and industry insiders alike."

I read along as Hunter spoke with added drama. I tried not to let the positive feedback get to my head, tamping down my excitement as I wiggled out of Hunter's grip. I didn't say a word, because what was there to say? I couldn't jump for joy just yet; I still had to prove myself—now more than ever. As the article said, I needed to show that I could handle the pressure.

"Baby, come on! This is amazing! It's going to throw you into the spotlight!"

"Hunter, it's just an article." I couldn't let someone's nice words get to me because I needed to focus on pushing harder to show them that he was right. I just needed to focus on hockey.

"Baby, stop and think about everything you've achieved. You've got good grades; you aced hockey and you're a great boyfriend."

I looked at him at the last remark and he simply glared at me, daring me to question it.

"I didn't ace my grades," I said instead.

"If you weren't so cute I'd punch you. You got high marks in all but one of your exams—and that was still well over a pass."

I rolled my eyes because we'd had this argument before. It was biochemistry, which made no sense to me whatsoever. I didn't remember learning any of the stuff in high school, and suddenly I had to teach myself a lot of nonsense the Australian school system failed to offer. If it hadn't been for Hunter, I would have failed.

So, I wasn't just angry at my grade—I was pissed that I couldn't show him how good of a tutor he was. I wanted to ace that stupid exam for him. He spent way more time than he had available teaching me and I'd let him down.

"Baby, you knew fuck-all to begin with. A 'B' is an achievement on its own. If you'd only gotten a pass, I would have been proud of you."

I hated that he knew me so well.

Cal appeared by the door, holding his bag in his hand. "Tyler, are you still good to drop me to the ice?" His bunky old car had broken down last week, and I promised to help him since he did the same for me. I checked the time, spitting out a curse when I realized I was behind schedule.

I quickly got myself ready and headed for the door. When Hunter stopped me with an arm around my waist, I tried to fight him—I didn't have time to be late. I needed to drop Cal off before we had to be ready for the trip to Minnesota for the Frozen Four.

I stopped fighting when I saw my large coffee thermos in his hand. "Take this, grumps." He swatted me on the ass and kissed my cheek. "You will be on time, and everything is going to be fine."

My anger and anxiety dispersed to make room for the tingling on my cheek.

Cal's competition wasn't too far from our college, and I drove in silence. Yes, I said *silence*. With *Cal* in the car.

"Okay, you've been M.I.A for a while now, and you're really quiet today. Have I done something to piss you off?"

Cal whipped his eyes to me, and it was then that I noticed the dark rings beneath them.

"What? No, of course not. I've just been busy with practice; this routine is kicking my ass."

Well, I at least knew he wasn't lying about that. The practice he required made me look like a slacker. He was up and out before me most days, only returning after Hunter and I had fallen asleep.

"Everything okay? Other than the routine?"

Cal looked out the window, and his silence made me glance over. He gnawed at the inside of his cheek. He didn't look like my full-of-life friend, and I suddenly felt a wave of guilt. I had been so swept up in my own shit that I hadn't made time for my best friend.

"Other than my piece of shit car breaking? Oh, and my boyfriend cheating on me—again."

Thankfully, I was caught by a red light which let me look at Cal when anger began to boil my blood. "What?"

"Can you tell me something? What is it about me that screams 'Hey, cheat on me'?"

"Nothing about you screams that, Cal. You're hot, funny, talented—and a great friend."

Cal rolled his eyes., "You've never made a pass at me."

I reared back in disbelief, flinching when a honk blasted behind me. I accelerated but let his words swim in my head, trying to find the appropriate answer.

"Cal, that doesn't reflect on you. Hunter, he—"

"Yeah, yeah, I know. Sorry, that was a dick thing to say. Hunter is your boo, your everything. I am just feeling insecure. Ignore me."

"Cal, those guys are dickheads."

"I knew Sunday golfer was, but Eric? I thought things were different."

I sighed, navigating my way into the skating rink parking lot.

"Eric was an attractive guy, but he didn't really match your energy."

I parked as Cal seemed to think that over. "Well, I suppose he was more my Joe to my Taylor than my Travis... Why didn't you say anything?"

"You were happy and that's all I could ever want for you. But next time I see that fuckwit, he'll find out what happens to people who hurt my best friend."

Cal leaned over the console and stamped a kiss to my cheek.

"Don't break your fist over someone like him. It just makes me wonder what is wrong with me, like am I bad in bed? Am I too much? Like what is it, Tyler, that makes these men cheat on me?"

"Nothing, Cal. There's nothing wrong with you. And I have seen your dance moves. With those hips, you *have* to be good in bed. I once remember you telling me you were a power bottom for a reason."

Something in there had its desired effect, and a wide smile brightened Cal's face. There was something wrong about a Cal Johnson not smiling that made things seem... wrong.

"You're right. Well, I am going to win this freaking comp and say goodbye to Miss Susie Q, and get signed to be the next top male figure skater. They can watch this hot ass of mine at the Olympics."

"Damn right." I smiled back and watched him get out of the car, making a show of spanking said ass and going on his way into the building.

I looked down at the dash clock. "Fucking shit!"

I was going to be late. I quickly reversed out of the car park, ignoring a couple of honks that came my way from whomever I cut off. I lifted my hand in apology and got the heck out of there.

My phone rang over the speakers, Hunter's name flashing on the screen.

"Aussie, everything okay?"

"Be there soon; I got a bit distracted. Cal needed a pep talk." I sped through a yellow light and changed lanes, hearing the blast of a horn from the person behind me I cut off without meaning to.

"Please drive safe. Don't worry about Coach; I'll run interference." I heard the worry in his tone but kept my hurried pace, cursing the crazy roads of America. "For fuck's sake! Why can't your roads be simple like Perth!" I hit my hand against the steering wheel. Another horn blared, and I was unsure if it was at me. "Oh, common mate, the light's green!"

"Tyler, calm down. The last thing we need is you getting in an accident."

"Fine," I huffed. "See you soon." I hung up and continued my road rage towards the university ice rink.

I parked, seeing all the guys on the bus and both coaches looking at their watches. More choice curse words left my mouth as I got out of the car, grabbed my belongings, and ran to the bus, looking like a complete and utter drongo.

Coach's angry glare wasn't lost on me as I stowed my things and made for the door.

"If you think you won't be punished for your tardiness, Riley, you have another thing coming."

I mumbled an apology before jumping on the bus, heading straight for Hunter's worried face. I sat down with a ceremonious thud and felt his hand seek me out—but in my rotten mood, I shrugged him off. I could feel his gaze on me from the side of my head, along with many of the other teammates. I couldn't even bring myself to apologize to any of them.

Instead, I chucked my headphones in my ears and blasted music on our way to the airport. I heard the buzz of my phone and didn't dare look at it, knowing full well it was Hunter.

I sulked for the entire journey, thinking of all the ways Coach would punish me for being late.

Chapter Fifty

Hunter

I wanted to call Tyler out on his shit, I really did. But between the picking and nail-biting, my man was a nervous wreck. He hated letting anyone down, and on top of being removed from the starting line for the first round, he was punishing himself by chewing out his own ass.

We went straight to the rink from the airport for our allotted practice time. I could tell that Tyler was still in his head, but how he gritted his teeth proved his determination. Stone-faced, he called those plays like a pro. But I was worried he was pushing himself too hard. I stayed behind him as we walked to our hotel room after practice but kept enough distance. None of the team heckled him or bothered him about partying—they knew he meant business.

I followed him into our room, where I watched him hang his suit in the bathroom to steam with his shower. I knew his routine better than anything now; being each other's roommates, I had learned the exact order of what he would do during his unpacking. His pajamas and toiletries would come next. Then, he'd have a steaming hot shower where he would scrub every inch of his body before simply soaking up the heat.

If he had any sore muscles, he'd ice them after his shower while watching game tapes—the same ones he watched every night. Tyler studied each player, memorizing their every move. Then, if he had any energy to spare, we'd fall into bed together—but not before he checked his alarm multiple times.

Tyler was methodically undressing and folding his clothes neatly on the bathroom counter while he waited for the shower to heat. He no longer closed the door; a small, intimate thing that made my stupid little heart flutter. Even now with his underlying anger, he let me see glances of his bare ass in the mirror. Our eyes met, and where I expected to see that cute little frown line, I loved to tease him about—I only saw sadness. It only hung around for a moment before he looked away and stepped into the shower. Tyler's usual confident shoulders slumped, the fight seeming to have left him.

We couldn't have that.

I stripped, dumping my clothes on the floor and knowing I'd pay for it later. I got in the shower with him, moving in close and resting my chin on his shoulder as my hands found his waist. He relaxed into my touch, seeming to hold the weight of the world on his shoulders. I held him tighter when his breathing picked up and his hands began to shake.

"Baby, talk to me," I whispered in his ear. He shook his head against my collarbone, his longer hair moving with him. It fell in waves past his ears now; not long enough to tie back yet, but just enough to wrap around my fingers. I picked my hand up to tap at his temple. "What's going through here?"

I felt as he held his breath before he spoke.

"If we lose tomorrow, that is our last game together."

I flinched as if I'd been physically hit. I was certain we'd nail it, so the thought hadn't even crossed my mind. I was confident we'd at least make it to the final. After only three months on the ice together, we were killing it. All of the articles painted the two of us as some kind of dream team. Tyler might not buy into it, but I'd stashed away every one of those articles like secret entries in a diary, evidence of what we represent together in the game we both adore.

"We won't lose," I said, certain of the fact. He let out a choked sound, a half-sob half-laugh. But I didn't turn him to face me—not yet.

"Ever the optimist."

"I've got a good feeling, Aussie. We've had a killer season and we've taken out Minnesota every time."

"Yeah, I know." He resigned, but there was still no lightness in his tone. I held him tighter, hoping he would offload his thoughts.

"Boston, even if we snag this win, it's just another game, you know? I mean, I've been counting down the days, but I don't like the thought of not playing on a team with you."

For some reason, I felt like the last bit meant something more. As if the game were a metaphor for his life. Because after The Frozen Four, I was off to Vancouver. My bags were packed and sitting in his room. An annoying little reminder that we'd been trying our best to ignore.

"I know," was all I could say. I'd had four perfect months of knowing what it felt like to be this man's partner. We were a team, damn it. I wasn't ready to say goodbye.

I wasn't ready to give up these stolen moments.

My life once was a mixture of flinching to avoid the brutality of my father's hits and using sex and booze as some sad version of therapy. Then the man in my arms made it all go away. He showed me love and affection I didn't know I deserved; he showed me the true meaning of family. That man was my hero.

I finally turned him to face me, kissing away the wet paths down his cheeks; kissing away his sadness. Those three little words sat on the tip of my tongue, and I bit back the urge to set them free. We hadn't said them yet, and it was sort of an unspoken understanding that we hadn't. The closer I got to leaving, the more painful it became to admit it.

At least, that's what I was banking on. The way he reacted at that moment suggested he felt the same. Tyler's lips met mine, hot and heavy as our wet bodies writhed against each other. I wanted nothing more than to be fucked by my man tonight—even if it was just one more time.

We stumbled out of the shower, hardly any cleaner than we were before. I dragged him by the hand I had in his hair, the wet strands dripping over his body. He followed as I crashed onto the bed, mumbling the word "lube" against his lips. Tyler smiled against my mouth, leaping off the bed. He was only gone for a second, but my wet body felt cold without him. With the bottle in hand, he blanketed himself over me once more, attacking my mouth like he owned me. And in truth, he did.

"I need you this time, baby," I said, not missing the way those gorgeous eyes flared with heat. He needed the control, and I just needed him.

The room got hot; the air got heavy. Before we knew it, I cried out his name as we hurtled over the edge together. Quick and dirty—just how we needed it. We collapsed together, lips grazing over well-earned scars from prior games. Once we got cold and sticky, I brushed his hair away from his face, suggesting we hit the shower again.

We did things properly this time—only together. I washed his hair, then gave those tense shoulders a much-needed massage. Tyler, being the sweetheart he was, returned the favor.

After folding our laundry and setting multiple alarms to ensure no chance of being late, we snuggled up in the same double bed by the window—like always. That's where my man put on his tapes and curled up next to me. We watched, and I listened to his breakdown of plays. I always thought if playing hockey didn't work out for him, he'd make a great coach. He had a natural talent for reading the players, picking up on things that most couldn't without years of training.

Eventually, my baby fell asleep in my arms; lips slightly parted as always and those long, dark lashes fluttering against his freckled cheekbones. I fell asleep later than I should have, my mind wanting to savor every part of Tyler Riley.

I wasn't surprised when Tyler wiggled out of bed before either of our alarms. He was engrossed in studying plays, simultaneously maneuvering his hockey stick over the bathroom tiles. As I lay there, I observed the effortless dance of tendons and ligaments beneath his skin, akin to a seasoned pianist effortlessly playing Beethoven on a quiet Sunday morning. His gaze met mine, and an embarrassed smile played on his lips, yet it didn't quite reach those sad eyes.

To break the subtle tension, I got out of bed and noticed Tyler mimic me as I got dressed. We left the room together, heading for the ice in a routine that spoke more than words could ever convey.

I never imagined I'd feel more like a spectator than I did as we made our way to the hotel's foyer. Tyler's infectious smiles were directed at teammates, accompanied by heartfelt bro hugs for Jarman, Mouse, Amon, and Preston—those closest to him. The camaraderie extended to the entire team, but I found myself lingering at the periphery—and the others noticed. It was my final year at BU and in the past, it would have marked the end of my hockey career. I never thought things would turn out the way they had.

I was genuinely thrilled for the opportunity to join a pro team. Though my last altercation with my father and subsequent recovery worried me, Connor assured me that the Vancouver team was still more than satisfied with my performance. As I absorbed the atmosphere of my last year, I realized it wasn't just *my* farewell. Jarman and Mouse were also bidding adieu to their collegiate hockey careers. Mouse chattered away, detailing the arrival of his girlfriend to the competition. Jarman stood quietly to his side, and I found myself drawn to the friend I'd overlooked for far too long.

I stepped closer, placing a comforting hand on Jarman's shoulder. We watched together as Tyler gave Mouse every ounce of his focus—an unexpected moment where even the guy known for his witty banter received genuine attention.

"To think your guy is only going to have Amon next year," Jarman muttered. A wave of sadness washed over me at the realization. Cal was graduating as well, and my chest ached at the realization: that his dorm would be void of our presence. No me, no Cal—and no Jamie.

Jarman placed his hand over mine and squeezed, seeming to read my mind. "Have you told him yet?" I'd always wonder how Jarman got to be so perceptive.

I sighed and shook my head, just enough so Tyler didn't notice the movement. "Why not?"

Jarman kept his voice low as Tyler made his rounds through the team. For Mr. Serious, he had a way of connecting with each player, putting them at ease before every game. The curse of an empath, I suppose- feeding everyone from an empty plate.

"Because I leave after this, and who knows what we will be after…"

When I was met with silence, I pulled my gaze from Tyler to meet Jarman's sad eyes. "Sometimes, we just can't have what we love," he said matter-of-factly. I followed his attention to Mouse.

I returned the squeeze of a shoulder. "What are you going to do about that?"

Jarman didn't even flinch, not needing me to indicate what I meant by "that." He simply stared at his best friend with a sense of longing that made my heart ache even more. "He's going to work for his father, and his girlfriend is moving in with him. I don't know what I'll do yet—either a farm team or coaching. Either way, I'll be saying goodbye to Mouse. If I'm on a farm team, I'll keep my sexuality on the down low. If I wind up coaching, maybe I'll try to see if I can meet someone."

Sadness filled me on behalf of my friend, "Regardless, I hope that you get to experience being with someone you're attracted to, Jarman."

"Who said I haven't?" he snorted. "I just don't parade it around like you do."

I huffed a laugh, "And does Mouse know?"

Jarman didn't even look at me. "No, there's no point."

I nodded, a twinge of regret settling in that my friend had weathered this storm alone. "I've got your back, Jar. Wherever life takes you, just a call away, man."

Jarman responded with a playful pat on my ass, saying, "Same here. Glad we're wrapping it up this way."

Yet again, I found myself merely observing. My feet mechanically carried me towards the rink, but my mind seemed to linger behind, watching the scene unfold. It played out like a film—the love of my life caught up in conversation with Amon, my team hitting the ice together. The mental reel continued to capture those moments as we geared up, preparing for what could very well be the last game we'd ever play together.

That wasn't our last game.

It was evident from the first period. Every damn player had a surge of energy, making us quicker and sharper on the ice. An invisible thread seemed to connect us, flawlessly guiding us through our plays. Backward passes clicked and sliced through Minnesota's traffic. Minnesota was playing a hard game. Tyler was their primary target—but he was unfazed. He dodged their attempts, hitting back with hard hits—regulated, of course. If you didn't know any better, you'd think our Aussie hotshot had practiced as a lineman with the way he took down opponents.

Sure, we had our faults. I took a penalty for high sticking—a total accident I might add... he ran into the stick. Tyler got a penalty for tripping when a defenseman's legs got caught up in his stick. I watched as Tyler, true to form, unleashed a torrent of curses during his two minutes in the penalty box.

In those moments when we were off the ice, their star forward managed to score and put them on the board with a two-to-one lead. But they didn't know what they'd asked for by putting Tyler Riley in the penalty box—he emerged with a vengeance. His determination for perfection led him to seize a breakaway opportunity, showcasing his speed. He shot the puck right past the goalie, securing a two-goal lead before the buzzer sounded. Things looked good, but in hockey time, minutes felt like hours.

I was on Tyler's right-wing, observing as he charged toward the net with a Minnesota defenseman hot on his heels. I checked him, letting Tyler slide the puck to Colton. Cheers erupted as Colton scored, but no one got a chance to celebrate before a defenseman pinned Tyler against the boards. He barely flinched as his head hit the plexiglass. Instead, he spun and threw a punch.

Tyler was swearing bloody murder as I came in behind and cross-checked the defenseman's back. Like any hockey game, the sound of the final buzzer sent both teams erupting into a brawl. Hands grabbed at my shirt, bodies collided against my helmet, but my focus remained on Tyler, who was still stuck against the glass. That oversized defenseman rained down punches on him until his helmet flew off. Eventually, the refs intervened, and I reached Tyler, his eyes ablaze with fury, pointing towards number 25. The only injury to be seen was a small cut just above his eyebrow—that matched my own scar.

The feeling of my glove-free hand against his cheek brought him back down to earth.

"Let's get you cleaned up, Aus. We did it!" Unlike the exuberant celebration around us, Tyler's face remained emotionless as he let the team revel in victory.

CHAPTER FIFTY-ONE

Tyler

My head was still vibrating from that hit. As I stood under the locker room shower and watched bright red blood swirl around the drain, I convinced myself it was the result of the fury behind that punch. The team's concerned glances flickered over me a couple of times. I couldn't muster any joy at our victory. Not when it meant we were one game closer to witnessing Hunter leave.

I turned off the tap and wrapped a cheap white towel around my waist. Something about a locker room shower just never made me feel clean enough, and I was itching to get back to the hotel for a proper clean.

As I walked through the dressing area, I heard my name amongst the persistent ringing in my ears. I turned to see Coach glaring at me furiously.

"Get over here, Riley!" he barked. "You're bleeding all over the place. You need Baxter to check that out."

I tried to nod, but it only made my head swim, so I silently made my way to the team's physician. My split eyebrow had become a familiar spot for such hits. Could I truly be a hockey player without a scar in place of a piercing there?

"How are you feeling?" Baxter inquired. There was no way I was going to bring up the way my head was swimming—he'd instantly bench me.

"Fine. Just bandage me so I can rest up for tomorrow." I attempted a smile, hoping it hid the pain behind my eyes.

Baxter looked at me hard, and I gave him the eye contact he was after. I sighed with relief when he gave me a clear.

I got myself dressed, telling the team I would only celebrate once we were victorious against Merrimack the next day.

Yep—*that* Merrimack made it to the finals.

I beelined toward the lifts that led to our hotel room. I didn't need to look behind me to see if Hunter would follow—I knew he would. Part of me hoped he'd stay behind to spend some time with the team. I didn't want him to miss his last few moments with them because I was a little sad. Besides, we'd all meet at the hotel restaurant to share our last meal as a team. Next year, a whole new batch of players would replace the seniors heading off to the big scary world.

After another careful shower with my injury in mind, I got dressed once more.

I found myself feeling somewhat guilty as I made my way downstairs. The team scattered about the restaurant, spirits still soaring from the win. Hunter draped his arm over my shoulder. To everyone else, it seemed like nothing more than a friendly move, but I welcomed that physical connection.

"Alright, boys, take a seat," Coach boomed, and we all did. I sat between Hunter and Jarman, facing Mouse and Amon. Coach headed to one end of the table while Colton took the other and the rest of the team found their places.

"First, Captain, we thank you for all your work this year. This is one of our best seasons yet. I have been proud to have such a great bunch who have worked hard for the stats that they have. I'll give you the floor to say a few things."

Coach sat down, and I watched as Colton stood and adjusted his tie. "Well team, we did it! I have no doubt we'll crush Merrimack tomorrow—again. We know this team is scrappy, but we have the skill to put them in their place. It has been a great pleasure being captain, especially in our best season yet."

Hunter's hand squeezed my knee under the table, seemingly aware that despite everything, the tension between me and our captain was palpable. He didn't like me—that much was clear.

The coach took the spotlight once more. "Thank you, Colton. Well, I want to say it really has been a momentous year. I know quite a few of you are hoping for a contract—and I do not doubt that you'll get it. But I want to highlight someone: Tyler Riley. You were a bit quiet coming in, but since you've shown remarkable skills on the ice despite everything working against you. The way you jumped in headfirst, helping your teammates and proving your dedication to this team is commendable. I know we have one more game to play, but we've all voted. Tyler Riley—you're our player of the year."

My cheeks were on fire as Coach handed over a small medal. Whether it was from the praise or the dozen pairs of eyes on me, I wasn't sure—but I deflected anyway. "Thank you, everyone. Really, it was all you. It's been an amazing opportunity to play with such a talented group. Hockey is a high-stakes world where I come from, and you've helped me become a better player. So, yeah, I am just grateful. No matter the outcome of my hockey career, whether that is going back home or playing here, I am happy for this experience." Hunter's grip turned punishing at the mention of me moving back to Australia.

"Pfft, if any of us is making it to the big leagues Aus, it's you," Mouse called. "You've carried this team." Mouse continued despite the glare I was trying to send him across the table. If Colton fumed any harder, his head would explode.

The chorus of agreements should have warmed my heart, but I was stuck on the hurdles in my way—the NHL had never seemed so far out of reach.

Luckily, the rest of the dinner went by peacefully. I listened to Mouse ramble on and on and despite the dark cloud that was surrounding me, I couldn't help but smile. The guy could talk the ass off a donkey, but his energy was infectious.

I spun when a strange hand tapped my shoulder.

"Surprise," Cal said with spirit fingers. He stood there in his suit with an ear-to-ear grin. A gold metal hung around his neck. I already knew he'd won his competition—he updated me the second it happened—but typical Cal, he wore that medal with pride.

Good for him.

"I'm the reason you were late yesterday so I thought the least I could do is support you at your final game. Besides, I won't be able to soon. You're looking at a *signed* figure skater who's moving to Canada!"

My nails dug into my palm, the prospect of everything I was about to lose looming over me like a tidal wave. Without my crew around me when Mum died, I doubt I'd have made it through. They were my rock, keeping me focused on the goal and preventing me from wallowing in self-pity. This was what Mum always wanted for me—to play hockey with the best, to make friends outside of that small town I grew up in. But now, everyone was moving on with their lives—and I was getting left behind.

I bit the inside of my cheek, the pain distracting me long enough to put my game face on. I shot to my feet and excused myself from the table, racing upstairs to my room. My hands shook and my thoughts raced so fast it made me dizzy. I collapsed against the bed, sliding down to the floor, and dropping my head between my knees. My temples pounded, and I gripped my hair to distract myself from how it once again protested the thoughts in my mind. The overwhelming sense of being alone, of saying goodbye over and over and over again, swallowed me whole.

"I can't do this." The words hurt my throat, and I couldn't figure out why. The world was spinning beneath me with no way for me to stop it.

"Yes, you can, baby," Hunter whispered, crowding my space. "You have been doing this for a year. You've got this." I felt the words against my neck, and the restraints around me tightened. However, instead of feeling suffocated, it felt like they held me together.

"I can't, I can't, I can't." The words came out short and sharp as I tried to catch my breath.

"Baby..." Hunter's voice broke.

"Everyone is leaving, and I'll be alone. I just can't say goodbye, Hunter, I can't!" I tried to wiggle out of his grip, but his strong arms didn't let me. The words hurt too much. It would be selfish to ask him to stay.

"I was stupid, so stupid. I never thought about what it would mean to lose you."

"Baby," he said again as if he were at a loss for words. He gripped me tighter, his lips brushing against the side of my head.

That bubble grew in my chest until it burst and a sob broke free. My eyes hurt and my throat burned. I berated myself for getting into this mess. I berated Hunter for not giving me a reason to hate him. I should have resisted the pull. Yet, as he held me tighter amid my sobs, I acknowledged there was no chance I could have refused him. Initially, he was broody, sarcastic, a lone wolf. But I'd let myself fall for the man who whispered sweet nothings to me as I drifted off to sleep, the man who'd become my family. He infused my life with so much joy that I found myself crumpled on the ground, weeping for just one more day, one more month... one more *anything* with him.

Because he was the one. The one for me. I'd known it from that first "one more time." The weight of it all poured out of me, and instead of pushing him away, I found myself clinging to him for dear life.

"It's not going to be the same without you," I sobbed. "I don't know how I am going to do this, Hunt. I don't know. I'm scared."

Rough hands maneuvered me, and I let him move me where he wanted until I straddled his lap. His hands cradled my face, but I couldn't bring myself to look at him—that would be letting him see right into my feelings.

"Baby, look at me."

I shook my head, tears spilling down my cheeks and over his fingers.

"Please, look at me, baby."

Unable to fight his pull any longer, I gazed into those golden eyes that glittered in the dim hotel lamp light.

"That's it," he praised, then his voice turned stern. "Now listen to me. You are *not* losing me; no distance will change the way I feel about you. Do I know what it will look like? No, but I know how I feel. I'll spend every moment I can with you, whether on the phone or in person. Your friends aren't leaving you either. Whether you get signed tomorrow or lead this team to more victories, you *will* succeed. And you most definitely won't be alone."

The determination in his eyes kept me from protesting.

"And no matter where I am, Aus, I am *yours*. If you want to move on, I'll accept that but know that there will be no one else for me. I'll have you whichever way I can until we're together again. Either way, know this isn't our last time."

I took in his features, counting the little scars decorating his face. Some were hidden in the beard he'd let grow out—a tradition for the end of the season. I memorized his olive skin and dark hair, which had recently been cut but was still long enough for me to grab onto. I didn't hate it; he was all man. The only man I could ever see as being mine. Our lips collided, but he kept the kiss sweet

"As much as I want you, I just want to hold you tonight, baby. You're exhausted, and you also took a good knock to the head today. Not to mention that panic attack and don't think I haven't seen you nursing that headache. If it wasn't our last game tomorrow, I would be asking you to sit this one out. This isn't our last night together. Tomorrow, we will be the winners of the Frozen Four and I'll make love to you in ways you never even imagined."

I couldn't help but laugh. "You'd better, hotshot." I stayed right where we were, resting my head against his shoulder. I was tired, really fucking tired. I felt Hunter gather me up and tuck me into him on the mattress—I didn't even question how he could lift me. Hunter was nothing if not superhuman in my eyes.

I woke up to the echoing sound of both our alarms. I smiled, knowing that he was the one to set them the night before. Despite my throbbing headache, I gathered my thoughts, acknowledging that my usual pre-game routine had been abandoned last night. I looked over to the spare bed seeing my workout clothes folded and waiting with my full water bottle sitting on top—even my smartwatch had been put on the charger. I moved into the bathroom, sure that there would be clothes scattered on the floor—a particular pet peeve of mine—but was surprised to find it spotless.

Hunter's arms encircled my waist, and his lips met the nape of my neck. "Everything to your liking, baby?" he teased. I melted into his touch. Without Hunter, I wondered how chaotic my high-strung, type-A personality might become.

"Thank you—for everything," I expressed, hoping he understood the true weight of those words. His lips brushed my cheek before he moved away to get ready.

There was no room for sentimental moments. It was time for each of us to prepare for the game in our own way. Like two sheepdogs doing a job, we collected what we needed and made our way to channel our buzzing energy.

The sight that greeted us was a mix of excitement—mostly from Mouse—and nervous anticipation from our teammates. Pre-workouts were done, game suits were on, and Colton was giving his pep talk. The team responded with stick bangs, but that nervous energy lingered. This particular team unsettled us the most, and doubts were beginning to take root.

"I want to say," I started "This season has been the best I've ever played. Each and every one of you has what it takes to beat those guys out there. Forget about the stats, the agents, the cameras. Focus on the chemistry we've built. When you step onto that ice, think about your teammate beside you. Make this your best game ever. Let's make this a memory to last a lifetime."

Amid catcalls and stick banging came, "We're not here to fuck with spiders! Let's show them what BU is made of."

The team dispersed from the benches, and I watched everyone head down to the ice, exuding enthusiasm. A hand rested on the back of my neck, and Hunter's scent enveloped me as he leaned into my ear.

"That mouth of yours has *so* many talents, baby," he remarked, giving me a wink and swatting my ass with his stick as he walked past me.

"Win this game with me, Boston, and I'll show you what else this mouth can do," I teased, enjoying the way the tips of his ears reddened. We stepped onto the ice behind our team for the last time, determined to make it a night to remember. I resolved to tell my broody Bostoner that I loved him tonight—regardless of the game's outcome.

There was no doubt I had a target on my back. It felt like I was evading hits more than I was going after the puck. The thudding in my noggin fought for attention, as I tried to clear my head and read the play, a task that used to come naturally. But whatever strategy we were employing, it was working—kind of. The first period ticked away, and it was a scoreless game. While their defense was stellar, ours matched up. The buzzer sounded and I welcomed the twenty-minute breather. How we managed to avoid turning the game into a fistfight was beyond me.

I plonked myself down on the bench and guzzled from a bottle of water, hoping it would shake off the dizziness. "You okay?" Hunter whispered.

I nodded. "Yep, just trying to evade them tearing me a new asshole," I replied.

Hunter growled. "Those guys are on you—hard. I feel like I'm playing chasey all night with how they're trying to keep you off goal. Not to mention, that ass is mine."

I bit back a grin as I gave him a playful elbow to his ribs.

Coach ran through a play refresh, adjusting the lines so Jarman and Hunter could tag team and work with Colton and I.

As we hit the ice, the change in lines rattled the opposition. They weren't expecting the switch-up. I won the faceoff, breaking away to score a goal and finally put a point on the board. However, the shift in lines led to miscommunication between Hunter and Colton which, resulted in Merrimack shooting their own goal. I took numerous shots, but the defense's focus on me prevented any successful contacts.

A rough hit from Zane left me rattled on the ice. His sneers mirrored those from before, but their impact was no longer the same. In truth, I had what he wanted—*multiple* things he wanted: the guy, and the game. I forced myself off the board and returned to the bench for the line change, watching as Amon and Mouse took a crack at the net.

"You okay, Aussie?" Hunter asked. "That was a big hit." I nodded, eyes following the puck like a dog playing fetch.

Baxter's hand on my shoulder captured my attention. "Need a concussion check? You were slow to get up."

He didn't *have* to ask; he could pull me from the game off that alone. "Nah mate, really, I'm fine. He winded me a little, is all."

Baxter studied my eyes, searching for any hint of a lie. Whatever he saw made his shoulders relax. "Okay, but if you have any signs, I need you to tell me, okay?"

I nodded, shaking off the voice in the back of my head that said I was taking a huge risk.

As the third period rolled around, it was make or break. The score stood at one-all, and our lines showed weariness from the relentless hits. We needed to muster every ounce of energy we had left so I boldly approached the heads of the team. "Coach?"

"Yeah, kid?"

"I need you to put Hunter back on my line." I got the whiteboard and drew out my idea, shifting the play away from the top shooters because they were on us like a huntsman in the dunny. "I don't think they'll anticipate it." I gestured out the play and watched as he considered it.

I let out a sigh of relief when he nodded. "Okay, but when I say so."

CHAPTER FIFTY-TWO

Hunter

I never thought I'd say it, but I was desperate for that game to end. It was supposed to be my last game with Tyler and once upon a time I wanted it to last... but he wasn't looking good. He was pushing himself beyond his limits—and Merrimack was determined to take him down.

But give my man his credit; he took no one's shit. In those last few minutes, he grappled for the puck, pulling off plays I could only ever dream of. Merrimack was on him like he was a number one draft pick in his first year of the league. He wasn't a defenseman, but he damn sure acted like it. With just five minutes left, there was a risk of overtime if the game continued.

Tyler and Jarman hit the ice running on the shift change, with Jarman working his ass off to keep players off Tyler. As Jarman struggled for the puck against the boards, Tyler shoved his way behind him, ready for the pass. The Merrimack defenseman cross-checked Jarman—causing him to grab the back of his head, blood stained his fingers as he pulled his hand away. Mayhem ensued before the refs got involved. Jarman skated to the bench holding the back of his neck, and the penalty was called in the last few minutes of the game. Coach tapped me on the shoulder, showing me a play I didn't expect. I nodded and took to the ice.

That game felt like the longest in my life—but that two minute power play was over before I could blink. It was a seamless tape to tape between Colton and Tyler, and the defenseman was doing everything in his power to disrupt our rhythm. The clock was ticking, and the final seconds were closing in. Though Tyler didn't look at me, I could sense the buzzing energy as he showcased that fancy footwork he was known for, skillfully maneuvering the puck away from the relentless defenseman.

All eyes were on Tyler as he dazzled with occasional glances at Colton, who anticipated the puck. In those last few crucial seconds, I spotted the defenseman closing in on Tyler. Colton vociferously called for the puck. With a swift flick of the wrist, the puck met my stick, and I took the shot.

The whoosh of the puck through the air was followed by a thunderous crash. A cheer erupted, only to fall to an eerie silence.

I turned, ready to celebrate the win with my man.

Only to freeze. On the screen, the playback unfolded: the puck reached me and the impactful hit from Zane. Tyler, with one skate on the ice, lost his footing in a collision that resembled a stampeding horse meeting a rickety lawn chair. His helmet went flying upon impact and he slid, crashing into the boards with a sickening crack.

Blinking back to the present, I heard the murmurs of the crowd as Tyler remained motionless on the ice. The rush of medics and our teammates beat me to him, and the atmosphere shifted from victory to concern in a flash.

I sprang into action, shoving my way past the men. My gaze dropped, and there was Baxter kneeling next to my man. He laid flat on his stomach while Baxter tried to rouse him. Blood stained the ice, and I struggled to push the stubborn ref out of the way so I could reach Tyler. Arms surrounded me—I wasn't sure who they belonged to. "Get off me! Tyler!" I shouted, hoping my voice would be the one to make those pretty eyes open. "Get up! Get up!" The call for a stretcher came and took my breath away.

"Hey, let the medics help him, man,"

I shook my head and shrugged the hand away. "No, I need to be with him. I need to be with him." I scrambled, feeling myself being dragged backward. Medics rushed in, hushed tones filling the space as they maneuvered him onto the board.

Helmet off, gloves tossed aside, I pulled at my hair as I watched the scene unfold. The team of medics began to carry him off the ice—I was quick to follow.

"Tyler, I am right here. I am not going anywhere." The words left my mouth like a mantra, hoping he could hear me past the chaos of people seeking a response from him. I didn't move to brush away the tears streaming down my cheeks, instead licking the salty flavor from my lips.

I shot toward Baxter. "I need to be with him. Please, he has no family here. Let me go with him."

Baxter looked at me with sad eyes; I could see he felt partly to blame—we all were. I knew he wasn't feeling his best. "Get your skates off; they're taking him to the hospital."

I'd never moved so fast in my life. Mouse, Amon, and Jarmon assisted, taking off my skates and passing me sneakers, which I hastily put on. Soon, I found myself in the back of an ambulance in my full hockey kit.

"Baby?" I took his hand, my heart breaking when he didn't grip mine in return. I glanced up at the paramedic, who looked far too sympathetic for my liking. "Is he going to be okay?"

"His vitals are okay..."

But I knew that tone.

I suddenly understood how Tyler felt when I was in the hospital. If he felt half as scared as I was, I knew I had a lifetime of making it up to him. The blood crusted in his auburn hair made me feel sick as I leaned into his ear. "Baby, please be okay. You need to come out of this; Jamie needs his brother. *I* need you. I love you. I love you so much, and I know this is way too late to be saying this. Please, please just wake up and let me say it to your face, okay?" My voice turned into more of a rasp than a coherent sound as my throat constricted.

From the moment we arrived at the hospital, it was a whirlwind. They wheeled him away and sent me to a waiting room where I paced back and forth in full hockey gear for what felt like hours.

I felt a tap on my shoulder, and when I turned around, half the team stood behind me. Preston handed over my kit bag and led me to a nearby restroom to change and freshen up. I spared only a brief glance in the mirror, confirming that I looked as pathetic as I felt. Stepping out of the bathroom, I headed towards the crowd forming for the man who seemed oblivious to how much he mattered.

A cluster of hockey players challenged the limited space but despite the nurses' growing agitation, we stayed. Even Coach joined us, tapping his phone against his palm with a frown etched on his features.

Cal approached me, his hand resting on my shoulder. "I spoke to Jamie. Their Auntie has called the hospital and listed you as his emergency contact, so they'll be updating you." Thoughts of Tyler's brother, alone in Australia, intensified the ache in my heart.

An hour later, the team was officially asked to leave. Though I was grateful for the relative silence, my phone and keys rattled in my pocket with the nervous jiggle of my leg. Eventually, a nurse emerged with a tablet. Lips moved, presumably uttering my name, but the sound failed to register as panic tightened its grip on my chest.

"Hunter Graves?" I nodded, rendered speechless.

"Tyler is currently under observation; he's still unconscious. Our main concern was the concussion and the stitches he needed on the back of his head. Other than game-related bruises, he's okay, and his vitals are stable. We anticipate he'll regain consciousness once his body is ready, but we're closely monitoring him in case of any changes."

"When do you think he'll wake up?"

The subtle change in her expression wasn't lost on me. "That's hard to say, Mr. Graves; head injuries are unpredictable. It could be a few hours or even days. We're vigilant in case any developments require further intervention, but, for now, it's a waiting game."

"So, what? I just have to play the role of the worried partner while my boyfriend is unconscious, like some tragic movie?" I snapped, overwhelmed by the clichéd scenario unfolding. It felt like a combination of every tragic rom-com I'd ever seen.

"I can't guarantee the outcome, Mr. Graves, but his vitals are promising. With time, we hope he'll wake up on his own."

I suppressed an eye roll and refrained from expressing my frustration. She then asked if I wanted to see him, and my incredulous look conveyed the absurdity of the question.

I followed her down a seemingly endless hallway before she gestured to a closed door and left me alone. As I stepped inside, my heart stuttered at the sight of Tyler—paler under the harsh fluorescent lights, the monitors beeping steadily, and an absence of his usual vibrancy. His long eyelashes, which normally fluttered, were still against his cheeks. Sitting there, holding his hand, I hoped that last night wouldn't be our last.

Twenty-four hours of hell was the only way to describe the day that followed. Exhaustion clung to me, yet sleep remained elusive. I rested my head on his torso, attempting to catch his familiar scent through the overpowering smell of antiseptic.

"Baby, please," I surrendered. The floodgates opened, releasing all the emotions I'd tried so hard to keep bottled up. Tears streamed down, and I couldn't remember the last time I cried so much. Drifting in and out of sleep, I dreamt of Tyler's fingers gently threading through my hair, the sound of his voice, and the comforting sight of his blue-green eyes. I'd taken too long to tell that man I loved him, and my mind and body craved his presence. His voice echoed through the darkness of my dreams, as a sweet torment.

"Boston, time to wake up."

My eyes fluttered open, the symphony of sounds reminding me of where I was. Glancing at Tyler, I feared encountering the vacant expression that often accompanied consciousness after an ordeal like that. Instead, I was met with his bleary eyes, and impulsively our lips met in a kiss. He responded with a groan and as I pulled back, his pain-laden smile tugged at my heartstrings.

"God, I'm torn between being ecstatic that you're awake and ready to rip you a new one for scaring the shit out of me, baby."

His lip quirked. "You still owe me a last time, remember? So, if it's ripping a new one, I know how I'd prefer you do it."

Laughter bubbled up, and I planted a light kiss on his lips. "I love you." The words spilled out, and Tyler's eyes glossed over. My gut twisted with anticipation, but before I could reassure him that he didn't need to reciprocate just yet, his hand found my hoodie and clung on.

"I love you too, Boston. Have for some time now." Despite myself, I closed my eyes, wanting to capture this moment.

As I leaned in for another kiss, the commotion from the hallway reached us, and I pulled back just in time before Cal and Jarman barged through the door.

"Oh, thank sweet baby Jesus, you're okay!" Cal's voice reached new heights as he rushed across the room. Tyler endured Cal's exuberance—with a grimace—and I shot warning daggers in his direction. "Sorry, sorry, subtle was never my middle name." Cal kissed the top of Tyler's head and settled down. Jarman chuckled. "You know, Aus, I'm going to have to teach you not to take a hit with your head."

I sought my guy's reaction, finding only that heart-stopping smirk on his face. "Think you might, aye."

CHAPTER FIFTY-THREE

Tyler

"Hey," I said, observing my brother's face tighten at the sight of me in a hospital room. I spoke up again before he could say anything. "I'm fine, James, just a concussion. I'll be out of here today."

"You scared me, Ty," he scolded.

I closed my eyes, understanding the fear firsthand. Hunter had kept them updated on my condition, but I hadn't mustered the courage to call home, avoiding the face of a little brother who feared losing yet another family member. The worry that someone would be taken away from us seemed ingrained in our very beings.

"I know, but I'm okay. No serious injuries, just a bump to the head."

Jamie gave me a look that conveyed every word.

"You get punched as a hobby," I pointed out, and he rolled his eyes.

"You wear knives on your feet and crash into people."

Touché.

"I'm sorry I got hurt."

"Yeah, I know. Just not sorry for playing the game. I hate worrying all the time, you know?"

Oh, I knew all too well—and I hoped he saw it in my face.

"I miss you." His words hit me square in the chest.

"I miss you, too."

"Will you come home for the summer? Well, your summer. I know Holden would love to have you watch them play."

I hadn't made plans yet, but I needed to decide quickly. Vacating my dorm for the summer meant finding somewhere to stay—but saying goodbye was never my strong suit.

"I haven't made plans yet, but as soon as I do, I will let you know."

Disappointment flooded his features. "Yeah, okay. I gotta go. Love you."

The call disconnected.

I sat in relative silence having been disconnected from most of the monitors. Hunter had—reluctantly — returned to the hotel to clean up, but with gratitude from Jarman and Cal. Not that I wanted him to leave, but in truth, the guy bloody stank.

I heard footsteps and looked to the door, staring into the broad, tall presence of Connor Bellamy.

"Hell of a way to end the season, kid." He smiled and came to sit beside me. As usual in his presence, my tongue felt heavy in my mouth—completely unrelated to the concussion. Likely sensing my dumbfounded expression at his unexpected visit, he took mercy on me and smiled. "Regardless of the ending, that was some game—one of the best I have seen in a while."

I managed a smile, or as close to it as I could muster. "Thanks."

"Well, I won't stay long. I know you are set to leave today according to your coach, so I thought I would pop in." Leaning forward, he rested his elbows on his knees, giving me direct eye contact that made me bristle. "You've spared me the heavy lifting; your performance this season stands as a testament to your capabilities. Your stats have outshone those of top draft picks. The Vancouver franchise has expressed keen interest in having you at their training camp this fall, allowing ample time for your recovery from this setback. Following that, there's a possibility of securing a spot on their roster. Initial talks suggest a shorter contract, given your relatively recent entry onto the scene, but it's still a significant opportunity. Alternatively, we can explore the option of placement with their farm team—along with your teammate. If neither aligns with your goals, there's always the option to return for another season here, potentially attracting more offers from other teams. The market might not be fully ready for you yet; not many are in the rebuilding phase, and I'm aware they have been eyeing a few other players."

I probably looked like a dork sitting there with that dumb grin plastered across my face. I reckon my gob was hanging open, but I couldn't be certain because my heartbeat was louder than a kookaburra's laugh. Instead of getting my head around the hockey details like I should've, the strongest and most crystal-clear thought was about a golden-eyed

Boston boy who just signed a contract with that very team.

"Fuck, yes!" I managed to get out.

Connor laughed. "Yes to what?"

I blinked at him like *he* was an idiot. "The training and the league, and if you can get me on the farm team, that's fine. Honestly, if I could just focus on hockey alone, it would be one weight off my shoulders." Connor nodded, a smile of understanding on his face.

Yet again breaking the silence that bordered on awkward, he said, "I like you, kid, and I would like to be your agent—officially. If you're happy, I could have a contract drawn up and I'll get you to that fall training. If you prove yourself like you have so far, a ticket to play pro awaits."

I agreed without hesitation. Somehow, sharing the same agent as Hunter was comforting; it felt like I was closer to him. Connor promised to have the contract in my inbox by the end of the day, leaving my future held firmly in his hands.

Hunter buzzed with energy as he took me to the airport, where we caught a flight back home. Despite the bit of information I was sitting on that threatened to burst out of me, I was exhausted. However, I wanted to tell him in the right moment—in our home, which might not be mine much longer. If it wasn't, I at least wanted the send-off to be right.

The entire journey was a blur of brushing hands and stolen kisses. "God, why did you have to get hit like that? I'm *dying* for your body," Hunter whispered in my ear, and, as always, its effect on me was noticeable, as my body seemed to have a Hunter radar, reacting to every little thing he did.

"Hasn't stopped us before…" I prodded, regretting our night of nothing but cuddles before the last game more than anything right now.

"Tell me you don't have a headache right now. You've winced at every noise so far. If you think either one of us is pounding the other tonight, you're mad. I'm just going to be happy to kiss you properly in the privacy of our bedroom."

An unguarded smile spread across my lips. "*Our* bedroom." We hadn't discussed when everything became ours. It was an unspoken agreement, just like I understood that he loved me without words.

He grabbed my hand as we entered the quiet dorm, Cal and Jarman sat on the couch watching some Hallmark crap that Cal loved. Both guys shot up and Cal kissed me on my cheek, "So glad you're okay."

Jarman squeezed my shoulder in lieu of words.

"Come on, baby." Hunter took my hand, kissing the bumps of my knuckles one by one, guiding me in the direction of our room. Once behind our closed door, he wrapped me in his arms. "Love you," he whispered, almost tentatively. I pulled back to see the heartbreak in his eyes; he was supposed to be flying to Canada soon.

I took his face, savoring the connection of our lips that brought both elation and comfort to my body. "I don't know about you, but I need to shower off the hospital and airport muck."

Hunter moaned in response, sounding more like a pained groan. I couldn't help but suppress the light laughter bubbling within me. It dawned on me that I never laughed more freely than when I was with that man. With that in mind, I guided him back through the living room to the bathroom, disregarding the playful catcalls from Cal and the amused scoffs of laughter from Jarman.

I stripped him of his clothes, needing to feel his skin against mine. Hunter, though, showed a lot more care while he undressed me. I knew I looked forward to when he could manhandle me but, in that moment, I didn't mind the soft glide of his calloused fingers against my skin, the light brush of his lips against my bruised flesh that had taken too many hits. I pulled him into the shower, and we moaned at the scalding pressure from the water.

There was something about knowing another's body and having them know yours. Like many times before, our hands cleaned each other, our lips met one another and brushed over each other's bruises, and showed our love without words; in a way that was purely *us*. I had the only man I would ever want.

Once warmed by the water and each other's touch that admittedly led to us stroking each other off with pure desperation, we collapsed onto the fresh bed sheets I found myself curling into Hunter's chest, finding my home in his arms. The silence was easy and at the count of his heartbeats, I found my moment.

Chapter Fifty-Four

Hunter

My body begged for sleep, eyelids growing heavier with each passing second.

Though I could feel the energy buzzing from the man next to me, telling me he was ready for anything but. Despite molding his body to mine, creating a perfect blend of soft skin and hard edges, there was a rigid edge that told me his mind was racing.

"Baby? Your thoughts are loud enough to be broadcasted across the ESPN network. Care to share?"

As he propped himself up on my chest, I couldn't help but notice a glint in his eye—a sort of youthful excitement that hadn't graced us nearly enough. His tousled hair sticking out in every direction should have been amusing but on him, it came off as oddly charming.

"How do you feel about spending summer and autumn with me?"

I gazed at him, attempting to read between the lines. He knew I was planning to spend the fall training and as for the summer, I wasn't sure how long I'd need to get set up in Vancouver.

"Baby..." I coaxed, trying to get him to explain further.

"Well, I can help you set yourself up over the summer. I love Canada and well, I was hoping I could stay with you when I go to the autumn training camp for Vancouver... Then there's a chance I could sign a contract and..."

Tyler kept speaking but anything else he said blurred together. Amidst the astonishment, I recognized the moment to curb my baby's stream of plans and the looming meticulous details. I ate his words as I sealed my lips against his, excitement coursing through my veins. I searched those pretty eyes for any chance of a lie

"Is this true? Don't fuck with me, baby."

His smile was like lightning shooting through my veins. "Vancouver is in a rebuilding year; they need some rookies. The training camp is where they're choosing. Bellamy said there might be a slot on the farm team if not. I have to prove my—"

I cut him off again with another kiss. My hands found their way into his hair, and my tongue tangled with his, savoring the fresh peppermint and my man.

"Fuck, I don't think I've ever been so happy in my life," I mumbled against his lips.

That was what I wanted to do the moment I scored that goal, and it was taken from me with one hit. Every hardship we'd faced led up to that moment. The version of me from the start of the season would think it was all too good to be true. But after months of waiting for the puck to drop, I learned that he would be right there to give it back to me. Somehow, I knew, no matter where we'd be, he would always come back to me. Our future wasn't promised with trades to worry about, but I had just been promised more time with him—however long it was

The smile of his lips against mine brought tears to my eyes. "Me neither Boston. You smashed into my life and made it complete. I selfishly want it all, Boston, but with you. I just want it all with you."

Our lips spoke the rest of the words until the excitement turned into a comforting silence. "One more time" no longer meant treating each time like it was our last. It meant that we simply couldn't get enough, and we planned to have each other time and time again.

Epilogue

Hunter

"Baby, can you just chill out?" I laughed as Tyler bustled around the house we temporarily called home.

"No! Have you seen my Monday underwear? I can't go to our Monday training without it; it's just not right."

Jarman, who'd taken one of our spare rooms, leaned in the doorway hiding his smile behind his coffee. Cal sat beside him, looking like he wanted to say something, but a quick glance from me made him think twice. Tyler was dead serious, after all.

"I thought Australians were supposed to be easygoing?" I teased, and he shot me a look that could put me six feet under.

"I *am* easygoing. But it's a crime to wear Tuesday underwear on a Monday."

My laughter burst out uncontrollably. "Or you could just wear plain underwear like a normal person."

"Fuck off, you know this is my thing. You have your own superstitions I have mine—mine is just less smelly."

He had a point. Many hockey players had lucky undergarments, even if they got a bit ripe during long road trips. With a sigh, I joined the hunt for the missing Monday underwear.

"Fucking Mondays, it's always Mondays," Tyler mumbled to himself and I couldn't help but find his frustration endearing. Despite his high-strung ways, Tyler was surprisingly easygoing—except for his particular need to have things a certain way.

I headed to my wardrobe, digging through the clean laundry he'd asked me to put away—which I swiftly stowed there in my not-so-clever way of avoiding chores. Grabbing the underwear discreetly, I pretended to find them by magic just as Tyler stopped short and stared at me.

"Ugh, give me those! We'll discuss that later. I don't want to be late." Tyler snatched the underwear and stuffed them into his bag which, like always, Mr. Perfect had meticulously organized. Meanwhile, I couldn't even find my own hand in my bag if left to my own devices.

"Baby, we're going to be half an hour early." I checked the time, confirming that it only took fifteen minutes to drive to the rink. We were already ahead of schedule.

"Good. They need to know we like to be early; it's a good impression to make." Tyler stormed to the living room, grabbed his pre-prepared kit bag by the door, saluted our still-amused roommates, and left me behind.

"Hurry up, babe! I'm not waiting for you!" At least he hadn't forgotten about me.

"Yeah, go on, *babe*; can't be the second person on the ice," Jarman joked earning a playful finger.

"You're just jealous. Wait until the day you have one of your own."

I left with a wave and chuckled at Tyler nervously tapping his fingers on the steering wheel while waiting for me in the car. I kind of loved that something's never changed, even his crazy need for perfection. I'd eased it a little, even getting him to watch the occasional movie with me instead of hockey tapes. In reality, he fell asleep halfway through. Though I didn't mind—he was adorable when he slept.

Tyler

A much-needed break had me eagerly anticipating my return to the ice. I'd been kidding myself when I thought I could give that up. My life had felt almost complete over the summer, with my guy—a summer romance that would undoubtedly go down as the hottest and most swoon-worthy of all summers. As we navigated the training camp, all eyes were on us. Connor Bellamy had come to watch both Hunter and me working together, showcasing that we were the two winning rookies. Hunter already had a ticket to the minor league and after the training camp, he would be heading for preseason training. Now, I had to hope I would either follow him or get called up.

Skating off the ice for the last time at training camp with sweat pouring off me, showed how I'd given my all on that ice. We finished with a scrimmage, facing off against some other determined young players who playfully chirped at me to head back home to Australia. But proving people wrong was my jam, and even though I wasn't raised in the hockey capitals of the world, I knew I was just as seasoned and disciplined as the rest of them. Hunter gave my shoulder a reassuring squeeze, and the look in his eyes sent my heart into overdrive.

We came out on top in the scrimmage, and if I thought getting back on the ice was awesome, hitting the ice with my man... that was absolutely stella. Our chemistry had us owning the other team; nothing beat our combo, and I hoped the team managers from both sides caught on to that.

As we stepped into the locker room, my name echoed through the air, and I turned to see Connor motioning for me to join him. I glanced at Hunter, who offered me a reassuring smile and a casual, "You got this, baby," as he swatted me on the ass with his stick.

As I followed Connor into the hallway, he patted my shoulder. "Kid, you really put it all on the ice today." I nodded and tried to catch my breath.

A suited man approached, triggering a surge of anxiety and hope. This was the moment—deciding if I would stay in Vancouver or return to Boston. I wondered if Hunter felt the same way. We briefly considered talking about it that morning but brushed it off instead.

"Mr. Riley, that was some hockey I just watched."

I managed a breathless, "Thank you, sir." I fought the urge to jiggle my legs, determined to remain composed.

"How do you feel about showing that energy and talent on the ice for the preseason?"

I nodded, though my expression couldn't conceal the questions whirling in my mind. While I knew the players on the ice and grasped the game like a skilled chess player, the politics eluded me. The man in the suit was virtually a stranger to me.

He chuckled, before introducing himself. "Sorry, I'm Jerard Lucas, the team manager for Vancouver's Voyagers NHL team, and we would like you to sign a temporary contract. I want to see you in the preseason and evaluate your performance in the big leagues. If you showcase the same grit I saw today, we'll sign you for a set number of games post-preseason. If you maintain your promise, an official signing will follow. If that doesn't pan out, there may be a spot for you on our minor league team. With your confidence, we want to put you to the test. We're in a rebuilding year, taking a cautious approach to long-term commitments until we're confident you can perform."

Before I could respond, Connor interjected, "he's the real deal. Outstanding academic performance with top grades and he held the highest scoring average in the college league. Plus, his other stats followed the same impressive trajectory. Forward the offer, and I'll engage in further discussions with Tyler. As you rightly pointed out, he's weighing other factors, but longevity in one place is always a solid choice. Trust me, committing to him for the long term won't be a decision you'll regret."

I sensed my agent wasn't entirely pleased with the straightforward approach, but I embraced it, as it only added fuel to my determination to stay. "Mr. Lucas, I'm here to prove that I'm the best damn player you can choose. No messing around, no messing up. I want the team to recognize the asset they have, and I'll go above and beyond to be their best addition. "

Mr. Lucas seemed to fight back a smile. "Good. I hope to see you for preseason training, Mr. Riley."

"I'll be there early and with bells on."

Connor shot me a warning glance and I realized then that it was his role to do the talking, so I closed my mouth, allowing the typical goodbye handshakes to unfold. "I like you, kid, but please let me do the talking next time." I offered an apologetic smile in place of a verbal answer. "I'll review the contract and send it to you. It's a good offer, and I know if anyone is going to show them up, it will be you."

I nodded, expressed my gratitude, and practically sprinted back to the locker room. Hunter emerged from the showers and disregarding the clunky and disgusting gear still on me, I rushed over and pulled him into my arms. "Guess who gets to play a preseason in the NHL?"

I pulled back then, eagerly awaiting his reaction. His eyes widened, matching his smile. I had never been more excited to spend more time with my golden-eyed man. "I knew you could do it!"

Sensing his desire to maul me like a bear, I pulled back and whispered in his ear. "How about we get Cal and Jarman to vacate the house tonight, and we celebrate, just you and me, one more time before we become *professional* hockey players."

"I'm down for one more time."

Hunter's smile told the whole story; he was everything. The excitement was palpable and despite the hurdles, we still had each other, hockey, and so much more than just one more time.

The end... for now.

A note from Rory

Thank you so much for reading. I'm incredibly grateful to this beautiful community for embracing my characters and inspiring me to bring this book to fruition. A special shoutout to my amazing editor, Rae – your guidance and support made all the difference. And to all the readers, I apologize for the tissue bill! If you're curious about Jarman and Mouse, stay tuned – their story is up next!

www.ingramcontent.com/pod-product-compliance
Lightning Source LLC
Chambersburg PA
CBHW061117100726
47911CB00013B/579